HADJI MURAD
AND OTHER STORIES

T0343610

HADJI MURAD
AND OTHER STORIES

Leo Tolstoy

Translated from the Russian by
Louise and Aylmer Maude
and Nigel J. Cooper

Selected and with a preface by
Sharon Cameron

riverrun

The translation first published in 2001 by Alfred A. Knopf
This edition published in 2022 by

riverrun

An imprint of

Quercus Editions Limited
Carmelite House
50 Victoria Embankment
London EC4Y 0DZ

An Hachette UK company

A CIP catalogue record for this book is available
from the British Library

PB ISBN 978 1 52941 055 6
EBOOK ISBN 978 1 52941 056 3

10 9 8 7 6 5 4 3

Typeset by CC Book Production
Printed and bound in Great Britain by Clays Ltd, Elcograf S.p.A.

Papers used by riverrun are from well-managed forests and other responsible sources.

Contents

Preface

LEO TOLSTOY (1828–1910) was born to Russian aristocrats on the family estate, Yasnaya Polyana, eight miles from Moscow. By the end of his life he had written in many genres for different audiences. He wrote 'God Sees the Truth but Waits'(1872) and 'A Prisoner in the Caucasus' (1872) for children, and folkloric fables for all, among them 'The Three Hermits' (1886) and 'Alyosha Gorshok' (1905). He wrote ethical treatises: *What Then Must We Do?* (1882), in which he argued against the injustices of contemporary Russian society, urging intellectuals, aristocrats, and artists who exploit the poor working on their behalf to see that such a division of labour blights their own spiritual welfare; and in *Why Do Men Stupefy Themselves?* (1891), he maintained that the aim of alcohol, opium, and other drugs is to permit actions that violate reason and conscience. *What Is Religion and of What Does Its Essence Consist?* (1902), 'The Kingdom of Heaven Is Within You' (1893), and 'An Appeal to the Clergy' (1902) shocked the

Russian Orthodox Church – which excommunicated him – by announcing that Church doctrine and rituals, the belief in Christ's divine origin, in such miracles as 'the turning of water into wine' and even in 'the resurrection of Jesus himself', are 'fairy-tales' extraneous to the essence of religion, which is discovered only in the love preached by the Gospels. In the didactic 'What Is Art?' (1898), Tolstoy answered: 'an infection', in which the author inflames an audience to share his feelings. Tolstoy also wrote essays on vegetarianism (1891), against capital punishment (1900), and on the education of peasant children: 'Who Should Learn Writing of Whom; Peasant Children of Us, or We of Peasant Children?' (1862) is an early essay whose counter-intuitive conclusion might give a reader pause about the periodization of Tolstoy's thinking, which is in some ways continuous. The tenets of Tolstoy's ethical, social, and religious writing are reflected in many of his post-1880s stories, and anticipated by *A Confession* (1882), in which he rejected the Orthodox Church, his own debauched way of living, and the fame that followed the titanic *War and Peace* (1865–69) and *Anna Karenina* (1875–78). In an 1878 letter to his editor, Nikolai Strakhov, Tolstoy called the energy that fuelled his famous novels 'the energy of delusion'. Yet he is celebrated for these novels. He himself could not assign *War and Peace* to any 'existing genre'. It is 'neither novel, nor tale, nor long poem, nor history'. In their unwavering gaze at the disparity between what is abstract or imaginary and what is actual, Tolstoy's stories are also *sui generis*.

As in *War and Peace*, in the sketch 'Sevastopol in May 1855'

(1855) the arc of a historical event, here the Crimean War, indiscriminately shapes destinies. In the battle scenes 'vanity, the wish to shine, the hope of rewards, of gaining a reputation' mingle with chaos and terror. Thus Adjutant Kalugin, 'who always boasted that he never even stooped', finds himself in a 'trench almost on all fours' as a bomb 'whizzed near him . . . He was surprised at himself but no longer strove to master his feelings.' Sentences that amass quantities – the fates of 'hundreds of men with curses or prayers on their parched lips' who 'crawled, writhed, and groaned'; 'a heap of corpses'; 'a million fires flashed from all sides' – shift to close-ups of individual confusion in which no one can fathom what will happen, or what *has* happened, to him. In 'What Men Live By' (1881), no man knows 'whether, when evening comes, he will need boots for his body, or slippers for his corpse'. When a bomb explodes near Captain Praskukhin, he thinks, 'Thank God, I'm only bruised,' though in fact he had been 'killed on the spot by a bomb-splinter in the middle of his chest', while Lieutenant-Captain Mikhaylov – sure he is dying: '"That's the soul passing," he thought' – is only 'slightly wounded in the head by a stone'. The technique of juxtaposing panoptic scenes of carnage with their reflection in the consciousness of multiple characters, each experiencing disorientation in his own flawed way, is amplified on the vaster canvas of *War and Peace*, but 'Sevastopol in May 1855' has an analogous feel of inclusiveness.

Throughout Tolstoy's stories, there is inclusiveness of a

different order – not the pairing of wide-angle and close-up lenses that melds communal and personal nightmares, but an array of calamities from which there seems no escape. 'Oh, my God, what is it for?' moans the invalid whose lungs are failing in 'Three Deaths' (1859), because 'the word "die" . . . frightened her'. 'This is impossible . . . There must be some remedy for it,' Eugene, in 'The Devil' (1890), says to himself, 'walking up and down in his room', tormented by an 'almost insane' lust for Stepanida, the peasant who was his mistress before his marriage to Liza, now five months pregnant. In 'The Kreutzer Sonata' (1889), Pozdnyshev is intoxicated by the fantasy of his wife's infidelity with a violinist: 'The more I gazed at those imaginary pictures, the stronger grew my belief in their reality.' Their 'vividness . . . seemed to serve as proof that what I imagined was real'. In 'Polikushka' (1863), delusion slides into hypocrisy when the mistress of a large estate laments the 'evil' of 'dreadful money' after a peasant's loss of fifteen hundred rubles leads to a hanging and a baby's drowning. Her display of empathy for the well-being of her serfs (she 'would do everything in my power . . . sacrifice everything' to keep them from 'harm') does not blind the reader to the emptiness of that hyperbole, because she will not spend 'three hundred rubles' to save her serfs from a conscription, which will almost certainly end in death. In 'Father Sergius' (1898), penance for such posturing is deluded – as when, to chastise his pride, his atheism, his coldness, his attraction to a feeble-minded girl, his seductive thought of suicide, Sergius cuts off 'the forefinger of his left hand . . . below the second joint', but cannot cut off his transgressive thoughts.

Tolstoy's antidotes to delusion, fear, jealousy, and even madness have a common ethical thread pulled through the fabric of very different narrative structures, themes, and genres, whether realist, didactic, or parabolic. In the stark form of homily that shapes Tolstoy's late stories, life considered as one's own has no rational meaning. Thus, in the fable 'Esarhaddon, King of Assyria' (1903), an old man tells the King that his enemy 'Lailie is you, and the warriors you put to death were you also. And not the warriors only, but the animals which you slew . . . Life is one in them all, and yours is but a portion of this same common life.' Narrative structure dramatizes that realization in the rival logics of violence and love that shape the two halves of 'The Forged Coupon' (1904). Stepan's indiscriminate enmity towards all leads to a series of thefts and murders, and has a domino effect in crimes perpetrated by his victims, until he encounters Mariya Semyonovna, who – before he slits her throat – admonishes: 'Have pity on yourself . . . it's your own soul you are destroying.' When her benevolence dawns on him, the domino effect of love transforms not only him but his fellow prison inmates, who 'began to understand this new world of spiritual aspirations which had formerly seemed . . . alien'.

How truth thickens and deepens when it migrates from didactic fable to the raw experience of a visceral awakening is one of the thrills of Tolstoy's stories. Insight can bypass thought and rise up mutely in an instant, as in 'Master and Man' (1895), or seem as though it will never arrive, as in 'The Death of Ivan Ilych' (1886). In 'Master and Man' the miserly Vasili Andreevich's 'sole aim' is to calculate 'how much money he had made and might still make . . . how much other people he knew had made', and 'how he, like them, might still make much more'. When he sets out with his peasant Nikita to buy land for which he plans to offer 'only a third of its real value', they get lost in dark, cold, 'drifting snow' and 'wind [that] blew in their faces'. In the blizzard, the men sink into a ravine and begin to freeze to death until, 'with the same resolution with which he used to strike hands when making a good purchase, [Vasili] began raking the snow off Nikita' and 'lay down on top of him . . . it seemed to him that he was Nikita and Nikita was he, and that his life was not in himself but in Nikita'. Comparably, in 'Memoirs of a Madman' (1884), the fear of death 'tearing asunder within me' inexplicably dissolves before a greater mystery, while in 'How Much Land Does a Man Need?' (1886), Pahom believes he can outrun fear by dint of physical prowess. Though he dreams of a man 'prostrate on the ground', and even sees that 'the man was dead, and that it was himself' lying there, he waves away the premonition that he could become such a man, and muses: 'What things one does dream.'

'The Death of Ivan Ilych' exposes the illusions of everyday existence behind such incredulity – the zeal for comfort, pleasure, money, property, and status, which is incompatible with a finality that renders acquisitions paltry. The pity of such ambitions is signalled in Tolstoy's startling sentence, 'Ivan Ilych's life had been most simple and most ordinary and therefore most terrible'. Viktor Shklovsky underscores Tolstoy's conviction that in the 'most ordinary . . . the habitual, nothing amaz[es]' or even penetrates. He writes that, in 'The Death of Ivan Ilych', when, Tolstoy 'rip[s] off the mask of all that is mundane', a flood of sensation immediately testifies to the deception of the 'ordinary', which stupefies with its abstractions, hypocrisy, and platitudes. Nowhere is there more visceral intensity than in the torment of Ivan Ilych's shock that death, an unnameable '*It*', could come to *him*, 'little Vanya', who once had 'a mamma and a papa'. Yet death's insistent presence does not exhaust itself: '*It* would come and stand before him and look at him, and he would be petrified and the light would die out of his eyes, and he would again begin asking himself whether *It* alone was true.' Above all, there is no response that could assuage what he sees: 'what was worst of all was that *It* drew his attention to itself not in order to make him take some action, but only so that he should look at *It*, look it straight in the face', and 'suffer inexpressibly'. Only unflinching, acquiescent to mental and physical pain, stripped of consolation, can Ivan Ilych see that 'all that for which he had lived . . . was not real at all, but a terrible and huge deception which had hidden both life and death'. For the critic Natalie Repin, therefore, the question is not 'whether there is life after death', but 'whether there could be life before [the lived immediacy of] death'. Ivan Ilych's dying, unmediated by screens, prompts the memory of other palpable experiences: 'the raw shrivelled French plums of his childhood', the 'flavour and the flow of saliva when he sucked their pits', and, in 'the present', the pressure of 'the button on the back of the sofa and the creases in its morocco'. The same sensory awareness prompts him suddenly to see past his own suffering to his family's misery ('Yes, I am making them wretched') and to experience a common wonder, his capacity to feel for them. The flavour of the plums Ivan Ilych sucked as a child, and the terrible *It* that is death, though antitheses, are more like each other than the damasks, plants, rugs, positions, pleasures in which he has shrouded himself. In 'The Death of Ivan Ilych' life and death converge beneath the surface of unlikeness to disclose the essential strangeness of their connection.

'There is always at the centre' of Tolstoy's writing, Virginia Woolf wrote, some character 'who gathers into himself all experience, turns the world round between his fingers, and never ceases to ask, even as he enjoys it, what is the meaning of it'. Tolstoy's stories – in which nothing but artifice seems omitted – also include experience that is meaningless, even nonsensical, as when this locution pops into the mind of a cavalry officer in 'Two Hussars' (an early story from 1856): '"I have ruined my youth!" he suddenly said to himself, not because he really thought he had ruined his youth ... but because the phrase happened to occur to him.' Or as when, in 'The Devil', Eugene (who that morning 'rode' out to his 'fallow land which was to be sprinkled with phosphates', to revitalize the soil) returns home to Liza, his pregnant wife, and, still obsessed with his mistress, 'repeat[s] a phrase he had just uttered ... The phrase was: "phosphates justify" – what or to whom, he neither knew nor reflected.' 'Phosphates', plant nutrients, are lodged in Eugene's mind from the visit to his fields, where they will be disseminated so seedlings can grow. Coupled with 'justify', the agricultural moves to a juridical, even a theological, context, where the phrase is intoned as a mantra. Approaching the house, Eugene sees that 'they were beating a carpet on the grass', and marvels:

> 'What a house cleaning Liza has undertaken! ... Phosphates justify ... Yes, I must change my boots, or else "phosphates justify", that is, smell of manure, and the manageress is in such a condition ... Because a new little Irtenev is growing there inside her,' he thought. 'Yes, phosphates justify.'

The association of soil and womb is warranted by the fertilization of each. But nothing *justifies* Eugene's consuming lust for his mistress when a 'little Irtenev' is 'growing', or explains the logic of the unnerving mantra whose repetitions derange his thinking. 'Phosphates justify' is like a maxim with a meaningful sound, but a different kind of nonsense from 'I have ruined my youth'. Tolstoy's stories voice thoughts that barge unharnessed into consciousness, as in 'Two Hussars', or as in 'The Devil', whose conflict erupts in a stutter – two examples from Tolstoy's vast repertoire of surprises by which everyday sense is punctured, riddled, or broken open to arresting new associations and energies.

The majority of the stories collected here were written after 1880; after, that is, the spiritual crisis Tolstoy documented in *A Confession*. They appear in these volumes in roughly chronological order, with the exception of 'Family Happiness' (1859), which I have moved to Volume Two, where it precedes 'The Devil' (1890) and 'The Kreutzer Sonata' (1889), Tolstoy's other unhappy-marriage stories, written thirty years later.

With the exception of 'Family Happiness' (translated by J. D. Duff) and 'After the Ball', 'The Forged Coupon', 'Alyosha Gorshok', and 'What For?' (translated by Nigel J. Cooper), the stories in this edition are translated by Louise and Aylmer Maude, of whom Tolstoy wrote: 'Better translators . . . could not be invented.' The Maudes were friends of Tolstoy and translated his major works. Aylmer Maude, who also wrote a classic two-volume biography of Tolstoy, supplied the notes for the stories translated by the Maudes; Nigel Cooper annotated those which he translated.

Sharon Cameron

A List of Tartar Words Used in 'Hadji Murad'

Throughout this edition I have tried to avoid the use of Russian words, employing their English equivalents wherever possible. In the following story, however, Tolstoy makes use of a number of Tartar words which he does not translate. As there are generally no one- or two-word equivalents for them in English, it would be difficult to avoid following his example and retaining these Tartar words. I have therefore done so, and the reader should refer to the following alphabetical list when he encounters one of them that needs explanation.

Aylmer Maude

Aoul	A Tartar village.
Bar	Have.
Beshmet	A Tartar undergarment with sleeves.
Burka	A long round felt cape.
Dzhigit	The same as a *brave* among the Red Indians, but the word is inseparably connected with the idea of skilful horsemanship.
Ghazavat	Holy War against the infidels.
Imam	The leader in the Holy War, uniting in himself supreme spiritual and temporal power.
Khansha	Khan's wife.
Kizyak	A fuel made of straw and manure.
Kunak	A sworn friend, an adopted brother.
Murid	A disciple or follower: 'One who desires' to find the way in Muridism.
Muridism	Almost identical with Sufism.
Murshid	'One who shows' the way in Muridism.
Naib	A Tartar lieutenant or governor.
Pilau	An oriental dish, prepared with rice and mutton or chicken.
Saklya	A Caucasian house, clay-plastered and often built of earth.
Shariat	The written Mohammedan law.
Tarikat	'The Path' leading to the higher life.
Yok	No, not.

Hadji Murad

I

I WAS RETURNING HOME by the fields. It was midsummer, the hay harvest was over and they were just beginning to reap the rye. At that season of the year there is a delightful variety of flowers – red, white, and pink scented tufty clover; milk-white ox-eye daisies with their bright yellow centres and pleasant spicy smell; yellow honey-scented rape blossoms; tall campanulas with white and lilac bells, tulip-shaped; creeping vetch; yellow, red, and pink scabious; faintly scented, neatly arranged purple plantains with blossoms slightly tinged with pink; cornflowers, the newly opened blossoms bright blue in the sunshine but growing paler and redder towards evening or when growing old; and delicate almond-scented dodder flowers that withered quickly. I gathered myself a large nosegay and was going home when I noticed in a ditch, in full bloom, a beautiful thistle plant of the crimson variety, which in our neighbourhood they call 'Tartar' and carefully avoid when mowing – or, if they do happen to cut it down, throw out from among the grass for fear of pricking their hands. Thinking to pick this thistle and put it in the centre of my nosegay, I climbed down into the ditch, and after driving away a velvety humble-bee that had penetrated deep into one of the flowers and had there fallen sweetly asleep, I set to work to pluck the flower. But this proved a very difficult task. Not only did the stalk prick on every side – even through the handkerchief I wrapped round my hand – but it was so tough that I had to struggle with it for nearly five minutes, breaking the fibres one by one; and when I had at last plucked it, the stalk was all frayed and the flower itself no longer seemed so fresh and beautiful. Moreover, owing to its coarseness and stiffness, it did not seem in place among the delicate blossoms of my nosegay. I threw it away feeling sorry to have vainly destroyed a flower that looked beautiful in its proper place.

'But what energy and tenacity! With what determination it defended itself, and how dearly it sold its life!' thought I, remembering the effort it had cost me to pluck the flower. The way home led across black-earth fields that had just been ploughed up. I ascended the dusty path. The ploughed field belonged to a landed proprietor and was so large that on both sides and before me to the top of the hill nothing was visible but evenly furrowed and moist earth. The land was well tilled and nowhere was there a blade of grass or any kind of plant to be seen, it was all black. 'Ah, what a destructive creature is man . . . How many different plant-lives he destroys to support his own existence!' thought I, involuntarily looking around for some living thing in this lifeless black field. In front of me to the right of the road I saw some kind of little clump, and drawing nearer I found it was the same kind of thistle as that which I had vainly plucked and thrown away. This 'Tartar' plant had three branches. One was broken and stuck out like the stump of a mutilated arm. Each of the other two bore a flower, once red but now blackened. One stalk was broken, and half of it hung down with a soiled flower at its tip. The other, though also soiled with black mud, still stood erect. Evidently a cartwheel had passed over the plant but it had risen again, and that was why, though erect, it stood twisted to one side, as if a piece of its body had been torn from it, its bowels drawn out, an arm torn off, and one of its eyes plucked out. Yet it stood firm and did not surrender to man who had destroyed all its brothers around it . . .

'What vitality!' I thought. 'Man has conquered everything and destroyed millions of plants, yet this one won't submit.' And I remembered a Caucasian episode of years ago, which I had partly seen myself, partly heard of from eye-witnesses, and in part imagined.

The episode, as it has taken shape in my memory and imagination, was as follows.

It happened towards the end of 1851.

On a cold November evening Hadji Murad rode into Makhmet, a hostile Chechen *aoul* that lay some fifteen miles from

Russian territory and was filled with the scented smoke of burning *kizyak*. The strained chant of the muezzin had just ceased, and through the clear mountain air, impregnated with *kizyak* smoke, above the lowing of the cattle and the bleating of the sheep that were dispersing among the *saklyas* (which were crowded together like the cells of a honeycomb), could be clearly heard the guttural voices of disputing men, and sounds of women's and children's voices rising from near the fountain below.

This Hadji Murad was Shamil's *naib*, famous for his exploits, who used never to ride out without his banner and some dozens of *murids*, who caracoled and showed off before him. Now wrapped in hood and *burka*, from under which protruded a rifle, he rode, a fugitive, with one *murid* only, trying to attract as little attention as possible and peering with his quick black eyes into the faces of those he met on his way.

When he entered the *aoul*, instead of riding up the road leading to the open square, he turned to the left into a narrow side-street, and on reaching the second *saklya*, which was cut into the hillside, he stopped and looked round. There was no one under the penthouse in front, but on the roof of the *saklya* itself, behind the freshly plastered clay chimney, lay a man covered with a sheepskin. Hadji Murad touched him with the handle of his leather-plaited whip and clicked his tongue, and an old man, wearing a greasy old *beshmet* and a nightcap, rose from under the sheepskin. His moist red eyelids had no lashes, and he blinked to get them unstuck. Hadji Murad, repeating

4

the customary '*Selaam aleikum!*' uncovered his face. '*Aleikum, selaam!*' said the old man, recognizing him, and smiling with his toothless mouth. And raising himself on his thin legs he began thrusting his feet into the wooden-heeled slippers that stood by the chimney. Then he leisurely slipped his arms into the sleeves of his crumpled sheepskin, and going to the ladder that leant against the roof he descended backwards. While he dressed and as he climbed down he kept shaking his head on its thin, shrivelled sunburnt neck and mumbling something with his toothless mouth. As soon as he reached the ground he hospitably seized Hadji Murad's bridle and right stirrup; but the strong active *murid* had quickly dismounted and, motioning the old man aside, took his place. Hadji Murad also dismounted, and walking with a slight limp, entered under the penthouse. A boy of fifteen, coming quickly out of the door, met him and wonderingly fixed his sparkling eyes, black as ripe sloes, on the new arrivals.

'Run to the mosque and call your father,' ordered the old man as he hurried forward to open the thin, creaking door into the *saklya*.

As Hadji Murad entered the outer door, a slight, spare, middle-aged woman in a yellow smock, red *beshmet*, and wide blue trousers came through an inner door carrying cushions.

'May thy coming bring happiness!' said she, and bending nearly double began arranging the cushions along the front wall for the guest to sit on.

5

'May thy sons live!' answered Hadji Murad, taking off his *burka*, his rifle, and his sword, and handing them to the old man who carefully hung the rifle and sword on a nail beside the weapons of the master of the house, which were suspended between two large basins that glittered against the clean clay-plastered and carefully whitewashed wall.

Hadji Murad adjusted the pistol at his back, came up to the cushions, and wrapping his Circassian coat closer round him, sat down. The old man squatted on his bare heels beside him, closed his eyes, and lifted his hands palms upwards. Hadji Murad did the same; then after repeating a prayer they both stroked their faces, passing their hands downwards till the palms joined at the end of their beards.

'*Ne habar?*' ('Is there anything new?') asked Hadji Murad, addressing the old man.

'*Habar yok*' ('Nothing new'), replied the old man, looking with his lifeless red eyes not at Hadji Murad's face but at his breast. 'I live at the apiary and have only today come to see my son . . . He knows.'

Hadji Murad, understanding that the old man did not wish to say what he knew and what Hadji Murad wanted to know, slightly nodded his head and asked no more questions.

'There is no good news,' said the old man. 'The only news is that the hares keep discussing how to drive away the eagles, and the eagles tear first one and then another of them. The other day the Russian dogs burnt the hay in the

Mitchit *aoul* . . . May their faces be torn!' he added hoarsely and angrily.

Hadji Murad's *murid* entered the room, his strong legs striding softly over the earthen floor. Retaining only his dagger and pistol, he took off his *burka*, rifle, and sword as Hadji Murad had done, and hung them up on the same nails as his leader's weapons.

'Who is he?' asked the old man, pointing to the newcomer.

'My *murid*. Eldar is his name,' said Hadji Murad.

'That is well,' said the old man, and motioned Eldar to a place on a piece of felt beside Hadji Murad. Eldar sat down, crossing his legs and fixing his fine ram-like eyes on the old man who, having now started talking, was telling how their brave fellows had caught two Russian soldiers the week before and had killed one and sent the other to Shamil in Veden.

Hadji Murad heard him absently, looking at the door and listening to the sounds outside. Under the penthouse steps were heard, the door creaked, and Sado, the master of the house, came in. He was a man of about forty, with a small beard, long nose, and eyes as black, though not as glittering, as those of his fifteen-year-old son who had run to call him home and who now entered with his father and sat down by the door. The master of the house took off his wooden slippers at the door, and pushing his old and much-worn cap to the back of his head (which had remained unshaved so long that it was beginning to be overgrown with black hair), at once squatted down in front of Hadji Murad.

He too lifted his hands palms upwards, as the old man had done, repeated a prayer, and then stroked his face downwards. Only after that did he begin to speak. He told how an order had come from Shamil to seize Hadji Murad alive or dead, that Shamil's envoys had left only the day before, that the people were afraid to disobey Shamil's orders, and that therefore it was necessary to be careful.

'In my house,' said Sado, 'no one shall injure my *kunak* while I live, but how will it be in the open fields? . . . We must think it over.'

Hadji Murad listened with attention and nodded approvingly. When Sado had finished he said:

'Very well. Now we must send a man with a letter to the Russians. My *murid* will go but he will need a guide.'

'I will send brother Bata,' said Sado. 'Go and call Bata,' he added, turning to his son.

The boy instantly bounded to his nimble feet as if he were on springs, and swinging his arms, rapidly left the *saklya*. Some ten minutes later he returned with a sinewy, short-legged Chechen, burnt almost black by the sun, wearing a worn and tattered yellow Circassian coat with frayed sleeves, and crumpled black leggings.

Hadji Murad greeted the newcomer, and again without wasting a single word, immediately asked:

'Canst thou conduct my *murid* to the Russians?'

'I can,' gaily replied Bata. 'I can certainly do it. There is

8

not another Chechen who would pass as I can. Another might agree to go and might promise anything, but would do nothing; but I can do it!'

'All right,' said Hadji Murad. 'Thou shalt receive three for thy trouble,' and he held up three fingers.

Bata nodded to show that he understood, and added that it was not money he prized, but that he was ready to serve Hadji Murad for the honour alone. Everyone in the mountains knew Hadji Murad, and how he slew the Russian swine.

'Very well ... A rope should be long but a speech short,' said Hadji Murad.

'Well then I'll hold my tongue,' said Bata.

'Where the river Argun bends by the cliff,' said Hadji Murad, 'there are two stacks in a glade in the forest – thou knowest?'

'I know.'

'There my four horsemen are waiting for me,' said Hadji Murad.

'Aye,' answered Bata, nodding.

'Ask for Khan Mahoma. He knows what to do and what to say. Canst thou lead him to the Russian commander, Prince Vorontsov?'

'Yes, I'll take him.'

'Canst thou take him and bring him back again?'

'I can.'

'Then take him there and return to the wood. I shall be there too.'

'I will do it all,' said Bata, rising, and putting his hands on his heart he went out.

Hadji Murad turned to his host.

'A man must also be sent to Chekhi,' he began, and took hold of one of the cartridge pouches of his Circassian coat, but let his hand drop immediately and became silent on seeing two women enter the *saklya*.

One was Sado's wife – the thin middle-aged woman who had arranged the cushions. The other was quite a young girl, wearing red trousers and a green *beshmet*. A necklace of silver coins covered the whole front of her dress, and at the end of the short but thick plait of hard black hair that hung between her thin shoulder-blades a silver ruble was suspended. Her eyes, as sloe-black as those of her father and brother, sparkled brightly in her young face which tried to be stern. She did not look at the visitors, but evidently felt their presence.

Sado's wife brought in a low round table on which stood tea, pancakes in butter, cheese, *churek* (that is, thinly rolled-out bread), and honey. The girl carried a basin, a ewer, and a towel.

Sado and Hadji Murad kept silent as long as the women, with their coin ornaments tinkling, moved softly about in their red soft-soled slippers, setting out before the visitors the things they had brought. Eldar sat motionless as a statue, his ram-like eyes fixed on his crossed legs, all the time the women were in the *saklya*. Only after they had gone and their soft footsteps could no longer be heard behind the door, did he give a sigh of relief.

Hadji Murad having pulled out a bullet from one of the cartridge-pouches of his Circassian coat, and having taken out a rolled-up note that lay beneath it, held it out, saying:

'To be handed to my son.'

'Where must the answer be sent?'

'To thee; and thou must forward it to me.'

'It shall be done,' said Sado, and placed the note in a cartridge-pocket of his own coat. Then he took up the metal ewer and moved the basin towards Hadji Murad.

Hadji Murad turned up the sleeves of his *beshmet* on his white muscular arms, held out his hands under the clear cold water which Sado poured from the ewer, and having wiped them on a clean unbleached towel, turned to the table. Eldar did the same. While the visitors ate, Sado sat opposite and thanked them several times for their visit. The boy sat by the door never taking his sparkling eyes off Hadji Murad's face, and smiled as if in confirmation of his father's words.

Though he had eaten nothing for more than twenty-four hours Hadji Murad ate only a little bread and cheese; then, drawing out a small knife from under his dagger, he spread some honey on a piece of bread.

'Our honey is good,' said the old man, evidently pleased to see Hadji Murad eating his honey. 'This year, above all other years, it is plentiful and good.'

'I thank thee,' said Hadji Murad and turned from the table. Eldar would have liked to go on eating but he followed his leader's example, and having moved away from the table, handed him the ewer and basin.

Sado knew that he was risking his life by receiving such a guest in his house, for after his quarrel with Shamil the latter had issued a proclamation to all the inhabitants of Chechnya forbidding them to receive Hadji Murad on pain of death. He knew that the inhabitants of the *aoul* might at any moment become aware of Hadji Murad's presence in his house and might demand his surrender. But this not only did not frighten Sado, it even gave him pleasure: he considered it his duty to protect his guest though it should cost him his life, and he was proud and pleased with himself because he was doing his duty.

'Whilst thou art in my house and my head is on my shoulders no one shall harm thee,' he repeated to Hadji Murad.

Hadji Murad looked into his glittering eyes and understanding that this was true, said with some solemnity:

'Mayest thou receive joy and life!'

Sado silently laid his hand on his heart in token of thanks for these kind words.

Having closed the shutters of the *saklya* and laid some sticks in the fireplace, Sado, in an exceptionally bright and animated mood, left the room and went into that part of his *saklya* where his family all lived. The women had not yet gone to sleep, and were talking about the dangerous visitors who were spending the night in their guest-chamber.

II

AT VOZDVIZHENSK, the advanced fort situated some ten miles from the *aoul* in which Hadji Murad was spending the night, three soldiers and a non-commissioned officer left the fort and went beyond the Shahgirinsk Gate. The soldiers, dressed as Caucasian soldiers used to be in those days, wore sheepskin coats and caps, and boots that reached above their knees, and they carried their cloaks tightly rolled up and fastened across their shoulders. Shouldering arms, they first went some five hundred paces along the road and then turned off it and went some twenty paces to the right – the dead leaves rustling under their boots – till they reached the blackened trunk of a broken plane-tree just visible through the darkness. There they stopped. It was at this plane-tree that an ambush party was usually placed.

The bright stars, that had seemed to be running along the tree-tops while the soldiers were walking through the forest, now stood still, shining brightly between the bare branches of the trees.

'A good job it's dry,' said the non-commissioned officer Panov, bringing down his long gun and bayonet with a clang from his shoulder and placing it against the plane-tree.

The three soldiers did the same.

'Sure enough I've lost it!' muttered Panov crossly. 'Must have left it behind or I've dropped it on the way.'

'What are you looking for?' asked one of the soldiers in a bright, cheerful voice.

'The bowl of my pipe. Where the devil has it got to?'

'Have you got the stem?' asked the cheerful voice.

'Here it is.'

'Then why not stick it straight into the ground?'

'Not worth bothering!'

'We'll manage that in a minute.'

Smoking in ambush was forbidden, but this ambush hardly deserved the name. It was rather an outpost to prevent the mountaineers from bringing up a cannon unobserved and firing at the fort as they used to. Panov did not consider it necessary to forgo the pleasure of smoking, and therefore accepted the cheerful soldier's offer. The latter took a knife from his pocket and made a small round hole in the ground. Having smoothed it, he adjusted the pipe-stem to it, then filled the hole with tobacco and pressed it down, and the pipe was ready. A sulphur match flared and for a moment lit up the broad-cheeked face of the soldier who lay on his stomach, the air whistled in the stem, and Panov smelt the pleasant odour of burning tobacco.

'Fixed it up?' said he, rising to his feet.

'Why, of course!'

'What a smart chap you are, Avdeev! . . . As wise as a judge! Now then, lad.'

Avdeev rolled over on his side to make room for Panov, letting smoke escape from his mouth.

Panov lay down prone, and after wiping the mouthpiece with his sleeve, began to inhale.

When they had had their smoke the soldiers began to talk.

'They say the commander has had his fingers in the cash-box again,' remarked one of them in a lazy voice. 'He lost at cards, you see.'

'He'll pay it back again,' said Panov.

'Of course he will! He's a good officer,' assented Avdeev.

'Good! good!' gloomily repeated the man who had started the conversation. 'In my opinion the company ought to speak to him. "If you've taken the money, tell us how much and when you'll repay it."'

'That will be as the company decides,' said Panov, tearing himself away from the pipe.

'Of course. "The community is a strong man,"' assented Avdeev, quoting a proverb.

'There will be oats to buy and boots to get towards spring. The money will be wanted, and what shall we do if he's pocketed it?' insisted the dissatisfied one.

'I tell you it will be as the company wishes,' repeated Panov. 'It's not the first time: he takes it and gives it back.'

In the Caucasus in those days each company chose men to manage its own commissariat. They received six rubles, fifty kopeks a month per man from the treasury, and catered for the company. They planted cabbages, made hay, had their own carts, and prided themselves on their well-fed horses. The company's money was kept in a chest of which the commander had the key, and it often happened that he borrowed from the chest. This had just happened again, and the soldiers were talking about it. The morose soldier, Nikitin, wished to demand an account from the commander, while Panov and Avdeev considered that unnecessary.

After Panov, Nikitin had a smoke, and then spreading his cloak on the ground sat down on it leaning against the trunk of the plane-tree. The soldiers were silent. Far above their heads the crowns of the trees rustled in the wind and suddenly, above this incessant low rustling, rose the howling, whining, weeping, and chuckling of jackals.

'Just listen to those accursed creatures – how they caterwaul!'

'They're laughing at you because your mouth's all on one side,' remarked the high voice of the third soldier, an Ukrainian.

All was silent again, except for the wind that swayed the branches, now revealing and now hiding the stars.

'I say, Panov,' suddenly asked the cheerful Avdeev, 'do you ever feel dull?'

'Dull, why?' replied Panov reluctantly.

'Well, I do . . . I feel so dull sometimes that I don't know what I might not be ready to do to myself.'

'There now!' was all Panov replied.

'That time when I drank all the money it was from dullness. It took hold of me . . . took hold of me till I thought to myself, "I'll just get blind drunk!"'

'But sometimes drinking makes it still worse.'

'Yes, that's happened to me too. But what is a man to do with himself?'

'But what makes you feel so dull?'

'What, me? . . . Why, it's the longing for home.'

'Is yours a wealthy home then?'

'No; we weren't wealthy, but things went properly – we lived well.' And Avdeev began to relate what he had already told Panov many times.

'You see, I went as a soldier of my own free will, instead of my brother,' he said. 'He has children. They were five in the family and I had only just married. Mother began begging me to go. So I thought, "Well, maybe they will remember what I've done." So I went to our proprietor . . . he was a good master and he said, "You're a fine fellow, go!" So I went instead of my brother.'

'Well, that was right,' said Panov.

'And yet, will you believe me, Panov, it's chiefly because of that that I feel so dull now? "Why did you go instead of your brother?" I say to myself. "He's living like a king now over there, while you have to suffer here"; and the more I think of it the worse I feel . . . It seems just a piece of ill-luck!'

Avdeev was silent.

'Perhaps we'd better have another smoke,' said he after a pause.

'Well then, fix it up!'

But the soldiers were not to have their smoke. Hardly had Avdeev risen to fix the pipe-stem in its place when above the rustling of the trees they heard footsteps along the road. Panov took his gun and pushed Nikitin with his foot.

Nikitin rose and picked up his cloak.

The third soldier, Bondarenko, rose also, and said:

'And I have dreamt such a dream, mates . . .'

'Sh!' said Avdeev, and the soldiers held their breath, listening. The footsteps of men in soft-soled boots were heard approaching. The fallen leaves and dry twigs could be heard rustling clearer and clearer through the darkness. Then came the peculiar guttural tones of Chechen voices. The soldiers could now not only hear men approaching, but could see two shadows passing through a clear space between the trees; one shadow taller than the other. When these shadows had come in line with the soldiers, Panov, gun in hand, stepped out on to the road, followed by his comrades.

'Who goes there?' cried he.

'Me, friendly Chechen,' said the shorter one. This was Bata. 'Gun, *yok!* . . . sword, *yok!*' said he, pointing to himself. 'Prince, want!'

The taller one stood silent beside his comrade. He too was unarmed.

'He means he's a scout, and wants the Colonel,' explained Panov to his comrades.

'Prince Vorontsov . . . much want! Big business!' said Bata.

'All right, all right! We'll take you to him,' said Panov. 'I say, you'd better take them,' said he to Avdeev, 'you and Bondarenko; and when you've given them up to the officer on duty come back again. Mind,' he added, 'be careful to make them keep in front of you!'

'And what of this?' said Avdeev, moving his gun and bayonet as though stabbing someone. 'I'd just give a dig, and let the steam out of him!'

'What'll he be worth when you've stuck him?' remarked Bondarenko.

'Now, march!'

When the steps of the two soldiers conducting the scouts could no longer be heard, Panov and Nikitin returned to their post.

'What the devil brings them here at night?' said Nikitin.

'Seems it's necessary,' said Panov. 'But it's getting chilly,' he added, and unrolling his cloak he put it on and sat down by the tree.

About two hours later Avdeev and Bondarenko returned.

'Well, have you handed them over?'

'Yes. They weren't yet asleep at the colonel's – they were taken straight in to him. And do you know, mates, those shaven-headed lads are fine!' continued Avdeev. 'Yes, really. What a talk I had with them!'

'Of course you'd talk,' remarked Nikitin disapprovingly.

'Really they're just like Russians. One of them is married.

"Molly," says I, *"bar?"* *"Bar,"* he says. Bondarenko, didn't I say *"bar?"* "Many *bar?"* "A couple," says he. A couple! Such a good talk we had! Such nice fellows!'

'Nice, indeed!' said Nikitin. 'If you met him alone he'd soon let the guts out of you.'

'It will be getting light before long,' said Panov.

'Yes, the stars are beginning to go out,' said Avdeev, sitting down and making himself comfortable.

And the soldiers were silent again.

III

THE WINDOWS of the barracks and the soldiers' houses had long been dark in the fort; but there were still lights in the windows of the best house.

In it lived Prince Simon Mikhailovich Vorontsov, Commander of the Kurin Regiment, an Imperial Aide-de-Camp and son of the Commander-in-Chief. Vorontsov's wife, Marya Vasilevna, a famous Petersburg beauty, was with him and they lived in this little Caucasian fort more luxuriously than anyone had ever lived there before. To Vorontsov, and even more to his wife, it seemed that they were not only living a very modest life, but one full of privations, while to the inhabitants of the place their luxury was surprising and extraordinary.

Just now, at midnight, the host and hostess sat playing cards with their visitors, at a card-table lit by four candles, in the spacious drawing-room with its carpeted floor and rich curtains drawn across the windows. Vorontsov, who had a long face and wore the insignia and gold cords of an aide-de-camp, was partnered by a shaggy young man of gloomy appearance, a graduate of Petersburg University whom Princess Vorontsov had lately had sent to the Caucasus to be tutor to her little son (born of her first marriage). Against them played two officers: one a broad, red-faced man, Poltoratsky, a company commander who had exchanged out of the Guards; and the other the regimental adjutant, who sat very straight on his chair with a cold expression on his handsome face.

Princess Marya Vasilevna, a large-built, large-eyed, black-browed beauty, sat beside Poltoratsky – her crinoline touching his legs – and looked over his cards. In her words, her looks, her smile, her perfume, and in every movement of her body, there was something that reduced Poltoratsky to obliviousness of everything except the consciousness of her nearness, and he made blunder after blunder, trying his partner's temper more and more.

'No . . . that's too bad! You've wasted an ace again,' said the regimental adjutant, flushing all over as Poltoratsky threw out an ace.

Poltoratsky turned his kindly, wide-set black eyes towards the dissatisfied adjutant uncomprehendingly, as though just aroused from sleep.

'Do forgive him!' said Marya Vasilevna, smiling. 'There, you see! Didn't I tell you so?' she went on, turning to Poltoratsky.

'But that's not at all what you said,' replied Poltoratsky, smiling.

'Wasn't it?' she queried, with an answering smile, which excited and delighted Poltoratsky to such a degree that he blushed crimson and seizing the cards began to shuffle.

'It isn't your turn to deal,' said the adjutant sternly, and with his white ringed hand he began to deal himself, as though he wished to get rid of the cards as quickly as possible.

The prince's valet entered the drawing-room and announced that the officer on duty wanted to speak to him.

'Excuse me, gentlemen,' said the prince, speaking Russian with an English accent. 'Will you take my place, Marya?'

'Do you all agree?' asked the princess, rising quickly and lightly to her full height, rustling her silks, and smiling the radiant smile of a happy woman.

'I always agree to everything,' replied the adjutant, very pleased that the princess – who could not play at all – was now going to play against him.

Poltoratsky only spread out his hands and smiled.

The rubber was nearly finished when the prince returned to the drawing-room, animated and obviously very pleased.

'Do you know what I propose?'

'What?'

'That we have some champagne.'

'I am always ready for that,' said Poltoratsky.

'Why not? We shall be delighted!' said the adjutant.

'Bring some, Vasili!' said the prince.

'What did they want you for?' asked Marya Vasilevna.

'It was the officer on duty and another man.'

'Who? What about?' asked Marya Vasilevna quickly.

'I mustn't say,' said Vorontsov, shrugging his shoulders.

'You mustn't say!' repeated Marya Vasilevna. 'We'll see about that.'

When the champagne was brought each of the visitors drank a glass, and having finished the game and settled the scores they began to take their leave.

'Is it your company that's ordered to the forest tomorrow?' the prince asked Poltoratsky as they said goodbye.

'Yes, mine . . . why?'

'Then we shall meet tomorrow,' said the prince, smiling slightly.

'Very pleased,' replied Poltoratsky, not quite understanding what Vorontsov was saying to him and preoccupied only by the thought that he would in a minute be pressing Marya Vasilevna's hand.

Marya Vasilevna, according to her wont, not only pressed his hand firmly but shook it vigorously, and again reminding him of his mistake in playing diamonds, she gave him what he took to be a delightful, affectionate, and meaning smile.

Poltoratsky went home in an ecstatic condition only to be

understood by people like himself who, having grown up and been educated in society, meet a woman belonging to their own circle after months of isolated military life, and moreover a woman like Princess Vorontsov.

When he reached the little house in which he and his comrade lived he pushed the door, but it was locked. He knocked, with no result. He felt vexed, and began kicking the door and banging it with his sword. Then he heard a sound of footsteps and Vovilo – a domestic serf of his – undid the cabin-hook which fastened the door.

'What do you mean by locking yourself in, blockhead?'

'But how is it possible, sir . . . ?'

'You're tipsy again! I'll show you "how it is possible"!' and Poltoratsky was about to strike Vovilo but changed his mind. 'Oh, go to the devil! . . . Light a candle.'

'In a minute.'

Vovilo was really tipsy. He had been drinking at the name-day party of the ordnance-sergeant, Ivan Petrovich. On returning home he began comparing his life with that of the latter. Ivan Petrovich had a salary, was married, and hoped in a year's time to get his discharge.

Vovilo had been taken 'up' when a boy – that is, he had been taken into his owner's household service – and now although he was already over forty he was not married, but lived a campaigning life with his harum-scarum young master. He was a good master, who seldom struck him, but what kind of a life was it? 'He promised to free me when we return from the Caucasus, but where am I to go with my freedom? ... It's a dog's life!' thought Vovilo, and he felt so sleepy that, afraid lest someone should come in and steal something, he fastened the hook of the door and fell asleep.

Poltoratsky entered the bedroom which he shared with his comrade Tikhonov.

'Well, have you lost?' asked Tikhonov, waking up.

'No, as it happens, I haven't. I've won seventeen rubles, and we drank a bottle of Cliquot!'

'And you've looked at Marya Vasilevna?'

'Yes, and I've looked at Marya Vasilevna,' repeated Poltoratsky.

'It will soon be time to get up,' said Tikhonov. 'We are to start at six.'

'Vovilo!' shouted Poltoratsky, 'see that you wake me up properly tomorrow at five!'

'How can I wake you if you fight?'

'I tell you you're to wake me! Do you hear?'

'All right.' Vovilo went out, taking Poltoratsky's boots and clothes with him. Poltoratsky got into bed and smoked a cigarette and put out his candle, smiling the while. In the dark he saw before him the smiling face of Marya Vasilevna.

*

The Vorontsovs did not go to bed at once. When the visitors had left, Marya Vasilevna went up to her husband and standing in front of him, said severely:

'*Eh bien! Vous allez me dire ce que c'est.*'

'*Mais, ma chère . . .*'

'*Pas de "ma chère"! C'était un émissaire, n'est-ce pas?*'

'*Quand même, je ne puis pas vous le dire.*'

'*Vous ne pouvez pas? Alors, c'est moi qui vais vous le dire!*'

'*Vous?*'*

'It was Hadji Murad, wasn't it?' said Marya Vasilevna, who had for some days past heard of the negotiations and thought that Hadji Murad himself had been to see her husband. Vorontsov could not altogether deny this, but disappointed her by saying that it was not Hadji Murad himself but only an emissary to announce that Hadji Murad would come to meet him next day at the spot where a wood-cutting expedition had been arranged.

In the monotonous life of the fortress the young Vorontsovs — both husband and wife — were glad of this occurrence, and it was already past two o'clock when, after speaking of the pleasure the news would give his father, they went to bed.

---

* 'Well now! You're going to tell me what it is.' / 'But, my dear . . .' / 'Don't "my dear" me! It was an emissary, wasn't it?' / 'Supposing it was, still I must not tell you.' / 'You must not? Well then, I will tell you!' / 'You?'

IV

AFTER THE three sleepless nights he had passed flying from the *murids* Shamil had sent to capture him, Hadji Murad fell asleep as soon as Sado, having bid him goodnight, had gone out of the *saklya*. He slept fully dressed with his head on his hand, his elbow sinking deep into the red down-cushions his host had arranged for him.

At a little distance, by the wall, slept Eldar. He lay on his back, his strong young limbs stretched out so that his high chest, with the black cartridge-pouches sewn into the front of his white Circassian coat, was higher than his freshly shaven, blue-gleaming head, which had rolled off the pillow and was thrown back. His upper lip, on which a little soft down was just appearing, pouted like a child's, now contracting and now expanding, as though he were sipping something. Like Hadji Murad he slept with pistol and dagger in his belt. The sticks in the grate burnt low, and a night-light in a niche in the wall gleamed faintly.

In the middle of the night the floor of the guest-chamber creaked, and Hadji Murad immediately rose, putting his hand to his pistol. Sado entered, treading softly on the earthen floor.

'What is it?' asked Hadji Murad, as if he had not been asleep at all.

'We must think,' replied Sado, squatting down in front of him. 'A woman from her roof saw you arrive and told her husband,

and now the whole *aoul* knows. A neighbour has just been to tell my wife that the Elders have assembled in the mosque and want to detain you.'

'I must be off!' said Hadji Murad.

'The horses are saddled,' said Sado, quickly leaving the *saklya*.

'Eldar!' whispered Hadji Murad. And Eldar, hearing his name, and above all his master's voice, leapt to his feet, setting his cap straight as he did so.

Hadji Murad put on his weapons and then his *burka*. Eldar did the same, and they both went silently out of the *saklya* into the penthouse. The black-eyed boy brought their horses. Hearing the clatter of hoofs on the hard-beaten road, someone stuck his head out of the door of a neighbouring *saklya*, and a man ran up the hill towards the mosque, clattering with his wooden shoes. There was no moon, but the stars shone brightly in the black sky so that the outlines of the *saklya* roofs could be seen in the darkness, the mosque with its minarets in the upper part of the village rising above the other buildings. From the mosque came a hum of voices.

Quickly seizing his gun, Hadji Murad placed his foot in the narrow stirrup, and silently and easily throwing his body across, swung himself onto the high cushion of the saddle.

'May God reward you!' he said, addressing his host while his right foot felt instinctively for the stirrup, and with his whip he lightly touched the lad who held his horse, as a sign that he should let go. The boy stepped aside, and the horse, as if it knew what it had to do, started at a brisk pace down the lane towards the principal street. Eldar rode behind him. Sado in his sheepskin followed, almost running, swinging his arms and crossing now to one side and now to the other of the narrow side-street. At the place where the streets met, first one moving shadow and then another appeared in the road.

'Stop ... who's that? Stop!' shouted a voice, and several men blocked the path.

Instead of stopping, Hadji Murad drew his pistol from his belt and increasing his speed rode straight at those who blocked the way. They separated, and without looking round he started down the road at a swift canter. Eldar followed him at a sharp trot. Two shots cracked behind them and two bullets whistled past without hitting either Hadji Murad or Eldar. Hadji Murad continued riding at the same pace, but having gone some three hundred yards he stopped his slightly panting horse and listened.

In front of him, lower down, gurgled rapidly running water. Behind him in the *aoul* cocks crowed, answering one another. Above these sounds he heard behind him the approaching tramp of horses and the voices of several men. Hadji Murad touched his horse and rode on at an even pace. Those behind him galloped and soon overtook him. They were some twenty mounted men, inhabitants of the *aoul*, who had decided to detain Hadji Murad or at least to make a show of detaining him in order to justify themselves in Shamil's eyes. When they came near enough to be seen in the darkness, Hadji Murad stopped, let go his bridle, and with an accustomed movement of his left hand unbuttoned the cover of his rifle, which he drew forth with his right. Eldar did the same.

'What do you want?' cried Hadji Murad. 'Do you wish to take me? . . . Take me, then!' and he raised his rifle. The men from the *aoul* stopped, and Hadji Murad, rifle in hand, rode down into the ravine. The mounted men followed him but did not draw any nearer. When Hadji Murad had crossed to the other side of the ravine the men shouted to him that he should hear what they had to say. In reply he fired his rifle and put his horse to a gallop. When he reined it in his pursuers were no longer within hearing and the crowing of the cocks could also no longer be heard; only the murmur of the water in the forest sounded more distinctly and now and then came the cry of an owl. The black wall of the forest appeared quite close. It was in this forest that his *murids* awaited him.

On reaching it Hadji Murad paused, and drawing much air into his lungs he whistled and then listened silently. The next minute he was answered by a similar whistle from the forest. Hadji Murad turned from the road and entered it. When he had gone about a hundred paces he saw among the trunks of the trees a bonfire, the shadows of some men sitting round it, and, half lit-up by the firelight, a hobbled horse which was saddled. Four men were seated by the fire.

One of them rose quickly, and coming up to Hadji Murad

took hold of his bridle and stirrup. This was Hadji Murad's sworn brother who managed his household affairs for him.

'Put out the fire,' said Hadji Murad, dismounting.

The men began scattering the pile and trampling on the burning branches.

'Has Bata been here?' asked Hadji Murad, moving towards a *burka* that was spread on the ground.

'Yes, he went away long ago with Khan Mahoma.'

'Which way did they go?'

'That way,' answered Khanefi pointing in the opposite direction to that from which Hadji Murad had come.

'All right,' said Hadji Murad, and unslinging his rifle he began to load it.

'We must take care – I have been pursued,' he said to a man who was putting out the fire.

This was Gamzalo, a Chechen. Gamzalo approached the *burka*, took up a rifle that lay on it wrapped in its cover, and without a word went to that side of the glade from which Hadji Murad had come.

When Eldar had dismounted he took Hadji Murad's horse, and having reined up both horses' heads high, tied them to two trees. Then he shouldered his rifle as Gamzalo had done and went to the other side of the glade. The bonfire was extinguished, the forest no longer looked as black as before, but in the sky the stars still shone, though faintly.

Lifting his eyes to the stars and seeing that the Pleiades had already risen halfway up the sky, Hadji Murad calculated that it must be long past midnight and that his nightly prayer was long overdue. He asked Khanefi for a ewer (they always carried one in their packs), and putting on his *burka* went to the water.

Having taken off his shoes and performed his ablutions, Hadji Murad stepped onto the *burka* with bare feet and then squatted down on his calves, and having first placed his fingers in his ears and closed his eyes, he turned to the south and recited the usual prayer.

When he had finished he returned to the place where the saddle-bags lay, and sitting down on the *burka* he leant his elbows on his knees and bowed his head and fell into deep thought.

Hadji Murad always had great faith in his own fortune. When planning anything he always felt in advance firmly convinced of success, and fate smiled on him. It had been so, with a few rare exceptions, during the whole course of his stormy military life; and so he hoped it would be now. He pictured to himself how – with the army Vorontsov would place at his disposal – he would march against Shamil and take him prisoner, and revenge himself on him; and how the Russian Tsar would reward him and how he would again rule not only over Avaria, but over the whole of Chechnya, which would submit to him. With these thoughts he unwittingly fell asleep.

He dreamt how he and his brave followers rushed at Shamil with songs and with the cry, 'Hadji Murad is coming!' and how they seized him and his wives and how he heard the wives crying and sobbing. He woke up. The song, *Lya-il-allysha*, and the cry, 'Hadji Murad is coming!' and the weeping of Shamil's wives, was the howling, weeping, and laughter of jackals that awoke him. Hadji Murad lifted his head, glanced at the sky which, seen between the trunks of the trees, was already growing light in the east, and inquired after Khan Mahoma of a *murid* who sat at some distance from him. On hearing that Khan Mahoma had not yet returned, Hadji Murad again bowed his head and at once fell asleep.

He was awakened by the merry voice of Khan Mahoma returning from his mission with Bata. Khan Mahoma at once sat down beside Hadji Murad and told him how the soldiers had met them and had led them to the prince himself, and how pleased the prince was and how he promised to meet them in the morning where the Russians would be felling trees beyond the Mitchik in the Shalin glade. Bata interrupted his fellow-envoy to add details of his own.

Hadji Murad asked particularly for the words with which Vorontsov had answered his offer to go over to the Russians, and Khan Mahoma and Bata replied with one voice that the prince promised to receive Hadji Murad as a guest, and to act so that it should be well for him.

Then Hadji Murad questioned them about the road, and when Khan Mahoma assured him that he knew the way well and would conduct him straight to the spot, Hadji Murad took out some money and gave Bata the promised three rubles. Then

33

he ordered his men to take out of the saddle-bags his gold-ornamented weapons and his turban, and to clean themselves up so as to look well when they arrived among the Russians.

While they cleaned their weapons, harness, and horses, the stars faded away, it became quite light, and an early morning breeze sprang up.

V

EARLY IN THE morning, while it was still dark, two companies carrying axes and commanded by Poltoratsky marched six miles beyond the Shahgirinsk Gate, and having thrown out a line of sharpshooters set to work to fell trees as soon as the day broke. Towards eight o'clock the mist which had mingled with the perfumed smoke of the hissing and crackling damp green branches on the bonfires began to rise and the wood-fellers — who till then had not seen five paces off but had only heard one another — began to see both the bonfires and the road through the forest, blocked with fallen trees. The sun now appeared like a bright spot in the fog and now again was hidden.

In the glade, some way from the road, Poltoratsky, his subaltern Tikhonov, two officers of the 3rd Company, and Baron Freze, an ex-officer of the Guards and a fellow-student of Poltoratsky's at the Cadet College, who had been reduced to the ranks for fighting a duel, were sitting on drums. Bits of paper that had contained food, cigarette stumps, and empty bottles, lay scattered around them. The officers had had some vodka and were now eating, and drinking porter. A drummer was uncorking their third bottle.

Poltoratsky, although he had not had enough sleep, was in that peculiar state of elation and kindly careless gaiety which he always felt when he found himself among his soldiers and with his comrades where there was a possibility of danger.

The officers were carrying on an animated conversation, the subject of which was the latest news: the death of General Sleptsov. None of them saw in this death that most important moment of a life, its termination and return to the source whence it sprang – they saw in it only the valour of a gallant officer who rushed at the mountaineers sword in hand and hacked them desperately.

Though all of them – and especially those who had been in action – knew and could not help knowing that in those days in the Caucasus, and in fact anywhere and at any time, such hand-to-hand hacking as is always imagined and described never occurs (or if hacking with swords and bayonets ever does occur, it is only those who are running away that get hacked), that fiction of hand-to-hand fighting endowed them with the calm pride and cheerfulness with which they sat on the drums – some with a jaunty air, others on the contrary in a very modest pose, and drank and joked without troubling about death, which might overtake them at any moment as it had overtaken Sleptsov. And in the midst of their talk, as if to confirm their expectations, they heard to the left of the road the pleasant stirring sound of a rifle-shot; and a bullet, merrily whistling somewhere in the misty air, flew past and crashed into a tree.

'Hullo!' exclaimed Poltoratsky in a merry voice; 'why that's at our line . . . There now, Kostya,' and he turned to Freze, 'now's your chance. Go back to the company. I will lead the whole company to support the cordon and we'll arrange a battle that will be simply delightful . . . and then we'll make a report.'

Freze jumped to his feet and went at a quick pace towards the smoke-enveloped spot where he had left his company.

Poltoratsky's little Kabarda dapple-bay was brought to him, and he mounted and drew up his company and led it in the direction whence the shots were fired. The outposts stood on the skirts of the forest in front of the bare descending slope of a ravine. The wind was blowing in the direction of the forest, and not only was it possible to see the slope of the ravine, but the opposite side of it was also distinctly visible. When Poltoratsky rode up to the line the sun came out from behind the mist, and on the other side of the ravine, by the outskirts of a young forest, a few horsemen could be seen at a distance of a quarter of a mile. These were the Chechens who had pursued Hadji Murad and wanted to see him meet the Russians. One of them fired at the line. Several soldiers fired back. The Chechens retreated and the firing ceased.

But when Poltoratsky and his company came up he nevertheless gave orders to fire, and scarcely had the word been passed than along the whole line of sharpshooters the incessant, merry, stirring rattle of our rifles began, accompanied by pretty dissolving cloudlets of smoke. The soldiers, pleased to have some distraction, hastened to load and fired shot after shot. The Chechens evidently caught the feeling of excitement, and leaping forward one after another fired a few shots at our men. One of these shots wounded a soldier. It was that same Avdeev who had lain in ambush the night before.

When his comrades approached him he was lying prone, holding his wounded stomach with both hands, and rocking himself with a rhythmic motion moaned softly. He belonged to Poltoratsky's company, and Poltoratsky, seeing a group of soldiers collected, rode up to them.

'What is it, lad? Been hit?' said Poltoratsky. 'Where?'

Avdeev did not answer.

'I was just going to load, your Honour, when I heard a click,' said a soldier who had been with Avdeev; 'and I look and see he's dropped his gun.'

'Tut, tut, tut!' Poltoratsky clicked his tongue. 'Does it hurt much, Avdeev?'

'It doesn't hurt but it stops me walking. A drop of vodka now, your Honour!'

Some vodka (or rather the spirit drunk by the soldiers in the Caucasus) was found, and Panov, severely frowning, brought

Avdeev a can-lid full. Avdeev tried to drink it but immediately handed back the lid.

'My soul turns against it,' he said. 'Drink it yourself.'

Panov drank up the spirit.

Avdeev raised himself but sank back at once. They spread out a cloak and laid him on it.

'Your Honour, the Colonel is coming,' said the sergeant-major to Poltoratsky.

'All right. Then will you see to him?' said Poltoratsky, and flourishing his whip he rode at a fast trot to meet Vorontsov.

Vorontsov was riding his thoroughbred English chestnut gelding, and was accompanied by the adjutant, a Cossack, and a Chechen interpreter.

'What's happening here?' asked Vorontsov.

'Why, a skirmishing party attacked our advanced line,' Poltoratsky answered.

'Come, come – you arranged the whole thing yourself!'

'Oh no, Prince, not I,' said Poltoratsky with a smile; 'they pushed forward of their own accord.'

'I hear a soldier has been wounded?'

'Yes, it's a great pity. He's a good soldier.'

'Seriously?'

'Seriously, I believe . . . in the stomach.'

'And do you know where I am going?' Vorontsov asked.

'I don't.'

'Can't you guess?'

'No.'

'Hadji Murad has surrendered and we are now going to meet him.'

'You don't mean to say so?'

'His envoy came to me yesterday,' said Vorontsov, with difficulty repressing a smile of pleasure. 'He will be waiting for me at the Shalin glade in a few minutes. Place sharpshooters as far as the glade, and then come and join me.'

'I understand,' said Poltoratsky, lifting his hand to his cap, and rode back to his company. He led the sharpshooters to the right himself, and ordered the sergeant-major to do the same on the left side.

The wounded Avdeev had meanwhile been taken back to the fort by some of the soldiers.

On his way back to rejoin Vorontsov, Poltoratsky noticed behind him several horsemen who were overtaking him. In front on a white-maned horse rode a man of imposing appearance. He wore a turban and carried weapons with gold ornaments. This man was Hadji Murad. He approached Poltoratsky and said something to him in Tartar. Raising his eyebrows, Poltoratsky made a gesture with his arms to show that he did not understand, and smiled. Hadji Murad gave him smile for smile, and that smile struck Poltoratsky by its childlike kindliness. Poltoratsky had never expected to see the terrible mountain chief look like that. He had expected to see a morose, hard-featured man, and here was a vivacious person whose smile was so kindly that

39

Poltoratsky felt as if he were an old acquaintance. He had only one peculiarity: his eyes, set wide apart, which gazed from under their black brows calmly, attentively, and penetratingly into the eyes of others.

Hadji Murad's suite consisted of five men, among them Khan Mahoma, who had been to see Prince Vorontsov that night. He was a rosy, round-faced fellow with black lashless eyes and a beaming expression, full of the joy of life. Then there was the Avar Khanefi, a thick-set, hairy man, whose eyebrows met. He was in charge of all Hadji Murad's property and led a stud-bred horse which carried tightly packed saddle-bags. Two men of the suite were particularly striking. The first was a Lesghian: a youth, broad-shouldered but with a waist as slim as a woman's, beautiful ram-like eyes, and the beginnings of a brown beard. This was Eldar. The other, Gamzalo, was a Chechen with a short red beard and no eyebrows or eyelashes; he was blind in one eye and had a scar across his nose and face. Poltoratsky pointed out Vorontsov, who had just appeared on the road. Hadji Murad rode to meet him, and putting his right hand on his heart said something in Tartar and stopped. The Chechen interpreter translated.

'He says, "I surrender myself to the will of the Russian Tsar. I wish to serve him," he says. "I wished to do so long ago but Shamil would not let me."'

Having heard what the interpreter said, Vorontsov stretched out his hand in its wash-leather glove to Hadji Murad. Hadji

Murad looked at it hesitatingly for a moment and then pressed it firmly, again saying something and looking first at the interpreter and then at Vorontsov.

'He says he did not wish to surrender to anyone but you, as you are the son of the Sirdar and he respects you much.'

Vorontsov nodded to express his thanks. Hadji Murad again said something, pointing to his suite.

'He says that these men, his henchmen, will serve the Russians as well as he.'

Vorontsov turned towards them and nodded to them too. The merry, black-eyed, lashless Chechen, Khan Mahoma, also nodded and said something which was probably amusing, for the hairy Avar drew his lips into a smile, showing his ivory-white teeth. But the red-haired Gamzalo's one red eye just glanced at Vorontsov and then was again fixed on the ears of his horse.

When Vorontsov and Hadji Murad with their retinues rode back to the fort, the soldiers released from the lines gathered in groups and made their own comments.

'What a lot of men that damned fellow has destroyed! And now see what a fuss they will make of him!'

'Naturally. He was Shamil's right hand, and now — no fear!'

'Still there's no denying it! he's a fine fellow — a regular *dzhigit!*'

'And the red one! He squints at you like a beast!'

'Ugh! He must be a hound!'

They had all specially noticed the red one. Where the

wood-felling was going on the soldiers nearest to the road ran out to look. Their officer shouted to them, but Vorontsov stopped him.

'Let them have a look at their old friend.'

'You know who that is?' he added, turning to the nearest soldier, and speaking the words slowly with his English accent.

'No, your Excellency.'

'Hadji Murad . . . Heard of him?'

'How could we help it, your Excellency? We've beaten him many a time!'

'Yes, and we've had it hot from him too.'

'Yes, that's true, your Excellency,' answered the soldier, pleased to be talking with his chief.

Hadji Murad understood that they were speaking about him, and smiled brightly with his eyes.

Vorontsov returned to the fort in a very cheerful mood.

VI

YOUNG VORONTSOV was much pleased that it was he, and no one else, who had succeeded in winning over and receiving Hadji Murad – next to Shamil Russia's chief and most active enemy. There was only one unpleasant thing about it: General Meller-Zakomelsky was in command of the army at Vozdvizhensk, and the whole affair ought to have been carried out through him. As Vorontsov had done everything himself without reporting it there might be some unpleasantness, and this thought rather interfered with his satisfaction. On reaching his house he entrusted Hadji Murad's henchmen to the regimental adjutant and himself showed Hadji Murad into the house.

Princess Marya Vasilevna, elegantly dressed and smiling, and her little son, a handsome curly-headed child of six, met Hadji Murad in the drawing-room. The latter placed his hands on his heart, and through the interpreter – who had entered with him – said with solemnity that he regarded himself as the prince's *kunak*, since the prince had brought him into his own house; and that a *kunak*'s whole family was as sacred as the *kunak* himself.

Hadji Murad's appearance and manners pleased Marya Vasilevna, and the fact that he flushed when she held out her large white hand to him inclined her still more in his favour. She invited him to sit down, and having asked him whether he drank coffee, had some served. He, however, declined it when it came. He understood a little Russian but could not speak it. When something was said which he could not understand he smiled, and his smile pleased Marya Vasilevna just as it had pleased Poltoratsky. The curly-haired, keen-eyed little boy (whom his mother called Bulka) standing beside her did not take his eyes off Hadji Murad, whom he had always heard spoken of as a great warrior.

Leaving Hadji Murad with his wife, Vorontsov went to his office to do what was necessary about reporting the fact of Hadji

Murad's having come over to the Russians. When he had written a report to the general in command of the left flank – General Kozlovsky – at Grozny, and a letter to his father, Vorontsov hurried home, afraid that his wife might be vexed with him for forcing on her this terrible stranger, who had to be treated in such a way that he should not take offence, and yet not too kindly. But his fears were needless. Hadji Murad was sitting in an armchair with little Bulka, Vorontsov's stepson, on his knee, and with bent head was listening attentively to the interpreter who was translating to him the words of the laughing Marya Vasilevna. Marya Vasilevna was telling him that if every time a *kunak* admired anything of his he made him a present of it, he would soon have to go about like Adam . . .

When the prince entered, Hadji Murad rose at once and, surprising and offending Bulka by putting him off his knee, changed the playful expression of his face to a stern and serious one. He only sat down again when Vorontsov had himself taken a seat.

Continuing the conversation he answered Marya Vasilevna by telling her that it was a law among his people that anything your *kunak* admired must be presented to him.

'Thy son, *kunak*!' he said in Russian, patting the curly head of the boy who had again climbed on his knee.

'He is delightful, your brigand!' said Marya Vasilevna to her husband in French. 'Bulka has been admiring his dagger, and he has given it to him.'

Bulka showed the dagger to his father. '*C'est un objet de prix!*' added she.

'*Il faudra trouver l'occasion de lui faire cadeau,*'* said Vorontsov.

Hadji Murad, his eyes turned down, sat stroking the boy's curly hair and saying: '*Dzhigit, dzhigit!*'

'A beautiful, beautiful dagger,' said Vorontsov, half drawing out the sharpened blade which had a ridge down the centre. 'I thank thee!'

'Ask him what I can do for him,' he said to the interpreter.

The interpreter translated, and Hadji Murad at once replied that he wanted nothing but that he begged to be taken to a place where he could say his prayers.

Vorontsov called his valet and told him to do what Hadji Murad desired.

As soon as Hadji Murad was alone in the room allotted to him his face altered. The pleased expression, now kindly and now stately, vanished, and a look of anxiety showed itself. Vorontsov had received him far better than Hadji Murad had expected. But the better the reception the less did Hadji Murad trust Vorontsov and his officers. He feared everything: that he might be seized, chained, and sent to Siberia, or simply killed; and therefore he was on his guard. He asked Eldar, when the latter entered his room, where his *murids* had been put and whether their arms had been taken from them, and where the horses were. Eldar

---

* 'It is a thing of value.' / 'We must find an opportunity to make him a present.'

reported that the horses were in the prince's stables; that the men had been placed in a barn; that they retained their arms, and that the interpreter was giving them food and tea.

Hadji Murad shook his head in doubt, and after undressing said his prayers and told Eldar to bring him his silver dagger. He then dressed, and having fastened his belt sat down on the divan with his legs tucked under him, to await what might befall him.

At four in the afternoon the interpreter came to call him to dine with the prince.

At dinner he hardly ate anything except some *pilau*, to which he helped himself from the very part of the dish from which Marya Vasilevna had helped herself.

'He is afraid we shall poison him,' Marya Vasilevna remarked to her husband. 'He has helped himself from the place where I took my helping.' Then instantly turning to Hadji Murad she asked him through the interpreter when he would pray again. Hadji Murad lifted five fingers and pointed to the sun. 'Then it will soon be time,' and Vorontsov drew out his watch and pressed a spring. The watch struck four and one quarter. This evidently surprised Hadji Murad, and he asked to hear it again and to be allowed to look at the watch.

'*Voilà l'occasion! Donnez-lui la montre*,'* said the princess to her husband.

---

* 'This is the opportunity! Give him the watch.'

Vorontsov at once offered the watch to Hadji Murad.

The latter placed his hand on his breast and took the watch. He touched the spring several times, listened, and nodded his head approvingly.

After dinner, Meller-Zakomelsky's aide-de-camp was announced.

The aide-de-camp informed the prince that the general, having heard of Hadji Murad's arrival, was highly displeased that this had not been reported to him, and required Hadji Murad to be brought to him without delay. Vorontsov replied that the general's command should be obeyed, and through the interpreter informed Hadji Murad of these orders and asked him to go to Meller with him.

When Marya Vasilevna heard what the aide-de-camp had come about, she at once understood that unpleasantness might arise between her husband and the general, and in spite of all her husband's attempts to dissuade her, decided to go with him and Hadji Murad.

'*Vous feriez bien mieux de rester – c'est mon affaire, non pas la vôtre . . .*'

'*Vous ne pouvez pas m'empêcher d'aller voir madame la générale!*'*

---

* 'You would do much better to remain at home . . . this is my business, and not yours.' / 'You cannot prevent my going to see the general's wife!'

'You could go some other time.'

'But I wish to go now!'

There was no help for it, so Vorontsov agreed, and they all three went.

When they entered, Meller with sombre politeness conducted Marya Vasilevna to his wife and told his aide-de-camp to show Hadji Murad into the waiting-room and not let him out till further orders.

'Please . . .' he said to Vorontsov, opening the door of his study and letting the prince enter before him.

Having entered the study he stopped in front of Vorontsov and, without offering him a seat, said:

'I am in command here and therefore all negotiations with the enemy have to be carried on through me! Why did you not report to me that Hadji Murad had come over?'

'An emissary came to me and announced his wish to capitulate only to me,' replied Vorontsov growing pale with excitement, expecting some rude expression from the angry general and at the same time becoming infected with his anger.

'I ask you why I was not informed?'

'I intended to inform you, Baron, but . . .'

'You are not to address me as "Baron", but as "Your Excellency"!' And here the baron's pent-up irritation suddenly broke out and he uttered all that had long been boiling in his soul.

'I have not served my sovereign twenty-seven years in order

that men who began their service yesterday, relying on family connections, should give orders under my very nose about matters that do not concern them!'

'Your Excellency, I request you not to say things that are incorrect!' interrupted Vorontsov.

'I am saying what is correct, and I won't allow . . .' said the general, still more irritably.

But at that moment Marya Vasilevna entered, rustling with her skirts and followed by a modest-looking little lady, Meller-Zakomelsky's wife.

'Come, come, Baron! Simon did not wish to displease you,' began Marya Vasilevna.

'I am not speaking about that, Princess . . .'

'Well, well, let's forget it all! . . . You know, "A bad peace is better than a good quarrel!" . . . Oh dear, what am I saying?' and she laughed.

The angry general capitulated to the enchanting laugh of the beauty. A smile hovered under his moustache.

'I confess I was wrong,' said Vorontsov, 'but——'

'And I too got rather carried away,' said Meller, and held out his hand to the prince.

Peace was re-established, and it was decided to leave Hadji Murad with the general for the present, and then to send him to the commander of the left flank.

Hadji Murad sat in the next room and though he did not understand what was said, he understood what it was necessary

49

for him to understand – namely, that they were quarrelling about him, that his desertion of Shamil was a matter of immense importance to the Russians, and that therefore not only would they not exile or kill him, but that he would be able to demand much from them. He also understood that though Meller-Zakomelsky was the commanding-officer, he had not as much influence as his subordinate Vorontsov, and that Vorontsov was important and Meller-Zakomelsky unimportant; and therefore when Meller-Zakomelsky sent for him and began to question him, Hadji Murad bore himself proudly and ceremoniously, saying that he had come from the mountains to serve the White Tsar and would give account only to his Sirdar, meaning the commander-in-chief, Prince Vorontsov senior, in Tiflis.

VII

THE WOUNDED Avdeev was taken to the hospital – a small wooden building roofed with boards at the entrance of the fort – and was placed on one of the empty beds in the common ward. There were four patients in the ward: one ill with typhus and in high fever; another, pale, with dark shadows under his eyes, who had ague, was just expecting another attack and yawned continually; and two more who had been wounded in a raid three weeks before: one in the hand – he was up – and the other in the shoulder. The latter was sitting on a bed. All of them except the typhus patient surrounded and questioned the newcomer and those who had brought him.

'Sometimes they fire as if they were spilling peas over you, and nothing happens . . . and this time only about five shots were fired,' related one of the bearers.

'Each man gets what fate sends!'

'Oh!' groaned Avdeev loudly, trying to master his pain when they began to place him on the bed; but he stopped groaning when he was on it, and only frowned and moved his feet continually. He held his hands over his wound and looked fixedly before him.

The doctor came, and gave orders to turn the wounded man over to see whether the bullet had passed out behind.

'What's this?' the doctor asked, pointing to the large white scars that crossed one another on the patient's back and loins.

'That was done long ago, your Honour!' replied Avdeev with a groan.

They were scars left by the flogging Avdeev had received for the money he drank.

Avdeev was again turned over, and the doctor probed in his stomach for a long time and found the bullet, but failed to extract it. He put a dressing on the wound, and having stuck plaster over it went away. During the whole time the doctor was probing and bandaging the wound Avdeev lay with clenched teeth and closed eyes, but when the doctor had gone he opened them and looked around as though amazed. His eyes were turned on the other patients and on the surgeon's orderly, though he seemed to see not them but something else that surprised him.

His friends Panov and Serogin came in, but Avdeev continued to lie in the same position looking before him with surprise. It was long before he recognized his comrades, though his eyes gazed straight at them.

'I say, Peter, have you no message to send home?' said Panov.

Avdeev did not answer, though he was looking Panov in the face.

'I say, haven't you any orders to send home?' again repeated Panov, touching Avdeev's cold, large-boned hand.

Avdeev seemed to come to.

'Ah! . . . Panov!'

'Yes, I'm here . . . I've come! Have you nothing for home? Serogin would write a letter.'

'Serogin . . .' said Avdeev moving his eyes with difficulty towards Serogin, 'will you write? . . . Well then, write so: "Your son," say, "Peter, has given orders that you should live long.* He envied his brother" . . . I told you about that today . . . "and now he is himself glad. Don't worry him . . . Let him live. God grant it him. I am glad!" Write that.'

Having said this he was silent for some time with his eyes fixed on Panov.

'And did you find your pipe?' he suddenly asked.

---

* A popular expression, meaning that the sender of the message is already dead.

Panov did not reply.

'Your pipe . . . your pipe! I mean, have you found it?' Avdeev repeated.

'It was in my bag.'

'That's right! . . . Well, and now give me a candle to hold . . . I am going to die,' said Avdeev.

Just then Poltoratsky came in to inquire after his soldier.

'How goes it, my lad! Badly?' said he.

Avdeev closed his eyes and shook his head negatively. His broad-cheeked face was pale and stern. He did not reply, but again said to Panov:

'Bring a candle . . . I am going to die.'

A wax taper was placed in his hand but his fingers would not bend, so it was placed between them and held up for him.

Poltoratsky went away, and five minutes later the orderly put his ear to Avdeev's heart and said that all was over.

Avdeev's death was described in the following manner in the report sent to Tiflis:

'*23rd Nov.* – Two companies of the Kurin Regiment advanced from the fort on a wood-felling expedition. At midday a considerable number of mountaineers suddenly attacked the wood-fellers. The sharpshooters began to retreat, but the 2nd Company charged with the bayonet and overthrew the mountaineers. In this affair two privates were slightly wounded and one killed. The mountaineers lost about a hundred men killed and wounded.'

VIII

ON THE DAY Peter Avdeev died in the hospital at Vozdvizhensk, his old father with the wife of the brother in whose stead he had enlisted, and that brother's daughter – who was already approaching womanhood and almost of age to get married – were threshing oats on the hard-frozen threshing-floor.

There had been a heavy fall of snow the previous night, followed towards morning by a severe frost. The old man woke when the cocks were crowing for the third time, and seeing the bright moonlight through the frozen window-panes got down from the stove, put on his boots, his sheepskin coat and cap, and went out to the threshing-floor. Having worked there for a couple of hours he returned to the hut and awoke his son and the women. When the woman and the girl came to the threshing-floor they found it ready swept, with a wooden shovel sticking in the dry white snow, beside which were birch brooms with the twigs upwards and two rows of oat-sheaves laid ears to ears in a long line the whole length of the clean threshing-floor. They chose their flails and started threshing, keeping time with their triple blows. The old man struck powerfully with his heavy flail, breaking the straw, the girl struck the ears from above with measured blows, and the daughter-in-law turned the oats over with her flail.

The moon had set, dawn was breaking, and they were

finishing the line of sheaves when Akim, the eldest son, in his sheepskin and cap, joined the threshers.

'What are you lazing about for?' shouted his father to him, pausing in his work and leaning on his flail.

'The horses had to be seen to.'

'"Horses seen to"!' the father repeated, mimicking him.

'The old woman will look after them . . . Take your flail! You're getting too fat, you drunkard!'

'Have you been standing me treat?' muttered the son.

'What?' said the old man, frowning sternly and missing a stroke.

The son silently took a flail and they began threshing with four flails.

'*Trak, tapatam . . . trak, tapatam . . . trak . . .*' came down the old man's heavy flail after the three others.

'Why, you've got a nape like a goodly gentleman! . . . Look here, my trousers have hardly anything to hang on!' said the old man, omitting his stroke and only swinging his flail in the air so as not to get out of time.

They had finished the row, and the women began removing the straw with rakes.

'Peter was a fool to go in your stead. They'd have knocked the nonsense out of you in the army, and he was worth five of such as you at home!'

'That's enough, father,' said the daughter-in-law, as she threw aside the binders that had come off the sheaves.

'Yes, feed the six of you and get no work out of a single one! Peter used to work for two. He was not like . . .'

Along the trodden path from the house came the old man's wife, the frozen snow creaking under the new bark shoes she wore over her tightly wound woollen leg-bands.* The men were shovelling the unwinnowed grain into heaps, the woman and the girl sweeping up what remained.

'The Elder has been and orders everybody to go and work for the master, carting bricks,' said the old woman. I've got breakfast ready . . . Come along, won't you?'

'All right . . . Harness the roan and go,' said the old man to Akim, 'and you'd better look out that you don't get me into trouble as you did the other day! . . . I can't help regretting Peter!'

'When he was at home you used to scold him,' retorted Akim. 'Now he's away you keep nagging at me.'

'That shows you deserve it,' said his mother in the same angry tones. 'You'll never be Peter's equal.'

'Oh, all right,' said the son.

'"All right", indeed! You've drunk the meal, and now you say "all right"!'

'Let bygones be bygones!' said the daughter-in-law.

The disagreements between father and son had begun long ago – almost from the time Peter went as a soldier. Even then the old man felt that he had parted with an eagle for a cuckoo.

---

* Worn by Russian peasants instead of stockings.

It is true that it was right – as the old man understood it – for a childless man to go in place of a family man. Akim had four children and Peter had none; but Peter was a worker like his father, skilful, observant, strong, enduring, and above all industrious. He was always at work. If he happened to pass by where people were working he lent a helping hand as his father would have done, and took a turn or two with the scythe, or loaded a cart, or felled a tree, or chopped some wood. The old man regretted his going away, but there was no help for it. Conscription in those days was like death. A soldier was a severed branch, and to think about him at home was to tear one's heart uselessly. Only occasionally, to prick his elder son, did the father mention him, as he had done that day. But his mother often thought of her younger son, and for a long time – more than a year now – she had been asking her husband to send Peter a little money, but the old man had made no response.

The Kurenkovs were a well-to-do family and the old man had some savings hidden away, but he would on no account have consented to touch what he had laid by. Now however the old woman having heard him mention their younger son, made up her mind to ask him again to send him at least a ruble after selling the oats. This she did. As soon as the young people had gone to work for the proprietor and the old folk were left alone together, she persuaded him to send Peter a ruble out of the oats-money.

So when ninety-six bushels of the winnowed oats had been

packed onto three sledges lined with sacking carefully pinned together at the top with wooden skewers, she gave her husband a letter the church clerk had written at her dictation, and the old man promised when he got to town to enclose a ruble and send it off to the right address.

The old man, dressed in a new sheepskin with a homespun cloak over it, his legs wrapped round with warm white woollen leg-bands, took the letter, placed it in his wallet, said a prayer, got into the front sledge, and drove to town. His grandson drove in the last sledge. When he reached town the old man asked the inn-keeper to read the letter to him, and listened to it attentively and approvingly.

In her letter Peter's mother first sent him her blessing, then greetings from everybody and the news of his godfather's death, and at the end she added that Aksinya (Peter's wife) had not wished to stay with them but had gone into service, where they heard she was living honestly and well. Then came a reference to the present of a ruble, and finally a message which the old woman, yielding to her sorrow, had dictated with tears in her eyes and the church clerk had taken down exactly, word for word:

'One thing more, my darling child, my sweet dove, my own Peterkin! I have wept my eyes out lamenting for thee, thou light of my eyes. To whom hast thou left me? . . .' At this point the old woman had sobbed and wept, and said: 'That will do!' So the words stood in the letter; but it was not fated that Peter should receive the news of his wife's having left home, nor the present of the ruble, nor his mother's last words. The letter with the money in it came back with the announcement that Peter had been killed in the war, 'defending his Tsar, his Fatherland, and the Orthodox Faith'. That is how the army clerk expressed it.

The old woman, when this news reached her, wept for as long as she could spare time, and then set to work again. The very next Sunday she went to church and had a requiem chanted and Peter's name entered among those for whose souls prayers were to be said, and she distributed bits of holy bread to all the good people in memory of Peter, the servant of God.

Aksinya, his widow, also lamented loudly when she heard of the death of her beloved husband with whom she had lived but one short year. She regretted her husband and her own ruined life, and in her lamentations mentioned Peter's brown locks and his love, and the sadness of her life with her little orphaned Vanka, and bitterly reproached Peter for having had pity on his brother but none on her – obliged to wander among strangers!

But in the depth of her soul Aksinya was glad of her husband's death. She was pregnant a second time by the shopman with whom she was living, and no one would now have a right to scold her, and the shopman could marry her as he had said he would when he was persuading her to yield.

IX

MICHAEL SEMENOVICH VORONTSOV, being the son of the Russian Ambassador, had been educated in England and possessed a European education quite exceptional among the higher Russian officials of his day. He was ambitious, gentle and kind in his manner with inferiors, and a finished courtier with superiors. He did not understand life without power and submission. He had obtained all the highest ranks and decorations and was looked upon as a clever commander, and even as the conqueror of Napoleon at Krasnoe.*

In 1852 he was over seventy, but young for his age, he moved briskly, and above all was in full possession of a facile, refined, and agreeable intellect which he used to maintain his power and strengthen and increase his popularity. He possessed large means – his own and his wife's (who had been a Countess Branitski) – and received an enormous salary as Viceroy, and he spent a great part of his means on building a palace and laying out a garden on the south coast of the Crimea.

On the evening of 4 December 1852, a courier's troyka drew up before his palace in Tiflis. An officer, tired and black with

---

* A town thirty miles south-west of Smolensk, at which, in November 1812, the rear-guard of Napoleon's army was defeated during the retreat from Moscow. It is mentioned in *War and Peace*.

dust, sent by General Kozlovsky with the news of Hadji Murad's surrender to the Russians, entered the wide porch, stretching the stiffened muscles of his legs as he passed the sentinel. It was six o'clock, and Vorontsov was just going in to dinner when he was informed of the courier's arrival. He received him at once, and was therefore a few minutes late for dinner.

When he entered the drawing-room the thirty persons invited to dine, who were sitting beside Princess Elizabeth Ksaverevna Vorontsova, or standing in groups by the windows, turned their faces towards him. Vorontsov was dressed in his usual black military coat, with shoulder-straps but no epaulettes, and wore the White Cross of the Order of St George at his neck.

His clean-shaven, foxlike face wore a pleasant smile as, screwing up his eyes, he surveyed the assembly. Entering with quick soft steps he apologized to the ladies for being late, greeted the men, and approaching Princess Manana Orbelyani – a tall, fine, handsome woman of oriental type about forty-five years of age – he offered her his arm to take her in to dinner. Princess Elizabeth Ksaverevna Vorontsova gave her arm to a red-haired general with bristly moustaches who was visiting Tiflis. A Georgian prince offered his arm to Princess Vorontsova's friend, Countess Choiseuil. Doctor Andreevsky, the aide-de-camp, and others, with ladies or without, followed these first couples. Footmen in livery and knee-breeches drew back and replaced the guests' chairs when they sat down, while the major-domo ceremoniously ladled out steaming soup from a silver tureen.

Vorontsov took his place in the centre of one side of the long table, and his wife sat opposite, with the general on her right. On the prince's right sat his lady, the beautiful Orbelyani; and on his left was a graceful, dark, red-cheeked Georgian woman, glittering with jewels and incessantly smiling.

'*Excellentes, chère amie!*' replied Vorontsov to his wife's inquiry about what news the courier had brought him. '*Simon a eu de la chance!*'* And he began to tell aloud, so that everyone could hear, the striking news (for him alone not quite unexpected, because negotiations had long been going on) that Hadji Murad, the bravest and most famous of Shamil's officers, had come over to the Russians and would in a day or two be brought to Tiflis.

Everybody – even the young aides-de-camp and officials who sat at the far ends of the table and who had been quietly laughing at something among themselves – became silent and listened.

'And you, General, have you ever met this Hadji Murad?' asked the princess of her neighbour, the carroty general with the bristly moustaches, when the prince had finished speaking.

'More than once, Princess.'

And the general went on to tell how Hadji Murad, after the mountaineers had captured Gergebel in 1843, had fallen upon General Pahlen's detachment and killed Colonel Zolotukhin almost before their very eyes.

Vorontsov listened to the general and smiled amiably,

---

* 'Excellent, my dear! . . . Simon has had good luck.'

evidently pleased that the latter had joined in the conversation. But suddenly his face assumed an absent-minded and depressed expression.

The general, having started talking, had begun to tell of his second encounter with Hadji Murad.

'Why, it was he, if your Excellency will please remember,' said the general, 'who arranged the ambush that attacked the rescue party in the "Biscuit" expedition.'

'Where?' asked Vorontsov, screwing up his eyes.

What the brave general spoke of as the 'rescue' was the affair in the unfortunate Dargo campaign in which a whole detachment, including Prince Vorontsov who commanded it, would certainly have perished had it not been rescued by the arrival of fresh troops. Everyone knew that the whole Dargo campaign under Vorontsov's command – in which the Russians lost many killed and wounded and several cannon – had been a shameful affair, and therefore if anyone mentioned it in Vorontsov's presence they did so only in the aspect in which Vorontsov had reported it to the Tsar – as a brilliant achievement of the Russian army. But the word 'rescue' plainly indicated that it was not a brilliant victory but a blunder costing many lives. Everybody understood this and some pretended not to notice the meaning of the general's words, others nervously waited to see what would follow, while a few exchanged glances and smiled. Only the carroty general with the bristly moustaches noticed nothing, and carried away by his narrative quietly replied:

'At the rescue, your Excellency.'

Having started on his favourite theme, the general recounted circumstantially how Hadji Murad had so cleverly cut the detachment in two that if the rescue party had not arrived (he seemed to be particularly fond of repeating the word 'rescue') not a man in the division would have escaped, because . . . He did not finish his story, for Manana Orbelyani having understood what was happening, interrupted him by asking if he had found comfortable quarters in Tiflis. The general, surprised, glanced at everybody all round and saw his aides-de-camp from the end of the table looking fixedly and significantly at him, and he suddenly understood! Without replying to the princess's question, he frowned, became silent, and began hurriedly swallowing the delicacy that lay on his plate, the appearance and taste of which both completely mystified him.

Everybody felt uncomfortable, but the awkwardness of the situation was relieved by the Georgian prince – a very stupid man but an extraordinarily refined and artful flatterer and courtier – who sat on the other side of Princess Vorontsova. Without seeming to have noticed anything he began to relate how Hadji Murad had carried off the widow of Akhmet Khan of Mekhtuli.

'He came into the village at night, seized what he wanted, and galloped off again with the whole party.'

'Why did he want that particular woman?' asked the princess.

'Oh, he was her husband's enemy, and pursued him but could

never once succeed in meeting him right up to the time of his death, so he revenged himself on the widow.'

The princess translated this into French for her old friend Countess Choiseuil, who sat next to the Georgian prince.

'*Quelle horreur!*'* said the countess, closing her eyes and shaking her head.

'Oh no!' said Vorontsov, smiling. 'I have been told that he treated his captive with chivalrous respect and afterwards released her.'

'Yes, for a ransom!'

'Well, of course. But all the same he acted honourably.'

These words of Vorontsov's set the tone for the further conversation. The courtiers understood that the more importance was attributed to Hadji Murad the better the prince would be pleased.

'The man's audacity is amazing. A remarkable man!'

'Why, in 1849 he dashed into Temir Khan Shura and plundered the shops in broad daylight.'

An Armenian sitting at the end of the table, who had been in Temir Khan Shura at the time, related the particulars of that exploit of Hadji Murad's.

In fact, Hadji Murad was the sole topic of conversation during the whole dinner.

Everybody in succession praised his courage, his ability,

---

* 'How horrible!'

and his magnanimity. Someone mentioned his having ordered twenty-six prisoners to be killed, but that too was met by the usual rejoinder, 'What's to be done? *À la guerre, comme à la guerre!*'*

'He is a great man.'

Had he been born in Europe he might have been another Napoleon,' said the stupid Georgian prince with a gift of flattery.

He knew that every mention of Napoleon was pleasant to Vorontsov, who wore the White Cross at his neck as a reward for having defeated him.

'Well, not Napoleon perhaps, but a gallant cavalry general if you like,' said Vorontsov.

'If not Napoleon, then Murat.'

'And his name is Hadji *Murad*!'

'Hadji Murad has surrendered and now there'll be an end to Shamil too,' someone remarked.

'They feel that now' (this 'now' meant under Vorontsov) 'they can't hold out,' remarked another.

'*Tout cela est grâce à vous!*'† said Manana Orbelyani.

Prince Vorontsov tried to moderate the waves of flattery which began to flow over him. Still, it was pleasant, and in the best of spirits he led his lady back into the drawing-room.

After dinner, when coffee was being served in the drawing-room, the prince was particularly amiable to everybody, and

---

* 'War is war.'

† 'All this is thanks to you!'

going up to the general with the red bristly moustaches he tried to appear not to have noticed his blunder.

Having made a round of the visitors he sat down to the card-table. He only played the old-fashioned game of ombre. His partners were the Georgian prince, an Armenian general (who had learnt the game of ombre from Prince Vorontsov's valet), and Doctor Andreevsky, a man remarkable for the great influence he exercised.

Placing beside him his gold snuff-box with a portrait of Alexander I on the lid, the prince tore open a pack of highly glazed cards and was going to spread them out, when his Italian valet, Giovanni, brought him a letter on a silver tray.

'Another courier, your Excellency.'

Vorontsov laid down the cards, excused himself, opened the letter, and began to read.

The letter was from his son, who described Hadji Murad's surrender and his own encounter with Meller-Zakomelsky.

The princess came up and inquired what their son had written.

'It's all about the same matter . . . *Il a eu quelques désagréments avec le commandant de la place. Simon a eu tort** . . . But "All's well that ends well",' he added in English, handing the letter to his wife; and turning to his respectfully waiting partners he asked them to draw cards.

---

* 'He has had some unpleasantness with the commandant of the place. Simon was in the wrong.'

67

When the first round had been dealt Vorontsov did what he was in the habit of doing when in a particularly pleasant mood: with his white, wrinkled old hand he took out a pinch of French snuff, carried it to his nose, and released it.

X

WHEN HADJI MURAD appeared at the prince's palace next day, the waiting-room was already full of people. Yesterday's general with the bristly moustaches was there in full uniform with all his decorations, having come to take leave. There was the commander of a regiment who was in danger of being court-martialled for misappropriating commissariat money, and there was a rich Armenian (patronized by Doctor Andreevsky) who wanted to obtain from the Government a renewal of his monopoly for the sale of vodka. There, dressed in black, was the widow of an officer who had been killed in action. She had come to ask for a pension, or for free education for her children. There was a ruined Georgian prince in a magnificent Georgian costume who was trying to obtain for himself some confiscated church property. There was an official with a large roll of paper containing a new plan for subjugating the Caucasus. There was also a Khan who had come solely to be able to tell his people at home that he had called on the prince.

They all waited their turn and were one by one shown into

the prince's cabinet and out again by the aide-de-camp, a handsome, fair-haired youth.

When Hadji Murad entered the waiting-room with his brisk though limping step all eyes were turned towards him and he heard his name whispered from various parts of the room.

He was dressed in a long white Circassian coat over a brown *beshmet* trimmed round the collar with fine silver lace. He wore black leggings and soft shoes of the same colour which were stretched over his instep as tight as gloves. On his head he wore a high cap draped turban-fashion – that same turban for which, on the denunciation of Akhmet Khan, he had been arrested by General Klugenau and which had been the cause of his going over to Shamil.

He stepped briskly across the parquet floor of the waiting-room, his whole slender figure swaying slightly in consequence of his lameness in one leg which was shorter than the other. His eyes, set far apart, looked calmly before him and seemed to see no one.

The handsome aide-de-camp, having greeted him, asked him to take a seat while he went to announce him to the prince, but Hadji Murad declined to sit down and, putting his hand on his dagger, stood with one foot advanced, looking round contemptuously at all those present.

The prince's interpreter, Prince Tarkhanov, approached Hadji Murad and spoke to him. Hadji Murad answered abruptly and unwillingly. A Kumyk prince, who was there to lodge a complaint against a police official, came out of the prince's room, and then the aide-de-camp called Hadji Murad, led him to the door of the cabinet, and showed him in.

The Commander-in-Chief received Hadji Murad standing beside his table, and his old white face did not wear yesterday's smile but was rather stern and solemn.

On entering the large room with its enormous table and great windows with green venetian blinds, Hadji Murad placed his small sunburnt hands on his chest just where the front of his white coat overlapped, and lowering his eyes began, without hurrying, to speak distinctly and respectfully, using the Kumyk dialect which he spoke well.

'I place myself under the powerful protection of the great Tsar and of yourself,' said he, 'and promise to serve the White Tsar in faith and truth to the last drop of my blood, and I hope to be useful to you in the war with Shamil who is my enemy and yours.'

Having heard the interpreter out, Vorontsov glanced at Hadji Murad and Hadji Murad glanced at Vorontsov.

The eyes of the two men met, and expressed to each other much that could not have been put into words and that was not at all what the interpreter said. Without words they told each other the whole truth. Vorontsov's eyes said that he did not believe a single word Hadji Murad was saying, and that he knew he was and always would be an enemy to everything Russian and had surrendered only because he was obliged to.

Hadji Murad understood this and yet continued to give assurances of his fidelity. His eyes said, 'That old man ought to be thinking of his death and not of war, but though he is old he is cunning, and I must be careful.' Vorontsov understood this also, but nevertheless spoke to Hadji Murad in the way he considered necessary for the success of the war.

'Tell him', said Vorontsov, 'that our sovereign is as merciful as he is mighty and will probably at my request pardon him and take him into his service . . . Have you told him?' he asked, looking at Hadji Murad . . . 'Until I receive my master's gracious decision, tell him I take it on myself to receive him and make his sojourn among us pleasant.'

Hadji Murad again pressed his hands to the centre of his chest and began to say something with animation.

'He says', the interpreter translated, 'that formerly, when he governed Avaria in 1839, he served the Russians faithfully and would never have deserted them had not his enemy, Akhmet Khan, wishing to ruin him, calumniated him to General Klugenau.'

'I know, I know,' said Vorontsov (though if he had ever known he had long forgotten it). 'I know,' he repeated, sitting down and motioning Hadji Murad to the divan that stood beside the wall. But Hadji Murad did not sit down. Shrugging his powerful shoulders as a sign that he could not bring himself to sit in the presence of so important a man, he went on, addressing the interpreter:

'Akhmet Khan and Shamil are both my enemies. Tell the prince that Akhmet Khan is dead and I cannot revenge myself on him, but Shamil lives and I will not die without taking vengeance on him,' said he, knitting his brows and tightly closing his mouth.

'Yes, yes; but how does he want to revenge himself on Shamil?' said Vorontsov quietly to the interpreter. 'And tell him he may sit down.'

Hadji Murad again declined to sit down, and in answer to the question replied that his object in coming over to the Russians was to help them to destroy Shamil.

'Very well, very well,' said Vorontsov; 'but what exactly does he wish to do? . . . Sit down, sit down!'

Hadji Murad sat down, and said that if only they would send him to the Lesghian line and would give him an army, he would guarantee to raise the whole of Daghestan and Shamil would then be unable to hold out.

'That would be excellent . . . I'll think it over,' said Vorontsov.

The interpreter translated Vorontsov's words to Hadji Murad.

Hadji Murad pondered.

'Tell the Sirdar one thing more,' Hadji Murad began again, 'that my family are in the hands of my enemy, and that as long as they are in the mountains I am bound and cannot serve him. Shamil would kill my wife and my mother and my children if I went openly against him. Let the prince first exchange my family for the prisoners he has, and then I will destroy Shamil or die!'

'All right, all right,' said Vorontsov. 'I will think it over . . .

Now let him go to the chief of the staff and explain to him in detail his position, intentions, and wishes.'

Thus ended the first interview between Hadji Murad and Vorontsov.

That evening an Italian opera was performed at the new theatre, which was decorated in oriental style. Vorontsov was in his box when the striking figure of the limping Hadji Murad wearing a turban appeared in the stalls. He came in with Loris-Melikov,* Vorontsov's aide-de-camp, in whose charge he was placed, and took a seat in the front row. Having sat through the first act with oriental Mohammedan dignity, expressing no pleasure but only obvious indifference, he rose and looking calmly round at the audience went out, drawing to himself everybody's attention.

The next day was Monday and there was the usual evening party at the Vorontsovs'. In the large brightly lighted hall a band was playing, hidden among trees. Young women and women not very young wearing dresses that displayed their bare necks, arms, and breasts, turned round and round in the embrace of men in bright uniforms. At the buffet, footmen in red swallow-tail coats and wearing shoes and knee-breeches, poured out champagne and served sweetmeats to the ladies. The 'Sirdar's' wife also, in spite of her age, went about half-dressed among the visitors

---

* Count Michael Tarielovich Loris-Melikov, who afterwards became Minister of the Interior and framed the Liberal *ukase* [decree] which was signed by Alexander II on the day that he was assassinated.

smiling affably, and through the interpreter said a few amiable words to Hadji Murad who glanced at the visitors with the same indifference he had shown yesterday in the theatre. After the hostess, other half-naked women came up to him and all of them stood shamelessly before him and smilingly asked him the same question: How he liked what he saw? Vorontsov himself, wearing gold epaulettes and gold shoulder-knots with his white cross and ribbon at his neck, came up and asked him the same question, evidently feeling sure, like all the others, that Hadji Murad could not help being pleased at what he saw. Hadji Murad replied to Vorontsov as he had replied to them all, that among his people nothing of the kind was done, without expressing an opinion as to whether it was good or bad that it was so.

Here at the ball Hadji Murad tried to speak to Vorontsov about buying out his family, but Vorontsov, pretending that he had not heard him, walked away, and Loris-Melikov afterwards told Hadji Murad that this was not the place to talk about business.

When it struck eleven Hadji Murad, having made sure of the time by the watch the Vorontsovs had given him, asked Loris-Melikov whether he might now leave. Loris-Melikov said he might, though it would be better to stay. In spite of this Hadji Murad did not stay, but drove in the phaeton placed at his disposal to the quarters that had been assigned to him.

XI

ON THE FIFTH day of Hadji Murad's stay in Tiflis Loris-Melikov, the Viceroy's aide-de-camp, came to see him at the latter's command.

'My head and my hands are glad to serve the Sirdar,' said Hadji Murad with his usual diplomatic expression, bowing his head and putting his hands to his chest. 'Command me!' said he, looking amiably into Loris-Melikov's face.

Loris-Melikov sat down in an armchair placed by the table and Hadji Murad sank onto a low divan opposite and, resting his hands on his knees, bowed his head and listened attentively to what the other said to him.

Loris-Melikov, who spoke Tartar fluently, told him that though the prince knew about his past life, he yet wanted to hear the whole story from himself.

'Tell it me, and I will write it down and translate it into Russian and the prince will send it to the Emperor.'

Hadji Murad remained silent for a while (he never interrupted anyone but always waited to see whether his collocutor had not something more to say), then he raised his head, shook back his cap, and smiled the peculiar childlike smile that had captivated Marya Vasilevna.

'I can do that,' said he, evidently flattered by the thought that his story would be read by the Emperor.

'Thou must tell me' (in Tartar nobody is addressed as 'you') 'everything, deliberately from the beginning,' said Loris-Melikov drawing a notebook from his pocket.

'I can do that, only there is much — very much — to tell! Many events have happened!' said Hadji Murad.

'If thou canst not do it all in one day thou wilt finish it another time,' said Loris-Melikov.

'Shall I begin at the beginning?'

'Yes, at the very beginning . . . where thou wast born and where thou didst live.'

Hadji Murad's head sank and he sat in that position for a long time. Then he took a stick that lay beside the divan, drew a little knife with an ivory gold-inlaid handle, sharp as a razor, from under his dagger, and started whittling the stick with it and speaking at the same time.

'Write: Born in Tselmess, a small *aoul*, "the size of an ass's head", as we in the mountains say,' he began. 'Not far from it, about two cannon-shots, lies Khunzakh where the Khans lived. Our family was closely connected with them.

'My mother, when my eldest brother Osman was born, nursed the eldest Khan, Abu Nutsal Khan. Then she nursed the second son of the Khan, Umma Khan, and reared him; but Akhmet my second brother died, and when I was born and the Khansha bore Bulach Khan, my mother would not go as wet-nurse again. My father ordered her to, but she would not. She said: "I should again kill my own son, and I will not go." Then my father, who was passionate, struck her with a dagger and would have killed her had they not rescued her from him. So she did not give me up, and later on she composed a song . . . but I need not tell that.'

'Yes, you must tell everything. It is necessary,' said Loris-Melikov.

Hadji Murad grew thoughtful. He remembered how his mother had laid him to sleep beside her under a fur coat on the roof of the *saklya*, and he had asked her to show him the place in her side where the scar of her wound was still visible.

He repeated the song, which he remembered:

> '*My white bosom was pierced by the blade of bright steel,*
> *But I laid my bright sun, my dear boy, close upon it*
> *Till his body was bathed in the stream of my blood.*
> *And the wound healed without aid of herbs or of grass.*
> *As I feared not death, so my boy will ne'er fear it.*'

'My mother is now in Shamil's hands,' he added, 'and she must be rescued.'

He remembered the fountain below the hill, when holding on to his mother's *sharovary* (loose Turkish trousers) he had gone with her for water. He remembered how she had shaved his head for the first time, and how the reflection of his round bluish head in the shining brass vessel that hung on the wall had astonished him. He remembered a lean dog that had licked his face. He remembered the strange smell of the *lepeshki* (a kind of flat cake) his mother had given him – a smell of smoke and of sour milk. He remembered how his mother had carried him in a basket on her back to visit his grandfather at the farmstead. He remembered his wrinkled grandfather with his grey hairs, and how he had hammered silver with his sinewy hands.

'Well, so my mother did not go as nurse,' he said with a jerk of his head, 'and the Khansha took another nurse but still remained fond of my mother, and my mother used to take us children to the Khansha's palace, and we played with her children and she was fond of us.

'There were three young Khans: Abu Nutsal Khan my brother Osman's foster-brother; Umma Khan my own sworn brother; and Bulach Khan the youngest – whom Shamil threw over the precipice. But that happened later.

'I was about sixteen when *murids* began to visit the *aouls*. They beat the stones with wooden scimitars and cried, "Mussulmans, *Ghazavat!*" The Chechens all went over to Muridism and the Avars began to go over too. I was then living in the palace like a brother of the Khans. I could do as I liked, and I became rich. I had horses and weapons and money. I lived for pleasure and had no care, and went on like that till the time when Kazi-Mulla, the Imam, was killed and Hamzad succeeded him. Hamzad sent envoys to the Khans to say that if they did not join the *Ghazavat* he would destroy Khunzakh.

'This needed consideration. The Khans feared the Russians,

but were also afraid to join in the Holy War. The old Khansha sent me with her second son, Umma Khan, to Tiflis to ask the Russian Commander-in-Chief for help against Hamzad. The Commander-in-Chief at Tiflis was Baron Rosen. He did not receive either me or Umma Khan. He sent word that he would help us, but did nothing. Only his officers came riding to us and played cards with Umma Khan. They made him drunk with wine and took him to bad places, and he lost all he had to them at cards. His body was as strong as a bull's and he was as brave as a lion, but his soul was weak as water. He would have gambled away his last horses and weapons if I had not made him come away.

'After visiting Tiflis my ideas changed and I advised the old Khansha and the Khans to join the *Ghazavat* . . .'

'What made you change your mind?' asked Loris-Melikov. 'Were you not pleased with the Russians?'

Hadji Murad paused.

'No, I was not pleased,' he answered decidedly, closing his eyes. 'And there was also another reason why I wished to join the *Ghazavat*.'

'What was that?'

'Why, near Tselmess the Khan and I encountered three *murids*, two of whom escaped but the third one I shot with my pistol.

'He was still alive when I approached to take his weapons. He looked up at me, and said, "Thou hast killed me . . . I am

79

happy; but thou art a Mussulman, young and strong. Join the *Ghazavat!* God wills it!"'

'And did you join it?'

'I did not, but it made me think,' said Hadji Murad, and he went on with his tale.

'When Hamzad approached Khunzakh we sent our Elders to him to say that we would agree to join the *Ghazavat* if the Imam would send a learned man to explain it to us. Hamzad had our Elders' moustaches shaved off, their nostrils pierced, and cakes hung to their noses, and in that condition he sent them back to us.

'The Elders brought word that Hamzad was ready to send a sheik to teach us the *Ghazavat*, but only if the Khansha sent him her youngest son as a hostage. She took him at his word and sent her youngest son, Bulach Khan. Hamzad received him well and sent to invite the two elder brothers also. He sent word that he wished to serve the Khans as his father had served their father ... The Khansha was a weak, stupid, and conceited woman, as all women are when they are not under control. She was afraid to send away both sons and sent only Umma Khan. I went with him. We were met by *murids* about a mile before we arrived and they sang and shot and caracoled around us, and when we drew near, Hamzad came out of his tent and went up to Umma Khan's stirrup and received him as a Khan. He said, "I have not done any harm to thy family and do not wish to do any. Only do not kill me and do not prevent my bringing the people over to the *Ghazavat*, and I will serve you with my whole army as my father served your father! Let me live in your house and I will help you with my advice, and you shall do as you like!"

'Umma Khan was slow of speech. He did not know how to reply and remained silent. Then I said that if this was so, let Hamzad come to Khunzakh and the Khansha and the Khans would receive him with honour . . . But I was not allowed to finish — and here I first encountered Shamil, who was beside the Imam. He said to me, "Thou hast not been asked . . . It was the Khan!"

'I was silent, and Hamzad led Umma Khan into his tent. Afterwards Hamzad called me and ordered me to go to Khunzakh with his envoys. I went. The envoys began persuading the Khansha to send her eldest son also to Hamzad. I saw there was treachery and told her not to send him; but a woman has as much sense in her head as an egg has hair. She ordered her son to go. Abu Nutsal Khan did not wish to. Then she said, "I see thou art afraid!" Like a bee she knew where to sting him most painfully. Abu Nutsal Khan flushed and did not speak to her any more, but ordered his horse to be saddled. I went with him.

'Hamzad met us with even greater honour than he had shown Umma Khan. He himself rode out two rifle-shot lengths down the hill to meet us. A large party of horsemen with their banners followed him, and they too sang, shot, and caracoled.

'When we reached the camp, Hamzad led the Khan into his tent and I remained with the horses . . .

'I was some way down the hill when I heard shots fired in Hamzad's tent. I ran there and saw Umma Khan lying prone in a pool of blood, and Abu Nutsal was fighting the *murids*. One of his cheeks had been hacked off and hung down. He supported it with one hand and with the other stabbed with his dagger at all who came near him. I saw him strike down Hamzad's brother and aim a blow at another man, but then the *murids* fired at him and he fell.'

Hadji Murad stopped and his sunburnt face flushed a dark red and his eyes became bloodshot.

'I was seized with fear and ran away.'

'Really? . . . I thought thou never wast afraid,' said Loris-Melikov.

'Never after that . . . Since then I have always remembered that shame, and when I recalled it I feared nothing!'

XII

'BUT ENOUGH! It is time for me to pray,' said Hadji Murad drawing from an inner breast-pocket of his Circassian coat Vorontsov's repeater watch and carefully pressing the spring. The repeater struck twelve and a quarter. Hadji Murad listened with his head on one side, repressing a childlike smile.

'*Kunak* Vorontsov's present,' he said, smiling.

'It is a good watch,' said Loris-Melikov. 'Well then, go thou and pray, and I will wait.'

'*Yakshi*. Very well,' said Hadji Murad and went to his bed-room.

Left by himself, Loris-Melikov wrote down in his notebook the chief things Hadji Murad had related, and then lighting a cigarette began to pace up and down the room. On reaching the door opposite the bedroom he heard animated voices speaking rapidly in Tartar. He guessed that the speakers were Hadji Murad's *murids*, and opening the door he went in to them.

The room was impregnated with that special leathery acid smell peculiar to the mountaineers. On a *burka* spread out on the floor sat the one-eyed, red-haired Gamzalo, in a tattered greasy *beshmet*, plaiting a bridle. He was saying something excitedly, speaking in a hoarse voice, but when Loris-Melikov entered he immediately became silent and continued his work without paying any attention to him.

In front of Gamzalo stood the merry Khan Mahoma showing his white teeth, his black lashless eyes glittering, and saying something over and over again. The handsome Eldar, his sleeves turned up on his strong arms, was polishing the girths of a saddle suspended from a nail. Khanefi, the principal worker and manager of the household, was not there, he was cooking their dinner in the kitchen.

'What were you disputing about?' asked Loris-Melikov after greeting them.

'Why, he keeps on praising Shamil,' said Khan Mahoma

giving his hand to Loris-Melikov. 'He says Shamil is a great man, learned, holy, and a *dzhigit.*'

'How is it that he has left him and still praises him?'

'He has left him and still praises him,' repeated Khan Mahoma, his teeth showing and his eyes glittering.

'And does he really consider him a saint?' asked Loris-Melikov.

'If he were not a saint the people would not listen to him,' said Gamzalo rapidly.

'Shamil is no saint, but Mansur was!' replied Khan Mahoma. 'He was a real saint. When he was Imam the people were quite different. He used to ride through the *aouls* and the people used to come out and kiss the hem of his coat and confess their sins and vow to do no evil. Then all the people – so the old men say – lived like saints: not drinking, nor smoking, nor neglecting their prayers, and forgiving one another their sins even when blood had been spilt. If anyone then found money or anything, he tied it to a stake and set it up by the roadside. In those days God gave the people success in everything – not as now.'

'In the mountains they don't smoke or drink now,' said Gamzalo.

'Your Shamil is a *lamorey*,' said Khan Mahoma, winking at Loris-Melikov. (*Lamorey* was a contemptuous term for a mountaineer.)

'Yes, *lamorey* means mountaineer,' replied Gamzalo. 'It is in the mountains that the eagles dwell.'

'Smart fellow! Well hit!' said Khan Mahoma with a grin, pleased at his adversary's apt retort.

Seeing the silver cigarette-case in Loris-Melikov's hand, Khan Mahoma asked for a cigarette, and when Loris-Melikov remarked that they were forbidden to smoke, he winked with one eye and jerking his head in the direction of Hadji Murad's bedroom replied that they could do it as long as they were not seen. He at once began smoking – not inhaling – and pouting his red lips awkwardly as he blew out the smoke.

'That is wrong!' said Gamzalo severely, and left the room. Khan Mahoma winked in his direction, and while smoking asked Loris-Melikov where he could best buy a silk *beshmet* and a white cap.

'Why, hast thou so much money?'

'I have enough,' replied Khan Mahoma with a wink.

'Ask him where he got the money,' said Eldar, turning his handsome smiling face towards Loris-Melikov.

'Oh, I won it!' said Khan Mahoma quickly, and related how while walking in Tiflis the day before he had come upon a group of men – Russians and Armenians – playing at *orlyanka* (a kind of heads-and-tails). The stake was a large one: three gold pieces and much silver. Khan Mahoma at once saw what the game consisted in, and jingling the coppers he had in his pocket he went up to the players and said he would stake the whole amount.

'How couldst thou do it? Hadst thou so much?' asked Loris-Melikov.

'I had only twelve kopeks,' said Khan Mahoma, grinning.

'But if thou hadst lost?'

'Why, this!' said Khan Mahoma pointing to his pistol.

'Wouldst thou have given that?'

'Give it indeed! I should have run away, and if anyone had tried to stop me I should have killed him – that's all!'

'Well, and didst thou win?'

'Aye, I won it all and went away!'

Loris-Melikov quite understood what sort of men Khan Mahoma and Eldar were. Khan Mahoma was a merry fellow, careless and ready for any spree. He did not know what to do with his superfluous vitality. He was always gay and reckless, and played with his own and other people's lives. For the sake of that sport with life he had now come over to the Russians, and for the same sport he might go back to Shamil tomorrow.

Eldar was also quite easy to understand. He was a man entirely devoted to his *murshid*; calm, strong, and firm.

The red-haired Gamzalo was the only one Loris-Melikov did not understand. He saw that that man was not only loyal to Shamil but felt an insuperable aversion, contempt, repugnance, and hatred for all Russians, and Loris-Melikov could therefore not understand why he had come over to them. It occurred to him that, as some of the higher officials suspected, Hadji Murad's surrender and his tales of hatred of Shamil might be false, and that perhaps he had surrendered only to spy out the Russians' weak spots that, after escaping back to the mountains, he might be able to direct his forces accordingly. Gamzalo's whole person strengthened this suspicion.

'The others, and Hadji Murad himself, know how to hide their intentions, but this one betrays them by his open hatred,' thought he.

Loris-Melikov tried to speak to him. He asked whether he did not feel dull. 'No, I don't!' he growled hoarsely without stopping his work, and glancing at his questioner out of the corner of his one eye. He replied to all Loris-Melikov's other questions in a similar manner.

While Loris-Melikov was in the room Hadji Murad's fourth *murid* came in, the Avar Khanefi; a man with a hairy face and neck and an arched chest as rough as if it were overgrown with moss. He was strong and a hard worker, always engrossed in his duties, and like Eldar unquestioningly obedient to his master.

When he entered the room to fetch some rice, Loris-Melikov stopped him and asked where he came from and how long he had been with Hadji Murad.

'Five years,' replied Khanefi. 'I come from the same *aoul* as he. My father killed his uncle and they wished to kill me,' he said calmly, looking from under his joined eyebrows straight into Loris-Melikov's face. 'Then I asked them to adopt me as a brother.'

'What do you mean by "adopt as a brother"?'

'I did not shave my head nor cut my nails for two months,

and then I came to them. They let me in to Patimat, his mother, and she gave me the breast and I became his brother.'

Hadji Murad's voice could be heard from the next room and Eldar, immediately answering his call, promptly wiped his hands and went with large strides into the drawing-room.

'He asks thee to come,' said he, coming back.

Loris-Melikov gave another cigarette to the merry Khan Mahoma and went into the drawing-room.

XIII

WHEN LORIS-MELIKOV entered the drawing-room Hadji Murad received him with a bright face.

'Well, shall I continue?' he asked, sitting down comfortably on the divan.

'Yes, certainly,' said Loris-Melikov. 'I have been in to have a talk with thy henchmen . . . One is a jolly fellow!' he added.

'Yes, Khan Mahoma is a frivolous fellow,' said Hadji Murad.

'I liked the young handsome one.'

'Ah, that's Eldar. He's young but firm — made of iron!'

They were silent for a while.

'So I am to go on?'

'Yes, yes!'

'I told thee how the Khans were killed . . . Well, having killed them Hamzad rode into Khunzakh and took up his quarters in their palace. The Khansha was the only one of the family left alive. Hamzad sent for her. She reproached him, so he winked to his *murid* Aseldar, who struck her from behind and killed her.'

'Why did he kill her?' asked Loris-Melikov.

'What could he do? . . . Where the forelegs have gone the hind legs must follow! He killed off the whole family. Shamil killed the youngest son – threw him over a precipice . . .

'Then the whole of Avaria surrendered to Hamzad. But my brother and I would not surrender. We wanted his blood for the blood of the Khans. We pretended to yield, but our only thought was how to get his blood. We consulted our grandfather and decided to await the time when he would come out of his palace, and then to kill him from an ambush. Someone overheard us and told Hamzad, who sent for grandfather and said, "Mind, if it be true that thy grandsons are planning evil against me, thou and they shall hang from one rafter. I do God's work and cannot be hindered Go, and remember what I have said!"

'Our grandfather came home and told us.

'Then we decided not to wait but to do the deed on the first day of the feast in the mosque. Our comrades would not take part in it but my brother and I remained firm.

'We took two pistols each, put on our *burkas*, and went to the mosque. Hamzad entered the mosque with thirty *murids*. They all had drawn swords in their hands. Aseldar, his favourite *murid* (the one who had cut off the Khansha's head), saw us, shouted to us to take off our *burkas*, and came towards me. I had my dagger in my hand and I killed him with it and rushed at Hamzad; but my brother Osman had already shot him. He was still alive and rushed at my brother dagger in hand, but I gave him a finishing blow on the head. There were thirty *murids* and we were only two. They killed my brother Osman, but I kept them at bay, leapt through the window, and escaped.

'When it was known that Hamzad had been killed all the people rose. The *murids* fled and those of them who did not flee were killed.'

Hadji Murad paused, and breathed heavily.

'That was very good,' he continued, 'but afterwards everything was spoilt.

'Shamil succeeded Hamzad. He sent envoys to me to say that I should join him in attacking the Russians, and that if I refused he would destroy Khunzakh and kill me.

'I answered that I would not join him and would not let him come to me . . .'

'Why didst thou not go with him?' asked Loris-Melikov.

Hadji Murad frowned and did not reply at once.

'I could not. The blood of my brother Osman and of Abu Nutsal Khan was on his hands. I did not go to him. General Rosen sent me an officer's commission and ordered me to govern Avaria. All this would have been well but that Rosen appointed as Khan of Kazi-Kumukh, first Mahomet-Murza, and afterwards Akhmet Khan, who hated me. He had been trying to get the Khansha's daughter, Sultanetta, in marriage for his son, but she would not give her to him, and he believed me to be the cause of this . . . Yes, Akhmet Khan hated me and sent his henchmen to kill me, but I escaped from them. Then he spoke ill of me to General Klugenau. He said that I told the Avars not to supply wood to the Russian soldiers, and he also said that I had donned a turban – this one' (Hadji Murad touched his turban) 'and that this meant that I had gone over to Shamil. The general did not believe him and gave orders that I should not be touched. But when the general went to Tiflis, Akhmet Khan did as he pleased. He sent a company of soldiers to seize me, put me in chains, and tied me to a cannon.

'So they kept me six days,' he continued. 'On the seventh day they untied me and started to take me to Temir Khan Shura. Forty soldiers with loaded guns had me in charge. My hands were tied and I knew that they had orders to kill me if I tried to escape.

'As we approached Mansokha the path became narrow, and on the right was an abyss about a hundred and twenty yards deep. I went to the right – to the very edge. A soldier wanted to stop me, but I jumped down and pulled him with me. He was killed outright but I, as you see, remained alive.

'Ribs, head, arms, and leg – all were broken! I tried to crawl but grew giddy and fell asleep. I awoke wet with blood. A shepherd saw me and called some people who carried me to an *aoul*. My ribs and head healed, and my leg too, only it has remained short,' and Hadji Murad stretched out his crooked leg. 'It still serves me, however, and that is well,' said he.

'The people heard the news and began coming to me. I recovered and went to Tselmess. The Avars again called on me to rule over them,' he went on, with tranquil, confident pride, 'and I agreed.'

He rose quickly and taking a portfolio out of a saddle-bag, drew out two discoloured letters and handed one of them to Loris-Melikov. They were from General Klugenau. Loris-Melikov read the first letter, which was as follows:

'Lieutenant Hadji Murad, thou hast served under me and I was satisfied with thee and considered thee a good man.

'Recently Akhmet Khan informed me that thou art a traitor, that thou hast donned a turban and hast intercourse with Shamil, and that thou hast taught the people to disobey the Russian Government. I ordered thee to be arrested and brought before me but thou fledst. I do not know whether this is for thy good or not, as I do not know whether thou art guilty or not.

'Now hear me. If thy conscience is pure, if thou art not guilty in anything towards the great Tsar, come to me, fear no one. I am thy defender. The Khan can do nothing to thee, he is himself under my command, so thou hast nothing to fear.'

Klugenau added that he always kept his word and was just, and he again exhorted Hadji Murad to appear before him.

When Loris-Melikov had read this letter Hadji Murad, before handing him the second one, told him what he had written in reply to the first.

'I wrote that I wore a turban not for Shamil's sake but for

my soul's salvation; that I neither wished nor could go over to Shamil, because he had caused the death of my father, my brothers, and my relations; but that I could not join the Russians because I had been dishonoured by them. (In Khunzakh, a scoundrel had spat on me while I was bound, and I could not join your people until that man was killed.) But above all I feared that liar, Akhmet Khan.

'Then the general sent me this letter,' said Hadji Murad, handing Loris-Melikov the other discoloured paper.

'Thou hast answered my first letter and I thank thee,' read Loris-Melikov. 'Thou writest that thou art not afraid to return but that the insult done thee by a certain giaour prevents it, but I assure thee that the Russian law is just and that thou shalt see him who dared to offend thee punished before thine eyes. I have already given orders to investigate the matter.

'Hear me, Hadji Murad! I have a right to be displeased with thee for not trusting me and my honour, but I forgive thee, for I know how suspicious mountaineers are in general. If thy conscience is pure, if thou hast put on a turban only for thy soul's salvation, then thou art right and mayst look me and the Russian Government boldly in the eye. He who dishonoured thee shall, I assure thee, be punished and *thy property shall be restored to thee*, and thou shalt see and know what Russian law is. Moreover we Russians look at things differently, and thou hast not sunk in our eyes because some scoundrel has dishonoured thee.

'I myself have consented to the Chimrints wearing turbans,

and I regard their actions in the right light, and therefore I repeat that thou hast nothing to fear. Come to me with the man by whom I am sending thee this letter. He is faithful to me and is not the slave of thy enemies, but is the friend of a man who enjoys the special favour of the Government.'

Further on Klugenau again tried to persuade Hadji Murad to come over to him.

'I did not believe him,' said Hadji Murad when Loris-Melikov had finished reading, 'and did not go to Klugenau. The chief thing for me was to revenge myself on Akhmet Khan, and that I could not do through the Russians. Then Akhmet Khan surrounded Tselmess and wanted to take me or kill me. I had too few men and could not drive him off, and just then came an envoy with a letter from Shamil promising to help me to defeat and kill Akhmet Khan and making me ruler over the whole of Avaria. I considered the matter for a long time and then went over to Shamil, and from that time I have fought the Russians continually.'

Here Hadji Murad related all his military exploits, of which there were very many and some of which were already familiar to Loris-Melikov. All his campaigns and raids had been remarkable for the extraordinary rapidity of his movements and the boldness of his attacks, which were always crowned with success.

'There never was any friendship between me and Shamil,' said Hadji Murad at the end of his story, 'but he feared me and needed me. But it so happened that I was asked who should be Imam after Shamil, and I replied: "He will be Imam whose sword is sharpest!"

'This was told to Shamil and he wanted to get rid of me. He sent me into Tabasaran. I went, and captured a thousand sheep and three hundred horses, but he said I had not done the right thing and dismissed me from being *Naib*, and ordered me to send him all the money. I sent him a thousand gold pieces. He sent his *murids* and they took from me all my property. He demanded that I should go to him, but I knew he wanted to kill me and I did not go. Then he sent to take me. I resisted and went over to Vorontsov. Only I did not take my family. My mother, my wives, and my son are in his hands. Tell the Sirdar that as long as my family is in Shamil's power I can do nothing.'

'I will tell him,' said Loris-Melikov.

'Take pains, try hard! . . . What is mine is thine, only help me with the prince! I am tied up and the end of the rope is in Shamil's hands,' said Hadji Murad concluding his story.

XIV

ON 20 DECEMBER Vorontsov wrote to Chernyshov, the Minister of War. The letter was in French:

'I did not write to you by the last post, dear Prince, as I wished first to decide what we should do with Hadji Murad, and for the last two or three days I have not been feeling quite well.

'In my last letter I informed you of Hadji Murad's arrival here. He reached Tiflis on the 8th, and next day I made his acquaintance, and during the following seven or eight days have spoken to him and considered what use we can make of him in the future, and especially what we are to do with him at present, for he is much concerned about the fate of his family, and with every appearance of perfect frankness says that while they are in Shamil's hands he is paralysed and cannot render us any service or show his gratitude for the friendly reception and forgiveness we have extended to him.

'His uncertainty about those dear to him makes him restless, and the persons I have appointed to live with him assure me that he does not sleep at night, eats hardly anything, prays continually, and asks only to be allowed to ride out accompanied by several Cossacks – the sole recreation and exercise possible for him and made necessary to him by lifelong habit. Every day he comes to me to know whether I have any news of his family, and to ask me to have all the prisoners in our hands collected and offered to Shamil in exchange for them. He would also give a little money. There are people who would let him have some for the purpose. He keeps repeating to me: "Save my family and then give me a chance to serve thee" (preferably, in his opinion, on the Lesghian line), "and if within a month I do not render you great service, punish me as you think fit." I reply that to me all this appears very just, and that many among us would even not trust him so long as his family remain in the mountains and are not in our hands as hostages, and that I will do everything possible to collect the prisoners on our frontier, that I have no power under our laws to give him money for the ransom of his family in addition to the sum he may himself be able to raise, but that I may perhaps find some other means of helping him. After that I told him frankly that in my opinion Shamil would not in any case give up the family, and that Shamil might tell him so straight out and promise him a full pardon and his former posts, and might threaten if Hadji Murad did not return, to kill his mother, his wives, and his six children. I asked him whether he could say frankly what he would do if he received such an announcement from Shamil. He lifted his eyes and arms to heaven, and said that everything is in God's hands, but that he would never surrender to his foe, for he is certain Shamil would not forgive him and he would therefore not have long to live. As to the destruction of his family, he did not think Shamil would act so rashly: firstly, to avoid making him a yet more desperate and dangerous foe, and secondly, because there were many people, and even very influential people, in Daghestan, who would dissuade Shamil from such a course. Finally, he repeated several times that whatever God might decree for him in the future, he was at present interested in nothing but his family's ransom, and he implored me in God's name to help him and allow him to return to the neighbourhood of the Chechnya, where he could, with the help and consent of our commanders, have some intercourse with his family and regular news of their condition and of the best means to liberate them. He said that many people, and even some *Naibs* in that part of the enemy's territory, were more or less attached to him, and that among the whole of the population already subjugated by Russia or neutral it would be easy with our help to establish relations very useful for the attainment of the aim which gives him no peace day or night, and the attainment of which would set him at ease and make it possible for him to act for our good and win our confidence.

'He asks to be sent back to Grozny with a convoy of twenty or thirty picked Cossacks who would serve him as a protection against foes and us as a guarantee of his good faith.

'You will understand, dear Prince, that I have been much perplexed by all this, for do what I will a great responsibility rests on me. It would be in the highest degree rash to trust him entirely, yet in order to deprive him of all means of escape we should have to lock him up, and in my opinion that would be both unjust and impolitic. A measure of that kind, the news of which would soon spread over the whole of Daghestan, would do us great harm by keeping back those who are now inclined more or less openly to oppose Shamil (and there are many such), and who are keenly watching to see how we treat the Imam's bravest and most adventurous officer now that he has found himself obliged to place himself in our hands. If we treat Hadji Murad as a prisoner all the good effect of the situation will be lost. Therefore I think that I could not act otherwise than as I have done, though at the same time I feel that I may be accused of having made a great mistake if Hadji Murad should take it into his head to escape again. In the service, and especially in a complicated situation such as this, it is difficult, not to say impossible, to follow any one straight path without risking mistakes and without accepting responsibility, but once a path seems to be the right one I must follow it, happen what may.

'I beg of you, dear Prince, to submit this to His Majesty the Emperor for his consideration; and I shall be happy if it pleases our most august monarch to approve my action.

'All that I have written above I have also written to Generals Zavodovsky and Kozlovsky, to guide the latter when communicating direct with Hadji Murad whom I have warned not to act or go anywhere without Kozlovsky's consent. I also told him that it would be all the better for us if he rode out with our convoy, as otherwise Shamil might spread a rumour that we were keeping him prisoner, but at the same time I made him promise never to go to Vozdvizhensk, because my son, to whom he first surrendered and whom he looks upon as his *kunak* (friend), is not the commander of that place and some unpleasant misunderstanding might easily arise. In any case Vozdvizhensk lies too near a thickly populated hostile settlement, while for the intercourse with his friends which he desires, Grozny is in all respects suitable.

'Besides the twenty chosen Cossacks who at his own request are to keep close to him, I am also sending Captain

Loris-Melikov – a worthy, excellent, and highly intelligent officer who speaks Tartar, and knows Hadji Murad well and apparently enjoys his full confidence. During the ten days that Hadji Murad has spent here, he has, however, lived in the same house with Lieutenant-Colonel Prince Tarkhanov, who is in command of the Shoushin District and is here on business connected with the service. He is a truly worthy man whom I trust entirely. He also has won Hadji Murad's confidence, and through him alone – as he speaks Tartar perfectly – we have discussed the most delicate and secret matters. I have consulted Tarkhanov about Hadji Murad, and he fully agrees with me that it was necessary either to act as I have done, or to put Hadji Murad in prison and guard him in the strictest manner (for if we once treat him badly he will not be easy to hold), or else to remove him from the country altogether. But these two last measures would not only destroy all the advantage accruing to us from Hadji Murad's quarrel with Shamil, but would inevitably check any growth of the present insubordination, and possible future revolt, of the people against Shamil's power. Prince Tarkhanov tells me he himself has no doubt of Hadji Murad's truthfulness, and that Hadji Murad is convinced that Shamil will never forgive him but would have him executed in spite of any promise of forgiveness. The only thing Tarkhanov has noticed in his intercourse with Hadji Murad that might cause any anxiety, is his attachment to his religion. Tarkhanov does not deny that Shamil might influence Hadji Murad from that side. But as I have already said, he will never persuade Hadji Murad that he will not take his life sooner or later should the latter return to him.

'This, dear Prince, is all I have to tell you about this episode in our affairs here.'

XV

THE REPORT was dispatched from Tiflis on 24 December 1851, and on New Year's Eve a courier, having overdriven a dozen horses and beaten a dozen drivers till they bled, delivered it to Prince Chernyshov who at that time was Minister of War; and on 1 January 1852 Chernyshov took Vorontsov's report, among other papers, to the Emperor Nicholas.

Chernyshov disliked Vorontsov because of the general respect in which the latter was held and because of his immense wealth, and also because Vorontsov was a real aristocrat while Chernyshov, after all, was a *parvenu*, but especially because the Emperor was particularly well disposed towards Vorontsov. Therefore at every opportunity Chernyshov tried to injure Vorontsov.

When he had last presented a report about Caucasian affairs he had succeeded in arousing Nicholas's displeasure against Vorontsov because – through the carelessness of those in command – almost the whole of a small Caucasian detachment had been destroyed by the mountaineers. He now intended to present the steps taken by Vorontsov in relation to Hadji

Murad in an unfavourable light. He wished to suggest to the Emperor that Vorontsov always protected and even indulged the natives to the detriment of the Russians, and that he had acted unwisely in allowing Hadji Murad to remain in the Caucasus for there was every reason to suspect that he had only come over to spy on our means of defence, and that it would therefore be better to transport him to Central Russia and make use of him only after his family had been rescued from the mountaineers and it had become possible to convince ourselves of his loyalty.

Chernyshov's plan did not succeed merely because on that New Year's Day Nicholas was in particularly bad spirits, and out of perversity would not have accepted any suggestion whatever from anyone, least of all from Chernyshov whom he only tolerated – regarding him as indispensable for the time being but looking upon him as a blackguard, for Nicholas knew of his endeavours at the trial of the Decembrists* to secure the conviction of Zachary Chernyshov, and of his attempt to obtain Zachary's property for himself. So thanks to Nicholas's ill temper Hadji Murad remained in the Caucasus, and his circumstances were not changed as they might have been had Chernyshov presented his report at another time.

*

---

* The military conspirators who tried to secure a Constitution for Russia in 1825, on the accession of Nicholas I.

It was half-past nine o'clock when through the mist of the cold morning (the thermometer showed 13 degrees below zero Fahrenheit) Chernyshov's fat, bearded coachman, sitting on the box of a small sledge (like the one Nicholas drove about in) with a sharp-angled, cushion-shaped azure velvet cap on his head, drew up at the entrance of the Winter Palace and gave a friendly nod to his chum, Prince Dolgoruky's coachman – who having brought his master to the palace had himself long been waiting outside, in his big coat with the thickly wadded skirts, sitting on the reins and rubbing his numbed hands together. Chernyshov had on a long cloak with a large cape and a fluffy collar of silver beaver, and a regulation three-cornered hat with cocks' feathers. He threw back the bearskin apron of the sledge and carefully disengaged his chilled feet, on which he had no over-shoes (he prided himself on never wearing any). Clanking his spurs with an air of bravado he ascended the carpeted steps and passed through the hall door which was respectfully opened for him by the porter, and entered the hall. Having thrown off his cloak which an old Court lackey hurried forward to take, he went to a mirror and carefully removed the hat from his curled wig. Looking at himself in the mirror, he arranged the hair on his temples and the tuft above his forehead with an accustomed movement of his old hands, and adjusted his cross, the shoulder-knots of his uniform, and his large-initialled epaulettes, and then went up the gently ascending carpeted stairs, his not very reliable old legs feebly mounting the shallow steps. Passing the

Court lackeys in gala livery who stood obsequiously bowing, Chernyshov entered the waiting-room. He was respectfully met by a newly appointed aide-de-camp of the Emperor's in a shining new uniform with epaulettes and shoulder-knots, whose face was still fresh and rosy and who had a small black moustache, and the hair on his temples brushed towards his eyes in the same way as the Emperor.

Prince Vasili Dolgoruky, Assistant-Minister of War, with an expression of *ennui* on his dull face – which was ornamented with similar whiskers, moustaches, and temple tufts brushed forward like Nicholas's – greeted him.

'*L'empereur?*' said Chernyshov, addressing the aide-de-camp and looking inquiringly towards the door leading to the cabinet.

'*Sa majesté vient de rentrer,*'* replied the aide-de-camp, evidently enjoying the sound of his own voice, and stepping so softly and steadily that had a tumbler of water been placed on his head none of it would have been spilt, he approached the door and disappeared, his whole body evincing reverence for the spot he was about to visit.

Dolgoruky meanwhile opened his portfolio to see that it contained the necessary papers, while Chernyshov, frowning, paced up and down to restore the circulation in his numbed feet, and thought over what he was about to report to the Emperor. He was near the door of the cabinet when it opened again and the

* 'The Emperor?' / 'His Majesty has just returned.'

aide-de-camp, even more radiant and respectful than before, came out and with a gesture invited the Minister and his assistant to enter.

The Winter Palace had been rebuilt after a fire some considerable time before this, but Nicholas was still occupying rooms in the upper storey. The cabinet in which he received the reports of his ministers and other high officials was a very lofty apartment with four large windows. A big portrait of the Emperor Alexander I hung on the front side of the room. Two bureaux stood between the windows, and several chairs were ranged along the walls. In the middle of the room was an enormous writing-table, with an armchair before it for Nicholas, and other chairs for those to whom he gave audience.

Nicholas sat at the table in a black coat with shoulder-straps but no epaulettes, his enormous body – with his overgrown stomach tightly laced in – was thrown back, and he gazed at the newcomers with fixed, lifeless eyes. His long pale face, with its enormous receding forehead between the tufts of hair which were brushed forward and skilfully joined to the wig that covered his bald patch, was specially cold and stony that day. His eyes, always dim, looked duller than usual, the compressed lips under his upturned moustaches, the high collar which supported his chin, and his fat freshly shaven cheeks on which symmetrical sausage-shaped bits of whiskers had been left, gave his face a dissatisfied and even irate expression. His bad mood was caused by fatigue, due to the fact that he had been to a masquerade the night before, and while walking about as was his wont in his Horse Guards' uniform with a bird on the helmet, among the public which crowded round and timidly made way for his enormous, self-assured figure, he had again met the mask who at the previous masquerade had aroused his senile sensuality by her whiteness, her beautiful figure, and her tender voice. At that former masquerade she had disappeared after promising to meet him at the next one.

At yesterday's masquerade she had come up to him, and this time he had not let her go, but had led her to the box specially kept ready for that purpose, where he could be alone with her. Having arrived in silence at the door of the box Nicholas looked round to find the attendant, but he was not there. He frowned and pushed the door open himself, letting the lady enter first.

'*Il y a quelqu'un!*'* said the mask, stopping short.

And the box actually was occupied. On the small velvet-covered sofa, close together, sat an Uhlan officer and a pretty, fair curly-haired young woman in a domino, who had removed her mask. On catching sight of the angry figure of Nicholas drawn up to its full height, she quickly replaced her mask, but the Uhlan officer, rigid with fear, gazed at Nicholas with fixed eyes without rising from the sofa.

Used as he was to the terror he inspired in others, that terror always pleased Nicholas, and by way of contrast he sometimes liked to astound those plunged in terror by addressing kindly

---

* 'There's someone there!'

words to them. He did so on this occasion.

'Well, friend,' said he to the officer, 'you are younger than I and might give up your place to me!'

The officer jumped to his feet, and growing first pale and then red and bending almost double, he followed his partner silently out of the box, leaving Nicholas alone with his lady.

She proved to be a pretty, twenty-year-old virgin, the daughter of a Swedish governess. She told Nicholas how when quite a child she had fallen in love with him from his portraits; how she adored him and had made up her mind to attract his attention at any cost. Now she had succeeded and wanted nothing more – so she said.

The girl was taken to the place where Nicholas usually had rendezvous with women, and there he spent more than an hour with her.

When he returned to his room that night and lay on the hard narrow bed about which he prided himself, and covered himself with the cloak which he considered to be (and spoke of as being) as famous as Napoleon's hat, it was a long time before he could fall asleep. He thought now of the frightened and elated expression on that girl's fair face, and now of the full, powerful shoulders of his established mistress, Nelidova, and he compared the two. That profligacy in a married man was a bad thing did not once enter his head, and he would have been greatly surprised had anyone censured him for it. Yet though convinced that he had acted rightly, some kind of unpleasant after-taste remained, and to stifle that feeling he dwelt on a thought that always tranquillized him – the thought of his own greatness.

Though he had fallen asleep so late, he rose before eight, and after attending to his toilet in the usual way – rubbing his big well-fed body all over with ice – and saying his prayers (repeating those he had been used to from childhood – the prayer to the Virgin, the Apostles' Creed, and the Lord's Prayer, without attaching any kind of meaning to the words he uttered), he went out through the smaller portico of the palace onto the embankment in his military cloak and cap.

On the embankment he met a student in the uniform of the School of Jurisprudence, who was as enormous as himself. On recognizing the uniform of that school, which he disliked for its freedom of thought, Nicholas frowned, but the stature of the student and the painstaking manner in which he drew himself up and saluted, ostentatiously sticking out his elbow, mollified his displeasure.

'Your name?' said he.

'Polosatov, your Imperial Majesty.'

'. . . fine fellow!'

The student continued to stand with his hand lifted to his hat. Nicholas stopped.

'Do you wish to enter the army?'

'Not at all, your Imperial Majesty.'

'Blockhead!' And Nicholas turned away and continued his

walk, and began uttering aloud the first words that came into his head.

'Kopervine ... Kopervine—' he repeated several times (it was the name of yesterday's girl). 'Horrid ... horrid—' He did not think of what he was saying, but stifled his feelings by listening to the words.

'Yes, what would Russia be without me?' said he, feeling his former dissatisfaction returning. 'What would – not Russia alone but Europe be, without me?' and calling to mind the weakness and stupidity of his brother-in-law the King of Prussia, he shook his head.

As he was returning to the small portico, he saw the carriage of Helena Pavlovna,* with a red-liveried footman, approaching the Saltykóv entrance of the palace.

Helena Pavlovna was to him the personification of that futile class of people who discussed not merely science and poetry, but even the ways of governing men: imagining that they could govern themselves better than he, Nicholas, governed them! He knew that however much he crushed such people they reappeared again and again, and he recalled his brother, Michael Pavlovich, who had died not long before. A feeling of sadness and vexation came over him and with a dark frown he again began whispering the first words that

---

* Widow of Nicholas's brother Michael: a clever, well-educated woman, interested in science, art, and public affairs.

came into his head, which he only ceased doing when he re-entered the palace.

On reaching his apartments he smoothed his whiskers and the hair on his temples and the wig on his bald patch, and twisted his moustaches upwards in front of the mirror, and then went straight to the cabinet in which he received reports.

He first received Chernyshov, who at once saw by his face, and especially by his eyes, that Nicholas was in a particularly bad humour that day, and knowing about the adventure of the night before he understood the cause. Having coldly greeted him and invited him to sit down, Nicholas fixed on him a lifeless gaze. The first matter Chernyshov reported upon was a case of embezzlement by commissariat officials which had just been discovered; the next was the movement of troops on the Prussian frontier; then came a list of rewards to be given at the New Year to some people omitted from a former list; then Vorontsov's report about Hadji Murad; and lastly some unpleasant business concerning an attempt by a student of the Academy of Medicine on the life of a professor.

Nicholas heard the report of the embezzlement silently with compressed lips, his large white hand – with one ring on the fourth finger – stroking some sheets of paper, and his eyes steadily fixed on Chernyshov's forehead and on the tuft of hair above it.

Nicholas was convinced that everybody stole. He knew he would have to punish the commissariat officials now, and decided to send them all to serve in the ranks, but he also knew that this would not prevent those who succeeded them from acting in the same way. It was a characteristic of officials to steal, but it was his duty to punish them for doing so, and tired as he was of that duty he conscientiously performed it.

'It seems there is only one honest man in Russia!' said he.

Chernyshov at once understood that this one honest man was Nicholas himself, and smiled approvingly.

'It looks like it, your Imperial Majesty,' said he.

'Leave it – I will give a decision,' said Nicholas, taking the document and putting it on the left side of the table.

Then Chernyshov reported about the rewards to be given and about moving the army on the Prussian frontier.

Nicholas looked over the list and struck out some names, and then briefly and firmly gave orders to move two divisions to the Prussian frontier. He could not forgive the King of Prussia for granting a Constitution to his people after the events of 1848, and therefore while expressing most friendly feelings to his brother-in-law in letters and conversation, he considered it necessary to keep an army near the frontier in case of need. He might want to use these troops to defend his brother-in-law's throne if the people of Prussia rebelled (Nicholas saw a readiness for rebellion everywhere) as he had used troops to suppress the rising in Hungary a few years previously. They were also of use to give more weight and influence to such advice as he gave to the King of Prussia.

'Yes – what would Russia be like now if it were not for me?' he again thought.

'Well, what else is there?' said he.

'A courier from the Caucasus,' said Chernyshov, and he reported what Vorontsov had written about Hadji Murad's surrender.

'Well, well!' said Nicholas. 'It's a good beginning!'

'Evidently the plan devised by your Majesty begins to bear fruit,' said Chernyshov.

This approval of his strategic talents was particularly pleasant to Nicholas because, though he prided himself upon them, at the bottom of his heart he knew that they did not really exist, and he now desired to hear more detailed praise of himself.

'How do you mean?' he asked.

'I mean that if your Majesty's plans had been adopted before, and we had moved forward slowly and steadily, cutting down forests and destroying the supplies of food, the Caucasus would have been subjugated long ago. I attribute Hadji Murad's surrender entirely to his having come to the conclusion that they can hold out no longer.'

'True,' said Nicholas.

Although the plan of a gradual advance into the enemy's territory by means of felling forests and destroying the food supplies was Ermolov's and Velyaminov's plan, and was quite contrary to Nicholas's own plan of seizing Shamil's place of residence and destroying that nest of robbers – which was the plan on which the Dargo expedition in 1845 (that cost so many lives) had been undertaken – Nicholas nevertheless attributed to himself also the plan of a slow advance and a systematic felling of forests and devastation of the country. It would seem that to believe the plan of a slow movement by felling forests and destroying food supplies to have been his own would have necessitated hiding the fact that he had insisted on quite contrary operations in 1845. But he did not hide it and was proud of the plan of the 1845 expedition as well as of the plan of a slow advance – though the two were obviously contrary to one another. Continual brazen flattery from everybody round him in the teeth of obvious facts had brought him to such a state that he no longer saw his own inconsistencies or measured his actions and words by reality, logic, or even simple common sense; but was quite convinced that all his orders, however senseless, unjust, and mutually contradictory they might be, became reasonable, just, and mutually accordant simply because he gave them. His decision in the case next reported to him – that of the student of the Academy of Medicine – was of that senseless kind.

The case was as follows: A young man who had twice failed in his examinations was being examined a third time, and when the examiner again would not pass him, the young man whose nerves were deranged, considering this to be an injustice, seized a pen-knife from the table in a paroxysm of fury, and rushing at the professor inflicted on him several trifling wounds.

'What's his name?' asked Nicholas.

'Bzhezovski.'

'A Pole?'

'Of Polish descent and a Roman Catholic,' answered Chernyshov.

Nicholas frowned. He had done much evil to the Poles. To justify that evil he had to feel certain that all Poles were rascals, and he considered them to be such and hated them in proportion to the evil he had done them.

'Wait a little,' he said, closing his eyes and bowing his head.

Chernyshov, having more than once heard Nicholas say so, knew that when the Emperor had to take a decision it was only necessary for him to concentrate his attention for a few moments and the spirit moved him, and the best possible decision presented itself as though an inner voice had told him what to do. He was now thinking how most fully to satisfy the feeling of hatred against the Poles which this incident had stirred up within him, and the inner voice suggested the following decision. He took the report and in his large handwriting wrote on its margin with three orthographical mistakes:

'Diserves deth, but, thank God, we have no capitle punishment, and it is not for me to introduce it. Make him run the gauntlet of a thousand men twelve times. – Nicholas.'

He signed, adding his unnaturally huge flourish.

Nicholas knew that twelve thousand strokes with the regulation rods were not only certain death with torture, but were a superfluous cruelty, for five thousand strokes were sufficient to kill the strongest man. But it pleased him to be ruthlessly cruel and it also pleased him to think that we have abolished capital punishment in Russia.

Having written his decision about the student, he pushed it across to Chernyshov.

'There,' he said, 'read it.'

Chernyshov read it, and bowed his head as a sign of respectful amazement at the wisdom of the decision.

'Yes, and let all the students be present on the drill-ground at the punishment,' added Nicholas.

'It will do them good! I will abolish this revolutionary spirit and will tear it up by the roots!' he thought.

'It shall be done,' replied Chernyshov; and after a short pause he straightened the tuft on his forehead and returned to the Caucasian report.

'What do you command me to write in reply to Prince Vorontsov's dispatch?'

'To keep firmly to my system of destroying the dwellings and food supplies in Chechnya and to harass them by raids,' answered Nicholas.

'And what are your Majesty's commands with reference to Hadji Murad?' asked Chernyshov.

'Why, Vorontsov writes that he wants to make use of him in the Caucasus.'

'Is it not dangerous?' said Chernyshov, avoiding Nicholas's gaze. 'Prince Vorontsov is too confiding, I am afraid.'

'And you – what do you think?' asked Nicholas sharply, detecting Chernyshov's intention of presenting Vorontsov's decision in an unfavourable light.

'Well, I should have thought it would be safer to deport him to Central Russia.'

'You would have thought!' said Nicholas ironically. 'But I don't think so, and agree with Vorontsov. Write to him accordingly.'

'It shall be done,' said Chernyshov, rising and bowing himself out.

Dolgoruky also bowed himself out, having during the whole audience only uttered a few words (in reply to a question from Nicholas) about the movement of the army.

After Chernyshov, Nicholas received Bibikov, General-Governor of the Western Provinces. Having expressed his approval of the measures taken by Bibikov against the mutinous peasants who did not wish to accept the Orthodox Faith, he ordered him to have all those who did not submit tried by court-martial. That was equivalent to sentencing them to run the gauntlet. He also ordered the editor of a newspaper to be sent to serve in the ranks of the army for publishing information about the transfer of several thousand State peasants to the Imperial estates.

'I do this because I consider it necessary,' said Nicholas, 'and I will not allow it to be discussed.'

Bibikov saw the cruelty of the order concerning the Uniate* peasants and the injustice of transferring State peasants (the only free peasants in Russia in those days) to the Crown, which meant making them serfs of the Imperial family. But it was impossible to express dissent. Not to agree with Nicholas's decisions would have meant the loss of that brilliant position which it had cost Bibikov forty years to attain and which he now enjoyed; and he therefore submissively bowed his dark head (already touched with grey) to indicate his submission and his readiness to fulfil the cruel, insensate, and dishonest supreme will.

Having dismissed Bibikov, Nicholas stretched himself, with a sense of duty well fulfilled, glanced at the clock, and went to get ready to go out. Having put on a uniform with epaulettes, orders, and a ribbon, he went out into the reception hall where more than a hundred persons – men in uniforms and women in elegant low-necked dresses, all standing in the places assigned to them – awaited his arrival with agitation.

He came out to them with a lifeless look in his eyes, his chest expanded, his stomach bulging out above and below its bandages, and feeling everybody's gaze tremulously and obsequiously fixed upon him he assumed an even more triumphant air. When his eyes met those of people he knew, remembering who was who, he stopped and addressed a few words to them sometimes in

---

* The Uniates acknowledge the Pope of Rome, though in other respects they are in accord with the Orthodox Russo-Greek Church.

Russian and sometimes in French, and transfixing them with his cold glassy eye listened to what they said.

Having received all the New Year congratulations he passed on to church, where God, through His servants the priests, greeted and praised Nicholas just as worldly people did; and weary as he was of these greetings and praises Nicholas duly accepted them. All this was as it should be, because the welfare and happiness of the whole world depended on him, and wearied though he was he would still not refuse the universe his assistance.

When at the end of the service the magnificently arrayed deacon, his long hair crimped and carefully combed, began the chant *Many Years*, which was heartily caught up by the splendid choir, Nicholas looked round and noticed Nelidova, with her fine shoulders, standing by a window, and he decided the comparison with yesterday's girl in her favour.

After Mass he went to the Empress and spent a few minutes in the bosom of his family, joking with the children and his wife. Then passing through the Hermitage,* he visited the Minister of the Court, Volkonski, and among other things ordered him to pay out of a special fund a yearly pension to the mother of yesterday's girl. From there he went for his customary drive.

Dinner that day was served in the Pompeian Hall. Besides the

---

* A celebrated museum and picture gallery in St Petersburg, adjoining the Winter Palace.

younger sons of Nicholas and Michael there were also invited Baron Lieven, Count Rzhevski, Dolgoruky, the Prussian Ambassador, and the King of Prussia's aide-de-camp.

While waiting for the appearance of the Emperor and Empress an interesting conversation took place between Baron Lieven and the Prussian Ambassador concerning the disquieting news from Poland.

'*La Pologne et le Caucase, ce sont les deux cautères de la Russie,*' said Lieven. '*Il nous faut cent mille hommes à peu près, dans chacun de ces deux pays.*'

The Ambassador expressed a fictitious surprise that it should be so.

'*Vous dites, la Pologne*—' began the Ambassador.

'*Oh, oui, c'était un coup de maître de Metternich de nous en avoir laissé l'embarras . . .*'*

At this point the Empress, with her trembling head and fixed smile, entered followed by Nicholas.

At dinner Nicholas spoke of Hadji Murad's surrender and said that the war in the Caucasus must now soon come to an end in consequence of the measures he was taking to limit the scope of the mountaineers by felling their forests and by his system of erecting a series of small forts.

---

* 'Poland and the Caucasus are Russia's two sores. We need about a hundred thousand men in each of those two countries.' / 'You say that Poland—' / 'Oh yes, it was a masterstroke of Metternich's to leave us the bother of it . . .'

The Ambassador, having exchanged a rapid glance with the aide-de-camp – to whom he had only that morning spoken about Nicholas's unfortunate weakness for considering himself a great strategist – warmly praised this plan which once more demonstrated Nicholas's great strategic ability.

After dinner Nicholas drove to the ballet where hundreds of women marched round in tights and scanty clothing. One of them specially attracted him, and he had the German ballet-master sent for and gave orders that a diamond ring should be presented to him.

The next day when Chernyshov came with his report, Nicholas again confirmed his order to Vorontsov – that now that Hadji Murad had surrendered, the Chechens should be more actively harassed than ever and the cordon round them tightened.

Chernyshov wrote in that sense to Vorontsov; and another courier, overdriving more horses and bruising the faces of more drivers, galloped to Tiflis.

XVI

IN OBEDIENCE to this command of Nicholas a raid was immediately made in Chechnya that same month, January 1852.

The detachment ordered for the raid consisted of four infantry battalions, two companies of Cossacks, and eight guns. The column marched along the road; and on both sides of it in a continuous line, now mounting, now descending, marched *Jägers* in high boots, sheepskin coats, and tall caps, with rifles on their shoulders and cartridges in their belts.

As usual when marching through a hostile country, silence was observed as far as possible. Only occasionally the guns jingled jolting across a ditch, or an artillery horse snorted or neighed, not understanding that silence was ordered, or an angry commander shouted in a hoarse subdued voice to his subordinates that the line was spreading out too much or marching too near or too far from the column. Only once was the silence broken, when from a bramble patch between the line and the column a gazelle with a white breast and grey back jumped out followed by a buck of the same colour with small backward-curving horns. Doubling up their forelegs at each big bound they took, the beautiful timid creatures came so close to the column that some of the soldiers rushed after them laughing and shouting, intending to bayonet them, but the gazelles turned back, slipped through the line of *Jägers*, and pursued by a few horsemen and the company's dogs, fled like birds to the mountains.

It was still winter, but towards noon, when the column (which had started early in the morning) had gone three miles, the sun had risen high enough and was powerful enough to make the men quite hot, and its rays were so bright that it was painful to look at the shining steel of the bayonets or at the reflections – like little suns – on the brass of the cannons.

The clear and rapid stream the detachment had just crossed

lay behind, and in front were tilled fields and meadows in shallow valleys. Farther in front were the dark mysterious forest-clad hills with crags rising beyond them, and farther still on the lofty horizon were the ever-beautiful ever-changing snowy peaks that played with the light like diamonds.

At the head of the 5th Company, Butler, a tall handsome officer who had recently exchanged from the Guards, marched along in a black coat and tall cap, shouldering his sword. He was filled with a buoyant sense of the joy of living, the danger of death, a wish for action, and the consciousness of being part of an immense whole directed by a single will. This was his second time of going into action and he thought how in a moment they would be fired at, and he would not only not stoop when the shells flew overhead, or heed the whistle of the bullets, but would carry his head even more erect than before and would look round at his comrades and the soldiers with smiling eyes, and begin to talk in a perfectly calm voice about quite other matters.

The detachment turned off the good road onto a little-used one that crossed a stubbly maize-field, and they were drawing near the forest when, with an ominous whistle, a shell flew past amid the baggage wagons – they could not see whence – and tore up the ground in the field by the roadside.

'It's beginning,' said Butler with a bright smile to a comrade who was walking beside him.

And so it was. After the shell a thick crowd of mounted

Chechens appeared with their banners from under the shelter of the forest. In the midst of the crowd could be seen a large green banner, and an old and very far-sighted sergeant-major informed the short-sighted Butler that Shamil himself must be there. The horsemen came down the hill and appeared to the right, at the highest part of the valley nearest the detachment, and began to descend. A little general in a thick black coat and tall cap rode up to Butler's company on his ambler, and ordered him to the right to encounter the descending horsemen. Butler quickly led his company in the direction indicated, but before he reached the valley he heard two cannon shots behind him. He looked round: two clouds of grey smoke had risen above two cannon and were spreading along the valley. The mountaineers' horsemen – who had evidently not expected to meet artillery – retired. Butler's company began firing at them and the whole ravine was filled with the smoke of powder. Only higher up above the ravine could the mountaineers be seen hurriedly retreating, though still firing back at the Cossacks who pursued them. The company followed the mountaineers farther, and on the slope of a second ravine came in view of an *aoul*.

Following the Cossacks, Butler and his company entered the *aoul* at a run, to find it deserted. The soldiers were ordered to burn the corn and the hay as well as the *saklyas*, and the whole *aoul* was soon filled with pungent smoke amid which the soldiers rushed about dragging out of the *saklyas* what they could find, and above all catching and shooting the fowls the mountaineers had not been able to take away with them.

The officers sat down at some distance beyond the smoke, and lunched and drank. The sergeant-major brought them some honeycombs on a board. There was no sign of any Chechens and early in the afternoon the order was given to retreat. The companies formed into a column behind the *aoul* and Butler happened to be in the rear-guard. As soon as they started Chechens appeared, following and firing at the detachment, but they ceased this pursuit as soon as they came out into an open space.

Not one of Butler's company had been wounded, and he returned in a most happy and energetic mood. When after fording the same stream it had crossed in the morning, the detachment spread over the maize-fields and the meadows, the singers* of each company came forward and songs filled the air.

'Very diff'rent, very diff'rent, *Jägers* are, *Jägers* are!' sang Butler's singers, and his horse stepped merrily to the music. Trezorka, the shaggy grey dog belonging to the company, ran in front, with his tail curled up with an air of responsibility like a commander. Butler felt buoyant, calm, and joyful. War presented itself to him as consisting only in his exposing himself to danger and to possible death, thereby gaining rewards and the respect of his comrades here, as well as of his friends in Russia. Strange to say, his imagination never pictured the other aspect of war: the

---

* Each regiment had a choir of singers.

death and wounds of the soldiers, officers, and mountaineers. To retain his poetic conception he even unconsciously avoided looking at the dead and wounded. So that day when we had three dead and twelve wounded, he passed by a corpse lying on its back and did not stop to look, seeing only with one eye the strange position of the waxen hand and a dark red spot on the head. The hillsmen appeared to him only as mounted *dzhigits* from whom he had to defend himself.

'You see, my dear sir,' said his major in an interval between two songs, 'it's not as it is with you in Petersburg – "Eyes right! Eyes left!" Here we have done our job, and now we go home and Masha will set a pie and some nice cabbage soup before us. That's life – don't you think so? – Now then! *As the Dawn was Breaking*!' He called for his favourite song.

There was no wind, the air was fresh and clear and so transparent that the snow hills nearly a hundred miles away seemed quite near, and in the intervals between the songs the regular sound of the footsteps and the jingle of the guns was heard as a background on which each song began and ended. The song that was being sung in Butler's company was composed by a cadet in honour of the regiment, and went to a dance tune. The chorus was: 'Very diff'rent, very diff'rent, *Jägers* are, *Jägers* are!'

Butler rode beside the officer next in rank above him, Major Petrov, with whom he lived, and he felt he could not be thankful enough to have exchanged from the Guards and come to the Caucasus. His chief reason for exchanging was that he had lost all he had at cards and was afraid that if he remained there he would be unable to resist playing though he had nothing more to lose. Now all that was over, his life was quite changed and was such a pleasant and brave one! He forgot that he was ruined, and forgot his unpaid debts. The Caucasus, the war, the soldiers, the officers – those tipsy, brave, good-natured fellows – and Major Petrov himself, all seemed so delightful that sometimes it appeared too good to be true that he was not in Petersburg – in a room filled with tobacco-smoke, turning down the corners of cards* and gambling, hating the holder of the bank and feeling a dull pain in his head – but was really here in this glorious region among these brave Caucasians.

The major and the daughter of a surgeon's orderly, formerly known as Masha, but now generally called by the more respectful name of Marya Dmitrievna, lived together as man and wife. Marya Dmitrievna was a handsome, fair-haired, very freckled, childless woman of thirty. Whatever her past may have been she was now the major's faithful companion and looked after him like a nurse – a very necessary matter, since he often drank himself into oblivion.

When they reached the fort everything happened as the major had foreseen. Marya Dmitrievna gave him and Butler, and two other officers of the detachment who had been invited,

---

* A way of doubling one's stake at the game of *shtos*.

a nourishing and tasty dinner, and the major ate and drank till he was unable to speak, and then went off to his room to sleep.

Butler, having drunk rather more chikhir wine than was good for him, went to his bedroom, tired but contented, and hardly had time to undress before he fell into a sound, dreamless, and unbroken sleep with his hand under his handsome curly head.

XVII

THE *AOUL* which had been destroyed was that in which Hadji Murad had spent the night before he went over to the Russians. Sado and his family had left the *aoul* on the approach of the Russian detachment, and when he returned he found his *saklya* in ruins – the roof fallen in, the door and the posts supporting the penthouse burnt, and the interior filthy. His son, the hand-some bright-eyed boy who had gazed with such ecstasy at Hadji Murad, was brought dead to the mosque on a horse covered with a *burka*: he had been stabbed in the back with a bayonet. The dignified woman who had served Hadji Murad when he was at the house now stood over her son's body, her smock torn in front, her withered old breasts exposed, her hair down, and she dug her nails into her face till it bled, and wailed incessantly. Sado, taking a pick-axe and spade, had gone with his relatives to dig a grave for his son. The old grandfather sat by the wall of the ruined *saklya* cutting a stick and gazing stolidly in front of him. He had only just returned from the apiary. The two stacks of hay there had been burnt, the apricot- and cherry-trees he had planted and reared were broken and scorched, and worse still all the beehives and bees had been burnt. The wailing of the women and the little children, who cried with their mothers, mingled with the lowing of the hungry cattle for whom there was no food. The bigger children, instead of playing, followed their elders with frightened eyes. The fountain was polluted, evidently on purpose, so that the water could not be used. The mosque was polluted in the same way, and the Mullah and his assistants were cleaning it out. No one spoke of hatred of the Russians. The feeling experienced by all the Chechens, from the youngest to the oldest, was stronger than hate. It was not hatred, for they did not regard those Russian dogs as human beings, but it was such repulsion, disgust, and perplexity at the senseless cruelty of these creatures, that the desire to exterminate them — like the desire to exterminate rats, poisonous spiders, or wolves — was as natural an instinct as that of self-preservation.

The inhabitants of the *aoul* were confronted by the choice of remaining there and restoring with frightful effort what had been produced with such labour and had been so lightly and senselessly destroyed, facing every moment the possibility of a repetition of what had happened; or to submit to the Russians — contrary to their religion and despite the repulsion and contempt they felt for them. The old men prayed, and unanimously decided to send envoys to Shamil asking him for help.

Then they immediately set to work to restore what had been destroyed.

XVIII

ON THE MORNING after the raid, not very early, Butler left the house by the back porch meaning to take a stroll and a breath of fresh air before breakfast, which he usually had with Petrov. The sun had already risen above the hills and it was painful to look at the brightly lit-up white walls of the houses on the right side of the street. But then as always it was cheerful and soothing to look to the left, at the dark receding and ascending forest-clad hills and at the dim line of snow peaks, which as usual pretended to be clouds. Butler looked at these mountains, inhaling deep breaths and rejoicing that he was alive, that it was just he that was alive, and that he lived in this beautiful place.

He was also rather pleased that he had behaved so well in yesterday's affair both during the advance and especially during the retreat when things were pretty hot; he was also pleased to remember how Masha (or Marya Dmitrievna), Petrov's mistress, had treated them at dinner on their return after the raid, and how she had been particularly nice and simple with everybody, but specially kind – as he thought – to him.

Marya Dmitrievna with her thick plait of hair, her broad shoulders, her high bosom, and the radiant smile on her kindly freckled face, involuntarily attracted Butler, who was a healthy young bachelor. It sometimes even seemed to him that she wanted him, but he considered that that would be doing his good-natured simple-hearted comrade a wrong, and he maintained a simple, respectful attitude towards her and was pleased with himself for doing so.

He was thinking of this when his meditations were disturbed by the tramp of many horses' hoofs along the dusty road in front of him, as if several men were riding that way. He looked up and saw at the end of the street a group of horsemen coming towards him at a walk. In front of a score of Cossacks rode two men: one in a white Circassian coat with a tall turban on his head, the other an officer in the Russian service, dark, with an aquiline nose, and much silver on his uniform and weapons. The man with the turban rode a fine chestnut horse with mane and tail of a lighter shade, a small head, and beautiful eyes. The officer's was a large, handsome Karabakh horse. Butler, a lover of horses, immediately recognized the great strength of the first horse and stopped to learn who these people were.

The officer addressed him. 'This the house of commanding officer?' he asked, his foreign accent and his words betraying his foreign origin.

Butler replied that it was. 'And who is that?' he added, coming nearer to the officer and indicating the man with the turban.

'That Hadji Murad. He come here to stay with the commander,' said the officer.

Butler knew about Hadji Murad and about his having come over to the Russians, but he had not at all expected to see him here in this little fort. Hadji Murad gave him a friendly look.

'Good day, *kotkildy*,' said Butler, repeating the Tartar greeting he had learnt.

'*Saubul!*' ('Be well!') replied Hadji Murad, nodding. He rode up to Butler and held out his hand, from two fingers of which hung his whip.

'Are you the chief?' he asked.

'No, the chief is in here. I will go and call him,' said Butler addressing the officer, and he went up the steps and pushed the door. But the door of the visitors' entrance, as Marya Dmitrievna called it, was locked, and as it still remained closed after he had knocked, Butler went round to the back door. He called his orderly but received no reply, and finding neither of the two orderlies he went into the kitchen, where Marya Dmitrievna – flushed, with a kerchief tied round her head and her sleeves rolled up on her plump white arms – was rolling pastry, white as her hands, and cutting it into small pieces to make pies of.

'Where have the orderlies gone to?' asked Butler.

'Gone to drink,' replied Marya Dmitrievna. 'What do you want?'

'To have the front door opened. You have a whole horde of mountaineers in front of your house. Hadji Murad has come!'

'Invent something else!' said Marya Dmitrievna, smiling.

'I am not joking, he is really waiting by the porch!'

'Is it really true?' said she.

'Why should I wish to deceive you? Go and see, he's just at the porch!'

'Dear me, here's a go!' said Marya Dmitrievna pulling down her sleeves and putting up her hand to feel whether the hairpins in her thick plait were all in order. 'Then I will go and wake Ivan Matveich.'

'No, I'll go myself. And you, Bondarenko, go and open the door,' said he to Petrov's orderly who had just appeared.

'Well, so much the better!' said Marya Dmitrievna and returned to her work.

When he heard that Hadji Murad had come to his house, Ivan Matveich Petrov, the major, who had already heard that Hadji Murad was in Grozny, was not at all surprised. Sitting up in bed he rolled a cigarette, lit it, and began to dress, loudly clearing his throat and grumbling at the authorities who had sent 'that devil' to him.

When he was ready he told his orderly to bring him some medicine. The orderly knew that 'medicine' meant vodka, and brought some.

'There is nothing so bad as mixing,' muttered the major when he had drunk the vodka and taken a bite of rye bread. 'Yesterday I drank a little chikhir and now I have a headache . . . Well, I'm ready,' he added, and went to the parlour, into which Butler had already shown Hadji Murad and the officer who accompanied him.

The officer handed the major orders from the commander of the left flank to the effect that he should receive Hadji Murad and should allow him to have intercourse with the mountaineers through spies, but was on no account to allow him to leave the fort without a convoy of Cossacks.

Having read the order the major looked intently at Hadji Murad and again scrutinized the paper. After passing his eyes several times from one to the other in this manner, he at last fixed them on Hadji Murad and said:

'*Yakshi, Bek; yakshi!*' ('Very well, sir, very well!') 'Let him stay here, and tell him I have orders not to let him out – and what is commanded is sacred! Well, Butler, where do you think we'd better lodge him? Shall we put him in the office?'

Butler had not time to answer before Marya Dmitrievna – who had come from the kitchen and was standing in the doorway – said to the major:

'Why? Keep him here! We will give him the guest-chamber and the store-room. Then at any rate he will be within sight,' said she, glancing at Hadji Murad; but meeting his eyes she turned quickly away.

'Do you know, I think Marya Dmitrievna is right,' said Butler.

'Now then, now then, get away! Women have no business here,' said the major frowning.

During the whole of this discussion Hadji Murad sat with his hand on the hilt of his dagger and a faint smile of contempt on his lips. He said it was all the same to him where he lodged, and that he wanted nothing but what the Sirdar had permitted – namely, to have communication with the mountaineers, and that he therefore wished they should be allowed to come to him.

The major said this should be done, and asked Butler to entertain the visitors till something could be got for them to eat and their rooms prepared. Meantime he himself would go across to the office to write what was necessary and to give some orders.

Hadji Murad's relations with his new acquaintances were at once very clearly defined. From the first he was repelled by and contemptuous of the major, to whom he always behaved very haughtily. Marya Dmitrievna, who prepared and served up his food, pleased him particularly. He liked her simplicity and especially the – to him – foreign type of her beauty, and he was influenced by the attraction she felt towards him and unconsciously conveyed. He tried not to look at her or speak to her, but his eyes involuntarily turned towards her and followed her movements. With Butler, from their first acquaintance, he immediately made friends and talked much and willingly with him, questioning him about his life, telling him of his own, communicating to him the news the spies brought him of his family's condition, and even consulting him as to how he ought to act.

The news he received through the spies was not good. During the first four days of his stay in the fort they came to see him twice and both times brought bad news.

XIX

HADJI MURAD'S family had been removed to Vedeno soon after his desertion to the Russians, and were there kept under guard awaiting Shamil's decision. The women – his old mother Patimat and his two wives with their five little children – were kept under guard in the *saklya* of the officer Ibrahim Raschid, while Hadji Murad's son Yusuf, a youth of eighteen, was put in prison – that is, into a pit more than seven feet deep, together with seven criminals, who like himself were awaiting a decision as to their fate.

The decision was delayed because Shamil was away on a campaign against the Russians.

On 6 January 1852, he returned to Vedeno after a battle, in which according to the Russians he had been vanquished and had fled to Vedeno; but in which according to him and all the *murids* he had been victorious and had repulsed the Russians. In this battle he himself fired his rifle – a thing he seldom did – and drawing his sword would have charged straight at the Russians had not the *murids* who accompanied him held him back. Two of them were killed on the spot at his side.

It was noon when Shamil, surrounded by a party of *murids* who caracoled around him firing their rifles and pistols and continually singing *Lya illyah il Allah!* rode up to his place of residence.

All the inhabitants of the large *aoul* were in the street or on their roofs to meet their ruler, and as a sign of triumph they also fired off rifles and pistols. Shamil rode a white Arab steed which pulled at its bit as it approached the house. The horse had no gold or silver ornaments, its equipment was of the simplest – a delicately worked red leather bridle with a stripe down the middle, metal cup-shaped stirrups, and a red saddlecloth showing a little from under the saddle. The Imam wore a brown cloth cloak lined with black fur showing at the neck and sleeves, and was tightly girded round his long thin waist with a black strap which held a dagger. On his head he wore a tall cap with flat crown and black tassel, and round it was wound a white turban, one end of which hung down on his neck. He wore green slippers, and black leggings trimmed with plain braid.

He wore nothing bright – no gold or silver – and his tall, erect, powerful figure, clothed in garments without any ornaments, surrounded by *murids* with gold and silver on their clothes and weapons, produced on the people just the impression and influence he desired and knew how to produce. His pale face framed by a closely trimmed reddish beard, with his small eyes always screwed up, was as immovable as though hewn out of stone. As he rode through the *aoul* he felt the gaze of a thousand eyes turned eagerly on him, but he himself looked at no one.

Hadji Murad's wives had come out into the penthouse with the rest of the inmates of the *saklya* to see the Imam's entry. Only Patimat, Hadji Murad's old mother, did not go out but remained sitting on the floor of the *saklya* with her grey hair down, her long arms encircling her thin knees, blinking with her fiery black eyes as she watched the dying embers in the fireplace. Like her son she had always hated Shamil, and now she hated him more than ever and had no wish to see him. Neither did Hadji Murad's son see Shamil's triumphal entry. Sitting in the dark and fetid pit he heard the firing and singing, and endured tortures such as can only be felt by the young who are full of vitality and deprived of freedom. He only saw his unfortunate, dirty, and exhausted fellow-prisoners – embittered and for the most part filled with hatred of one another. He now passionately envied those who, enjoying fresh air and light and freedom, caracoled on fiery steeds around their chief, shooting and heartily singing: *Lya illyah il Allah!*

When he had crossed the *aoul* Shamil rode into the large courtyard adjoining the inner court where his seraglio was. Two armed Lesghians met him at the open gates of this outer court, which was crowded with people. Some had come from distant parts about their own affairs, some had come with petitions, and some had been summoned by Shamil to be tried and sentenced. As the Imam rode in, they all respectfully saluted him with their hands on their breasts, some of them kneeling down and remaining on their knees while he rode across the court from the outer to the inner gates. Though he recognized among the people who waited in the court many whom he disliked, and many tedious petitioners who wanted his attention, Shamil passed them all with the same immovable, stony expression on his face, and having entered the inner court dismounted at the penthouse in front of his apartment, to the left of the gate. He was worn out, mentally rather than physically, by the strain of the campaign, for in spite of the public declaration that he had been victorious he knew very well that his campaign had been unsuccessful, that many Chechen *aouls* had been burnt down and ruined, and that the unstable and fickle Chechens were wavering and those nearest the border line were ready to go over to the Russians.

All this had to be dealt with, and it oppressed him, for at that moment he did not wish to think at all. He only desired one thing: rest and the delights of family life, and the caresses of his favourite wife, the black-eyed quick-footed eighteen-year-old Aminal, who at that very moment was close at hand behind the fence that divided the inner court and separated the men's from the women's quarters (Shamil felt sure she was there with his other wives, looking through a chink in the fence while he dismounted). But not only was it impossible for him to go to her, he could not even lie down on his feather cushions and rest from his fatigues; he had first of all to perform the midday rites for which he had just then not the least inclination, but which as the religious leader of the people he could not omit, and which moreover were as necessary to him himself as his daily food. So he performed his ablutions and said his prayers and summoned those who were waiting for him.

The first to enter was Jemal Eddin, his father-in-law and teacher, a tall grey-haired good-looking old man with a beard white as snow and a rosy red face. He said a prayer and began questioning Shamil about the incidents of the campaign and telling him what had happened in the mountains during his absence.

Among events of many kinds – murders connected with blood-feuds, cattle-stealing, people accused of disobeying the Tarikat (smoking and drinking wine) – Jemal Eddin related how Hadji Murad had sent men to bring his family over to the Russians, but that this had been detected and the family had been brought to Vedeno where they were kept under guard and awaited the Imam's decision. In the next room, the guest-chamber, the Elders were assembled to discuss all these affairs, and Jemal Eddin advised Shamil to finish with them and let them go that same day, as they had already been waiting three days for him.

After eating his dinner – served to him in his room by Zeidat, a dark, sharp-nosed, disagreeable-looking woman whom he did not love but who was his eldest wife – Shamil passed into the guest-chamber.

The six old men who made up his council – white, grey, or red-bearded, with tall caps on their heads, some with turbans and some without, wearing new *beshmets* and Circassian coats girdled with straps on which their daggers were suspended – rose to greet him on his entrance. Shamil towered a head above them all. On entering the room he, as well as all the others, lifted his hands, palms upwards, closed his eyes and recited a prayer, and then stroked his face downwards with both hands, uniting them at the end of his beard. Having done this they all sat down, Shamil on a larger cushion than the others, and discussed the various cases before them.

In the case of the criminals the decisions were given according to the Shariat: two were sentenced to have a hand cut off for stealing, one man to be beheaded for murder, and three were pardoned. Then they came to the principal business: how to stop the Chechens from going over to the Russians. To counteract that tendency Jemal Eddin drew up the following proclamation:

'I wish you eternal peace with God the Almighty!

'I hear that the Russians flatter you and invite you to surrender to them. Do not believe what they say, and do not surrender but endure. If ye be not rewarded for it in this life ye shall receive your reward in the life to come. Remember what happened before when they took your arms from you! If God had not brought you to reason then, in 1840, ye would now be soldiers, and your wives would be dishonoured and would no longer wear trousers.

'Judge of the future by the past. It is better to die in enmity with the Russians than to live with the Unbelievers. Endure for a little while and I will come with the Koran and the sword and will lead you against the enemy. But now I strictly command you not only to entertain no intention, but not even a thought, of submitting to the Russians!'

Shamil approved this proclamation, signed it, and had it sent out.

After this business they considered Hadji Murad's case. This was of the utmost importance to Shamil. Although he did not wish to admit it, he knew that if Hadji Murad with his agility, boldness, and courage, had been with him, what had now happened in Chechnya would not have occurred. It would therefore be well to make it up with Hadji Murad and have the benefit of his services again. But as this was not possible it would never do to allow him to help the Russians, and therefore he must be enticed back and killed. They might accomplish this either by sending a man to Tiflis who would kill him there, or by inducing him to come back and then killing him. The only means of doing the latter was by making use of his family and especially his son, whom Shamil knew he loved passionately. Therefore they must act through the son.

When the councillors had talked all this over, Shamil closed his eyes and sat silent.

The councillors knew that this meant that he was listening to the voice of the Prophet, who spoke to him and told him what to do.

After five minutes of solemn silence Shamil opened his eyes, and narrowing them more than usual, said:

'Bring Hadji Murad's son to me.'

'He is here,' replied Jemal Eddin, and in fact Yusuf, Hadji Murad's son, thin, pale, tattered, and evil-smelling, but still handsome in face and figure, with black eyes that burnt like his grandmother Patimat's, was already standing by the gate of the outside court waiting to be called in.

Yusuf did not share his father's feelings towards Shamil. He did not know all that had happened in the past, or if he knew it, not having lived through it he still did not understand why his father was so obstinately hostile to Shamil. To him who wanted only one thing – to continue living the easy, loose life that, as the *naib*'s son, he had led in Khunzakh – it seemed quite unnecessary to be at enmity with Shamil. Out of defiance and a spirit of contradiction to his father he particularly admired Shamil, and shared the ecstatic adoration with which he was regarded in the mountains. With a peculiar feeling of tremulous veneration for the Imam he now entered the guest-chamber. As he stopped by the door he met the steady gaze of Shamil's half-closed eyes. He paused for a moment, and then approached Shamil and kissed his large, long-fingered hand.

'Thou art Hadji Murad's son?'

'I am, Imam.'

'Thou knowest what he has done?'

'I know, Imam, and deplore it.'

'Canst thou write?'

'I was preparing myself to be a Mullah—'

'Then write to thy father that if he will return to me now, before the Feast of Bairam, I will forgive him and everything shall be as it was before; but if not, and if he remains with the Russians –' and Shamil frowned sternly – 'I will give thy grandmother, thy mother, and the rest to the different *aouls*, and thee I will behead!'

Not a muscle of Yusuf's face stirred, and he bowed his head to show that he understood Shamil's words.

'Write that and give it to my messenger.'

Shamil ceased speaking, and looked at Yusuf for a long time in silence.

'Write that I have had pity on thee and will not kill thee, but will put out thine eyes as I do to all traitors! . . . Go!'

While in Shamil's presence Yusuf appeared calm, but when he had been led out of the guest-chamber he rushed at his attendant, snatched the man's dagger from its sheath and tried to stab himself, but he was seized by the arms, bound, and led back to the pit.

That evening at dusk after he had finished his evening prayers, Shamil put on a white fur-lined cloak and passed out to the other side of the fence where his wives lived, and went straight to Aminal's room, but he did not find her there. She was with the older wives. Then Shamil, trying to remain unseen, hid behind the door and stood waiting for her. But Aminal was angry with him because he had given some silk stuff to Zeidat and not to her. She saw him come out and go into her room looking for her, and she purposely kept away. She stood a long time at the door of Zeidat's room, laughing softly at Shamil's white figure that kept going in and out of her room.

Having waited for her in vain, Shamil returned to his own apartments when it was already time for the midnight prayers.

XX

HADJI MURAD had been a week in the major's house at the fort. Although Marya Dmitrievna quarrelled with the shaggy Khanefi (Hadji Murad had only brought two of his *murids*, Khanefi and Eldar, with him) and had turned him out of her kitchen — for which he nearly killed her — she evidently felt a particular respect and sympathy for Hadji Murad. She now no longer served him his dinner, having handed that duty over to Eldar, but she seized every opportunity of seeing him and rendering him service. She always took the liveliest interest in the negotiations about his family, knew how many wives and children he had, and their ages, and each time a spy came to see him she inquired as best she could into the results of the negotiations.

Butler during that week had become quite friendly with Hadji Murad. Sometimes the latter came to Butler's room, sometimes Butler went to Hadji Murad's: sometimes they conversed by the help of the interpreter, and sometimes they got on as best they could with signs and especially with smiles.

Hadji Murad had evidently taken a fancy to Butler, as could be gathered from Eldar's relations with the latter. When Butler entered Hadji Murad's room Eldar met him with a pleased smile showing his glittering teeth, and hurried to put down a cushion for him to sit on and to relieve him of his sword if he was wearing one.

Butler also got to know, and became friendly with, the shaggy Khanefi, Hadji Murad's sworn brother. Khanefi knew many mountain songs and sang them well, and to please Butler, Hadji Murad often made Khanefi sing, choosing the songs he considered best. Khanefi had a high tenor voice and sang with extraordinary clearness and expression. One of the songs Hadji Murad specially liked impressed Butler by its solemnly mournful tone and he asked the interpreter to translate it.

The subject of the song was the very blood-feud that had existed between Khanefi and Hadji Murad. It ran as follows:

> '*The earth will dry on my grave,*
> *Mother, my Mother!*
> *And thou wilt forget me!*
> *And over me rank grass will wave,*
> *Father, my Father!*
> *Nor wilt thou regret me*
> *When tears cease thy dark eyes to lave,*
> *Sister, dear Sister!*
> *No more will grief fret thee!*
>
> '*But thou, my Brother the elder, wilt never forget,*
> *With vengeance denied me!*

And thou, my Brother the younger, wilt ever regret,
Till thou liest beside me!

'Hotly thou camest, O death-bearing ball that I spurned,
For thou wast my slave!
And thou, black earth, that battle-steed trampled and churned,
Wilt cover my grave!

'Cold art Thou, O Death, yet I was thy Lord and thy Master!
My body sinks fast to the earth, my soul to Heaven flies faster.'

Hadji Murad always listened to this song with closed eyes and when it ended on a long gradually dying note he always remarked in Russian:

'Good song! Wise song!'

After Hadji Murad's arrival and his intimacy with him and his *murids*, the poetry of the stirring mountain life took a still stronger hold on Butler. He procured for himself a *beshmet* and a Circassian coat and leggings, and imagined himself a mountaineer living the life those people lived.

On the day of Hadji Murad's departure the major invited several officers to see him off. They were sitting, some at the table where Marya Dmitrievna was pouring out tea, some at another table on which stood vodka, chikhir, and light refreshments, when Hadji Murad dressed for the journey came limping into the room with soft, rapid footsteps.

They all rose and shook hands with him. The major offered him a seat on the divan, but Hadji Murad thanked him and sat down on a chair by the window.

The silence that followed his entrance did not at all abash him. He looked attentively at all the faces and fixed an indifferent gaze on the tea-table with the samovar and refreshments. Petrovsky, a lively officer who now met Hadji Murad for the first time, asked him through the interpreter whether he liked Tiflis.

'*Alya!*' he replied.

'He says "Yes",' translated the interpreter.

'What did he like there?'

Hadji Murad said something in reply.

'He liked the theatre best of all.'

'And how did he like the ball at the house of the commander-in-chief?'

Hadji Murad frowned. 'Every nation has its own customs! Our women do not dress in such a way,' said he, glancing at Marya Dmitrievna.

'Well, didn't he like it?'

'We have a proverb,' said Hadji Murad to the interpreter, '"The dog gave meat to the ass and the ass gave hay to the dog, and both went hungry",' and he smiled. 'Its own customs seem good to each nation.'

The conversation went no farther. Some of the officers took tea, some other refreshments. Hadji Murad accepted the tumbler of tea offered him and put it down before him.

'Won't you have cream and a bun?' asked Marya Dmitrievna, offering them to him.

Hadji Murad bowed his head.

'Well, I suppose it is goodbye!' said Butler, touching his knee. 'When shall we meet again?'

'Goodbye, goodbye!' said Hadji Murad, in Russian, with a smile. '*Kunak bulug*. Strong *kunak* to thee! Time – *ayda* – go!' and he jerked his head in the direction in which he had to go.

Eldar appeared in the doorway carrying something large and white across his shoulder and a sword in his hand. Hadji Murad beckoned to him and he crossed the room with big strides and handed him a white *burka* and the sword. Hadji Murad rose, took the *burka*, threw it over his arm, and saying something to the interpreter handed it to Marya Dmitrievna.

'He says thou hast praised the *burka*, so accept it,' said the interpreter.

'Oh, why?' said Marya Dmitrievna blushing.

'It is necessary. Like Adam,' said Hadji Murad.

'Well, thank you,' said Marya Dmitrievna, taking the *burka*. 'God grant that you rescue your son,' she added. '*Ulan yakshi*. Tell him that I wish him success in releasing his son.'

Hadji Murad glanced at Marya Dmitrievna and nodded his head approvingly. Then he took the sword from Eldar and handed it to the major. The major took it and said to the interpreter, 'Tell him to take my chestnut gelding. I have nothing else to give him.'

Hadji Murad waved his hand in front of his face to show that he did not want anything and would not accept it. Then, pointing first to the mountains and then to his heart, he went out.

All the household followed him as far as the door, while the officers who remained inside the room drew the sword from its scabbard, examined its blade, and decided that it was a real Gurda.*

Butler accompanied Hadji Murad to the porch, and then came a very unexpected incident which might have ended fatally for Hadji Murad had it not been for his quick observation, determination, and agility.

The inhabitants of the Kumukh *aoul*, Tash-Kichu, which was friendly to the Russians, respected Hadji Murad greatly and had often come to the fort merely to look at the famous *naib*. They had sent messengers to him three days previously to ask him to visit their mosque on the Friday. But the Kumukh princes who lived in Tash-Kichu hated Hadji Murad because there was a blood-feud between them, and on hearing of this invitation they announced to the people that they would not allow him to enter the mosque. The people became excited and a fight occurred between them and the princes' supporters. The Russian authorities pacified the mountaineers and sent word to Hadji Murad not to go to the mosque.

---

* A highly prized quality of blade.

Hadji Murad did not go and everyone supposed that the matter was settled.

But at the very moment of his departure, when he came out into the porch before which the horses stood waiting, Arslan Khan, one of the Kumukh princes and an acquaintance of Butler and the major, rode up to the house.

When he saw Hadji Murad he snatched a pistol from his belt and took aim, but before he could fire, Hadji Murad in spite of his lameness rushed down from the porch like a cat towards Arslan Khan who missed him.

Seizing Arslan Khan's horse by the bridle with one hand, Hadji Murad drew his dagger with the other and shouted something to him in Tartar.

Butler and Eldar both ran at once towards the enemies and caught them by the arms. The major, who had heard the shot, also came out.

'What do you mean by it, Arslan – starting such a nasty business on my premises?' said he, when he heard what had happened. 'It's not right, friend! "To the foe in the field you need not yield!" – but to start this kind of slaughter in front of my house—'

Arslan Khan, a little man with black moustaches, got off his horse pale and trembling, looked angrily at Hadji Murad, and went into the house with the major. Hadji Murad, breathing heavily and smiling, returned to the horses.

'Why did he want to kill him?' Butler asked the interpreter.

'He says it is a law of theirs,' the interpreter translated Hadji

Murad's reply. 'Arslan must avenge a relation's blood and so he tried to kill him.'

'And supposing he overtakes him on the road?' asked Butler.

Hadji Murad smiled.

'Well, if he kills me it will prove that such is Allah's will . . . Goodbye,' he said again in Russian, taking his horse by the withers. Glancing round at everybody who had come out to see him off, his eyes rested kindly on Marya Dmitrievna.

'Goodbye, my lass,' said he to her. 'I thank you.'

'God help you – God help you to rescue your family!' repeated Marya Dmitrievna.

He did not understand her words, but felt her sympathy for him and nodded to her.

'Mind, don't forget your *kunak*,' said Butler.

'Tell him I am his true friend and will never forget him,' answered Hadji Murad to the interpreter, and in spite of his short leg he swung himself lightly and quickly into the high saddle, barely touching the stirrup, and automatically feeling for his dagger and adjusting his sword. Then, with that peculiarly proud look with which only a Caucasian hill-man sits his horse – as though he were one with it – he rode away from the major's house. Khanefi and Eldar also mounted and having taken a friendly leave of their hosts and of the officers, rode off at a trot, following their *murshid*.

As usual after a departure, those who remained behind began to discuss those who had left.

'Plucky fellow! He rushed at Arslan Khan like a wolf! His face quite changed!'

'But he'll be up to tricks – he's a terrible rogue, I should say,' remarked Petrovsky.

'It's a pity there aren't more Russian rogues of such a kind!' suddenly put in Marya Dmitrievna with vexation. 'He has lived a week with us and we have seen nothing but good from him. He is courteous, wise, and just,' she added.

'How did you find that out?'

'No matter, I did find it out!'

'She's quite smitten, and that's a fact!' said the major, who had just entered the room.

'Well, and if I am smitten? What's that to you? Why run him down if he's a good man? Though he's a Tartar he's still a good man!'

'Quite true, Marya Dmitrievna,' said Butler, 'and you're quite right to take his part!'

XXI

LIFE IN OUR advanced forts in the Chechen lines went on as usual. Since the events last narrated there had been two alarms when the companies were called out and militiamen galloped about; but both times the mountaineers who had caused the excitement got away, and once at Vozdvizhensk they killed a

Cossack and succeeded in carrying off eight Cossack horses that were being watered. There had been no further raids since the one in which the *aoul* was destroyed, but an expedition on a large scale was expected in consequence of the appointment of a new commander of the left flank, Prince Baryatinsky. He was an old friend of the Viceroy's and had been in command of the Kabarda Regiment. On his arrival at Grozny as commander of the whole left flank he at once mustered a detachment to continue to carry out the Tsar's commands as communicated by Chernyshov to Vorontsov. The detachment mustered at Vozdvizhensk left the fort and took up a position towards Kurin, where the troops were encamped and were felling the forest. Young Vorontsov lived in a splendid cloth tent, and his wife, Marya Vasilevna, often came to the camp and stayed the night. Baryatinsky's relations with Marya Vasilevna were no secret to anyone, and the officers who were not in the aristocratic set and the soldiers abused her in coarse terms – for her presence in camp caused them to be told off to lie in ambush at night. The mountaineers were in the habit of bringing guns within range and firing shells at the camp. The shells generally missed their aim and therefore at ordinary times no special measures were taken to prevent such firing, but now men were placed in ambush to hinder the mountaineers from injuring or frightening Marya Vasilevna with their cannon. To have to be always lying in ambush at night to save a lady from being frightened, offended and annoyed them, and therefore the soldiers, as well as the officers not admitted to the higher society, called Marya Vasilevna bad names.

Having obtained leave of absence from his fort, Butler came to the camp to visit some old messmates from the cadet corps and fellow-officers of the Kurin Regiment who were serving as adjutants and orderly officers. When he first arrived he had a very good time. He put up in Poltoratsky's tent and there met many acquaintances who gave him a hearty welcome. He also called on Vorontsov, whom he knew slightly, having once served in the same regiment with him. Vorontsov received him very kindly, introduced him to Prince Baryatinsky, and invited him to the farewell dinner he was giving in honour of General Kozlovsky, who until Baryatinsky's arrival had been in command of the left flank.

The dinner was magnificent. Special tents were erected in a line, and along the whole length of them a table was spread as for a dinner-party, with dinner-services and bottles. Everything recalled life in the Guards in Petersburg. Dinner was served at two o'clock. Kozlovsky sat in the middle on one side, Baryatinsky on the other. At Kozlovsky's right and left hand sat the Vorontsovs, husband and wife. All along the table on both sides sat the officers of the Kabarda and Kurin Regiments. Butler sat next to Poltoratsky and they both chatted merrily and drank with the officers around them. When the roast was served and the orderlies had gone round and filled the champagne glasses, Poltoratsky said to Butler, with real anxiety:

'Our Kozlovsky will disgrace himself!'

'Why?'

'Why, he'll have to make a speech, and what good is he at that? . . . It's not as easy as capturing entrenchments under fire! And with a lady beside him too, and these aristocrats!'

'Really it's painful to look at him,' said the officers to one another. And now the solemn moment had arrived. Baryatinsky rose and lifting his glass, addressed a short speech to Kozlovsky. When he had finished, Kozlovsky – who always had a trick of using the word 'how' superfluously – rose and stammeringly began:

'In compliance with the august will of His Majesty I am leaving you – parting from you, gentlemen,' said he. 'But consider me as always remaining among you. The truth of the proverb, how "One man in the field is no warrior", is well known to you, gentlemen . . . Therefore, how every reward I have received . . . how all the benefits showered on me by the great generosity of our sovereign the Emperor . . . how all my position – how my good name . . . how everything decidedly . . . how . . .' (here his voice trembled) '. . . how I am indebted to you for it, to you alone, my friends!' The wrinkled face puckered up still more, he gave a sob, and tears came into his eyes. 'How from my heart I offer you my sincerest, heartfelt gratitude!'

Kozlovsky could not go on but turned round and began to embrace the officers. The princess hid her face in her handkerchief. The prince blinked, with his mouth drawn awry. Many of the officers' eyes grew moist and Butler, who had hardly known Kozlovsky, could also not restrain his tears. He liked all this very much.

Then followed other toasts. Healths were drunk to Baryatinsky, Vorontsov, the officers, and the soldiers, and the visitors left the table intoxicated with wine and with the military elation to which they were always so prone. The weather was wonderful, sunny and calm, and the air fresh and bracing. Bonfires crackled and songs resounded on all sides. It might have been thought that everybody was celebrating some joyful event. Butler went to Poltoratsky's in the happiest, most emotional mood. Several officers had gathered there and a card-table was set. An adjutant started a bank with a hundred rubles. Two or three times Butler left the tent with his hand gripping the purse in his trousers-pocket, but at last he could resist the temptation no longer, and despite the promise he had given to his brother and to himself not to play, he began to do so. Before an hour was past, very red, perspiring, and soiled with chalk, he was sitting with both elbows on the table and writing on it – under cards bent for 'corners' and 'transports'* – the figures of his stakes. He had already lost so much that he was afraid to count up what was scored against him. But he knew without counting that all the pay he could draw in advance, added to the value of his horse, would not

---

* These expressions relate to the game of *shtos*. By turning down 'corners' of his card a player increased his stake two- or threefold. A 'transport' increased it sixfold.

suffice to pay what the adjutant, a stranger to him, had written down against him. He would still have gone on playing, but the adjutant sternly laid down the cards he held in his large clean hands and added up the chalked figures of the score of Butler's losses. Butler, in confusion, began to make excuses for being unable to pay the whole of his debt at once, and said he would send it from home. When he said this he noticed that everybody pitied him and that they all – even Poltoratsky – avoided meeting his eye. That was his last evening there. He reflected that he need only have refrained from playing and gone to the Vorontsovs who had invited him, and all would have been well, but now it was not only not well – it was terrible.

Having taken leave of his comrades and acquaintances he rode home and went to bed, and slept for eighteen hours as people usually sleep after losing heavily. From the fact that he asked her to lend him fifty kopeks to tip the Cossack who had escorted him, and from his sorrowful looks and short answers, Marya Dmitrievna guessed that he had lost at cards and she reproached the major for having given him leave of absence.

When he woke up at noon next day and remembered the situation he was in he longed again to plunge into the oblivion from which he had just emerged, but it was impossible. Steps had to be taken to repay the four hundred and seventy rubles he owed to the stranger. The first step he took was to write to his brother, confessing his sin and imploring him, for the last time, to lend him five hundred rubles on the security of the mill they still owned in common. Then he wrote to a stingy relative asking her to lend him five hundred rubles at whatever rate of interest she liked. Finally he went to the major, knowing that he – or rather Marya Dmitrievna – had some money, and asked him to lend him five hundred rubles.

'I'd let you have them at once,' said the major, 'but Masha won't! These women are so close-fisted – who the devil can understand them? . . . And yet you must get out of it somehow, devil take him! . . . Hasn't that brute the canteen-keeper got something?'

But it was no use trying to borrow from the canteen-keeper, so Butler's salvation could only come from his brother or his stingy relative.

XXII

NOT HAVING attained his aim in Chechnya, Hadji Murad returned to Tiflis and went every day to Vorontsov's, and whenever he could obtain audience he implored the Viceroy to gather together the mountaineer prisoners and exchange them for his family. He said that unless that were done his hands were tied and he could not serve the Russians and destroy Shamil as he desired to do. Vorontsov vaguely promised to do what he could, but put it off, saying that he would decide when General Argutinski reached Tiflis and he could talk the matter over with him.

Then Hadji Murad asked Vorontsov to allow him to go to live for a while in Nukha, a small town in Transcaucasia where he thought he could better carry on negotiations about his family with Shamil and with the people who were attached to himself. Moreover Nukha, being a Mohammedan town, had a mosque where he could more conveniently perform the rites of prayer demanded by the Mohammedan law. Vorontsov wrote to Petersburg about it but meanwhile gave Hadji Murad permission to go to Nukha.

For Vorontsov and the authorities in Petersburg, as well as for most Russians acquainted with Hadji Murad's history, the whole episode presented itself as a lucky turn in the Caucasian war, or simply as an interesting event. For Hadji Murad it was a terrible crisis in his life – especially latterly. He had escaped from the mountains partly to save himself and partly out of hatred of Shamil, and difficult as this flight had been he had attained his object, and for a time was glad of his success and really devised a plan to attack Shamil, but the rescue of his family – which he had thought would be easy to arrange – had proved more difficult than he expected.

Shamil had seized the family and kept them prisoners, threatening to hand the women over to the different *aouls* and to blind or kill the son. Now Hadji Murad had gone to Nukha intending to try by the aid of his adherents in Daghestan to rescue his family from Shamil by force or by cunning. The last spy who had come to see him in Nukha informed him that the Avars, who were devoted to him, were preparing to capture his family and themselves bring them over to the Russians, but that there were not enough of them and they could not risk making the attempt in Vedeno, where the family was at present imprisoned, but could do so only if the family were moved from Vedeno to some other place – in which case they promised to rescue them on the way.

Hadji Murad sent word to his friends that he would give three thousand rubles for the liberation of his family.

At Nukha a small house of five rooms was assigned to Hadji Murad near the mosque and the Khan's palace. The officers in charge of him, his interpreter, and his henchmen, stayed in the same house. Hadji Murad's life was spent in the expectation and reception of messengers from the mountains and in rides he was allowed to take in the neighbourhood.

On 24 April, returning from one of these rides, Hadji Murad learnt that during his absence an official sent by Vorontsov had arrived from Tiflis. In spite of his longing to know what message the official had brought him he went to his bedroom and repeated his noonday prayer before going into the room where the officer in charge and the official were waiting. This room served him both as drawing- and reception-room. The official who had come from Tiflis, Councillor Kirillov, informed Hadji Murad of Vorontsov's wish that he should come to Tiflis on the 12th to meet General Argutinski.

'*Yakshi!*' said Hadji Murad angrily. The councillor did not please him. 'Have you brought money?'

'I have,' answered Kirillov.

'For two weeks now,' said Hadji Murad, holding up first both hands and then four fingers. 'Give here!'

'We'll give it you at once,' said the official, getting his purse out of his travelling-bag. 'What does he want with the money?' he went on in Russian, thinking that Hadji Murad would not understand. But Hadji Murad had understood, and glanced angrily at him. While getting out the money the councillor, wishing to begin a conversation with Hadji Murad in order to have something to tell Prince Vorontsov on his return, asked through the interpreter whether he was not feeling dull there. Hadji Murad glanced contemptuously out of the corner of his eye at the fat, unarmed little man dressed as a civilian, and did not reply. The interpreter repeated the question.

'Tell him that I cannot talk with him! Let him give me the money!' and having said this, Hadji Murad sat down at the table ready to count it.

Hadji Murad had an allowance of five gold pieces a day, and when Kirillov had got out the money and arranged it in seven piles of ten gold pieces each and pushed them towards Hadji Murad, the latter poured the gold into the sleeve of his Circassian coat, rose, quite unexpectedly smacked Councillor Kirillov on his bald pate, and turned to go.

The councillor jumped up and ordered the interpreter to tell Hadji Murad that he must not dare to behave like that to him who held a rank equal to that of colonel! The officer in charge confirmed this, but Hadji Murad only nodded to signify that he knew, and left the room.

'What is one to do with him?' said the officer in charge. 'He'll stick his dagger into you, that's all! One cannot talk with those devils! I see that he is getting exasperated.'

As soon as it began to grow dusk two spies with hoods covering their faces up to their eyes, came to him from the hills. The officer in charge led them to Hadji Murad's room. One of them was a fleshy, swarthy Tavlinian, the other a thin old man. The news they brought was not cheering. Hadji Murad's friends who had undertaken to rescue his family now definitely refused to do so, being afraid of Shamil, who threatened to punish with most terrible tortures anyone who helped Hadji Murad. Having heard the messengers he sat with his elbows on his crossed legs, and bowing his turbaned head remained silent a long time.

He was thinking and thinking resolutely. He knew that he was now considering the matter for the last time and that it was necessary to come to a decision. At last he raised his head, gave each of the messengers a gold piece, and said: 'Go!'

'What answer will there be?'

'The answer will be as God pleases . . . Go!'

The messengers rose and went away, and Hadji Murad continued to sit on the carpet leaning his elbows on his knees. He sat thus a long time and pondered.

'What am I to do? To take Shamil at his word and return to him?' he thought. 'He is a fox and will deceive me. Even if he did not deceive me it would still be impossible to submit to that red liar. It is impossible . . . because now that I have been with the Russians he will not trust me,' thought Hadji Murad; and he remembered a Tavlinian fable about a falcon who had been caught and lived among men and afterwards returned to his own kind in the hills. He returned, wearing jesses with bells, and the other falcons would not receive him. 'Fly back to where they hung those silver bells on thee!' said they. 'We have no bells and no jesses.' The falcon did not want to leave his home and remained, but the other falcons did not wish to let him stay there and pecked him to death.

'And they would peck me to death in the same way,' thought Hadji Murad. 'Shall I remain here and conquer Caucasia for the Russian Tsar and earn renown, titles, riches?'

'That could be done,' thought he, recalling his interviews with Vorontsov and the flattering things the prince had said; 'but I must decide at once, or Shamil will destroy my family.'

That night he remained awake, thinking.

XXIII

BY MIDNIGHT his decision had been formed. He had decided that he must fly to the mountains, and break into Vedeno with the Avars still devoted to him, and either die or rescue his family. Whether after rescuing them he would return to the Russians or escape to Khunzakh and fight Shamil, he had not made up his mind. All he knew was that first of all he must escape from the Russians into the mountains, and he at once began to carry out his plan.

He drew his black wadded *beshmet* from under his pillow and went into his henchmen's room. They lived on the other side of the hall. As soon as he entered the hall, the outer door of which stood open, he was at once enveloped by the dewy freshness of the moonlit night and his ears were filled by the whistling and trilling of several nightingales in the garden by the house.

Having crossed the hall he opened the door of his henchmen's room. There was no light there, but the moon in its first quarter shone in at the window. A table and two chairs were standing on one side of the room, and four of his henchmen were lying on carpets or on *burkas* on the floor. Khanefi slept outside with the horses. Gamzalo heard the door creak, rose, turned round, and saw him. On recognizing him he lay down again, but Eldar, who lay beside him, jumped up and began putting on his *beshmet*, expecting his master's orders. Khan Mahoma and Bata slept on. Hadji Murad put down the *beshmet* he had brought on the table, which it hit with a dull sound, caused by the gold sewn up in it.

'Sew these in too,' said Hadji Murad, handing Eldar the gold pieces he had received that day. Eldar took them and at once went into the moonlight, drew a small knife from under his dagger and started unstitching the lining of the *beshmet*. Gamzalo raised himself and sat up with his legs crossed.

'And you, Gamzalo, tell the men to examine the rifles and pistols and get the ammunition ready. Tomorrow we shall go far,' said Hadji Murad.

'We have bullets and powder, everything shall be ready,' replied Gamzalo, and roared out something incomprehensible. He understood why Hadji Murad had ordered the rifles to be loaded. From the first he had desired only one thing – to slay and stab as many Russians as possible and to escape to the hills – and this desire had increased day by day. Now at last he saw that Hadji Murad also wanted this and he was satisfied.

When Hadji Murad went away Gamzalo roused his comrades, and all four spent the rest of the night examining their rifles, pistols, flints, and accoutrements; replacing what was damaged, sprinkling fresh powder onto the pans, and stoppering with bullets wrapped in oiled rags packets filled with the right amount of powder for each charge, sharpening their swords and daggers and greasing the blades with tallow.

Before daybreak Hadji Murad again came out into the hall to get water for his ablutions. The songs of the nightingales that had burst into ecstasy at dawn were now even louder and more incessant, while from his henchmen's room, where the daggers were being sharpened, came the regular screech and rasp of iron against stone.

Hadji Murad got himself some water from a tub, and was already at his own door when above the sound of the grinding he heard from his *murids'* room the high tones of Khanefi's voice singing a familiar song. He stopped to listen. The song told of how a *dzhigit*, Hamzad, with his brave followers captured a herd of white horses from the Russians, and how a Russian prince followed him beyond the Terek and surrounded him with an army as large as a forest; and then the song went on to tell how Hamzad killed the horses, entrenched his men behind this gory bulwark, and fought the Russians as long as they had bullets in their rifles, daggers in their belts, and blood in their veins. But before he died Hamzad saw some birds flying in the sky and cried to them:

> *'Fly on, ye winged ones, fly to our homes!*
> *Tell ye our mothers, tell ye our sisters,*
> *Tell the white maidens, that fighting we died*
> *For Ghazavat! Tell them our bodies*
> *Never will lie and rest in a tomb!*
> *Wolves will devour and tear them to pieces,*
> *Ravens and vultures will pluck out our eyes.'*

With that the song ended, and at the last words, sung to a mournful air, the merry Bata's vigorous voice joined in with a loud shout of *'Lya-il-lyakha-il Allakh!'* finishing with a shrill shriek. Then all was quiet again, except for the *tchuk, tchuk, tchuk, tchuk* and whistling of the nightingales from the garden and from behind the door the even grinding, and now and then the whiz, of iron sliding quickly along the whetstone.

Hadji Murad was so full of thought that he did not notice how he tilted his jug till the water began to pour out. He shook his head at himself and re-entered his room. After performing his morning ablutions he examined his weapons and sat down on his bed. There was nothing more for him to do. To be allowed to ride out he would have to get permission from the officer in charge, but it was not yet daylight and the officer was still asleep.

Khanefi's song reminded him of the song his mother had composed just after he was born – the song addressed to his father that Hadji Murad had repeated to Loris-Melikov.

And he seemed to see his mother before him – not wrinkled and grey-haired, with gaps between her teeth, as he had lately left her, but young and handsome, and strong enough to carry him in a basket on her back across the mountains to her father's when he was a heavy five-year-old boy.

And the recollection of himself as a little child reminded him of his beloved son, Yusuf, whose head he himself had shaved for the first time; and now this Yusuf was a handsome young *dzhigit*. He pictured him as he was when last he saw him on the day he left Tselmess. Yusuf brought him his horse and asked to be allowed to accompany him. He was ready dressed and armed, and led his own horse by the bridle, and his rosy handsome young face and the whole of his tall slender figure (he was taller than his father) breathed of daring, youth, and the joy of life. The breadth of his shoulders, though he was so young, the very wide youthful hips, the long slender waist, the strength of his long arms, and the power, flexibility, and agility of all his movements had always rejoiced Hadji Murad, who admired his son.

'Thou hadst better stay. Thou wilt be alone at home now. Take care of thy mother and thy grandmother,' said Hadji Murad. And he remembered the spirited and proud look and the flush of pleasure with which Yusuf had replied that as long as he lived no one should injure his mother or grandmother. All the same, Yusuf had mounted and accompanied his father as far as the stream. There he turned back, and since then Hadji Murad had not seen his wife, his mother, or his son. And it was this son whose eyes Shamil threatened to put out! Of what would be done to his wife Hadji Murad did not wish to think.

These thoughts so excited him that he could not sit still any longer. He jumped up and went limping quickly to the door, opened it, and called Eldar. The sun had not yet risen, but it was already quite light. The nightingales were still singing.

'Go and tell the officer that I want to go out riding, and saddle the horses,' said he.

XXIV

BUTLER'S ONLY consolation all this time was the poetry of warfare, to which he gave himself up not only during his hours of service but also in private life. Dressed in his Circassian costume, he rode and swaggered about, and twice went into ambush with Bogdanovich, though neither time did they discover or kill anyone. This closeness to and friendship with Bogdanovich, famed for his courage, seemed pleasant and warlike to Butler. He had paid his debt, having borrowed the money off a Jew at an enormous rate of interest – that is to say, he had postponed his difficulties but had not solved them. He tried not to think of his position, and to find oblivion not only in the poetry of warfare but also in wine. He drank more and more every day, and day by day grew morally weaker. He was now no longer the chaste Joseph he had been towards Marya Dmitrievna, but on the contrary began courting her grossly, meeting to his surprise with a strong and decided repulse which put him to shame.

At the end of April there arrived at the fort a detachment with which Baryatinsky intended to effect an advance right through Chechnya, which had till then been considered impassable. In that detachment were two companies of the Kabarda Regiment, and according to Caucasian custom these were treated as guests by the Kurin companies. The soldiers were lodged in the barracks, and were treated not only to supper, consisting of buckwheat-porridge and beef, but also to vodka. The officers shared the quarters of the Kurin officers, and as usual those in residence gave the newcomers a dinner at which the regimental singers performed and which ended up with a drinking-bout. Major Petrov, very drunk and no longer red but ashy pale, sat astride a chair and, drawing his sword, hacked at imaginary foes, alternately swearing and laughing, now embracing someone and now dancing to the tune of his favourite song.

> '*Shamil, he began to riot*
> *In the days gone by;*
> *Try, ry, rataty,*
> *In the years gone by!*'

Butler was there too. He tried to see the poetry of warfare in this also, but in the depth of his soul he was sorry for the major. To stop him, however, was quite impossible; and Butler, feeling that the fumes were mounting to his own head, quietly left the room and went home.

The moon lit up the white houses and the stones on the road. It was so light that every pebble, every straw, every little heap of dust was visible. As he approached the house he met Marya Dmitrievna with a shawl over her head and neck. After the rebuff she had given him Butler had avoided her, feeling rather ashamed, but now in the moonlight and after the wine he had drunk he was pleased to meet her and wished to make up to her again.

'Where are you off to?' he asked.

'Why, to see after my old man,' she answered pleasantly. Her rejection of Butler's advances was quite sincere and decided, but she did not like his avoiding her as he had done lately.

'Why bother about him? He'll soon come back.'

'But will he?'

'If he doesn't they'll bring him.'

'Just so . . . That's not right, you know! . . . But you think I'd better not go?'

'Yes, I do. We'd better go home.'

Marya Dmitrievna turned back and walked beside him. The moon shone so brightly that a halo seemed to move along the road round the shadows of their heads. Butler was looking at this halo and making up his mind to tell her that he liked her as much as ever, but he did not know how to begin. She waited for him to speak, and they walked on in silence almost to the house, when some horsemen appeared from round the corner. These were an officer with an escort.

'Who's that coming now?' said Marya Dmitrievna, stepping aside. The moon was behind the rider so that she did not recognize him until he had almost come up to them. It was Peter Nikolaevich Kamenev, an officer who had formerly served with the major and whom Marya Dmitrievna therefore knew.

'Is that you, Peter Nikolaevich?' said she, addressing him.

'It's me,' said Kamenev. 'Ah, Butler, how d'you do? . . . Not asleep yet? Having a walk with Marya Dmitrievna! You'd better look out or the major will give it you . . . Where is he?'

'Why, there . . . Listen!' replied Marya Dmitrievna pointing in the direction whence came the sounds of a *tulumbas** and songs. 'They're on the spree.'

---

* *Tulumbas*: a sort of kettledrum.

'Why? Are your people having a spree on their own?'

'No; some officers have come from Hasav-Yurt, and they are being entertained.'

'Ah, that's good! I shall be in time . . . I just want the major for a moment.'

'On business?' asked Butler.

'Yes, just a little business matter.'

'Good or bad?'

'It all depends . . . Good for us but bad for some people,' and Kamenev laughed.

By this time they had reached the major's house.

'Chikhirev,' shouted Kamenev to one of his Cossacks, 'come here!'

A Don Cossack rode up from among the others. He was dressed in the ordinary Don Cossack uniform with high boots and a mantle, and carried saddle-bags behind.

'Well, take the thing out,' said Kamenev, dismounting.

The Cossack also dismounted, and took a sack out of his saddle-bag. Kamenev took the sack from him and inserted his hand.

'Well, shall I show you a novelty? You won't be frightened, Marya Dmitrievna?'

'Why should I be frightened?' she replied.

'Here it is!' said Kamenev taking out a man's head and holding it up in the light of the moon. 'Do you recognize it?'

It was a shaven head with salient brows, black short-cut beard and moustaches, one eye open and the other half-closed.

The shaven skull was cleft, but not right through, and there was congealed blood in the nose. The neck was wrapped in a blood-stained towel. Notwithstanding the many wounds on the head, the blue lips still bore a kindly childlike expression.

Marya Dmitrievna looked at it, and without a word turned away and went quickly into the house.

Butler could not tear his eyes from the terrible head. It was the head of that very Hadji Murad with whom he had so recently spent his evenings in such friendly intercourse.

'What does this mean? Who has killed him?' he asked.

'He wanted to give us the slip, but was caught,' said Kamenev, and he gave the head back to the Cossack and went into the house with Butler.

'He died like a hero,' he added.

'But however did it all happen?'

'Just wait a bit. When the major comes I'll tell you all about it. That's what I am sent for. I take it round to all the forts and *aouls* and show it.'

The major was sent for, and came back accompanied by two other officers as drunk as himself, and began embracing Kamenev.

'And I have brought you Hadji Murad's head,' said Kamenev.

'No? . . . Killed?'

'Yes; wanted to escape.'

'I always said he would bamboozle them! . . . And where is it? The head, I mean Let's see it.'

The Cossack was called, and brought in the bag with the head. It was taken out and the major looked long at it with drunken eyes.

'All the same, he was a fine fellow,' said he. 'Let me kiss him!'

'Yes, it's true. It was a valiant head,' said one of the officers.

When they had all looked at it, it was returned to the Cossack who put it in his bag, trying to let it bump against the floor as gently as possible.

'I say, Kamenev, what speech do you make when you show the head?' asked an officer.

'No! . . . Let me kiss him. He gave me a sword!' shouted the major.

Butler went out into the porch.

Marya Dmitrievna was sitting on the second step. She looked round at Butler and at once turned angrily away again.

'What's the matter, Marya Dmitrievna?' asked he.

'You're all cut-throats! . . . I hate it! You're cut-throats, really,' and she got up.

'It might happen to anyone,' remarked Butler, not knowing what to say. 'That's war.'

'War? War, indeed! . . . Cut-throats and nothing else. A dead body should be given back to the earth, and they're grinning at it there! . . . Cut-throats, really,' she repeated, as she descended the steps and entered the house by the back door.

Butler returned to the room and asked Kamenev to tell them in detail how the thing had happened.

And Kamenev told them.

This is what had happened.

XXV

HADJI MURAD was allowed to go out riding in the neighbour-hood of the town, but never without a convoy of Cossacks. There was only half a troop of them altogether in Nukha, ten of whom were employed by the officers, so that if ten were sent out with Hadji Murad (according to the orders received) the same men would have had to go every other day. Therefore after ten had been sent out the first day, it was decided to send only five in future and Hadji Murad was asked not to take all his henchmen with him. But on April the 25th he rode out with all five. When he mounted, the commander, noticing that all five henchmen were going with him, told him that he was forbidden to take them all, but Hadji Murad pretended not to hear, touched his horse, and the commander did not insist.

With the Cossacks rode a non-commissioned officer, Nazarov, who had received the Cross of St George for bravery. He was a young, healthy, brown-haired lad, as fresh as a rose. He was the eldest of a poor family belonging to the sect of Old Believers, had grown up without a father, and had maintained his old mother, three sisters, and two brothers.

'Mind, Nazarov, keep close to him!' shouted the commander.

'All right, your Honour!' answered Nazarov, and rising in his stirrups and adjusting the rifle that hung at his back he started his fine large roan gelding at a trot. Four Cossacks followed him: Ferapontov, tall and thin, a regular thief and plunderer (it was he who had sold gunpowder to Gamzalo); Ignatov, a sturdy peasant who boasted of his strength, though he was no longer young and had nearly completed his service; Mishkin, a weakly lad at whom everybody laughed; and the young fair-haired Petrakov, his mother's only son, always amiable and jolly.

The morning had been misty, but it cleared up later on and the opening foliage, the young virgin grass, the sprouting corn, and the ripples of the rapid river just visible to the left of the road, all glittered in the sunshine.

Hadji Murad rode slowly along followed by the Cossacks and by his henchmen. They rode out along the road beyond the fort at a walk. They met women carrying baskets on their heads, soldiers driving carts, and creaking wagons drawn by buffaloes. When he had gone about a mile and a half Hadji Murad touched up his white Kabarda horse, which started at an amble that obliged the henchmen and Cossacks to ride at a quick trot to keep up with him.

'Ah, he's got a fine horse under him,' said Ferapontov. 'If only he were still an enemy I'd soon bring him down.'

'Yes, mate. Three hundred rubles were offered for that horse in Tiflis.'

'But I can get ahead of him on mine,' said Nazarov.

'You get ahead? A likely thing!'

Hadji Murad kept increasing his pace.

'Hey, *kunak*, you mustn't do that. Steady!' cried Nazarov, starting to overtake Hadji Murad.

Hadji Murad looked round, said nothing, and continued to ride at the same pace.

'Mind, they're up to something, the devils!' said Ignatov. 'See how they are tearing along.'

So they rode for the best part of a mile in the direction of the mountains.

'I tell you it won't do!' shouted Nazarov.

Hadji Murad did not answer or look round, but only increased his pace to a gallop.

'Humbug! You won't get away!' shouted Nazarov, stung to the quick. He gave his big roan gelding a cut with his whip and, rising in his stirrups and bending forward, flew full speed in pursuit of Hadji Murad.

The sky was so bright, the air so clear, and life played so joyously in Nazarov's soul as, becoming one with his fine strong horse, he flew along the smooth road behind Hadji Murad, that the possibility of anything sad or dreadful happening never occurred to him. He rejoiced that with every step he was gaining on Hadji Murad.

Hadji Murad judged by the approaching tramp of the big horse behind him that he would soon be overtaken, and seizing his pistol with his right hand, with his left he began slightly to rein in his Kabarda horse which was excited by hearing the tramp of hoofs behind it.

'You mustn't, I tell you!' shouted Nazarov, almost level with Hadji Murad and stretching out his hand to seize the latter's bridle. But before he reached it a shot was fired. 'What are you doing?' he screamed, clutching at his breast. 'At them, lads!' and he reeled and fell forward on his saddle-bow.

But the mountaineers were beforehand in taking to their weapons, and fired their pistols at the Cossacks and hewed at them with their swords.

Nazarov hung on the neck of his horse, which careered round his comrades. The horse under Ignatov fell, crushing his leg, and two of the mountaineers, without dismounting, drew their swords and hacked at his head and arms. Petrakov was about to rush to his comrade's rescue when two shots – one in his back and the other in his side – stung him, and he fell from his horse like a sack.

Mishkin turned round and galloped off towards the fortress. Khanefi and Bata rushed after him, but he was already too far away and they could not catch him. When they saw that they could not overtake him they returned to the others.

Petrakov lay on his back, his stomach ripped open, his young face turned to the sky, and while dying he gasped for breath like a fish.

Gamzalo having finished off Ignatov with his sword, gave a cut to Nazarov too and threw him from his horse. Bata took their cartridge-pouches from the slain. Khanefi wished to take Nazarov's horse, but Hadji Murad called out to him to leave it, and dashed forward along the road. His *murids* galloped after him, driving away Nazarov's horse that tried to follow them. They were already among rice-fields more than six miles from Nukha when a shot was fired from the tower of that place to give the alarm.

'O good Lord! O God! my God! What have they done?' cried the commander of the fort seizing his head with his hands when he heard of Hadji Murad's escape. 'They've done for me! They've let him escape, the villains!' cried he, listening to Mishkin's account.

An alarm was raised everywhere and not only the Cossacks of the place were sent after the fugitives but also all the militia that could be mustered from the pro-Russian *aouls*. A thousand-rubles reward was offered for the capture of Hadji Murad alive or dead, and two hours after he and his followers had escaped from the Cossacks more than two hundred mounted men were following the officer in charge at a gallop to find and capture the runaways.

After riding some miles along the high road Hadji Murad checked his panting horse, which, wet with sweat, had turned from white to grey.

To the right of the road could be seen the *saklyas* and minarets of the *aoul* Benerdzhik, on the left lay some fields, and beyond them the river. Although the way to the mountains lay to the right, Hadji Murad turned to the left, in the opposite direction, assuming that his pursuers would be sure to go to the right, while he, abandoning the road, would cross the Alazan and come out onto the high road on the other side where no one would expect him – ride along it to the forest, and then after recrossing the river make his way to the mountains.

Having come to this conclusion he turned to the left; but it proved impossible to reach the river. The rice-field which had to be crossed had just been flooded, as is always done in spring, and had become a bog in which the horses' legs sank above their pasterns. Hadji Murad and his henchmen turned now to the left, now to the right, hoping to find drier ground; but the field they were in had been equally flooded all over and was now saturated with water. The horses drew their feet out of the sticky mud into which they sank, with a pop like that of a cork drawn from a bottle, and stopped, panting, after every few steps. They struggled in this way so long that it began to grow dusk and they had still not reached the river. To their left lay a patch of higher ground overgrown with shrubs and Hadji Murad decided to ride in among these clumps and remain there till night to rest their exhausted horses and let them graze. The men themselves ate some bread and cheese they had brought with them. At last night came on and the moon that had been shining at first, hid behind the hill and it became dark. There were a great many nightingales in that neighbourhood and there were two of them in these shrubs. As long as Hadji Murad and his men were making a noise among the bushes the nightingales had been silent, but when they became still the birds again began to call to one another and to sing.

Hadji Murad, awake to all the sounds of night, listened to them involuntarily, and their trills reminded him of the song about Hamzad which he had heard the night before when he went to get water. He might now at any moment find himself in the position in which Hamzad had been. He fancied that it would be so, and suddenly his soul became serious. He spread out his *burka* and performed his ablutions, and scarcely had he finished before a sound was heard approaching their shelter. It was the sound of many horses' feet plashing through the bog.

The keen-sighted Bata ran out to one edge of the clump, and peering through the darkness saw black shadows, which were men on foot and on horseback. Khanefi discerned a similar crowd on the other side. It was Karganov, the military commander of the district, with his militia.

'Well, then, we shall fight like Hamzad,' thought Hadji Murad.

When the alarm was given, Karganov with a troop of militiamen and Cossacks had rushed off in pursuit of Hadji Murad, but had been unable to find any trace of him. He had already lost hope and was returning home when, towards evening, he met an old man and asked him if he had seen any horsemen about. The old man replied that he had. He had seen six horsemen floundering in the rice-field, and then had seen them enter the clump where he himself was getting wood. Karganov turned back, taking the old man with him, and seeing the hobbled horses he made sure that Hadji Murad was there. In the night he surrounded the clump and waited till morning to take Hadji Murad alive or dead.

Having understood that he was surrounded, and having discovered an old ditch among the shrubs, Hadji Murad decided to entrench himself in it and to resist as long as strength and ammunition lasted. He told his comrades this, and ordered them to throw up a bank in front of the ditch, and his henchmen at once set to work to cut down branches, dig up the earth with their daggers, and make an entrenchment. Hadji Murad himself worked with them.

As soon as it began to grow light the commander of the militia troop rode up to the clump and shouted:

'Hey! Hadji Murad, surrender! We are many and you are few!'

In reply came the report of a rifle, a cloudlet of smoke rose from the ditch and a bullet hit the militiaman's horse, which staggered under him and began to fall. The rifles of the militiamen who stood at the outskirt of the clump of shrubs began cracking in their turn, and their bullets whistled and hummed, cutting off leaves and twigs and striking the embankment, but not the men entrenched behind it. Only Gamzalo's horse, that had strayed from the others, was hit in the head by a bullet. It did not fall, but breaking its hobbles and rushing among the bushes it ran to the other horses, pressing close to them and watering the young grass with its blood. Hadji Murad and his men fired only when any of the militiamen came forward, and rarely missed their aim. Three militiamen were wounded, and the others, far from making up their minds to rush the entrenchment, retreated farther and farther back, only firing from a distance and at random.

So it continued for more than an hour. The sun had risen to about half the height of the trees, and Hadji Murad was already thinking of leaping on his horse and trying to make his way to the river, when the shouts were heard of many men who had just arrived. These were Hadji Aga of Mekhtuli with his followers. There were about two hundred of them. Hadji Aga had once been Hadji Murad's *kunak* and had lived with him in the mountains, but he had afterwards gone over to the Russians. With him was Akhmet Khan, the son of Hadji Murad's old enemy.

Like Karganov, Hadji Aga began by calling to Hadji Murad to surrender, and Hadji Murad answered as before with a shot.

'Swords out, my men!' cried Hadji Aga, drawing his own; and a hundred voices were raised by men who rushed shrieking in among the shrubs.

The militiamen ran in among the shrubs, but from behind the entrenchment came the crack of one shot after another. Some three men fell, and the attackers stopped at the outskirts of the clump and also began firing. As they fired they gradually approached the entrenchment, running across from behind one shrub to another. Some succeeded in getting across, others fell under the bullets of Hadji Murad or of his men. Hadji Murad fired without missing; Gamzalo too rarely wasted a shot, and shrieked with joy every time he saw that his bullet had hit its aim. Khan Mahoma sat at the edge of the ditch singing '*Il lyakha il Allakh!*' and fired leisurely, but often missed. Eldar's whole body trembled with impatience to rush dagger in hand at the enemy, and he fired often and at random, constantly looking round at Hadji Murad and stretching out beyond the entrenchment. The shaggy Khanefi, with his sleeves rolled up, did the duty of a servant even here. He loaded the guns which Hadji Murad and Khan Mahoma passed to him, carefully driving home with a ramrod the bullets wrapped in greasy rags, and pouring dry powder out of the powder-flask onto the pans. Bata did not remain in the ditch as the others did, but kept running to the horses, driving them away to a safer place and, shrieking incessantly, fired without using a prop for his gun. He was the first to be wounded. A bullet entered his neck and he sat down spitting blood and swearing. Then Hadji Murad was wounded, the bullet piercing his shoulder. He tore some cotton wool from the lining of his *beshmet*, plugged the wound with it, and went on firing.

'Let us fly at them with our swords!' said Eldar for the third time, and he looked out from behind the bank of earth ready to rush at the enemy; but at that instant a bullet struck him and he reeled and fell backwards onto Hadji Murad's leg. Hadji Murad glanced at him. His eyes, beautiful like those of a ram, gazed intently and seriously at Hadji Murad. His mouth, the upper lip pouting like a child's, twitched without opening. Hadji Murad drew his leg away from under him and continued firing.

Khanefi bent over the dead Eldar and began taking the unused ammunition out of the cartridge-cases of his coat.

Khan Mahoma meanwhile continued to sing, loading leisurely and firing. The enemy ran from shrub to shrub, hallooing and shrieking and drawing ever nearer and nearer.

Another bullet hit Hadji Murad in the left side. He lay down in the ditch and again pulled some cotton wool out of his *beshmet* and plugged the wound. This wound in the side was fatal and he felt that he was dying. Memories and pictures succeeded one another with extraordinary rapidity in his imagination. Now he saw the powerful Abu Nutsal Khan, dagger in hand and holding up his severed cheek he rushed at his foe; then he saw the weak, bloodless old Vorontsov with his cunning white face, and heard his soft voice; then he saw his son Yusuf, his wife Sofiat, and then the pale, red-bearded face of his enemy Shamil with its half-closed eyes. All these images passed through his mind without evoking any feeling within him – neither pity nor anger nor any kind of desire: everything seemed so insignificant in comparison with what was beginning, or had already begun, within him.

Yet his strong body continued the thing that he had commenced. Gathering together his last strength he rose from behind the bank, fired his pistol at a man who was just running towards him, and hit him. The man fell. Then Hadji Murad got quite out of the ditch, and limping heavily went dagger in hand straight at the foe.

Some shots cracked and he reeled and fell. Several militiamen with triumphant shrieks rushed towards the fallen body. But the body that seemed to be dead suddenly moved. First the uncovered, bleeding, shaven head rose; then the body with hands holding to the trunk of a tree. He seemed so terrible, that those who were running towards him stopped short. But suddenly a shudder passed through him, he staggered away from the tree and fell on his face, stretched out at full length like a thistle that had been mown down, and he moved no more.

He did not move, but still he felt.

When Hadji Aga, who was the first to reach him, struck him on the head with a large dagger, it seemed to Hadji Murad that someone was striking him with a hammer and he could not understand who was doing it or why. That was his last consciousness of any connection with his body. He felt nothing more and his enemies kicked and hacked at what had no longer anything in common with him.

Hadji Aga placed his foot on the back of the corpse and with two blows cut off the head, and carefully – not to soil his shoes with blood – rolled it away with his foot. Crimson blood spurted from the arteries of the neck, and black blood flowed from the head, soaking the grass.

Karganov and Hadji Aga and Akhmet Khan and all the militiamen gathered together – like sportsmen round a slaughtered animal – near the bodies of Hadji Murad and his men (Khanefi, Khan Mahoma, and Gamzalo they bound), and amid the powder-smoke which hung over the bushes they triumphed in their victory.

The nightingales, that had hushed their songs while the firing lasted, now started their trills once more: first one quite close, then others in the distance.

It was of this death that I was reminded by the crushed thistle in the midst of the ploughed field.

Two Old Men

The woman saith unto him, Sir, I perceive that thou art a prophet. Our fathers worshipped in this mountain: and ye say, that in Jerusalem is the place where men ought to worship. Jesus saith unto her, Woman, believe me, the hour cometh when neither in this mountain, nor in Jerusalem, shall ye worship the Father ... But the hour cometh, and now is, when the true worshippers shall worship the Father in spirit and truth: for such doth the Father seek to be his worshippers.

(John iv, 19–23)

I

THERE WERE ONCE two old men who decided to go on a pilgrimage to worship God at Jerusalem. One of them was a well-to-do peasant named Efim Tarasitch Shevelef. The other, Elisha Bodrof, was not so well off.

Efim was a staid man, serious and firm. He neither drank nor smoked nor took snuff, and had never used bad language in his life. He had twice served as village Elder, and when he left office his accounts were in good order. He had a large family: two sons and a married grandson, all living with him. He was hale, long-bearded and erect, and it was only when he was past sixty that a little grey began to show itself in his beard.

Elisha was neither rich nor poor. He had formerly gone out carpentering, but now that he was growing old he stayed at home and kept bees. One of his sons had gone away to find work, the other was living at home. Elisha was a kindly and cheerful old man. It is true he drank sometimes, and he took snuff, and was fond of singing; but he was a peaceable man, and lived on good terms with his family and with his neighbours. He was short and dark, with a curly beard, and, like his patron-saint Elisha, he was quite bald-headed.

The two old men had taken a vow long since and had arranged to go on a pilgrimage to Jerusalem together: but Efim could never spare the time; he always had so much business on hand; as soon as one thing was finished he started another. First he had to arrange his grandson's marriage; then to wait for his youngest son's return from the army, and after that he began building a new hut.

One holiday the two old men met outside the hut and, sitting down on some timber, began to talk.

'Well,' asked Elisha, 'when are we to fulfil our vow?'

Efim made a wry face.

'We must wait,' he said. 'This year has turned out a hard one for me. I started building this hut thinking it would cost me something over a hundred rubles, but now it's getting on for three hundred and it's still not finished. We shall have to wait till the summer. In summer, God willing, we will go without fail.'

'It seems to me we ought not to put it off, but should go at once,' said Elisha. 'Spring is the best time.'

'The time's right enough, but what about my building? How can I leave that?'

'As if you had no one to leave in charge! Your son can look after it.'

'But how? My eldest son is not trustworthy – he sometimes takes a glass too much.'

'Ah, neighbour, when we die they'll get on without us. Let your son begin now to get some experience.'

'That's true enough; but somehow when one begins a thing one likes to see it done.'

'Eh, friend, we can never get through all we have to do. The other day the women-folk at home were washing and house-cleaning for Easter. Here something needed doing, there something else, and they could not get everything done. So my eldest daughter-in-law, who's a sensible woman, says: "We may be thankful the holiday comes without waiting for us, or however hard we worked we should never be ready for it."'

Efim became thoughtful.

'I've spent a lot of money on this building,' he said, 'and one can't start on the journey with empty pockets. We shall want a hundred rubles apiece – and it's no small sum.'

Elisha laughed.

'Now, come, come, old friend!' he said, 'you have ten times as much as I, and yet you talk about money. Only say when we are to start, and though I have nothing now I shall have enough by then.'

Efim also smiled.

'Dear me, I did not know you were so rich!' said he. 'Why, where will you get it from?'

'I can scrape some together at home, and if that's not enough, I'll sell half a score of hives to my neighbour. He's long been wanting to buy them.'

'If they swarm well this year, you'll regret it.'

'Regret it! Not I, neighbour! I never regretted anything in my life, except my sins. There's nothing more precious than the soul.'

'That's so; still it's not right to neglect things at home.'

'But what if our souls are neglected? That's worse. We took the vow, so let us go! Now, seriously, let us go!'

II

ELISHA SUCCEEDED in persuading his comrade. In the morning, after thinking it well over, Efim came to Elisha.

'You are right,' said he, 'let us go. Life and death are in God's hands. We must go now, while we are still alive and have the strength.'

A week later the old men were ready to start. Efim had money enough at hand. He took a hundred rubles himself, and left two hundred with his wife.

Elisha, too, got ready. He sold ten hives to his neighbour, with any new swarms that might come from them before the summer. He took seventy rubles for the lot. The rest of the hundred rubles he scraped together from the other members of his household, fairly clearing them all out. His wife gave him all she had been saving up for her funeral; and his daughter-in-law also gave him what she had.

Efim gave his eldest son definite orders about everything: when and how much grass to mow, where to cart the manure, and how to finish off and roof the cottage. He thought out everything, and gave his orders accordingly. Elisha, on the other hand, only explained to his wife that she was to keep separate the swarms from the hives he had sold, and to be sure to let the neighbour have them all, without any tricks. As to household affairs, he did not even mention them.

'You will see what to do and how to do it, as the needs arise,' he said. 'You are the masters, and will know how to do what's best for yourselves.'

So the old men got ready. Their people baked them cakes, and made bags for them, and cut them linen for leg-bands.* They put on new leather shoes, and took with them spare shoes of plaited bark. Their families went with them to the end of the village and there took leave of them, and the old men started on their pilgrimage.

Elisha left home in a cheerful mood, and as soon as he was out of the village forgot all his home affairs. His only care was how to please his comrade, how to avoid saying a rude word to anyone, how to get to his destination and home again in peace and love. Walking along the road, Elisha would either whisper some prayer to himself or go over in his mind such of the lives of the saints as he was able to remember. When he came across anyone on the road, or turned in anywhere for the night, he tried to behave as gently as possible and to say a godly word. So he journeyed on, rejoicing. One thing only he could not do, he could not give up taking snuff. Though he had left his snuff-box behind, he hankered after it. Then a man he met on the road gave him some snuff; and every now and then he would lag behind (not to lead his comrade into temptation) and would take a pinch of snuff.

---

* Worn by Russian peasants instead of stockings.

Efim too walked well and firmly; doing no wrong and speaking no vain words, but his heart was not so light. Household cares weighed on his mind. He kept worrying about what was going on at home. Had he not forgotten to give his son this or that order? Would his son do things properly? If he happened to see potatoes being planted or manure carted, as he went along, he wondered if his son was doing as he had been told. And he almost wanted to turn back and show him how to do things, or even do them himself.

III

THE OLD MEN had been walking for five weeks, they had worn out their home-made bark shoes, and had to begin buying new ones when they reached Little Russia.* From the time they left home they had had to pay for their food and for their night's lodging, but when they reached Little Russia the people vied with one another in asking them into their huts. They took them in and fed them, and would accept no payment; and, more than that, they put bread or even cakes into their bags for them to eat on the road.

The old men travelled some five hundred miles in this manner

---

* Little Russia is situated in the south-western part of Russia, and consists of the Governments of Kief, Poltava, Tchernigof, and part of Kharkof and Kherson.

free of expense, but after they had crossed the next province, they came to a district where the harvest had failed. The peasants still gave them free lodging at night, but no longer fed them for nothing. Sometimes, even, they could get no bread: they offered to pay for it, but there was none to be had. The people said the harvest had completely failed the year before. Those who had been rich were ruined and had had to sell all they possessed; those of moderate means were left destitute, and those of the poor who had not left those parts, wandered about begging, or starved at home in utter want. In the winter they had had to eat husks and goosefoot.

One night the old men stopped in a small village; they bought fifteen pounds of bread, slept there, and started before sunrise, to get well on their way before the heat of the day. When they had gone some eight miles, on coming to a stream they sat down, and, filling a bowl with water, they steeped some bread in it, and ate it. Then they changed their leg-bands, and rested for a while. Elisha took out his snuff-box. Efim shook his head at him.

'How is it you don't give up that nasty habit?' said he.

Elisha waved his hand. 'The evil habit is stronger than I,' he said.

Presently they got up and went on. After walking for nearly another eight miles, they came to a large village and passed right through it. It had now grown hot. Elisha was tired out and wanted to rest and have a drink, but Efim did not stop. Efim was the better walker of the two, and Elisha found it hard to keep up with him.

'If I could only have a drink,' said he.

'Well, have a drink,' said Efim. 'I don't want any.'

Elisha stopped.

'You go on,' he said, 'but I'll just run in to the little hut there. I will catch you up in a moment.'

'All right,' said Efim, and he went on along the high road alone, while Elisha turned back to the hut.

It was a small hut plastered with clay, the bottom a dark colour, the top whitewashed; but the clay had crumbled away. Evidently it was long since it had been re-plastered, and the thatch was off the roof on one side. The entrance to the hut was through the yard. Elisha entered the yard, and saw, lying close to a bank of earth that ran round the hut, a gaunt, beardless man with his shirt tucked into his trousers, as is the custom in Little Russia.* The man must have lain down in the shade, but the sun had come round and now shone full on him. Though not asleep, he still lay there. Elisha called to him, and asked for a drink, but the man gave no answer.

'He is either ill or unfriendly,' thought Elisha; and going to the door he heard a child crying in the hut. He took hold of the ring that served as a door-handle, and knocked with it.

'Hey, masters!' he called. No answer. He knocked again with his staff.

'Hey, Christians!' Nothing stirred.

---

* In Great Russia the peasants let their shirt hang outside their trousers.

'Hey, servants of God!' Still no reply.

Elisha was about to turn away, when he thought he heard a groan the other side of the door.

'Dear me, some misfortune must have happened to the people? I had better have a look.'

And Elisha entered the hut.

IV

ELISHA TURNED the ring; the door was not fastened. He opened it and went along up the narrow passage. The door into the dwelling-room was open. To the left was a brick oven; in front against the wall was an icon-stand and a table before it; by the table was a bench on which sat an old woman, bareheaded and wearing only a single garment. There she sat with her head resting on the table, and near her was a thin, wax-coloured boy, with a protruding stomach. He was asking for something, pulling at her sleeve, and crying bitterly. Elisha entered. The air in the hut was very foul. He looked round, and saw a woman lying on the floor behind the oven: she lay flat on the ground with her eyes closed and her throat rattling, now stretching out a leg, now dragging it in, tossing from side to side; and the foul smell came from her. Evidently she could do nothing for herself and no one had been attending to her needs. The old woman lifted her head, and saw the stranger.

'What do you want?' said she. 'What do you want, man? We have nothing.'

Elisha understood her, though she spoke in the Little-Russian dialect.

'I came in for a drink of water, servant of God,' he said.

'There's no one – no one – we have nothing to fetch it in. Go your way.'

Then Elisha asked:

'Is there no one among you, then, well enough to attend to that woman?'

'No, we have no one. My son is dying outside, and we are dying in here.'

The little boy had ceased crying when he saw the stranger, but when the old woman began to speak, he began again, and clutching hold of her sleeve cried:

'Bread, Granny, bread.'

Elisha was about to question the old woman, when the man staggered into the hut. He came along the passage, clinging to the wall, but as he was entering the dwelling-room he fell in the corner near the threshold, and without trying to get up again to reach the bench, he began to speak in broken words. He brought out a word at a time, stopping to draw breath, and gasping.

'Illness has seized us . . . .' said he, 'and famine. He is dying . . . of hunger.'

And he motioned towards the boy, and began to sob.

Elisha jerked up the sack behind his shoulder and, pulling

the straps off his arms, put it on the floor. Then he lifted it onto the bench, and untied the strings. Having opened the sack, he took out a loaf of bread, and, cutting off a piece with his knife, handed it to the man. The man would not take it, but pointed to the little boy and to a little girl crouching behind the oven, as if to say:

'Give it to them.'

Elisha held it out to the boy. When the boy smelt bread, he stretched out his arms, and seizing the slice with both his little hands, bit into it so that his nose disappeared in the chunk. The little girl came out from behind the oven and fixed her eyes on the bread. Elisha gave her also a slice. Then he cut off another piece and gave it to the old woman, and she too began munching it.

'If only some water could be brought,' she said, 'their mouths are parched. I tried to fetch some water yesterday – or was it today – I can't remember, but I fell down and could go no further, and the pail has remained there, unless someone has taken it.'

Elisha asked where the well was. The old woman told him. Elisha went out, found the pail, brought some water, and gave the people a drink. The children and the old woman ate some more bread with the water, but the man would not eat.

'I cannot eat,' he said.

All this time the younger woman did not show any consciousness, but continued to toss from side to side. Presently Elisha went to the village shop and bought some millet, salt, flour, and oil. He found an axe, chopped some wood, and made a fire. The little girl came and helped him. Then he boiled some soup, and gave the starving people a meal.

V

THE MAN ATE a little, the old woman had some too, and the little girl and boy licked the bowl clean, and then curled up and fell fast asleep in one another's arms.

The man and the old woman then began telling Elisha how they had sunk to their present state.

'We were poor enough before,' said they, 'but when the crops failed, what we gathered hardly lasted us through the autumn. We had nothing left by the time winter came, and had to beg from the neighbours and from anyone we could. At first they gave, then they began to refuse. Some would have been glad enough to help us, but had nothing to give. And we were ashamed of asking: we were in debt all round, and owed money, and flour, and bread.'

'I went to look for work,' the man said, 'but could find none. Everywhere people were offering to work merely for their own keep. One day you'd get a short job, and then you might spend two days looking for work. Then the old woman and the girl went begging, further away. But they got very little; bread was so scarce. Still we scraped food together somehow, and hoped to struggle through till next harvest, but towards spring people ceased to give anything. And then this illness seized us. Things became worse and worse. One day we might have something to eat, and then nothing for two days. We began eating grass. Whether it was the grass, or what, made my wife ill, I don't know. She could not keep on her legs, and I had no strength left, and there was nothing to help us to recovery.'

'I struggled on alone for a while,' said the old woman, 'but at last I broke down too for want of food, and grew quite weak. The girl also grew weak and timid. I told her to go to the neighbours – she would not leave the hut, but crept into a corner and sat there. The day before yesterday a neighbour looked in, but seeing that we were ill and hungry she turned away and left us. Her husband has had to go away, and she has nothing for her own little ones to eat. And so we lay, waiting for death.'

Having heard their story, Elisha gave up the thought of overtaking his comrade that day, and remained with them all night. In the morning he got up and began doing the housework, just as if it were his own home. He kneaded the bread with the old woman's help, and lit the fire. Then he went with the little girl to the neighbours to get the most necessary things; for there was nothing in the hut: everything had been sold for bread – cooking utensils, clothing, and all. So Elisha began replacing what was necessary, making some things himself, and buying some. He remained there one day, then another, and then a third. The little boy picked up strength and, whenever Elisha sat down, crept along the bench and nestled up to him.

The little girl brightened up and helped in all the work, running after Elisha and calling:

'Daddy, daddy.'

The old woman grew stronger, and managed to go out to see a neighbour. The man too improved, and was able to get about, holding on to the wall. Only the wife could not get up, but even she regained consciousness on the third day, and asked for food.

'Well,' thought Elisha, 'I never expected to waste so much time on the way. Now I must be getting on.'

VI

THE FOURTH day was the feast day after the summer fast, and Elisha thought:

'I will stay and break the fast with these people. I'll go and buy them something, and keep the feast with them, and tomorrow evening I will start.'

So Elisha went into the village, bought milk, wheat-flour and dripping, and helped the old woman to boil and bake for the morrow. On the feast day Elisha went to church, and then broke the fast with his friends at the hut. That day the wife got up, and managed to move about a bit. The husband had shaved and put on a clean shirt, which the old woman had washed for him; and he went to beg for mercy of a rich peasant in the village to whom his plough-land and meadow were mortgaged. He went to beg the rich peasant to grant him the use of the meadow and field till after the harvest; but in the evening he came back very sad, and began to weep. The rich peasant had shown no mercy, but had said: 'Bring me the money.'

Elisha again grew thoughtful. 'How are they to live now?' thought he to himself. 'Other people will go haymaking, but there will be nothing for these to mow, their grass land is mortgaged. The rye will ripen. Others will reap (and what a fine crop mother earth is giving this year), but they have nothing to look forward to. Their three acres are pledged to the rich peasant. When I am gone, they'll drift back into the state I found them in.'

Elisha was in two minds, but finally decided not to leave that evening, but to wait until the morrow. He went out into the yard to sleep. He said his prayers, and lay down; but he could not sleep. On the one hand he felt he ought to be going, for he had spent too much time and money as it was; on the other hand he felt sorry for the people.

'There seems to be no end to it,' he said. 'First I only meant to bring them a little water and give them each a slice of bread: and just see where it has landed me. It's a case of redeeming the meadow and the corn-field. And when I have done that, I shall have to buy a cow for them, and a horse for the man to cart his sheaves. A nice coil you've got yourself into, brother Elisha! You've slipped your cables and lost your reckoning!'

Elisha got up, lifted his coat which he had been using for

a pillow, unfolded it, got out his snuff-box and took a pinch, thinking that it might perhaps clear his thoughts.

But no! He thought and thought, and came to no conclusion. He ought to be going; and yet pity held him back. He did not know what to do. He re-folded his coat and put it under his head again. He lay thus for a long time, till the cocks had already crowed once: then he was quite drowsy. And suddenly it seemed as if someone had roused him. He saw that he was dressed for the journey, with the sack on his back and the staff in his hand, and the gate stood ajar so that he could just squeeze through. He was about to pass out, when his sack caught against the fence on one side: he tried to free it, but then his leg-band caught on the other side and came undone. He pulled at the sack, and saw that it had not caught on the fence, but that the little girl was holding it and crying,

'Bread, daddy, bread!'

He looked at his foot, and there was the tiny boy holding him by the leg-band, while the master of the hut and the old woman were looking at him through the window.

Elisha awoke, and said to himself in an audible voice:

'Tomorrow I will redeem their corn-field, and will buy them a horse, and flour to last till the harvest, and a cow for the little ones; or else while I go to seek the Lord beyond the sea, I may lose Him in myself.'

Then Elisha fell asleep, and slept till morning. He awoke early, and going to the rich peasant, redeemed both the corn-field and the meadow land. He bought a scythe (for that also had been sold) and brought it back with him. Then he sent the man to mow, and himself went into the village. He heard that there was a horse and cart for sale at the public-house, and he struck a bargain with the owner, and bought them. Then he bought a sack of flour, put it in the cart, and went to see about a cow. As he was going along he overtook two women talking as they went. Though they spoke the Little-Russian dialect, he understood what they were saying.

'At first, it seems, they did not know him; they thought he was just an ordinary man. He came in to ask for a drink of water, and then he remained. Just think of the things he has bought for them! Why they say he bought a horse and cart for them at the publican's, only this morning! There are not many such men in the world. It's worth while going to have a look at him.'

Elisha heard and understood that he was being praised, and he did not go to buy the cow, but returned to the inn, paid for the horse, harnessed it, drove up to the hut, and got out. The people in the hut were astonished when they saw the horse. They thought it might be for them, but dared not ask. The man came out to open the gate.

'Where did you get a horse from, grandfather?' he asked.

'Why, I bought it,' said Elisha. 'It was going cheap. Go and cut some grass and put it in the manger for it to eat during the night. And take in the sack.'

The man unharnessed the horse, and carried the sack into

the barn. Then he mowed some grass and put it in the manger. Everybody lay down to sleep. Elisha went outside and lay by the roadside. That evening he took his bag out with him. When everyone was asleep, he got up, packed and fastened his bag, wrapped the linen bands round his legs, put on his shoes and coat, and set off to follow Efim.

VII

WHEN ELISHA had walked rather more than three miles it began to grow light. He sat down under a tree, opened his bag, counted his money, and found he had only seventeen rubles and twenty kopeks left.

'Well,' thought he, 'it is no use trying to cross the sea with this. If I beg my way it may be worse than not going at all. Friend Efim will get to Jerusalem without me, and will place a candle at the shrines in my name. As for me, I'm afraid I shall never fulfil my vow in this life. I must be thankful it was made to a merciful Master, and to one who pardons sinners.'

Elisha rose, jerked his bag well up on his shoulders, and turned back. Not wishing to be recognized by anyone, he made a circuit to avoid the village, and walked briskly homeward. Coming from home the way had seemed difficult to him, and he had found it hard to keep up with Efim, but now on his return journey, God helped him to get over the ground so that he hardly felt fatigue. Walking seemed like child's play. He went along swinging his staff, and did his forty to fifty miles a day.

When Elisha reached home the harvest was over. His family were delighted to see him again, and all wanted to know what had happened: Why and how he had been left behind? And why he had returned without reaching Jerusalem? But Elisha did not tell them.

'It was not God's will that I should get there,' said he. 'I lost my money on the way, and lagged behind my companion. Forgive me, for the Lord's sake!'

Elisha gave his old wife what money he had left. Then he questioned them about home affairs. Everything was going on well; all the work had been done, nothing neglected, and all were living in peace and concord.

Efim's family heard of his return the same day, and came for news of their old man; and to them Elisha gave the same answers.

'Efim is a fast walker. We parted three days before St Peter's day, and I meant to catch him up again, but all sorts of things happened. I lost my money, and had no means to get any further, so I turned back.'

The folks were astonished that so sensible a man should have acted so foolishly: should have started and not got to his destination, and should have squandered all his money. They wondered at it for a while, and then forgot all about it; and Elisha forgot it too. He set to work again on his homestead. With his son's help he cut wood for fuel for the winter. He and the women threshed the corn. Then he mended the thatch on the out-houses, put the bees under cover, and handed over to his neighbour the ten hives he had sold him in spring, and all the swarms that had come from them. His wife tried not to tell how many swarms there had been from these hives, but Elisha knew well enough from which there had been swarms and from which not. And instead of ten, he handed over seventeen swarms to his neighbour. Having got everything ready for the winter, Elisha sent his son away to find work, while he himself took to plaiting shoes of bark, and hollowing out logs for hives.

VIII

ALL THAT DAY while Elisha stopped behind in the hut with the sick people, Efim waited for him. He only went on a little way before he sat down. He waited and waited, had a nap, woke up again, and again sat waiting; but his comrade did not come. He gazed till his eyes ached. The sun was already sinking behind a tree, and still no Elisha was to be seen.

'Perhaps he has passed me,' thought Efim, 'or perhaps someone gave him a lift and he drove by while I slept, and did not see me. But how could he help seeing me? One can see so far here in the steppe. Shall I go back? Suppose he is on in front, we shall then miss each other completely and it will be still worse. I had better go on, and we shall be sure to meet where we put up for the night.'

He came to a village, and told the watchman, if an old man of a certain description came along, to bring him to the hut where Efim stopped. But Elisha did not turn up that night. Efim went on, asking all he met whether they had not seen a little, bald-headed, old man? No one had seen such a traveller. Efim wondered, but went on alone, saying:

'We shall be sure to meet in Odessa, or on board the ship,' and he did not trouble more about it.

On the way, he came across a pilgrim wearing a priest's coat, with long hair and a skull-cap such as priests wear. This pilgrim had been to Mount Athos, and was now going to Jerusalem for the second time. They both stopped at the same place one night, and, having met, they travelled on together.

They got safely to Odessa, and there had to wait three days for a ship. Many pilgrims from many different parts were in the same case. Again Efim asked about Elisha, but no one had seen him.

Efim got himself a foreign passport, which cost him five rubles. He paid forty rubles for a return ticket to Jerusalem, and bought a supply of bread and herrings for the voyage.

The pilgrim began explaining to Efim how he might get on to the ship without paying his fare; but Efim would not listen. 'No, I came prepared to pay, and I shall pay,' said he.

The ship was freighted, and the pilgrims went on board, Efim and his new comrade among them. The anchors were weighed, and the ship put out to sea.

All day they sailed smoothly, but towards night a wind arose, rain came on, and the vessel tossed about and shipped water. The people were frightened: the women wailed and screamed, and some of the weaker men ran about the ship looking for shelter. Efim too was frightened, but he would not show it, and remained at the place on deck where he had settled down when first he came on board, beside some old men from Tambof. There they sat silent, all night and all next day, holding on to their sacks. On the third day it grew calm, and on the fifth day they anchored at Constantinople. Some of the pilgrims went on shore to visit the Church of St Sophia, now held by the Turks. Efim remained on the ship, and only bought some white bread. They lay there for twenty-four hours, and then put to sea again. At Smyrna they stopped again; and at Alexandria; but at last they arrived safely at Jaffa, where all the pilgrims had to disembark. From there still it was more than forty miles by road to Jerusalem. When disembarking the people were again much frightened. The ship was high, and the people were dropped into boats, which rocked so much that it was easy to miss them and fall into the water. A couple of men did get a wetting, but at last all were safely landed.

They went on on foot, and at noon on the third day reached Jerusalem. They stopped outside the town, at the Russian inn, where their passports were endorsed. Then, after dinner, Efim visited the Holy Places with his companion, the pilgrim. It was not the time when they could be admitted to the Holy Sepulchre, but they went to the Patriarchate. All the pilgrims assembled there. The women were separated from the men, who were all told to sit in a circle, barefoot. Then a monk came in with a towel to wash their feet. He washed, wiped, and then kissed their feet, and did this to everyone in the circle. Efim's feet were washed and kissed, with the rest. He stood through vespers and matins, prayed, placed candles at the shrines, handed in booklets inscribed with his parents' names, that they might be mentioned in the church prayers. Here at the Patriarchate food and wine were given them. Next morning they went to the cell of Mary of Egypt, where she had lived doing penance. Here too they placed candles and had prayers read. From there they went to Abraham's Monastery, and saw the place where Abraham intended to slay his son as an offering to God. Then they visited the spot where Christ appeared to Mary Magdalene, and the Church of James, the Lord's brother. The pilgrim showed Efim all these places, and told him how much money to give at each place. At midday they returned to the inn and had dinner. As they were preparing to lie down and rest, the pilgrim cried out, and began to search his clothes, feeling them all over.

'My purse has been stolen, there were twenty-three rubles in it,' said he, 'two ten-ruble notes and the rest in change.'

He sighed and lamented a great deal, but as there was no help for it, they lay down to sleep.

IX

AS EFÍM lay there, he was assailed by temptation.

'No one has stolen any money from this pilgrim,' thought he, 'I do not believe he had any. He gave none away anywhere, though he made me give, and even borrowed a ruble off me.'

This thought had no sooner crossed his mind, than Efim rebuked himself, saying: 'What right have I to judge a man? It is a sin. I will think no more about it.' But as soon as his thoughts began to wander, they turned again to the pilgrim: how interested he seemed to be in money, and how unlikely it sounded when he declared that his purse had been stolen.

'He never had any money,' thought Efim. 'It's all an invention.'

Towards evening they got up, and went to midnight Mass at the great Church of the Resurrection, where the Lord's Sepulchre is. The pilgrim kept close to Efim and went with him everywhere. They came to the church; a great many pilgrims were there; some Russians and some of other nationalities: Greeks, Armenians, Turks, and Syrians. Efim entered the Holy Gates with the crowd. A monk led them past the Turkish sentinels, to the place where the Saviour was taken down from the cross and anointed, and where candles were burning in nine great candlesticks. The monk showed and explained everything. Efim offered a candle there. Then the monk led Efim to the right, up the steps to Golgotha, to the place where the cross had stood. Efim prayed there. Then they showed him the cleft where the ground had been rent asunder to its nethermost depths; then the place where Christ's hands and feet were nailed to the cross; then Adam's tomb, where the blood of Christ had dripped on to Adam's bones. Then they showed him the stone on which Christ sat when the crown of thorns was placed on His head; then the post to which Christ was bound when He was scourged. Then Efim saw the stone with two holes for Christ's feet. They were going to show him something else, but there was a stir in the crowd, and the people all hurried to the church of the Lord's Sepulchre itself. The Latin Mass had just finished there, and the Russian Mass was beginning. And Efim went with the crowd to the tomb cut in the rock.

He tried to get rid of the pilgrim, against whom he was still sinning in his mind, but the pilgrim would not leave him, but went with him to the Mass at the Holy Sepulchre. They tried to get to the front, but were too late. There was such a crowd that it was impossible to move either backwards or forwards. Efim stood looking in front of him, praying, and every now and then feeling for his purse. He was in two minds: sometimes he thought that the pilgrim was deceiving him, and then again he thought that if the pilgrim spoke the truth and his purse had really been stolen, the same thing might happen to himself.

X

EFÍM STOOD there gazing into the little chapel in which was the Holy Sepulchre itself with thirty-six lamps burning above it. As he stood looking over the people's heads, he saw something that surprised him. Just beneath the lamps in which the sacred fire burns, and in front of everyone, Efim saw an old man in a grey coat, whose bald, shining head was just like Elisha Bodrof.

'It is like him,' thought Efim, 'but it cannot be Elisha. He could not have got ahead of me. The ship before ours started a week sooner. He could not have caught that; and he was not on ours, for I saw every pilgrim on board.'

Hardly had Efim thought this, when the little old man began to pray, and bowed three times: once forwards to God, then once on each side – to the brethren. And as he turned his head to the right, Efim recognized him. It was Elisha Bodrof himself, with his dark, curly beard turning grey at the cheeks, with his brows, his eyes and nose, and his expression of face. Yes, it was he!

Efim was very pleased to have found his comrade again, and wondered how Elisha had got ahead of him.

'Well done, Elisha!' thought he. 'See how he has pushed ahead. He must have come across someone who showed him the way. When we get out, I will find him, get rid of this fellow in the skull-cap, and keep to Elisha. Perhaps he will show me how to get to the front also.'

Efim kept looking out, so as not to lose sight of Elisha. But when the Mass was over, the crowd began to sway, pushing forward to kiss the tomb, and pushed Efim aside. He was again seized with fear lest his purse should be stolen. Pressing it with his hand, he began elbowing through the crowd, anxious only to get out. When he reached the open, he went about for a long time searching for Elisha both outside and in the church itself. In the cells of the church he saw many people of all kinds, eating, and drinking wine, and reading and sleeping there. But Elisha was nowhere to be seen. So Efim returned to the inn without having found his comrade. That evening the pilgrim in the skull-cap did not turn up. He had gone off without repaying the ruble, and Efim was left alone.

The next day Efim went to the Holy Sepulchre again, with an old man from Tambof, whom he had met on the ship. He tried to get to the front, but was again pressed back; so he stood by a pillar and prayed. He looked before him, and there in the foremost place under the lamps, close to the very Sepulchre of the Lord, stood Elisha, with his arms spread out like a priest at the altar, and with his bald head all shining.

'Well, now,' thought Efim, 'I won't lose him!'

He pushed forward to the front, but when he got there, there was no Elisha: he had evidently gone away.

Again on the third day Efim looked, and saw at the Sepulchre, in the holiest place, Elisha standing in the sight of all men, his arms outspread, and his eyes gazing upwards as if he saw something above. And his bald head was all shining.

'Well, this time,' thought Efim, 'he shall not escape me! I will go and stand at the door, then we can't miss one another!'

Efim went out and stood by the door till past noon. Everyone had passed out, but still Elisha did not appear.

Efim remained six weeks in Jerusalem, and went everywhere: to Bethlehem, and to Bethany, and to the Jordan. He had a new shirt sealed at the Holy Sepulchre for his burial, and he took a bottle of water from the Jordan, and some holy earth, and bought candles that had been lit at the sacred flame. In eight places he inscribed names to be prayed for, and he spent all his money, except just enough to get home with. Then he started homeward. He walked to Jaffa, sailed thence to Odessa, and walked home from there on foot.

XI

EFÍM TRAVELLED the same road he had come by; and as he drew nearer home his former anxiety returned, as to how affairs were getting on in his absence. 'Much water flows away in a year,' the proverb says. It takes a lifetime to build up a homestead, but not long to ruin it, thought he. And he wondered how his son had managed without him, what sort of spring they were having, how the cattle had wintered, and whether the cottage was well finished. When Efim came to the district where he had parted from Elisha the summer before, he could hardly believe that the people living there were the same. The year before they had been starving, but now they were living in comfort. The harvest had been good, and the people had recovered, and had forgotten their former misery.

One evening Efim reached the very place where Elisha had remained behind; and as he entered the village, a little girl in a white smock ran out of a hut.

'Daddy, daddy, come to our house!'

Efim meant to pass on, but the little girl would not let him. She took hold of his coat, laughing, and pulled him towards the hut, where a woman with a small boy came out into the porch and beckoned to him.

'Come in, grandfather,' she said. 'Have supper and spend the night with us.'

So Efim went in.

'I may as well ask about Elisha,' he thought. 'I fancy this is the very hut he went to for a drink of water.'

The woman helped him off with the bag he carried, and gave him water to wash his face. Then she made him sit down to table, and set milk, curd-cakes and porridge before him. Efim thanked her, and praised her for her kindness to a pilgrim. The woman shook her head.

'We have good reason to welcome pilgrims,' she said. 'It was a pilgrim who showed us what life is. We were living forgetful of God, and God punished us almost to death. We reached such a pass last summer, that we all lay ill and helpless with nothing to eat. And we should have died, but that God sent an old man to help us – just such a one as you. He came in one day to ask for a drink of water, saw the state we were in, took pity on us, and remained with us. He gave us food and drink, and set us on our feet again; and he redeemed our land, and bought a cart and horse and gave them to us.'

Here the old woman entering the hut, interrupted the younger one and said:

'We don't know whether it was a man, or an angel from God. He loved us all, pitied us all, and went away without telling us his name, so that we don't even know whom to pray for. I can see it all before me now! There I lay waiting for death, when in comes a bald-headed old man. He was not anything much to look at, and he asked for a drink of water. I, sinner that I am, thought to myself: "What does he come prowling about here for?" And just think what he did! As soon as he saw us, he let down his bag, on this very spot, and untied it.'

Here the little girl joined in.

'No, Granny,' said she, 'first he put it down here in the middle of the hut, and then he lifted it onto the bench.'

And they began discussing and recalling all he had said and done, where he sat and slept, and what he had said to each of them.

At night the peasant himself came home on his horse, and he too began to tell about Elisha and how he had lived with them.

'Had he not come we should all have died in our sins. We

were dying in despair, murmuring against God and man. But he set us on our feet again; and through him we learnt to know God, and to believe that there is good in man. May the Lord bless him! We used to live like animals; he made human beings of us.'

After giving Efim food and drink, they showed him where he was to sleep; and lay down to sleep themselves.

But though Efim lay down, he could not sleep. He could not get Elisha out of his mind, but remembered how he had seen him three times at Jerusalem, standing in the foremost place.

'So that is how he got ahead of me,' thought Efim. 'God may or may not have accepted my pilgrimage, but He has certainly accepted his!'

Next morning Efim bade farewell to the people, who put some patties in his sack before they went to their work, and he continued his journey.

XII

EFÍM HAD been away just a year, and it was spring again when he reached home one evening. His son was not at home, but had gone to the public-house, and when he came back, he had had a drop too much. Efim began questioning him. Everything showed that the young fellow had been unsteady during his father's absence. The money had all been wrongly spent, and the work had been neglected. The father began to upbraid the son; and the son answered rudely.

'Why didn't you stay and look after it yourself?' he said. 'You go off, taking the money with you, and now you demand it of me!'

The old man grew angry, and struck his son.

In the morning Efim went to the village Elder to complain of his son's conduct. As he was passing Elisha's house, his friend's wife greeted him from the porch.

'How do you do, neighbour,' she said. 'How do you do, dear friend? Did you get to Jerusalem safely?'

Efim stopped.

'Yes, thank God,' he said. 'I have been there. I lost sight of your old man, but I hear he got home safely.'

The old woman was fond of talking:

'Yes, neighbour, he has come back,' said she. 'He's been back a long time. Soon after Assumption, I think it was, he returned. And we were glad the Lord had sent him back to us! We were dull without him. We can't expect much work from him any more, his years for work are past; but still he is the head of the household and it's more cheerful when he's at home. And how glad our lad was! He said, "It's like being without sunlight, when father's away!" It was dull without him, dear friend. We're fond of him, and take good care of him.'

'Is he at home now?'

'He is, dear friend. He is with his bees. He is hiving the

swarms. He says they are swarming well this year. The Lord has given such strength to the bees that my husband doesn't remember the like. "The Lord is not rewarding us according to our sins," he says. Come in, dear neighbour, he will be so glad to see you again.'

Efim passed through the passage into the yard and to the apiary, to see Elisha. There was Elisha in his grey coat, without any face-net or gloves, standing under the birch trees, looking upwards, his arms stretched out and his bald head shining, as Efim had seen him at the Holy Sepulchre in Jerusalem: and above him the sunlight shone through the birches as the flames of fire had done in the holy place, and the golden bees flew round his head like a halo, and did not sting him.

Efim stopped. The old woman called to her husband.

'Here's your friend come,' she cried.

Elisha looked round with a pleased face, and came towards Efim, gently picking bees out of his own beard.

'Good day, neighbour, good day, dear friend. Did you get there safely?'

'My feet walked there, and I have brought you some water from the river Jordan. You must come to my house for it. But whether the Lord accepted my efforts . . .'

'Well the Lord be thanked! May Christ bless you!' said Elisha.

Efim was silent for a while, and then added:

'My feet have been there, but whether my soul, or another's, has been there more truly . . .'

'That's God's business, neighbour, God's business,' interrupted Elisha.

'On my return journey I stopped at the hut where you remained behind . . .'

Elisha was alarmed, and said hurriedly:

'God's business, neighbour, God's business! Come into the cottage, I'll give you some of our honey.' And Elisha changed the conversation, and talked of home affairs.

Efim sighed, and did not speak to Elisha of the people in the hut, nor of how he had seen him in Jerusalem. But he now understood that the best way to keep one's vows to God and to do His will, is for each man while he lives to show love and do good to others.

The Forged Coupon

Part One

I

FYODOR MIKHAILOVICH SMOKOVNIKOV, the head of a government department, a man of incorruptible integrity and proud of it, a liberal of a gloomy cast of mind, and not only a free-thinker but a hater of any and every manifestation of religious feeling, which he regarded as a relic of primitive superstition, had returned home from his department in an extremely vexed state of mind. The Governor had sent him an utterly stupid memorandum from which it could have been inferred that Fyodor Mikhailovich had acted dishonestly. Fyodor Mikhailovich, furious at the suggestion, had lost no time in composing a biting and caustic reply.

Having got home, Fyodor Mikhailovich had the feeling that everything was happening to thwart him.

It was five minutes to five. He was expecting dinner to be served at once, but the dinner was not ready. Fyodor Mikhailovich banged the door and went off to his study. Someone knocked at the door. 'Who the devil is it now?' he thought, and called out:

'Who is it now?'

Into the room came Fyodor Mikhailovich's fifteen-year-old son, a grammar-school boy in the fifth year.

'What brings you here?'

'It's the first of the month today.'

'So, is it money you're after?'

By an established agreement, on the first day of each month the father gave his son an allowance of three rubles to spend on hobbies and amusements. Fyodor Mikhailovich frowned, reached for his wallet and fished out from it a two-and-a-half-ruble bond coupon,* then got out the purse in which he kept his small change and counted out a further fifty kopeks. His son remained silent and did not take the money.

'Please, Papa, can you let me have an advance?'

'What?'

'I wouldn't ask you, but I borrowed some money on my word of honour, I promised to pay it back. As a man of honour I

---

* A detachable voucher issued with government bonds and exchangeable for interest payments.

can't just . . . I only need another three rubles, honestly. I won't ask you . . . at least, I don't mean I won't ask you, it's simply that . . . Please, Papa.'

'You have already been told that—'

'Yes, Papa, I know, but it's just for this once, really . . .'

'You receive an allowance of three rubles, and it is always too little. When I was your age I didn't even get fifty kopeks.'

'But all my friends get more than I do now. Petrov and Ivanitsky actually have fifty rubles a month.'

'And I tell you that if that is the way you are going to behave, then you will end up as a swindler. That is all I have to say on the matter.'

'And what if it is? You'll never look at things from my point of view: it means I shall have to look like an absolute cad. It's all very well for you.'

'Get out of here, you good-for-nothing, get out!'

Fyodor Mikhailovich jumped up from his chair and rushed at his son.

'Get out. What you need is a good hiding.'

His son was both frightened and bitterly resentful, but his resentment outweighed his fear, and bowing his head he made hurriedly for the door. Fyodor Mikhailovich had no intention of hitting him, but he was enjoying his own anger and he continued shouting and cursing at his son as the latter made his retreat.

When the maid came to say that the dinner was ready to serve, Fyodor Mikhailovich stood up.

'At last,' he said. 'I've quite lost my appetite now.' And he walked scowling into the dining-room.

At the dinner-table his wife struck up a conversation but his growled reply was so curt and irritable that she fell silent. His son too did not look up from his plate and said nothing. They ate their meal in silence, then silently got up from the table and went their separate ways.

After dinner the schoolboy went back to his own room, took the coupon and the small change out of his pocket and threw them on the desk-table. Then he took off his school uniform and put on a jacket. For some time he pored over a battered Latin grammar, then he shut the door and fastened it on the hook, swept the money off the desk-top and into a drawer, took some cigarette papers out of the drawer, filled one with tobacco, plugged the cardboard mouthpiece with some cotton wool, and started to smoke.

He spent a further two hours or so sitting over his grammar and his exercise books but without taking anything in, then he stood up and began pacing to and fro across the room, stamping his heels and recalling everything that had passed between him and his father. His father's abusive words, and above all the spiteful expression on his father's face, came back to him just as if he was hearing and seeing it now. 'Good-for-nothing. What you need is a good hiding.' And the more he remembered, the more furious with his father he became. He remembered his father saying to him 'I can see how you will end up – as a swindler. Don't say I didn't warn you' – and – 'You'll end up as a swindler if you go on like this.' 'It's all right for him,' he thought, 'he's forgotten what it was like when he was young. And what are these crimes I have committed? Just going to the theatre, and running out of money, and borrowing some from Petya Grushetsky. What's so dreadful about that? Anybody else would have been sympathetic and asked me all about it, but all he does is rage at me and think of nobody but himself. Whenever he doesn't get what he wants he shouts the house down, but I, I am a swindler. No, my father he may be, but I don't love him. I don't know whether all fathers are the same as he is, but I don't love him.'

The maid knocked at his door. She had brought him a note. 'They said you were to reply at once.'

The note read: 'This is the third time I am having to ask you to return the six rubles you borrowed from me, but you keep trying to get out of it. That is not how honourable men behave. I ask you to send the money at once by the bearer of this note. I am extremely hard up myself. Surely you can get it? Your – depending whether you pay me or you don't – contemptuous or respectful friend, Grushetsky.'

'Well, what do you make of that? What a swine. He can't wait for a bit. I shall just have to have another try.'

Mitya went to see his mother. This was his last hope. His mother was a kind-hearted woman who found it hard to refuse him anything, and she might indeed have helped him, but just now she was anxious about the illness of her youngest child, two-year-old Petya. She was annoyed with Mitya for coming in and making a noise, and she turned down his request on the spot.

He muttered something under his breath and started to walk out of the room. Feeling sorry for her son, she called him back.

'Just a minute, Mitya,' she said. 'I haven't any money at the moment but I can get some tomorrow.'

But Mitya was still seething with bitter anger against his father.

'What's the use of telling me "tomorrow", when I need it right away? You may as well know that I am going to see a friend to ask him for it.'

He went out, banging the door.

'There's nothing else to be done. He'll tell me where I can go to pawn my watch,' he thought, feeling for the watch which he had in his pocket.

Mitya took the coupon and the change out of the desk drawer, put on his overcoat and set off to see his friend Makhin.

II

MAKHIN TOO was a schoolboy, but a sophisticated one. He played cards and knew women, and he always had money. He lived with his aunt. Mitya was aware that Makhin was a bad character, but when he was with him he automatically deferred to Makhin's authority. Makhin was at home, getting ready to go out to the theatre: his scruffy little room smelt of scented soap and eau-de-cologne.

'It's the last straw, my friend,' said Makhin when Mitya had told him his woeful story, shown him the coupon and the fifty kopeks, and explained that he was in need of nine rubles. 'You could actually pawn your watch, but there is an even better way,' said Makhin, winking his eye.

'What sort of a better way?'

'It's really very simple.' Makhin took the coupon. 'You just need to put in a figure one in front of the 2 r.50, and it will read 12 r.50.'

'But are there coupons for that amount?'

'Naturally there are, on thousand-ruble bonds. I passed off one myself once.'

'But surely it's not possible?'

'Well, shall we have a go?' said Makhin, taking a pen and smoothing out the coupon with a finger of his left hand.

'But it can't be right.'

'Oh, what nonsense.'

'He was quite right,' thought Mitya, remembering again the bad things his father had said about him: a swindler. 'I'll be a swindler now.' He looked Makhin in the face. Makhin was looking at him and smiling quietly.

'Well then, shall we have a go?'

'All right, go ahead.'

Makhin painstakingly traced out a figure one.

'Right, now we'll go to a shop. The one on the corner there that sells photographic supplies. I happen to need a frame, to go round this person here.'

He produced a mounted photograph of a young woman with large eyes, luxuriant hair and a magnificent bosom.

'A real peach, eh?'

'Yes, yes, absolutely. But all the same . . .'

'It's very simple. Let's go.'

Makhin put his coat on and the two of them went out together.

III

THE BELL over the door to the photographic shop gave a tinkle. The schoolboys entered and looked round the empty shop with its shelves of photographic supplies and glass display cases on the counters. From the door at the back of the shop emerged a plain-looking woman with a kindly face who took up her position behind the counter and asked them what they required.

'A nice little picture-frame, madame.'

'At what sort of price?' asked the lady, swiftly and expertly running her mittened hands with their swollen finger joints over the various types of frames. 'These are priced at fifty kopeks, these are a little dearer. And this one here is very nice, a new style — it costs one ruble twenty.'

'Very well, I'll take that one. But couldn't you knock it down a bit? I'll give you a ruble for it.'

'All the prices here are fixed,' said the lady with dignity.

'All right, as you wish,' said Makhin, putting the coupon down on the top of the display case. 'Please give me the frame and my change, and as quickly as you can, please. We don't want to be late for the theatre.'

'You have plenty of time yet,' said the lady, and she began examining the coupon with her shortsighted eyes.

'It'll look charming in that frame, won't it, eh?' said Makhin, turning to Mitya.

'Haven't you got any other money?' asked the sales-lady.

'That's just the problem. I haven't. My father gave it to me, and I need to get it changed.'

'And do you really not have a ruble and twenty kopeks on you?'

'I do have fifty kopeks. But what's the matter, are you afraid we are going to swindle you with forged money?'

'No, I didn't say that.'

'Well, let me have it back please. We'll find somewhere else to change it.'

'So how much do I have to give you?'

'Let's see now, it should come to eleven something.'

The sales-lady flicked the beads on her abacus, unlocked the bureau which served as a till, took out a ten-ruble note, and rummaging among the small change assembled a further six twenty-kopek and two five-kopek pieces.

'Would you kindly wrap it up for me please?' said Makhin, unhurriedly taking the money.

'Right away.'

The sales-lady wrapped up the frame and tied the package with string.

Mitya only began to breathe easily once more when the entrance bell had tinkled behind them and they had emergd into the street.

'Well now, here's ten rubles for you, and let me take the rest. I'll give it back.'

And Makhin went off to the theatre, leaving Mitya to go and see Grushetsky and settle up with him.

IV

AN HOUR after the boys had left the shop the owner returned home and started to count the takings.

'Oh, you stupid, muddling woman! What a fool you are!' he shouted at his wife as soon as he saw the coupon and immediately spotted the forgery. 'And why on earth have you been accepting coupons at all?'

'But I've been there when you have accepted them yourself, Zhenya, and they were twelve-ruble coupons just like this one,' said his wife, who was growing confused and angry and was on the point of bursting into tears. 'I don't know myself how they managed to take me in, those schoolboys. He was a handsome young man too, he really looked so *comme il faut*.'*

'And you're a simpleton *comme il faut*,' shouted her husband abusively as he went on counting the contents of the till. 'I accept a coupon when I know and can see clearly what is written on it. But you no doubt spend your whole life gazing at the ugly mugs of schoolboys.'

His wife could take no more of this, and she too lost her temper.

'There's a man for you! Always blaming other people – and when you go and lose fifty-four rubles at cards, that's a mere nothing!'

'I – that's a different matter altogether.'

'I'm not talking to you any longer,' said his wife, and she went off to her room and began to recall how her family had been against her becoming the wife of this man who was socially so much her inferior, and how she had herself insisted on the marriage; she recalled her child who had died, and her husband's indifference at this loss, and she felt such hatred of her husband that she thought how glad she would be if he were to die. But when she had thought that she became alarmed at her own feelings and hastened to get dressed and go out. When

___

* Gentlemanly, respectable.

her husband got back to their apartment she had already left. Without waiting for him she had put on her coat and driven by herself to the house of a teacher of French, an acquaintance of theirs, who had invited them to a social gathering that evening.

V

AT THE HOUSE of the French teacher, a Russian Pole, there was a formal tea party with sweet pastries, after which the guests sat down at several tables to play *vint*.*

The photographic-shop owner's wife was at a table with the host, an army officer and an elderly deaf lady in a wig who was the widow of a music-shop owner, and a passionate and very good card-player. The play was going in favour of the photographic supplier's wife: she made two slams. Beside her was a plate containing grapes and a pear, and she was now in a thoroughly cheerful mood.

'Why isn't Yevgeny Mikhailovich here yet?' asked the hostess from another table. 'We were counting on him for our fifth hand.'

'I expect he's got tied up in doing the accounts,' said Yevgeny Mikhailovich's wife. 'This is the day when he settles the accounts for the groceries and the firewood.'

And remembering the scene with her husband she frowned,

---

* A card-game resembling bridge.

and her hands in their mittens trembled from the resentment she felt towards him.

'Well, talk of the devil,' said the host, turning towards Yevgeny Mikhailovich, who had just walked in. 'What kept you?'

'Oh, various kinds of business,' replied Yevgeny Mikhailovich in a jovial voice, rubbing his hands together. And to his wife's surprise, he came over to her and said:

'You know that coupon – I managed to get rid of it.'

'Really?'

'Yes, I gave it to a peasant for some firewood.'

And with great indignation Yevgeny Mikhailovich told everybody the story – with additional details supplied by his wife – of how some unscrupulous schoolboys had managed to dupe his wife.

'Well now, let's get on with the main business,' he said, sitting down at the table when his turn arrived and shuffling the cards.

VI

YEVGENY MIKHAILOVICH had indeed managed to get rid of the coupon to a muzhik named Ivan Mironov in payment for some firewood.

Ivan Mironov's trade involved buying up single *sazhens** of

---

* *Sazhen*: a measure equivalent to 2.13 metres (here cubic).

firewood from the timber warehouses and delivering them to the townspeople; but he would divide the *sazhen* of wood into five parts, each of which he sold at the price a quarter-load would fetch in the woodyards. Early in the morning of this day which proved so ill-fated for him, Ivan Mironov had carted out an eighth-load intending to sell it, but he drove about until evening looking in vain for a customer. He continually came across experienced townsfolk who knew all about the tricks played by muzhik firewood-vendors and refused to believe his assurances that he had brought in this firewood from the country. He was getting really hungry and felt chilled to the marrow in his worn sheepskin jacket and his tattered cloth under-coat; by evening the temperature had dropped to twenty degrees of frost; and his little horse, which he had been driving pitilessly because he was at the point of selling it to the knacker, came to a complete standstill. So that Ivan Mironov was even ready to consider selling off the firewood at a loss, when he encountered Yevgeny Mikhailovich who had popped out to the tobacconist's and was now on his way home.

'Do you want some firewood, master? I'll let you have it cheap. My horse won't go any further.'

'And where are you from, then?'

'From the country, sir. My own firewood it is, and good and dry too.'

'We know your sort. Well, so what are you asking for it?' Ivan Mironov named an absurdly high sum, then started progressively to reduce it, and finally let the firewood go for his usual price.

'Just for you, master, seeing as it's not too far to deliver it,' he said.

Yevgeny Mikhailovich did not waste too much time bargaining since he was pleased at the thought that he would now be able to pass on the coupon. Somehow or other, hauling on the shafts of the cart himself, Ivan Mironov managed to drag the load into the courtyard of the house and personally unloaded it into the woodshed. There was no yardman about. At first Ivan Mironov was reluctant to accept the coupon, but Yevgeny Mikhailovich was so persuasive and looked to be such an important gentleman, that he agreed to take it.

Entering the maids' quarters from the back porch, Ivan Mironov crossed himself, wiped the melting icicles from his beard, and turning back the flap of his sheepskin jacket, drew out a small leather purse and took from it eight rubles and fifty kopeks in change. He handed over the money, and the coupon he rolled up in a piece of paper and put away in his purse.

Having thanked the gentleman in a manner befitting his rank, Ivan Mironov induced his wretched, doomed, frost-covered horse to get his legs moving, not by the whip but by the use of the whip handle, and drove the empty cart away in the direction of the tavern.

Once inside the tavern Ivan Mironov ordered himself eight kopeks' worth of vodka and tea, and when he had warmed himself up and even begun to perspire a little and was in a really cheerful state of mind, he fell to chatting with the yardman who was sitting at the same table. He soon warmed to the conversation and told the yardman all about himself: how he came from the village of Vasilyevskoye twelve versts from the town, how he had taken his share of the family goods and left his father and brothers, and was now living with his wife and two sons, the elder of whom was attending a trade school and so wasn't yet able to help him financially. He told him how he was staying in lodgings here in town and that tomorrow he was going to the knacker to sell his old hack, and he would see, but if it worked out all right he might buy himself a new horse. He told him how he had managed to put by some twenty-five rubles, and half the money was in the form of a coupon. He took out the coupon and showed it to the yardman. The yardman could not read or write but he said that he had changed money like that for the tenants and that it was good money, but there were forgeries about, and for that reason he advised him to be on the safe side and to get it changed here at the tavern bar. Ivan Mironov handed the coupon to the waiter and told him to bring back the cash to him, but the waiter did not bring back the money: instead the bald, shiny-faced tavern manager came over, holding the coupon in his pudgy hand.

'Your money's no good,' he said, pointing at the coupon but not returning it.

'That's good money – a gentleman gave it me.'

'This money is not good, it's counterfeit.'

'Well, if it's counterfeit, give it back to me.'

'No, my man, people like you need to be taught a lesson. You and your swindling friends have been tampering with it.'

'Let me have my money, what right have you got to do this?'

'Sidor, call the police,' said the barman to the waiter.

Ivan Mironov was drunk, and being drunk he was starting to get worked up. He seized the manager by the collar and shouted:

'Give it back, and I'll go and see the gentleman. I know where to find him.'

The manager struggled free of Ivan Mironov's grasp, tearing his shirt in the process.

'Ah, if that's how you want it – hold him!'

The waiter grabbed Ivan Mironov and at that moment the policeman appeared. Taking charge of the situation he listened to their explanations, then quickly brought things to a conclusion.

'Down to the station with you.'

The policeman put the coupon into his own wallet and led Ivan Mironov and his horse off to the police-station.

VII

IVAN MIRONOV spent the night in the cells at the police-station along with drunks and thieves. It was not until almost noon the next day that he was summoned to appear before the local police-officer. The officer questioned him and then sent him along with the constable to see the proprietor of the photographic shop. Ivan Mironov was able to remember the name of the street and the number of the house.

When the policeman had summoned the gentleman to the door and confronted him with the coupon and Ivan Mironov, who confirmed that this was the very gentleman who had given him the coupon, Yevgeny Mikhailovich put on an expression first of astonishment, and then of stern disapproval.

'Whatever are you talking about? You must be out of your mind. This is the first time I have ever set eyes on him.'

'Master, it's a sin to say that, remember we've all got to die,' said Ivan Mironov.

'What's the matter with him? You must have been dreaming. It was someone else you sold your firewood to,' said Yevgeny Mikhailovich. 'Anyway, wait there and I'll go and ask my wife if she bought any firewood yesterday.'

Yevgeny Mikhailovich went away and at once called the yardman to him. The yardman, Vasily, was a good-looking, unusually strong and nimble fellow, cheery in nature and something of a dandy. Yevgeny Mikhailovich told him that if anyone asked him where the last lot of firewood had come from he should say that they had got it from the woodyard and that they never bought firewood from muzhiks.

'There's a muzhik here claiming that I gave him a forged coupon. He's a muddle-headed peasant, but you're a man of understanding. So you tell him that we only ever buy our firewood from the woodyard. Oh, and I've been meaning for some time to give you this towards a new jacket,' added Yevgeny Mikhailovich, and he gave the yardman five rubles.

Vasily took the money, his eyes darting from the banknote to Yevgeny Mikhailovich's face, tossed back his hair and gave a slight smile.

'Everyone knows the common people are slow-witted. It's lack of education. Don't you worry, sir. I shall know well enough what to say.'

However tearfully Ivan Mironov begged Yevgeny Mikhailovich to acknowledge that the coupon was his, and the yardman to confirm what he was saying, both Yevgeny Mikhailovich and the yardman stuck to their line: they had never bought firewood off carts. And the policeman took Ivan Mironov back to the police-station where he was charged with forging a coupon.

Only by following the advice of his cell-mate, a drunken clerk, and by slipping the local police-officer a five-ruble note, did Ivan Mironov succeed in getting out of detention, minus his coupon and with just seven rubles instead of the twenty-five he had had the day before. Ivan Mironov used three of the seven rubles to get drunk, and with a face full of utter dejection and dead drunk he drove home to his wife.

His wife was pregnant and nearing her time, and she was feeling ill. She began swearing at her husband, he shoved her away, and she started hitting him. He did not retaliate, but lay belly down on the plank bed and wept loudly.

Only the next morning did his wife discover what had happened, and believing what her husband said, spent a long time cursing that brigand of a gentleman who had deceived her Ivan. And Ivan, who had now sobered up, remembered the advice of the factory-hand he had been drinking with the previous evening, and decided to go and find an *ablocate* and lodge a complaint.

VIII

THE ADVOCATE took on the case, not so much for any money he might make from it, but rather because he believed Ivan Mironov and was indignant at the way this muzhik had been so shamelessly defrauded.

Both parties were present at the hearing, and Vasily the yardman was the sole witness. At the hearing it all came out as it had done before. Ivan Mironov referred to God and to the fact that we shall all die. Yevgeny Mikhailovich, although uncomfortably aware of the unpleasantness and the danger of what he was doing, could not now alter his testimony, and he continued with an outwardly calm appearance to deny everything.

Vasily the yardman received a further ten rubles and went on asserting with a calm smile that he had never before so much as set eyes on Ivan Mironov. And when he was called to take the oath, although he quailed inwardly, he maintained a calm exterior as he repeated the words of the oath after the old priest specially brought in for this function, swearing on the cross and the Holy Gospel that he would tell the whole truth and nothing but the truth.

The proceedings ended with the judge dismissing the case brought by Ivan Mironov and decreeing that he was liable for court costs of five rubles, which Yevgeny Mikhailovich magnanimously paid on his behalf. Discharging Ivan Mironov, the judge admonished him to be more careful in future about making accusations against respectable people and said that he should be duly grateful that the court costs had been met for him and that he was not being prosecuted for slander, which could have led to his spending three months or more in prison.

'We humbly thank you, sir,' said Ivan Mironov, and shaking his head and sighing he left the courtroom.

It seemed as if the whole affair had ended well for Yevgeny Mikhailovich and for Vasily the yardman. But that was only how it looked. Something had actually happened which no one could see, something far more serious than anything merely human eyes could perceive.

It was more than two years now since Vasily had left his village and come to live in the town. With each year that passed he sent his father less and less of his earnings, and he did not get round to sending for his wife to come and join him, since he felt no need of her. Here in the town he had as many women as he could wish for, and not the sort of women who were anything like his old hag of a wife. With each year that passed Vasily forgot more and more the rules and standards of country life and became increasingly at home with the ways of the town. Back there in the country everything had been crude, dreary, impoverished and messy, but here everything was civilized, well-kept, clean and luxurious, as it ought to be. And he became more and more convinced that the country people lacked any understanding of life, like the beasts of the forest, whereas here – these people were real human beings. He read books by good authors, novels, and he went to theatrical performances at the People's House.* In his home village you would never see anything like that, not even in your dreams. In his village the old men would say: 'Live with your wife according to the law, work hard, don't eat too much and don't get above yourself'; but here people were clever, educated – and that meant they understood the real laws of life – and lived for their own pleasure. And it was all wonderful. Before the court case with the coupon Vasily had still not believed that the upper classes had no law governing the way they lived. He had always thought they must have some such law, although he did not know what it was. But this court hearing over the coupon, and most of all, his own perjury, which despite his fears had brought him no unpleasant repercussions but had actually earned him an extra

* An educational and cultural centre for working people.

ten rubles, convinced him that there were no laws at all, and that a man should simply live for his own pleasure. And so he did, and so he went on doing. To begin with he merely took a little extra profit on the purchases he made for the tenants, but this was not enough to meet all his expenses, so he began, whenever he could, to pilfer money and valuables from the tenants' apartments, and he even stole Yevgeny Mikhailovich's wallet. Yevgeny Mikhailovich, certain of Vasily's guilt, did not start proceedings against him, but gave him the sack.

Vasily had no desire to return home, but went on living in Moscow with his mistress while he looked for work. He found a low-paid job as a yardman to a small shopkeeper. Vasily started in the job, but the next month he was caught stealing sacks. His employer did not lodge an official complaint, but beat Vasily and threw him out. After this incident he was unable to find another job, his money was running out and he was getting short of clothes, so that in the end he was left with a single tattered coat, a pair of trousers and some down-at-heel shoes. His mistress abandoned him. But Vasily did not lose his bright and cheery disposition, and he waited until it was spring again, and then set off on foot for his home village.

IX

PYOTR NIKOLAYEVICH SVENTITSKY, a short stocky man who wore dark glasses (he had trouble with his eyes and was in danger of losing his sight altogether), got up as usual before daybreak, and after drinking a glass of tea, put on his knee-length sheepskin coat trimmed with lambskin and set off to make the rounds of his property.

Pyotr Nikolayevich had been a customs officer and in that profession he had saved up the sum of eighteen thousand rubles. He had retired some twelve years earlier, not quite of his own volition, and had bought the small estate of a young landowner who had squandered his fortune. Pyotr Nikolayevich had married when he was still in government service. His wife, the poor orphaned daughter of an old aristocratic family, was a sturdy, plump and attractive woman who had borne him no children. Pyotr Nikolayevich was a man thorough and persistent in all his dealings. Although he knew nothing about farming (he was the son of a minor Polish nobleman) he went into it so efficiently that in ten years his ramshackle estate of three hundred *desyatins** had become a model of its kind. All the structures he put up, from the house itself to the barn and the shelter for the fire-hose,

* One *desyatin* = 1.09 hectares or 2.7 acres.

were solid and reliable, covered with sheet-iron and regularly repainted. In the equipment shed there was an orderly array of carts, wooden and metal ploughs, and harrows. All the harnesses were kept well greased. The horses were of a modest size and almost always from his own stud, with light-brown coats and black mane and tail, sturdy and well-fed animals, matched in pairs. The threshing-machine operated in its own covered barn, the feed was stored in a special shed, and the manure slurry flowed away into a properly paved pit. The cows too were bred on the estate, not particularly large, but good milkers. The pigs were of an English breed. There was a poultry-yard with hens of particularly good egg-laying strains. The fruit-trees in the orchard were kept coated with grease and systematically replaced with new plants. Everything that could be seen was businesslike, clean, reliable and meticulous. Pyotr Nikolayevich took great delight in his estate and was proud of the fact that he had achieved all this not by treating his peasants oppressively, but on the contrary, by observing the strictest fairness in his dealings with them. Even in the society of the local nobility he maintained a moderate position that was more liberal than conservative, and invariably defended the common people to the advocates of serfdom. Treat them well, and they'll treat you well in return. True, he did not tolerate blunders and mistakes on the part of the men who worked for him and he would occasionally be seen in person urging them to greater efforts; he demanded hard work, but on the other hand the lodging and the victuals provided were of the very best, the wages were always paid on time, and on festival days he treated his men to vodka.

Stepping carefully over the melting snow – this was in February – Pyotr Nikolayevich made his way past the farm-hands' stable towards the large hut in which the farm-hands lived. It was still dark, all the darker because of the fog, but in the windows of the living-hut some light could be seen. The farm-hands were just getting up. He was intending to hurry them along: according to the work schedule six of them were to take a cart over to the copse and collect the last loads of firewood.

'What's this then?' he wondered, seeing the door of the stable wide open.

'Hey, who's in there?'

No one answered. Pyotr Nikolayevich went into the stable.

'Who's in there, I say?'

There was still no answer. It was dark in the stable, the ground beneath his feet was soft and there was a smell of manure. To the right of the doorway was a stall which should have been occupied by a pair of young chestnut horses. Pyotr Nikolayevich stretched out his hand – but the stall was empty. He felt in front of him with his foot. Perhaps the horses might be lying down. His foot encountered nothing but empty space. 'Where can they have taken them?' he thought. Could they have been taken out to be harnessed up? No, the sleigh was still there outside. He went outside again and called loudly: 'Hey, Stepan.'

Stepan was the head farm-hand. He was just emerging from the living-hut.

'Hello there!' Stepan called back cheerfully. 'Is that you, Pyotr Nikolaich? The lads are on their way.'

'Why have you left the stable door open?'

'The stable? I've no idea. Hey, Proshka, bring us a lantern here.' Proshka came running up with a lantern. They all went into the stable. Stepan realized at once what had occurred.

'We've had thieves here, Pyotr Nikolaich. The lock's been broken.'

'That can't be, surely.'

'They've taken them, the scoundrels. Mashka's gone, so is Hawk. No, he's over here. But Dapple isn't here. And neither is Beauty.'

Three horses were missing. Pyotr Nikolayevich did not say anything. He was frowning and breathing heavily.

'Ah, if I could get my hands on them . . . Who was on watch?'

'Pyetka. Pyetka fell asleep.'

Pyotr Nikolayevich reported the theft to the police, to the district police superintendent and to the head of the Zemstvo,* and he sent out his own men to look for the horses. But they were not found.

'Filthy peasants!' said Pyotr Nikolayevich, 'Doing this to me. Haven't I been good to them? Just you wait. Bandits they

---

* An elected district council which functioned in Russia from 1864 to 1917.

are, the lot of them. From now on you're going to get different treatment from me.'

X

BUT THE horses – three chestnuts – had already been taken to outlying places. Mashka they sold to some gypsies for eighteen rubles; the second horse, Dapple, was exchanged for a peasant's horse in a village forty versts away; and Beauty they simply rode until he dropped, then slaughtered him. They sold his hide for three rubles. The leader of this enterprise was Ivan Mironov. He had worked for Pyotr Nikolayevich in the past, knew his way round the estate, and had decided to get some of his money back. And had consequently thought up the whole plan.

After his misfortune with the forged coupon Ivan Mironov embarked on a long drinking bout and would have drunk away everything he possessed if his wife had not hidden from him the horse-collars, his clothes, and anything else he might have sold to buy vodka. All the time he was on his binge Ivan Mironov was thinking incessantly not just about the individual who had wronged him, but about all the masters, some of them worse than others, who only lived by what they could filch from the likes of him. On one occasion Ivan Mironov was drinking with some peasants who came from a place near Podolsk. And as they travelled along the road the muzhiks told him about how they had driven off some horses belonging to another muzhik. Ivan Mironov began ticking off those horse-thieves for committing such an offence against another muzhik. 'It's a sin,' he said. 'To a muzhik his horse is just like a brother, yet you go and deprive him of it. If you want to steal horses, then steal them from the masters. That's all those sons of bitches deserve anyway.' The further they went the more they talked, and the muzhiks from Podolsk said that if you wanted to steal horses from the gentry you had to be clever about it. You needed to know all about the lie of the land, and if you hadn't got someone on the inside, it couldn't be done. Then Ivan Mironov remembered about Sventitsky, on whose estate he had once lived and worked, and he remembered how Sventitsky had held back a ruble and a half from his wages to pay for a broken kingpin, and he remembered too the chestnut horses he had worked with on the farm.

Ivan Mironov went and saw Sventitsky on the pretext of looking for work, but in reality he was there to see how things were and find out all he could. Having done that, and discovered that there was no night-watchman and that the horses were kept in separate loose-boxes in the stable, he called in the horse-thieves and saw the whole business through.

After splitting the proceeds with the muzhiks from Podolsk Ivan Mironov returned to his village with five rubles. At home there was no work for him to do: he had no horse. And from that time on Ivan Mironov took to associating with horse-thieves and gypsies.

XI

PYOTR NIKOLAYEVICH SVENTITSKY did everything in his power to find the horse-thieves. He knew that the raid could not have been carried out without the help of one of his employees. And so he began to regard his farm-hands with suspicion and to inquire which of the farm-workers had not been sleeping at the farm on the night in question. He was told that Proshka Nikolayev had not spent that night at the farm. Proshka was a young fellow who had just returned from doing his military service, a good-looking, nimble fellow whom Pyotr Nikolayevich used to take with him on outings to serve as a coachman. The district superintendent of police was a friend of Pyotr Nikolayevich's, and he was also acquainted with the chief constable, the marshal of the nobility, the leader of the Zemstvo and the investigating magistrate. All these persons regularly came to his name-day celebrations and were familiar with his delicious fruit liqueurs and his pickled mush-rooms – white mushrooms, honey agarics and milk agarics. They all sympathized with him and attempted to offer him their help.

'There you are, and you are the one who is always defending the muzhiks,' said the district superintendent. 'I was telling the truth when I told you they were worse than wild animals. You can't do a thing with them unless you use the knout and the rod. So you say it was this Proshka, the one who rides out with you as coachman, do you?'

'Yes, he's the one.'

'Have him brought in here, please.'

Proshka was summoned and they began to question him.

'Where were you that night?'

Proshka tossed his hair back and flashed them a glance.

'At home.'

'What do you mean, "at home"? All the farm-hands say you were not there.'

'As you please, sir.'

'We're not talking about what I please. So where were you?'

'At home.'

'Very well, then. Constable, take this man to the district station.'

'As you please, sir.'

So Proshka still refused to say where he had been on the night of the raid, but the reason for his obstinacy was that he had spent the night with his girlfriend Parasha and he had promised not to give her away, so he did not do so. But there was no evidence. Proshka was released again. However, Pyotr Nikolayevich was sure that the raid had been wholly the work of this Prokofy Nikolayev, and from that time on he began to hate him. One day when Pyotr Nikolayevich had taken him out with him as coachman, he sent him off to the posting station to fetch the horses some fodder. Proshka, as was his custom, bought two measures of oats at a coaching-inn. He fed one-and-a-half measures to the horses and exchanged the remaining half-measure for vodka. Pyotr Nikolayevich found out about this and informed the local Justice of the Peace. The Justice of the Peace sentenced Proshka to three months in gaol. Prokofy was a man with a good opinion of himself. He considered himself superior to others and was proud of it. Being in prison was a humiliating experience for him. He could no longer give himself airs among his fellow-men, and he fell at once into a gloomy state of mind.

Proshka returned home from gaol embittered, not so much against Pyotr Nikolayevich, as against the world in general. As everyone said, after his time in prison Prokofy lost heart, and he took to drinking, was soon caught stealing clothes from a tradesman's wife, and again landed up in gaol.

Meanwhile all that Pyotr Nikolayevich could discover about the horses was that someone had come across the hide of a chestnut gelding, and Pyotr Nikolayevich identified it as Beauty's. And the impunity of these thieves came to exasperate Pyotr Nikolayevich more and more. Now he could not set eyes on muzhiks or even talk about them without being filled with anger, and whenever he had the chance he came down on them as hard as possible.

XII

ALTHOUGH, ONCE he had passed on the coupon, Yevgeny Mikhailovich had stopped thinking about it, his wife Mariya Vasilyevna was unable to forgive either herself for having been duped, or her husband for the cruel things he had said to her, or – and this was the main thing – those two young villains for having taken her in so cleverly.

From the day of the deception onwards she began to look very closely at any grammar-school boys she encountered. Once she actually met Makhin but did not recognize him because he saw her first and contorted his features so effectively that it completely altered his face. But when two weeks later she came face to face with Mitya Smokovnikov on the pavement, she recognized him at once. She let him go by, then turned on her heel and walked after him. On reaching the flat where he lived she made inquiries and found out whose son he was, and the next day she went to the grammar school, where in the entrance hall she met Mikhail Vvedensky, the scripture teacher. He inquired what he could do for her. She replied that she wanted to see the headmaster.

'Unfortunately the headmaster is not here – he is unwell; but perhaps I can help you, or take a message for him.'

Mariya Vasilyevna decided to tell the scripture teacher everything.

Father Vvedensky was a widower, a graduate from the theological academy, and a man of considerable self-esteem. The previous year he had come across Smokovnikov senior at a society meeting in the course of a discussion about religious belief, in which Smokovnikov had soundly trounced him on all points and exposed him to ridicule. As a result Vvedensky had resolved to keep a watchful eye on the son, and having detected in him the same indifference to the Divine Law that his unbelieving father had displayed, he began to persecute him, and even failed him in an examination.

Having found out from Mariya Vasilyevna about young Smokovnikov's escapade, Vvedensky could not help feeling a certain satisfaction, seeing in this incident a confirmation of his own prejudices concerning those immoral people who lacked the guidance of the Church, and he decided to make use of the incident in order, as he tried to assure himself, to reveal the dangers threatening all those who abandoned the Church and her ways – but in the depths of his soul he simply wanted to get his own back on a proud and self-confident atheist.

'Yes, it is very sad, very sad,' said Father Vvedensky, stroking the smooth edges of his pectoral cross. 'I am so glad you have entrusted this matter to me: as a servant of the Church I shall naturally try to make sure that the young man is not left without moral guidance, but I shall also do my best to make his edification as gentle as possible.'

'Yes, I shall act in a way which befits my calling,' said Father

Vvedensky to himself, thinking that he had now quite forgotten the father's hostility towards him and that he desired nothing but the moral good and salvation of the boy.

Next day during the scripture lesson Father Mikhail told his pupils all about the episode of the forged coupon and informed them that it was a grammar-school pupil who had been responsible for it.

'It was a vile, shameful act,' he said, 'but concealing it is even worse. If it was one of you who did this – which I cannot believe – then it would be better for him to own up to it than to hide his guilt.'

As he said this he was staring straight at Mitya Smokovnikov. Mitya went red and started to sweat, then he burst into tears and ran from the classroom.

When Mitya's mother heard about these events she persuaded her son to tell her the whole truth and then hurried off to the photographic supply shop. She paid back the twelve rubles fifty to the proprietor's wife and induced her to keep quiet about the schoolboy's name. She then instructed her son to deny everything, and on no account to make any confession to his father.

And indeed, when Fyodor Mikhailovich heard what had happened at the grammar school, and when his son on being questioned denied it all, he went to see the headmaster and explained the whole matter to him, saying that the scripture teacher's conduct had been deeply reprehensible and that he did not intend to let things rest there. The headmaster called in the scripture teacher and a heated exchange took place between him and Fyodor Mikhailovich.

'A stupid woman attempted to pin something on my son and then retracted her accusation, and you could find nothing better to do than to slander the honour of a thoroughly upright boy.'

'I did not slander him, and I will not permit you to speak to me in such a tone. You are forgetting my vocation.'

'I don't give a fig for your vocation.'

'Your deluded opinions, sir,' said the scripture teacher, his chin quivering so that his scanty little beard trembled in sympathy, 'your deluded opinions are well known to the whole town.'

'Gentlemen, Father,' said the headmaster, attempting to pacify the two disputants. But to pacify them was impossible.

'My holy vocation makes it my duty to concern myself with the moral and religious upbringing of the young.'

'Enough of this pretence. Do you think I don't know that you haven't a grain of genuine religious faith in you?'

'I consider it beneath me to continue talking to such a gentleman as you,' declared Father Mikhail, who had been particularly offended by Smokovnikov's last remark, since he knew that it was accurate. He had gone through the whole course at the theological academy and consequently had long since ceased to believe in what he professed and what he preached; in fact he believed only that everyone ought to make themselves believe those things which he had made himself believe.

Smokovnikov was not so much infuriated by the scripture teacher's behaviour, as by discovering this striking example of the clerical influence which was beginning to manifest itself throughout our society, and he told everyone about the incident.

Father Vvedensky on the other hand, seeing in it a demonstration of the nihilism and atheism which had taken hold not only of the younger generation but of the older one as well, became more and more convinced of the necessity of combating them. The more he condemned the unbelief of Smokovnikov and his kind, the more convinced he became of the firm and unshakable character of his own faith, and the less need he felt to test his faith or to reconcile it with his actual way of living. His faith, acknowledged by the world around him, was for him his principal weapon in his fight against those who denied it.

These thoughts, called forth by his clash with Smokovnikov, together with the disagreeable events at the grammar school which followed in its wake – namely, a reprimand and a caution from the school authorities – impelled him to take a decision which had been tantalizing him for a long time, since the death of his wife, in fact: to take monastic vows and thus opt for a career already followed by several of his fellow-students at the academy, one of whom was already a member of the hierarchy, another the superior of a monastery, and expected soon to be made a bishop.

Towards the end of the academic year Vvedensky left the grammar school, took his monastic vows and the new name of

Misail, and was very soon given the rectorship of a seminary in a town on the Volga.

XIII

MEANWHILE Vasily the yardman had set out on the highroad to the south.

By day he walked, and at night the local policeman would show him to the usual quarters provided for wanderers. Wherever he went people gave him bread, and sometimes even asked him in to have supper with them. In one village in the Oryol province where he was spending the night he was told that a merchant who had leased an orchard from the landowner was looking for fit young fellows as night-watchmen. Vasily was tired of living as a beggar but he did not want to go back to his village, so he went to see the merchant with the orchard and got himself taken on as a night-watchman at a wage of five rubles per month.

Vasily found life in his watchman's hut very pleasant, particularly when the sweet apples had begun to ripen and the other watchmen brought in huge trusses of fresh straw gathered from under the threshing-machine in the master's shed. He would lie the whole day long on the fresh, fragrant straw beside the still more fragrant piles of spring and winter windfall apples, just keeping an eye open to make sure the children were not pilfering the apples still on the trees, and whistling and singing songs. Singing songs Vasily was really good at. He had a fine voice. The women and girls would come up from the village to get some apples. Vasily would laugh and joke with them a bit and gave more or less apples in exchange for eggs or a few kopeks to whichever of them took his fancy – and then lie down again, only getting up to have his breakfast or his dinner or his supper.

Vasily possessed only one shirt, a pink cotton one full of holes, and he had nothing to put on his feet, but his body was strong and healthy, and when the porridge pot was taken off the fire Vasily would eat enough for three, so that the old man who was the chief watchman was always amazed at him. Vasily did not sleep at night and would whistle or call out to keep himself awake, and he could see a long way in the dark, like a cat. One night some big boys from the village climbed into the trees to shake the apples down. Vasily crept up and went for them; they did their best to beat him off but he sent them all flying, and took one of them back to the hut and handed him over to the master.

Vasily's first hut was at the far end of the orchard, but the second, where he lived for the sweet apple harvest, was only forty yards from the master's house. And in this hut Vasily enjoyed himself even more. All day long Vasily could see the gentlemen and the young ladies playing games, going out for drives or walks, and in the evenings and at night playing the piano or the violin, singing or dancing. He would see the students and the young ladies sitting in the windows snuggling up to one another, and then some of them would go for walks in the dark avenues of lime trees, where the moonlight only came through in streaks and patches. He would see the servants hurrying about with food and drink, he would see how the cooks, the laundresses, the stewards, the gardeners, the coachmen – all of them worked just to keep the masters supplied with food and drink and amusement. Sometimes the young gentlefolk would drop in to see him in his hut, and he would choose the finest apples, the ripe and rosy ones, to give to them, and the young ladies would bite into them there and then with a crunching noise, and praise the apples and say something – Vasily knew it was about him – in French, and get him to sing for them.

Vasily greatly admired this way of life, remembering the kind of life he had led in Moscow, and the thought that the beginning and the end of everything was to have money came more and more often into his head.

And Vasily began to think more and more about what he could do to get hold of some more money right away. He started to recall how he had made the odd profit before and he decided that that wasn't the way to go about it, just helping yourself to whatever was lying about; he needed to work out things in advance, to see what was what, and do a clean job leaving no evidence behind. Towards Christmas time they picked the last of the winter apples. The boss had made a good profit and he paid off all the watchmen, including Vasily, and thanked them.

Vasily put on the coat and the hat the young master had given him, but he did not go home, for the thought of that brutish, peasant life filled him with disgust – instead he went back to the town with the hard-drinking ex-conscripts who had worked alongside him as watchmen. Once back in the town he decided to break into and burgle the shop owned by his former employer who had beaten him and thrown him out without his wages. He knew the layout of the place and where the money was kept. He got one of the ex-soldiers to stand guard outside, and he himself smashed a window opening onto the yard, climbed in and took all the money. The thing was carried out skilfully, and no traces were found. Vasily got away with three hundred and seventy rubles. He gave a hundred to his assistant and went off with the rest to another town, where he went on a binge with his comrades and girlfriends.

XIV

MEANWHILE Ivan Mironov had become an accomplished, daring and successful horse-thief. His wife Afimya, who used to nag him on account of what she called his 'botched schemes', was now well pleased with her husband and even quite proud of him, for he was the owner of a sheepskin coat with a hood, and she had a shawl and a new fur coat.

Everyone in the village and surrounding district knew that there was never a horse-theft in which he was not somehow involved, but they were afraid to give evidence against him, and even when some suspicion did fall on him he invariably emerged without a stain on his character. His most recent theft had been from the night-grazing ground at Kolotovka. As far as possible Ivan Mironov liked to choose who to steal from, and he got particular satisfaction when his victims were landowners and merchants. But stealing from landowners and merchants was more difficult. And so when landowners' and merchants' horses were not accessible he would steal peasants' horses instead. Thus he stole from the night-grazing at Kolotovka as many horses as he could get hold of. This job, however, was carried out not by him, but by a skilful young fellow called Gerasim whom he had persuaded to do it. The muzhiks did not discover that their horses were gone until daybreak, and then they rushed off along all possible roads to look for them. The horses were in fact already hidden in a ravine in the middle of the state forest. Ivan Mironov planned to keep them there until the following night, then to make off with them to a yardman he knew in a place forty versts away. Ivan Mironov visited Gerasim in the forest and brought him some pie and vodka, returning home by a forest path on which he hoped not to meet anybody. Unfortunately for him he came up against a forest guard.

'Been out after mushrooms, have you?' asked the guard.

'Yes, but I haven't found any today,' replied Ivan Mironov, pointing to the bast basket which he had brought with him in case of need.

'That's right, it's not the mushroom season,' said the guard, 'but there'll be some coming up in Lent.' And he went on his way.

The forest guard realized that there was something suspicious here. There was no reason for Ivan Mironov to be out walking in the state forest early in the morning. The guard turned back and started to circle round through the trees. On getting near to the ravine he heard the sound of horses snorting and he crept up very quietly to the place the sound was coming from. The ground in the ravine was trampled by horses' hooves and it was all over horse droppings. A little further on Gerasim was sitting eating something, and there were two horses standing tethered to a tree.

The guard ran back to the village and fetched the village Elder, the constable and two witnesses. They approached the place where Gerasim was sitting from three directions, and seized him. Gerasim made no attempt to protest his innocence, but being drunk he at once confessed to everything. He told them that Ivan Mironov had got him drunk and talked him into doing the job, and had promised to come to the forest today to fetch the horses. The muzhiks left the horse and Gerasim where they were in the forest and set an ambush for Ivan Mironov. As soon as night had fallen they heard a whistle. Gerasim whistled back in reply. As soon as Ivan Mironov started to come down the slope they rushed at him, captured him and led him back to their village.

The next morning a crowd assembled in front of the Elder's

hut. Ivan Mironov was brought out and they began to interrogate him. Stepan Pelageyushkin, a tall, stooping, long-armed muzhik with a beaky nose and a dour expression, was the first to ask him a question. Stepan was an independent peasant who had completed his military service. He had not long since moved out of his father's house and was starting to do quite well, when his horse had been stolen from him. By working for a year in the mines Stepan managed to set himself up with two horses. Both of these had now been stolen.

'Tell me where my horses are,' began Stepan, pale with anger and glaring now at the ground, now straight into Ivan's face.

Ivan Mironov denied all knowledge of them. Then Stepan struck him in the face and broke his nose, from which the blood started to trickle.

'Tell me, or I'll kill you!'

Ivan Mironov bent his head but said nothing. Stepan struck him again with his long arm – once, then a second time. Ivan still did not speak, just swung his head from side to side.

'Come, all of you – beat him!' shouted the village Elder. And they all began to beat him. Ivan Mironov fell silently to the ground, then cried out: 'You barbarians, you devils, beat me to death then. I'm not scared of you.'

Then Stepan took hold of a stone from a pile he had ready, and he smashed Ivan Mironov's head in.

XV

IVAN MIRONOV'S murderers were brought to justice. Stepan
Pelageyushkin was among them. The charge brought against
him was particularly grave because they had all testified that
he was the one who had smashed Ivan Mironov's head in with
a stone. At his trial Stepan did not try to conceal anything, but
explained how when his last pair of horses had been stolen he
had reported it at the police-station, and they could probably
have tracked the horses down with the help of the gypsies, but
the district police-officer had not even seen him, and had made
no effort to organize a search.

'What were we supposed to do with a man of his sort? He'd
ruined us.'

'So why didn't the others beat him? Why just you?' asked
the prosecutor.

'That's not true. They all beat him, the village community
decided to do away with him. I was just the one who finished
him off. Why make him suffer more than necessary?'

The judges were struck by Stepan's utterly calm expression
as he described what he had done and how they had beaten Ivan
Mironov to death and how he had finished him off.

Stepan did not indeed see anything very dreadful in this
murder. When he was on his military service he had happened
to be one of the firing-squad when a soldier was executed, and

then, as also now at the murder of Ivan Mironov, he had seen nothing dreadful in it. If you killed a man, you killed a man. It's his turn today, tomorrow it may be mine.

Stepan's sentence was a light one: a year in prison. His peasant's clothes were taken away from him and put in the prison stores with a number attached to them, and they made him put on a prison overall and some slippers.

Stepan had never had much respect for the authorities, but now he was utterly convinced that everyone in authority, all the masters – apart from the Tsar, who pitied the common people and treated them justly – were all of them robbers, sucking the life-blood of the people. The stories told by the exiles and the hard-labour convicts he met in prison confirmed his view of things. One had been sentenced to exile with hard labour for having denounced the thievery of the local authorities, another for striking an official who was trying unlawfully to seize the property of some peasants, and a third, for forging banknotes. The gentry and the merchants, whatever they did, could get away with it, whereas the muzhiks who had nothing got sent off to prison to feed the lice on account of any little thing whatever.

Stepan's wife came to visit him from time to time in prison. With him away from home things had already been bad enough, but now she was ruined and destitute, and was reduced to begging with the children. The calamities afflicting his wife made Stepan even more bitter. His behaviour was vicious towards everyone he came into contact with in prison, and on one occasion he almost killed one of the cooks with an axe, for which he got an extra year on his sentence. During the course of that year he heard that his wife had died and his household no longer existed . . .

When Stepan had served his time he was summoned to the prison stores, and the clothes he had arrived in were taken down from a little shelf and given back to him.

'Where am I to go now?' he asked the quartermaster-sergeant as he put on his own clothes again.

'Home, of course.'

'I haven't got a home. I reckon I shall just have to go on the road. And rob people.'

'If you start robbing people, you'll soon be back in here again.'

'Well, what will be, will be.'

And Stepan went on his way. Despite what he had said, he set off in the direction of his home. He had nowhere else to go.

On his way there he happened to stop for the night at a coaching-inn with a pothouse attached, which he knew.

The inn was kept by a fat tradesman from Vladimir. He knew Stepan. And he knew that Stepan had got himself into prison through bad luck. So he let him stay the night.

This rich tradesman had run off with the wife of a peasant neighbour and was living with her as his wife and business partner.

Stepan knew all about this episode – how the tradesman had offended the muzhik in his honour, and how this wretched woman had walked out on her husband and had grown obese with good eating; and now there she was, sitting all fat and sweaty over her tea – and was kind enough to invite Stepan to have some with her. There were no other travellers staying at the inn. Stepan was allowed to sleep the night in the kitchen. Matryona cleared away all the dishes and went off to the maid's room. Stepan lay down on top of the stove, but he could not get to sleep, and kept snapping under his body the pieces of kindling which had been put there to dry. He could not get out of his head the image of the tradesman's fat paunch bulging out of the waist of his cotton shirt, faded with washing and re-washing. The idea kept coming into his head of taking a knife and slashing that paunch wide open and letting out the fatty intestines. And of doing the same to the woman too. One moment he was saying to himself: 'Come on now, devil take them, I shall be out of here tomorrow,' and the next moment he would remember Ivan Mironov and start thinking again about the tradesman's paunch and Matryona's white, sweaty throat. If he was going to kill one, he might as well kill them both. The cock crew for the second time. If he was going to do it, it had better be now, before it got light. He had noticed a knife the evening before, and an axe. He climbed down from the stove, picked up the axe and the knife and went out of the kitchen. Just as he had got out of the room he heard the click of the latch on another door. The tradesman opened the door and came out. Stepan had not meant to do it like this. He couldn't use the knife in this situation, so he swung the axe up and brought it down, splitting the man's head open. The tradesman collapsed against the lintel of the door and fell to the ground.

Stepan went into the maid's room. Matryona jumped up and stood there by the bed in her nightshirt. Stepan killed her too with the same axe. Then he lit a candle, took the money from the cash-desk, and made off.

XVI

IN THE chief town of a country district, in a house set somewhat apart from the other buildings, lived an old man who had been a civil servant in the days before he had taken to drink, his two daughters, and a son-in-law. The married daughter was also given to drinking and led a disreputable life, but the elder daughter Mariya Semyonovna, a thin, wrinkled woman of fifty whose husband had died, was their sole support on her pension of two hundred and fifty rubles a year. The whole family lived on this money. Mariya Semyonovna also did all the housework. She looked after her weak, drunken old father and her sister's baby, cooked and did the washing. And as is always the case in such situations, all three of them loaded all their wants and needs on to her, all three of them shouted abuse at her, and the son-in-law would even beat her when he was in a drunken state. She endured it all meekly and silently, and again, as is always the case, the more things she was expected to do, the more she managed to carry out. She even gave aid to the poor, to her own cost, giving away her clothing, and she helped to look after the sick.

On one occasion Mariya Semyonovna had a village tailor, a cripple who had lost one leg, staying in the house to do some work for her. He was altering her old father's coat and re-covering her sheepskin jacket with cloth for her to wear to market in the winter.

The crippled tailor was an intelligent and perceptive man who had met with a great variety of people in the course of his work, and because of his disability had to spend most of his time sitting down, which disposed him to do a lot of thinking. After living for a week in Mariya Semyonovna's household he was lost in wonderment for the life she led. Once she came into the kitchen where he was sewing, to wash some towels, and she chatted with him about his life, and how his brother had taken his share of the property and gone off to live on his own.

'I thought it would be better like that, but I'm still as poor as ever.'

'It's better not to change things, but to go on living as you've always lived,' said Mariya Semyonovna.

'That's what amazes me so much about you, Mariya Semyonovna, that you're always bustling about here and there worrying about other people's needs. But as I see it, you get precious little good back from them in return.'

Mariya Semyonovna did not answer.

'You must have decided that it's like it says in the holy books, that you'll get your reward in the next world.'

'We don't know about that,' said Mariya Semyonovna, 'but I'm sure it's better to live in that way.'

'And is that what it says in the holy books?'

'Yes, that's what it says,' she replied, and she read him the Sermon on the Mount from the Gospels. The tailor fell to thinking. And when he had been paid off and he had returned home he still kept thinking about what he had seen in Mariya Semyonovna's house, and about what she had said to him and read to him.

XVII

PYOTR NIKOLAYEVICH SVENTITSKY'S attitude towards the common people had changed completely, and so had their attitude towards him. Before a year was out they had felled twenty-seven of his oak trees and burnt down the barn and the threshing-floor, which were not insured. Pyotr Nikolayevich decided that it was impossible to go on living among these people.

About this time the Livyentsov family were seeking a steward to look after their estates, and the marshal of the nobility had recommended Pyotr Nikolayevich as being the best farmer in the district. The Livyentsov estates although enormous in size were not yielding any profit, and the peasants were helping themselves to everything they could. Pyotr Nikolayevich undertook to set everything to rights, and after letting his own estate to a tenant he set off with his wife to go and live on the Livyentsovs' land in the far-off Volga province.

Pyotr Nikolayevich had always been a lover of law and order, and now he was more unwilling than ever to tolerate these wild, uncivilized peasants who were illegally taking possession of property which did not belong to them. He was glad to have this chance to teach them a lesson and he set about his task with severity. One peasant he had imprisoned for the theft of forest timber, another he flogged with his own hand for not giving way to him on the road and failing to take off his hat. Concerning the meadows, about which there was a dispute, since the peasants regarded them as theirs, Pyotr Nikolayevich announced that if anyone let their cattle on to them, then he would have the animals impounded.

Spring came, and the peasants, as they had done in previous years, let their livestock out on to the manorial meadows. Pyotr Nikolayevich called all his farm-hands together and gave the order to drive the cattle and sheep into the manor farmyard. The muzhiks were out ploughing, so the farm-hands, despite the women's shrieks of protest, were able to drive the animals in. On getting back from their work the muzhiks gathered together and came across to the manor farmyard to demand that their livestock should be given back to them. Pyotr Nikolayevich came out to meet them carrying a rifle across his shoulders (he had just returned from making his tour of inspection on horseback) and informed them that he would only return their livestock to them on payment of a fine of fifty kopeks per horned beast and ten kopeks per sheep. The muzhiks began shouting that the meadows were theirs anyway, and had belonged to their fathers and their grandfathers before them, and that he had no right to go seizing other people's stock.

'Give us our cattle back, or it'll be the worse for you,' said one old man, going up to Pyotr Nikolayevich.

'It'll be the worse for me, will it?' cried Pyotr Nikolayevich, his face all pale, advancing on the old man.

'Give them back if you don't want to get hurt. Parasite.'

'What?' shouted Pyotr Nikolayevich, and he struck the old man in the face.

'You won't dare fight us. Come on, lads, take the cattle by force.'

The crowd surged forward. Pyotr Nikolayevich made as if to get out of the way, but they did not let him. He tried to force his way through. His rifle went off by accident, killing one of the peasants. A general riot broke out. Pyotr Nikolayevich was crushed to death. And five minutes later his mutilated body was dragged away and thrown into a ravine.

The murderers were brought before a military tribunal, and two of them were sentenced to death by hanging.

XVIII

IN THE VILLAGE where the tailor came from five wealthy peasants had leased from the landowner for eleven hundred rubles a hundred and five *desyatins* of rich arable land as black as tar and distributed it among the other muzhiks in parcels costing eighteen or fifteen rubles each. None of the allotments of land went for under twelve rubles. So that they made themselves a good profit. The muzhiks who had leased the land each took five *desyatins*, and this land cost them nothing at all. One of these five muzhiks died, and the others invited the crippled tailor to come in with them as a partner.

When the tenants began to divide up the land, the tailor did not join in drinking vodka with them, and when the discussion turned to the question of who should get how much land, the tailor said that they should allocate it equally, and without taking money they didn't need from the tenants, but only what they could afford.

'What do you mean?'

'If we don't do it like this, we are not acting like Christians. The other way may be all right for the masters, but we are Christian people. We should do things God's way. That's the law of Christ.'

'So where is this law written down, then?'

'In the holy book, in the Gospels. Why don't you come over to my place on Sunday, so we can talk about it?'

When Sunday came not all the peasants went to the tailor's house, but three of them did, and he started to read to them.

He read five chapters from the Gospel of Matthew, and then they started to discuss it. They all listened, but only one of them, Ivan Chuyev, really took it in. And he took it in to such an extent that he began trying to live his whole life according to God's way. And his family too began to live like that. He refused to take the extra land and kept only his proper share.

People began coming regularly to the tailor's house and to Ivan's house, and they began to understand, then they really grasped it, and they gave up smoking, and drinking, and swearing and using foul language, and they started helping one another. They also gave up going to church, and they took their household icons back to the priest. In the end seventeen households, comprising sixty-five people, were involved. The village priest was alarmed and he reported the matter to the bishop. The bishop considered what he should do, and he decided to send to the village Father Misail, who had formerly been a scripture teacher in a grammar school.

XIX

THE BISHOP invited Father Misail to sit down and began telling him about the strange new developments in his diocese.

'It is all the result of spiritual weakness and ignorance. Now you are a man of learning. I want you to go down there and call the people together and get the matter cleared up.'

'With your grace's blessing, I shall certainly try,' said Father Misail. He was glad to have this commission. Any situation in which he could demonstrate the strength of his faith gave him satisfaction. And in converting others he always managed to persuade himself even more thoroughly that he himself really believed.

'Please do your best, I am deeply troubled about my little flock,' said the bishop, unhurriedly accepting in his pudgy white hands the glass of tea which a lay brother had brought him.

'Why have you brought only one sort of jam? Go and get another,' he said to the lay brother. 'I really am deeply, deeply concerned about this matter,' he continued, addressing Misail.

Misail was glad of this opportunity to show his mettle. However, being a man of modest means he requested his travel expenses in advance, and since he feared that there might be some resistance from the uncouth peasantry, he requested that the Governor of the province should be asked to send an instruction to the local police to give him every assistance, should the need arise.

The bishop set up all the arrangements, and Misail, having with the help of the lay brother and the cook assembled the hamper and provisions so necessary for a journey to the back of beyond, set off for his appointed destination. As he started out on this official mission Misail was agreeably aware of the importance of the job he was engaged in, and also of the easing of any doubts he might have had concerning his own faith: he was, on the contrary, fully confident of its authenticity.

His thoughts were centred not on the essence of his faith – this he took to be axiomatic – but on the refutation of these objections which were being made to its outward forms.

XX

THE VILLAGE priest and his wife received Father Misail with great respect, and the day after his arrival they called all the people together in the church. Misail, wearing a brand-new silk cassock and a pectoral cross, his hair well combed, advanced to the ambo;* beside him stood the priest, a little further away the deacons and the choristers, and at the side-doors a few policemen had been stationed. The sectarians had also made their appearance, dressed in dirty, rough sheepskin coats.

After the set prayers were over Father Misail delivered a sermon in which he exhorted those who had fallen away to return to the bosom of Holy Mother Church, threatening them with the pains of hell and promising full absolution to all who repented.

The sectarians did not say anything, but when questioned they did reply.

---

* The raised platform from which the Scriptures were read and sermons preached.

To the question, why they had fallen away from the Church, they replied that in the church people worshipped wooden gods made by human hands, whereas not only was this not laid down in Holy Scripture, but in the prophecies it said just the opposite. When Father Misail asked Chuyev whether it was true that they referred to the holy icons as 'boards', Chuyev replied: 'That's right – just you take any icon you like and turn it round, and you'll see for yourself.' When they were asked why they did not recognize the priesthood, they replied that in Scripture it was written 'freely have ye received, freely give', but priests would only dispense their grace in return for money. To all Misail's attempts to support his position by reference to Holy Scripture, the tailor and Chuyev retorted calmly but firmly, referring to the same Scripture, of which they had a thorough grasp. Misail grew angry and threatened them with the secular authorities. To this the sectarians replied that Scripture said, 'If they have persecuted me, they will also persecute you.'

The encounter was inconclusive and the whole thing would have ended quietly, but the next day at Mass Father Misail preached a sermon about the pernicious influence of those who distort the truth, and how they deserved all kinds of retribution; and some of the peasants as they came out of the church started talking about how it would be good to teach the godless ones a lesson so that they wouldn't go on confusing the people. And that very day, while Father Misail was enjoying some appetizers of salmon and white fish with the rural dean and an inspector who had arrived from the local town, a disorder broke out in the village. The Orthodox folk had gathered together in a crowd in front of Chuyev's hut and were waiting for those inside to come out so that they could give them a good hiding. There were about twenty of the sectarians in there, both men and women. Father Misail's sermon, followed by this assemblage of the Orthodox and their threatening shouts, had aroused in the sectarians a fierceness which had not been there before. Evening had come and it was time for the peasant-women to milk the cows, but the Orthodox believers continued to stand there and wait, and when a young lad came out they started hitting him and drove him back into the house.

The sectarians were discussing what they ought to do, but they were unable to agree among themselves.

The tailor said that they should put up with whatever happened to them and not try to defend themselves. Chuyev, however, said that if they just put up with it they might all end up getting slaughtered, and he seized a poker and went out into the village street. The Orthodox believers hurled themselves upon him.

'All right then, let it be according to the Law of Moses,' he shouted, and he started hitting the Orthodox believers with the poker, putting out one man's eye in the process. The rest of the sectarians slipped out of the hut and returned to their homes.

Chuyev was put on trial for heresy and blasphemy, and sentenced to exile.

Father Misail, however, received an award and was made an archimandrite.

XXI

TWO YEARS before these events took place, a healthy attractive young woman of oriental looks named Turchaninova had come from the Don Cossack territory to St Petersburg to study at the university. In Petersburg she met a student named Tyurin, the son of a Zemstvo leader in the Simbirsk province, and fell in love with him, but her love for him was not of the usual womanly type, involving the desire to become his wife and the mother of his children, but a comradely love which drew its strength above all from a shared anger and detestation against the existing social order and the people who represented it, and from a consciousness of their own intellectual, educational and moral superiority to those people.

She was a gifted student, well able to memorize the contents of lectures and to pass examinations without much effort, and in addition she devoured enormous quantities of the most recently published books. She was sure that her vocation lay not in bearing and bringing up children – in fact she regarded such a vocation with disgust and contempt – but in destroying the present order of things which fettered the fine potential of the common people, and in pointing out to men and women the new path of life revealed to her by the most recent European writers. Full in figure, pale of skin, rosy-cheeked and attractive, with dark flashing eyes and a thick plait of dark hair, she aroused in men feelings which she had no desire to arouse and could not possibly share, utterly absorbed as she was by her task of agitation and argument. But all the same she found it pleasant to arouse such feelings, and for that reason although she did not deliberately dress to show herself off, neither did she neglect her appearance. She enjoyed being attractive, and indeed it gave her the chance of showing how much she looked down on that which other women held to be so important. In her views on the possible means of struggle against the existing order she went further than most of her associates, her friend Tyurin among them, and took it as read that all methods in the struggle were valid and to be used, up to and including murder. Yet Katya Turchaninova the revolutionary was still at heart a kind and unselfish woman, forever spontaneously putting the interests, enjoyment and well-being of other people before her own, and always glad of the chance to do something to make someone else happy, whether it was a child, an old person, or an animal.

Turchaninova spent the summer vacation period in a district town in the Volga province staying with a friend of hers who was a village schoolmistress. Tyurin was living in the same district, in his father's house. The three young people, and the local doctor too, met together frequently, lent each other books, argued, and fed one another's shared sense of social indignation. The Tyurins' property adjoined the Livyentsov estate where Pyotr Nikolayevich Sventitsky was now working as the steward. As soon as Pyotr Nikolayevich had arrived there and set about restoring order, young Tyurin, noting that the Livyentsovs' peasants had a spirit of independence and a firm resolve to stand up for their rights, began to take an interest in them and often walked over to the village to talk to the peasants, explaining to them the principles of socialism in general and of the nationalization of the land in particular.

When Pyotr Nikolayevich was murdered and the court case began, the trial gave the group of revolutionaries in the district town a powerful cause for agitation, and they denounced it outspokenly. Tyurin's visits to the village and his conversations with the peasants were referred to in the court proceedings. Tyurin's house was searched and some revolutionary pamphlets discovered, and he was arrested and taken away to Petersburg.

Turchaninova travelled to Petersburg after him and went to the prison to try to see him, but they would not permit her to see him on just any day, but only on a public visiting-day, and even then she was only allowed to talk to Tyurin through a double iron grille. This visit strengthened her feelings of moral outrage still further. Her indignation finally reached its climax when she was faced with a young and handsome officer of the gendarmes who was obviously ready to grant her some concessions, provided she would agree to certain proposals of his. This incident drove her to the highest pitch of fury and hatred against all representatives of authority. She went to the chief of police in order to lodge a complaint. The chief of police echoed the words of the gendarme: that there was nothing they could do, and that the matter was under the jurisdiction of the Minister. She sent in a written memorandum to the Minister requesting an interview; it was refused. Then she decided that a desperate act was called for, and she bought a revolver.

XXII

THE MINISTER was receiving visitors at his usual hour. After passing over three petitioners and talking for a while with a provincial governor, he went up to a pretty dark-eyed young woman in black who was standing there holding a piece of paper in her left hand. A lecherous glint appeared in the Minister's eyes at the sight of this charming petitioner, but remembering his position the Minister adopted a serious expression.

'And what can I do for you?' he asked, advancing towards her.

She made no reply, but swiftly drew out the revolver from beneath her cape, aimed it at the Minister's chest and fired, but she missed.

The Minister made a grab at her arm but she stepped back away from him and fired a second shot. The Minister fled. The young woman was immediately seized and held. She was shaking and unable to speak. Then suddenly she burst into hysterical laughter. The Minister had not even been wounded.

The woman was Turchaninova. She was sent to a special detention prison pending the investigation of her case. Meanwhile the Minister, who had received congratulations and commiserations from persons in the very highest places and even from the Sovereign himself, appointed a commission to investigate the conspiracy which had led to this attempt on his life.

There was of course no conspiracy whatever; but the officials of both the secret and civil police forces went assiduously to work to search out all the threads of the non-existent conspiracy, conscientiously justifying their salaries and their expenditure. Rising early in the morning when it was still dark, they conducted search after search, transcribed papers and books, perused diaries and private letters, and wrote out extracts from them in beautiful handwriting on the finest paper. They questioned Turchaninova any number of times and set up confrontations with witnesses in their efforts to get her to reveal the names of her accomplices.

The Minister was a kindly man at heart and felt very sorry for this healthy, attractive Cossack girl, but he told himself that he carried grave responsibilities to the state which he was bound to discharge, however painful this might prove to be. And when a former colleague of his, a court chamberlain who knew the Tyurin family, met him at a court ball and began to ask him about Tyurin and Turchaninova, the Minister shrugged his shoulders, crinkling the red sash he was wearing across his white waistcoat, and said:

'*Je ne demanderais pas mieux que de lâcher cette pauvre fillette, mais vous savez — le devoir.*'*

And meanwhile Turchaninova was sitting in her detention cell, exchanging occasional furtive tapped messages with her fellow-prisoners and reading the books she was given, but sometimes she would fall into a mood of fury and despair, beating on the walls with her fists, screaming and laughing.

XXIII

ONE DAY when Mariya Semyonovna had been to the local treasury office to draw her pension and was on her way home, she met a teacher whom she knew.

'Good day, Mariya Semyonovna, have you been to collect your pay then?' he called out to her from the opposite side of the road.

---

* 'I should like nothing better than to release the poor little girl, but you know how it is — one must stick to one's duty.'

'Yes, I have,' replied Mariya Semyonovna. 'It will do to plug a few gaps at least.'

'Well, you should have plenty to plug the gaps and still have some left over,' said the teacher, and he said goodbye to her and went on his way.

'Goodbye,' said Mariya Semyonovna, and as she was looking back at the teacher she walked straight into a tall man with extremely long arms and a stern face. As she came near to the house where she lived she was surprised to see this same long-armed man again. He watched her go into the house, stood there for a while, then turned and walked off.

At first Mariya Semyonovna felt alarmed, then her alarm turned to a sort of melancholy. But by the time she had gone inside and distributed little gifts to her old father and her little scrofulous nephew Fedya, and petted the little dog Trezorka, who yelped with delight, she was feeling cheerful again, and handing over the money to her father she got on with the housework, to which there never seemed to be an end.

The man she had bumped into was Stepan.

After leaving the coaching-inn where he had murdered the inn-keeper Stepan had not gone back to the town. And strange to say, not only did the memory of the inn-keeper's murder not distress him, but he actually found himself returning to it in his mind several times each day. It gave him pleasure to think that he was capable of doing the deed so cleanly and skilfully that no one would ever find him out or prevent him from doing the same thing again, to other people. As he sat in a tavern drinking his tea and his vodka he kept scrutinizing the people around him with the same thought always in mind: how he could set about murdering them. To find himself a bed for the night he went to the house of a man who came from his own district, a drayman. The drayman was out. He said he would wait and sat down to chat with the man's wife. Then, when she turned her back on him to tend the stove, it occurred to him that he could kill her. Surprised at himself, he shook his head, but then he took his knife from the top of his boot, threw her to the floor and cut her throat. The children started screaming, so he killed them too, and left the town at once that same day. Once out of the town he went into a village inn, where he stopped and had a good night's sleep.

The next day he walked back to the district town, and overheard Mariya Semyonovna's conversation with the teacher while he was walking down the street. He was frightened by the way she had stared at him, nevertheless he decided to break into her house and take the money which she had drawn. When night came he broke the lock and went upstairs into a bedroom. The first person to hear him was the younger, married daughter. She cried out. Stepan immediately cut her throat. The son-in-law woke up and grappled with him. He got hold of Stepan by the throat and struggled with him for quite some time, but Stepan was too strong for him. Having finished off the son-in-law Stepan, now in a state of some agitation and excited by the struggle, went behind a partition. On the other side of the partition Mariya Semyonovna was lying in bed. She raised herself on the bed and looked at Stepan with gentle, frightened eyes and crossed herself. Once again her look frightened Stepan. He lowered his gaze.

'Where's the money?' he asked without looking up.

She did not answer.

'Where's the money?' said Stepan, showing her the knife.

'What are you doing? You can't do this,' she said.

'Oh yes I can, and I will.'

Stepan moved nearer, intending to seize her arms so that she could not stop him doing what he intended to do, but she did not raise her hands, did not resist, but simply pressed her hands to her bosom, sighed heavily and repeated:

'Oh, what a great sin. What are you doing? Have pity on yourself. You think you are destroying others, but it's your own soul you are destroying. Oh, oh!' she screamed.

Stepan could not stand her voice or the look on her face any longer, and he slashed the knife right across her throat. — 'I haven't got time to waste chatting with you.' — She slumped back onto the pillows and began to wheeze, soaking one of the pillows with her blood. He turned away and walked through the bedrooms, collecting things as he went. When he had gathered up everything he wanted Stepan lit a cigarette, sat down for a moment, brushed down his clothes and then went out. He had thought he would get away with this murder just as easily as he had done with the previous ones, but even before he had reached the place where he planned to stay the night he suddenly felt so weary that he could hardly move a limb. He lay down in a ditch and stayed there for the rest of that night, the whole of the next day and the night that followed.

Part Two

I

AS HE LAY there in the ditch Stepan kept seeing before him Mariya Semyonovna's thin, meek, terrified face and hearing her voice: 'You can't do this,' her peculiar lisping, pathetic voice kept on repeating. And Stepan kept reliving over again everything he had done to her. He began to feel really frightened, and he shut his eyes, swaying his shaggy head from side to side in an attempt to shake these thoughts and memories out of it. And for a moment he managed to free himself from his memories, but in their place appeared first one black devil, then another, and after them still other black devils with red eyes, all pulling hideous faces and all saying the same thing: 'You did away with her – now do away with yourself, or we won't give you any peace.' And he would open his eyes and once again see her and hear her voice, and he was filled with pity for her, and with fear and loathing towards himself. And he would shut his eyes again, and again the black devils would be there.

Towards the evening of the second day he got to his feet and walked to the tavern nearby. Reaching the tavern with a great effort, he began drinking. Yet however much he drank, he was quite unable to get drunk. He sat silently at a table, downing one glass after another. Then into the tavern walked the village constable.

'And who might you be then?' inquired the constable.

'I'm the one who cut all those people's throats at the Dobrotvorovs' house the other night.'

They bound him, and after holding him for a day at the district police-station, sent him off to the main town of the province. The warden of the prison, recognizing him as a former prisoner and a trouble-maker who had now done something really bad, gave him a stern reception.

'You'd best get it into your head that you won't be pulling any tricks with me in charge,' said the warden in a hoarse wheezing voice, frowning and sticking out his lower jaw. 'And if I see you trying anything, I'll have you flogged. And you won't be escaping from this prison.'

'Why would I be escaping?' answered Stepan, looking at the ground. 'I gave myself up of my own accord.'

'That's enough back-chat from you. And when a superior is talking to you, look him in the eye,' shouted the warden, giving him a punch on the jaw.

At that moment Stepan was again seeing Mariya Semyonovna and hearing her voice. He heard nothing of what the warden had just been saying.

'What?' he asked, coming to his senses as he felt the blow on his chin.

'Come on, come on now – forward march, and none of your funny business.'

The warden was expecting Stepan to get violent, to hatch schemes with other prisoners, and to try and make a break for it. But there was nothing of that kind. Whenever the guard or the warden himself looked through the peephole in his cell door, Stepan would be sitting there on a sack stuffed with straw, his head propped up in his hands, whispering something to himself. When being questioned by the investigator he also behaved quite differently from the other prisoners: he seemed absent-minded, as if he did not hear the questions, and when he did grasp them he was so truthful in his answers that the investigator, accustomed as he was to contending with the ingenuity and cunning of accused prisoners, felt rather like a man climbing a staircase in the dark, who lifts his foot to find the next step, which turns out not to be there. Stepan gave a full account of all the murders he had committed, screwing up his brow and staring at a fixed point in space, and speaking in the simplest, most businesslike manner as he tried to recall all the details: 'He came out barefoot,' said Stepan, talking about the first murder, 'and he stood there in the doorway, and so I slashed him just the once and he started to wheeze, and I got straight on with it and dealt with his old woman.' And so he went on. When the public prosecutor made his round of the cells Stepan was asked if he had any complaints or if he needed anything. He answered that there was nothing he needed and that he wasn't being mistreated. The prosecutor walked a few steps down the stinking corridor, then stopped and asked the warden, who was accompanying him, how this prisoner was behaving.

'It's a most extraordinary thing,' replied the warden, gratified that Stepan had praised the way he was being treated. 'He's been with us for over a month now, and his behaviour is exemplary. I am just concerned that he may be thinking up something. He's a fearless fellow, and he's exceptionally strong.'

II

DURING HIS first month in prison Stepan was constantly tormented by the same thing: he could see the grey walls of his cell and hear the prison noises – the hum of voices on the common cell in the floor below him, the guard's footsteps in the corridor, the clangs that marked the passing of the hours – but at the same time he could see *her*, and that meek expression of hers which had already got the better of him when he had met her in the street, and the scraggy, wrinkled throat which he had slashed; and he could hear her touching, pitiful, lisping voice saying: '*You think you're destroying others, but it's your own soul you're destroying. You can't do this.*' Then the voice would fall silent, and those three would appear – the black devils. And they kept on appearing just the same, whether his eyes were open or shut. When his eyes were shut they looked more distinct. When Stepan opened his eyes the devils would blend into the doorways and the walls and vanish for a while, but then they came at him again, from in front of him and from both sides, making dreadful faces and repeating: 'Do away with yourself, do away with yourself. You could make a noose, you could start a fire.' And then Stepan would start to shake, and to repeat all the prayers he could remember – the Hail Mary and the Our Father – and at first that seemed to help him. As he recited the prayers he would start to recall his past life: his father and mother, his village, the dog Wolfcub, his grandad asleep on top of the stove, the upturned benches on which he had gone sledging with the other lads; and then he would recall the girls and their songs, and the horses, how they had been stolen and how they had managed to catch the horse-thief, and how he had finished the thief off with a stone. And he would recall his first term in prison and his release, and he would recall the fat inn-keeper and the drayman's wife and the children, and then once again he would recall *her*. And he would feel hot all over, and throw off his prison robe, leap up from his plank-bed and start pacing rapidly up and down his cramped cell like a wild animal in a cage, making a rapid turn each time he came up against the damp, oozing walls. And again he would start to recite his prayers, but the prayers were beginning to lose their effect.

One long autumn evening, when the wind was whistling and howling in the chimney-flues and he had had enough of pacing up and down his cell, he sat down on his bunk, and realizing that he could not go on struggling any longer, that the devils were too strong for him, he gave in to them. For some time he had had his eye on the stove-pipe. If he could wind some thin cord or some thin strips of cloth round it, it ought to hold. But he would need to go about it cleverly. So he set to work, and for two days he worked away to get some strips of linen from the palliasse he slept on (when the guard came in he covered the bunk with his dressing-gown). He tied the strips together with knots, double ones so that they would hold the weight of his body without pulling away. While he was busy with this task his torments abated. When everything was ready he made a noose, placed it round his neck, climbed up on to the bed and hanged himself. But his tongue had only just begun to protrude when the strips of cloth gave way, and he fell to the floor. Hearing the noise, the guard came running in. They summoned the medical orderly and took him off to the hospital. By the next day he was quite recovered, and was discharged from the hospital and placed not in a solitary cell, but in a communal one.

In the communal cell he lived as one of twenty inmates, but he lived there just as if he had been alone, seeing nobody, talking to nobody, and suffering the same mental torments as before. It was particularly bad for him when everyone else was sleeping and he could not, and as before he kept seeing *her* and hearing her voice, and then again the black devils would appear, with their dreadful eyes, mocking him.

Again, as before, he recited his prayers, and as before they were of no use.

On one occasion when, after he had said his prayers, she again appeared to him, he started to pray to her, to her little soul, praying that it would let him go, that it would forgive him. And when towards morning he collapsed onto his flattened straw palliasse, he fell fast asleep, and in his sleep he dreamt that she came towards him with her scraggy, wrinkled throat, all cut open.

'Please, will you forgive me?'

She looked at him with her meek look, and said nothing.

'Will you forgive me?'

And three times in the same way he begged her to forgive him. But she still said nothing. And then he woke up. From that time on he began to feel better: it was as though he had come to himself, and he looked round him, and for the first time he began to make friends with his cell-mates and to talk to them.

III

ONE OF THE prisoners in Stepan's communal cell was Vasily, who had again been caught stealing and had been sentenced to exile; another was Chuyev, who had likewise been sentenced to forcible resettlement. Vasily spent his time either singing songs in his splendid voice or telling his cell-mates the story of his adventures. Chuyev, on the other hand, was always working, or sewing away at some item of clothing or underwear, or reading the Gospels or the Psalms.

To Stepan's question as to why he was being exiled, Chuyev replied that it was because of his true faith in Christ and because the false priests could not bear to hear the spirit speaking through people such as he, who lived according to the Gospel, and thus showed up the priests for what they were. And when Stepan asked Chuyev what this Gospel law was, Chuyev explained to him how they had found out about this true faith from a one-legged tailor when they were sharing out some land.

'All right then, so what happens if you commit evil deeds?' asked Stepan.

'It tells you all about that.' And Chuyev proceeded to read to him:

'"When the Son of man shall come in his glory, and all the holy angels with him, then shall he sit upon the throne of his glory. And before him shall be gathered all nations; and he shall separate them one from another, as a shepherd divideth his sheep from the goats, and he shall set the sheep on his right hand, but the goats on the left. Then shall the King say unto them on his right hand, 'Come, ye blessed of my Father, inherit the kingdom prepared for you from the foundation of the world: for I was an hungred, and ye gave me meat; I was thirsty, and ye gave me drink; I was a stranger, and ye took me in; naked, and ye clothed me; I was sick, and ye visited me; I was in prison, and ye came unto me.' Then shall the righteous answer him, saying, 'Lord, when saw we thee an hungred, and fed thee? or thirsty, and gave thee drink? When saw we thee a stranger, and took thee in? or naked, and clothed thee? Or when saw we thee sick, or in prison, and came unto thee?' And the King shall answer and say unto them: 'Verily I say unto you, inasmuch as ye have done it unto one of the least of these my brethren, ye have done it unto me.' Then shall he say also unto them on the left hand: 'Depart from me, ye cursed, into everlasting fire, prepared for the devil and his angels: for I was an hungred, and ye gave me no meat; I was thirsty, and ye gave me no drink; I was a stranger, and ye took me not in; naked, and ye clothed me not; sick, and in prison, and ye visited me not.' Then shall they also answer him, saying: 'Lord, when saw we thee an hungred, or athirst, or a stranger, or naked, or sick, or in prison, and did not minister unto thee?' Then shall he answer them, saying: 'Verily I say unto you: inasmuch as ye did it not to one of the least of these, ye did it not to me.' And these shall go away into the everlasting punishment, but the righteous into life eternal.'"*

Vasily, who had been sitting on the floor opposite Chuyev and listening to him reading, nodded his handsome head approvingly.

'That's right,' he declared firmly, '"Go," he says, "ye accursed ones into everlasting punishment, you never fed anyone, you just

---

* Matthew xxv, 31–46.

stuffed your own bellies." That's just what they deserve. Here, let me have the book and I'll read some myself,' he added, wanting to show off his reading skills.

'But does it say there won't be any forgiveness?' asked Stepan, lowering his shaggy head and waiting quietly to listen to the reading.

'Just you wait a bit and hold your noise,' said Chuyev to Vasily, who was still going on about the rich not feeding the poor stranger and not visiting anybody in prison. 'Just wait, will you,' repeated Chuyev, leafing through the Gospels. Finding the place he was looking for, Chuyev smoothed out the pages with his large, powerful hand, grown quite white from his time in prison.

'"And there were also two other, malefactors, led with him" – with Christ, that is,' began Chuyev, '"to be put to death. And when they were come to the place, which is called the Skull, there they crucified him, and the malefactors, one on the right hand, and the other on the left.

'"Then said Jesus: 'Father, forgive them, for they know not what they do' . . . And the people stood beholding. And the rulers also with them derided him, saying: 'He saved others, let him save himself, if he be the Christ, the chosen of God.' And the soldiers also mocked him, coming to him and offering him vinegar, and saying: 'If thou be the king of the Jews, save thyself.' And a superscription also was written over him in letters of Greek, and Latin, and Hebrew: 'This is the king of the Jews.' And one of the malefactors which were hanged railed on him, saying: 'If thou be Christ, save thyself and us.' But the other answering, rebuked him, saying: 'Dost thou not fear God, seeing thou art in the same condemnation? And we indeed justly, for we receive the due reward for our deeds; but this man hath done nothing amiss.' And he said unto Jesus: 'Lord, remember me when thou comest into thy kingdom.' And Jesus said unto him: 'Verily I say unto thee: today shalt thou be with me in paradise.'"'*

Stepan said nothing, but sat deep in thought as though listening, although in fact he heard nothing more of what Chuyev was reading.

'So that is what the true faith is all about,' he thought. 'It's only the ones who have given food and drink to the poor and visited the prisoners who will be saved, and those who didn't do those things will go to hell. All the same, the thief only repented when he was already on the cross, and he still went to heaven.' He saw no contradiction in this; on the contrary, the one thing seemed to confirm the other: that the merciful would go to heaven, and the unmerciful to hell – that meant that everyone had better be merciful, and the fact that Christ forgave the thief meant that Christ himself was merciful. All this was quite new to Stepan; he was merely surprised that it had remained hidden from him until now. And he spent all his spare time with Chuyev, asking questions and listening to his replies. And as he listened

---

* Luke xxiii, 32–43.

he began to understand. He realized that the overall meaning of this teaching was that men were brothers, and ought to love and pity each other, and then it would be well with all of them. As he listened, he perceived as something forgotten, yet familiar, everything that confirmed the overall meaning of this teaching, and he allowed everything that did not confirm it to slip past his ears, attributing it to his own lack of understanding.

And from that time onwards Stepan became a different man.

IV

EVEN BEFORE this happened Stepan Pelageyushkin had been a docile prisoner, but now the warden, the orderlies and his fellow-prisoners were all amazed at the change which had come over him. Without being ordered, and even when it was not his turn, he carried out all the most arduous duties, among them the cleaning out of the night-bucket. Yet despite his submissiveness his cell-mates respected and feared him, knowing his force of will and his great physical strength, especially after an incident in which two vagrants attacked him and he fought them off, breaking the arm of one of them in the process. These vagrants had set out to beat a well-heeled young prisoner at cards and had taken from him everything he owned. Stepan had stood up for him and managed to get back from them the money they had won. The vagrants had started cursing him, and then tried to beat him up, but he had overpowered them both. When the warden tried to find out the cause of the quarrel, the vagrants had maintained that it was Pelageyushkin who had set upon them both. Stepan made no attempt to justify himself, but meekly accepted his punishment, which consisted of three days in the punishment block, followed by transfer to a solitary cell.

He found it hard to be in solitary confinement because it separated him from Chuyev and the Gospels; moreover, he was afraid that his visions of the woman he had killed and the black devils might start again. But his hallucinations did not return. His entire soul was now full of a new and joyful spirit. He would even have been glad of his isolation, if only he had been able to read and if he had possessed a copy of the Gospels. That the authorities would have provided him with, but he could not read.

As a boy he had begun to learn to read in the old-fashioned way, spelling out the letters – *az*, *buki*, *vyedi** – but not being very bright he got no further than the alphabet, was quite unable at that stage to grasp how words were strung together, and so remained illiterate. Now, however, he determined to do the job properly, and asked the orderly for a copy of the New Testament. The orderly brought him one and he set to work. He was able to recognize the letters, but he could make no progress towards putting them together. However much he racked his brains to

---

* The traditional names for a, b, v – the first letters of the Russian alphabet. Tolstoy promoted a more phonetic method of learning, and wrote several reading books.

understand how words could be composed out of individual letters, he could make nothing of it. He could not sleep at night, could not stop thinking about his problem, and lost his appetite for food, falling so low in spirits that he had a bad infestation of lice and could not get rid of them.

'Well then, have you still not got there?' the orderly asked him one day.

'No, I haven't.'

'But you know the Our Father, don't you?'

'Of course I know it.'

'So, just try reading that. Look, here it is' – and the orderly showed him the Lord's Prayer in the New Testament.

Stepan started to recite the Our Father, fitting the letters he knew to the sounds he knew. And suddenly the mystery of the combining of letters was opened to him, and he began to read. It was a tremendous joy to him. From that day he began reading, and the sense which emerged little by little from the painfully assembled words took on an even greater significance for him.

His isolation no longer weighed upon Stepan, it was a cause of rejoicing to him. He was entirely preoccupied with his task, and was not at all pleased when, to make room for some newly admitted politicals, he was moved back into the communal cell.

V

NOW IT WAS often not Chuyev, but Stepan who read the Gospels aloud in the cell, and although some of the prisoners sang bawdy songs, others listened to his reading and to the conversations which took place about what he had read. Two men in particular always listened to him attentively and in silence: one was the executioner Makhorkin who was doing hard labour for murder; the other was Vasily, who had been caught stealing and was being held in the same prison, awaiting trial. Makhorkin had twice fulfilled his duties as executioner during his stay in the prison, on both occasions in other towns where no one could be found to carry out the sentences the judges had imposed. The peasants who had murdered Pyotr Nikolayevich Sventitsky had been tried by a military tribunal and two of them had been condemned to death by hanging.

Makhorkin had been required to go to Penza to carry out his functions there. On previous occasions of this kind he had at once written to the Governor – he was unusually good at reading and writing – explaining that he had been commanded to go to Penza to carry out his duties and requesting the provincial chief to grant him the appropriate daily subsistence allowance; but this time he declared, to the astonishment of the prison director, that he would not go, and that never again would he be carrying out the duty of executioner.

'And have you forgotten the whip?' shouted the warden.

'The whip is the whip right enough, but killing's against the law.'

'So you've been picking up ideas from Pelageyushkin, have you? Quite the prison prophet he's become. Well, just you wait.'

VI

MEANWHILE MAKHIN, the grammar-school boy who had showed his friend how to forge the coupon, had left school and completed his course at the university Faculty of Law. Thanks to his success with women, including the former mistress of an elderly government minister who was a friend of his, he had while still quite a young man been made an examining magistrate. He was a dishonest man with considerable debts, a seducer of women and a gambler at cards, but he was a clever, quick-witted man with a retentive memory, and effective in his handling of legal cases.

He was examining magistrate in the district where Stepan Pelageyushkin was being tried. He had already been surprised during the first examination by Stepan's simple, accurate and level-headed replies to his questions. Makhin was almost unconsciously aware that this man standing before him shaven-headed and in shackles, who was brought here and guarded and would be taken away to be locked up again by two soldiers, this man was somehow perfectly free and existed on a moral level which he, Makhin, could not possibly attain. For this reason, as he examined the man he was obliged to keep on pulling himself together and urging himself on, so as not to get confused and to lose his way. He was struck by the manner in which Stepan spoke of the things he had done as of something which had happened long ago and which had been carried out not by him at all, but by another person.

'And you didn't feel sorry for them at all?' asked Makhin.

'No, I didn't feel sorry. I didn't understand at that time.'

'Well, and how do you feel towards them now?'

Stepan smiled sadly. 'Now, you could roast me alive, but I wouldn't do such a thing again.'

'And why is that?'

'Because I've come to see that all men are brothers.'

'All right, so I am your brother, am I?'

'Of course you are.'

'What, I am your brother, though I am condemning you to penal servitude?'

'That's only because you don't understand.'

'And what don't I understand?'

'You can't understand, if you are passing judgement on me.'

'Well, let us get on. So where did you go after that? . . .'

Makhin was struck most of all by what he learnt from the prison warden about Pelageyushkin's influence on the executioner

308

Makhorkin who, at the risk of corporal punishment, had refused
to carry out his official duties.

VII

AT AN EVENING party at the house of the Yeropkins, where
there were two marriageable daughters both of whom Makhin
was courting, after the singing of romances (at which the highly
musical Makhin distinguished himself as second singer and as
accompanist), Makhin was giving a faithful, detailed account –
his memory was excellent – and a quite impartial account, of
the strange criminal who had brought about the conversion of
the executioner. Makhin was able to remember and describe
everything so well, precisely because he was always utterly
impartial towards the people he had to deal with. He did not
and could not enter into the spiritual state of other people, and
for this reason he was extremely good at recalling everything
that had happened to them and all that they had done or said.

But Pelageyushkin had aroused his interest. He made no
attempt to put himself in Stepan's place but he could not help
wondering, 'What is going on in his mind?' and although he
came to no conclusions he felt that this was something of interest,
and so he was giving a thorough account of the whole case
at this soirée: the executioner's repudiation of his duties, the
warden's stories about Pelageyushkin's strange behaviour, his

reading of the Gospels, and the powerful influence he exerted on his fellow-prisoners.

Makhin's story intrigued everyone present, but it was of particular interest to the Yeropkins' younger daughter Liza, who was eighteen years old, had just completed her studies at a young ladies' academy, and was beginning to realize the darkness and narrowness of the thoroughly false environment in which she had been brought up – she was like a swimmer who had burst through the surface of the water and was eagerly gulping in the fresh air of life. She started to question Makhin about the details of the case and about how and why such a transformation had come upon Pelageyushkin, and Makhin told her what he had learnt from Pelageyushkin about his most recent murder, and how the meekness and docility of this extraordinarily good-hearted woman with no fear of death, whom he had murdered, had vanquished him and opened his eyes, and how his reading of the Gospels had then completed the process.

For a long time that night Liza Yeropkina could not get to sleep. For some months already a struggle had been going on within her between the life of fashionable society, in which her sister had been trying to involve her, and her attraction towards Makhin, which was mingled with a desire to reform him. And now it was this latter impulse which gained the upper hand. She had already heard something of the woman who had been murdered. Now, however, after that dreadful death and what Makhin had told her based on Pelageyushkin's account of it, she knew the whole story of Mariya Semyonovna in detail and she was deeply moved by all that she had learnt about her.

Liza felt an overwhelming desire to be a woman of the sort that Mariya Semyonovna had been. She was rich and she was afraid Makhin might be courting her simply for her money. And so she decided that she would give away the property she owned, and she confided her idea to Makhin.

Makhin was glad to have this opportunity of showing his disinterestedness, and he told Liza that he did not love her for her money, and this decision of hers, which seemed to him so magnanimous, moved him deeply. Meanwhile a struggle had begun between Liza and her mother (the estate had come to her from her father), who would not permit her to give her property away. Makhin gave Liza all the help he could. And the more he pursued this course of action, the more he began to understand this new world of spiritual aspirations which had formerly seemed to him so strange and alien, and which he now saw in Liza.

VIII

IN THE COMMUNAL cell everything had grown quiet. Stepan was lying in his place on the plank-bed, not yet asleep. Vasily went over to him, and tugging at his foot, gave him a wink as a sign that he should get up and come across to where he was standing. Stepan slipped down from the plank-bed and went up to Vasily.

'Well now, brother,' said Vasily, 'I want you to help me, if you will.'

'What sort of help do you need?'

'I'm thinking of escaping.'

And Vasily explained that he had made all the necessary preparations for an escape attempt.

'Tomorrow I'm going to stir up some trouble with them' – he pointed at the prisoners lying asleep. 'They'll complain about me to the orderlies. I'll be transferred to the cells upstairs and once I'm there I know what to do. But I'll be relying on you to give me a hand to get out of the mortuary.'

'I can do that. But where will you go?'

'I'll go wherever I feel like going. I reckon there's no lack of bad characters out there.'

'That's true, brother, but it's not for us to judge them.'

'What I mean is, I'm no murderer, am I? I've never done in a single soul, and what's a bit of stealing? What's so wrong about that? Aren't they always robbing poor devils like you and me?'

'That's their affair. They'll answer for it.'

'So are we just meant to stand there and watch them get on with it? Like, I cleaned out a church once. What harm did that do anybody? What I've got in mind now isn't to rob some measly little shop. I'm going to go for some big money, and then give it away to them as need it.'

At that moment one of the prisoners sat up on the plank-bed and began listening to what they were saying. Stepan and Vasily went their separate ways.

The next day Vasily did what he had planned to do. He began complaining about the bread, saying that it was not properly cooked, and he urged the other prisoners to call the warden in and lodge an official complaint. The warden arrived and shouted abuse at them, and on discovering that Vasily was the one behind the whole thing he gave orders that he should be put into solitary confinement in one of the cells on the floor above.

That was exactly what Vasily needed.

IX

VASILY WAS thoroughly familiar with the upstairs cell into which they had put him. He knew how the floor was constructed and as soon as he got in there he set about taking it up. When he had managed to worm his way under the floorboards he prised apart the panels which formed the ceiling of the room below and jumped down, into the mortuary. That day there was only one dead body lying on the mortuary table. In the mortuary they kept the sacks used for making the prisoners' palliasses. Vasily was aware of this and he was counting on it. The padlock on the door had been taken off and the hasp pushed inside. Vasily opened the door and went into the room at the end of the corridor, where a new latrine was being built. In the latrine there was a hole leading from the second floor down to the lowest one, the basement. Groping his way back to the door, Vasily went into the mortuary again, removed the shroud from the corpse, which felt icy cold (he touched it with his hand in taking the shroud off it), then took some sacks and tied them and the shroud together to form a rope, and lowered his rope down the latrine hole; then he made the rope fast round a cross-beam and climbed down it. The rope was not long enough to reach the floor. Just how much too short it was he did not know, but there was nothing for it, so he hung down as far as he could, then jumped.

He hurt his legs, but he could still walk. In the basement there were two windows. They were big enough for him to crawl through, but they were fitted with iron gratings. He had to get one of them out, but what with? Vasily began to fumble about. On the floor of the basement there were some sections of timber. He found one which had a pointed end and began using it to lever out the bricks which held the grating in place. He worked away at it for a long time. The cocks had crowed for the second time, but the grating still held. At last one side of it came loose. Vasily inserted his piece of timber into the gap and pushed hard on it; the whole grating came away, but a brick fell out and crashed to the floor. The sentries might have heard. Vasily froze. All was quiet. He climbed up into the window aperture, and out. To make his escape he still had to get over the prison wall. In one corner of the yard there stood a lean-to shed. He would have to climb on to the roof of this shed, and from there onto the top of the wall. He would need to take a piece of the timber with him, otherwise he would not be able to get on to the roof. Vasily crawled back through the window. He crawled out once more with a length of timber and froze, listening to find out where the sentry was. As far as he could judge, the sentry was walking along the far side of the square yard. Vasily approached the lean-to, placed the timber against it and started to climb up. The timber slipped, and fell to the ground. Vasily was in stockinged feet, with no shoes. He took off his socks so as to get a grip with his feet, put the timber in place once more, sprang onto it and managed to get his hand over the roof guttering. 'O Lord, don't let it come away, let it hold.' He gripped the guttering, then got one knee onto the roof. The sentry was coming. Vasily lay flat and froze. The sentry did not notice anything and continued on his way. Vasily leapt to his feet. The iron roof clattered beneath his feet. One more step, a second, and there was the wall in front of him. He could reach out and touch it. One hand, then the other, then he stretched up, and he was on the top of the wall. If only he didn't smash himself to bits now, jumping down. Vasily turned round, hung by both arms, stretched out as far as he could, and let go one hand, then the other. 'Lord be praised!' – he was on the ground. And the ground was soft.

His legs were undamaged and he ran off.

When he reached his house at the edge of the town Malanya opened the door to him, and he crawled under the warm patchwork quilt which was impregnated with the smell of sweat.

X

PYOTR NIKOLAYEVICH'S sturdy, attractive wife, ever placid, childless, plump, like a barren cow, watched from the window as the peasants murdered her husband and dragged his body away somewhere into the fields. The sensation of terror which Natalya Ivanovna (such was the name of Sventitsky's widow) experienced at the sight of this slaughter was – as is always the case – so powerful that it stifled all her other emotions. However, when the crowd of peasants had gone out of sight behind the garden fence and the hubbub of their voices had died away, and the barefooted girl Malanya, who worked for them, came running in wide-eyed as if to announce some glad tidings, with the news that they had murdered Pyotr Nikolayevich and thrown his body into the ravine, Natalya Ivanovna's initial feeling of terror began to be mingled with something different: a feeling of joy at her liberation from the despot, eyes hidden behind his tinted spectacles, who had kept her in slavery these past nineteen years. She was horrified at this feeling and did not even acknowledge it to herself, but tried all the more not to let anyone else know about it. When they washed his yellow, mutilated, hairy corpse and dressed it and placed it in the coffin she was overcome with horror, and she wept and sobbed. When the examining magistrate responsible for serious crimes came down and questioned her as a witness, she saw before her, right there in the investigator's office, the two peasants now in fetters who had been identified as the principal culprits. One of them was quite an old man, with a long, wavy white beard and a calm, sternly handsome face; the other looked like a gypsy, a youngish man with shining dark eyes and curly, tousled hair. She testified that as far as she knew these were the very same men who had been the first to seize Pyotr Nikolayevich by the arms, and despite the fact that the gypsy-like peasant turned his flashing eyes under his contorted brow directly upon her and said reproachfully 'It's a sin, lady! Ah, we shall all have to die one day' – in spite of that she felt no pity whatever for them. On the contrary, as the investigation went on there arose within her a feeling of hostility and a desire to revenge herself on her husband's murderers.

But when a month later the case, which had been transferred to a military tribunal, ended with eight men being condemned to penal servitude and the two men – the white-bearded old man and the dark-skinned 'gypsy lad', as they called him – being sentenced to be hanged, she experienced a most disagreeable feeling. But this disagreeable feeling of doubt was now quickly dissipated under the influence of the solemn ritual of the courtroom. If the higher authorities considered this to be necessary, then it must all be for the best.

The executions were to be carried out in the village. And returning from Mass one Sunday in her new dress and new shoes, Malanya informed her mistress that they were putting up a gallows, that an executioner was expected to arrive from Moscow by Wednesday, and that the two men's relatives were wailing without ceasing, so that you could hear them all over the village.

Natalya Ivanovna stayed indoors so as not to see the gallows or the local people, and her only wish was that what must be done should soon be over. She thought solely of herself, and not at all about the condemned men and their families.

XI

ON THE TUESDAY Natalya Ivanovna received a visit from the district superintendent, a friend of hers. Natalya Ivanovna entertained him with vodka and mushrooms she had pickled herself. The district superintendent drank his vodka and enjoyed some of the snacks, and then informed her that the executions would not be taking place tomorrow.

'What? How is that?'

'It's an extraordinary story. They have been unable to supply an executioner. There was one in Moscow but he, so my son tells me, got to reading the Gospels, and now he says that he can't kill anybody. He himself was condemned to hard labour for murder, but now all of a sudden – he can't kill someone even if it's legal. They told him he would be flogged. Flog me, he says, but I still can't do it.'

Natalya Ivanovna suddenly went red, and actually began to perspire because of what she was thinking.

'But would it be impossible to pardon them now?'

'How can they be pardoned when they have been sentenced by the court? Only the Tsar can grant pardons.'

'But how would the Tsar ever find out about them?'

'They have the right to appeal for mercy.'

'But it's on my account that they're being executed,' said Natalya Ivanovna, who was not very intelligent. 'And I forgive them.'

The district superintendent burst out laughing.

'Well then, why don't you lodge an appeal?'

'Can I do that?'

'Certainly you can.'

'But won't it be too late to get it to him now?'

'You could send it by telegram.'

'To the Tsar?'

'Of course, you can send a telegram even to the Tsar.' The discovery that the executioner had refused to do his duty and was ready to suffer rather than kill anybody brought about a sudden upheaval in Natalya Ivanovna's soul, and the feeling of sympathy and horror which had come close to breaking out on several occasions, now burst its way into the open and took possession of her.

'Filipp Vasilyevich my dear, please write the telegram for me. I want to ask the Tsar to show mercy to them.'

The district superintendent shook his head. 'What if we were to get into trouble over this?'

'But I'll be the one responsible. I won't say anything about you at all.'

'What a kind woman she is,' thought the district superintendent, 'a good-hearted woman. If only my wife was like that, it would be heaven – quite different from the way things are.'

And so the district superintendent composed a telegram to the Tsar: 'To His Imperial Majesty the Sovereign Emperor. Your Imperial Majesty's loyal subject, widow of the Collegiate Assessor Pyotr Nikolayevich Sventitsky who was murdered by peasants, prostrating herself at Your Imperial Majesty's sacred feet' (the district superintendent was particularly pleased with this bit of the telegram he had composed) 'begs You to have mercy on the men condemned to death, the peasants so-and-so and so-and-so, of such-and-such a province, region, district and village.'

The district superintendent sent off the telegram in person, and Natalya Ivanovna's soul was filled with joy and happiness. It seemed to her that if she, the widow of the murdered man, was ready to forgive and to ask for mercy, then the Tsar could not fail to show mercy too.

XII

LIZA YEROPKINA was living on a plateau of continuous exaltation. The further she travelled along the Christian way of life which had been revealed to her, the more certain was she that this way was the true one, and the more jubilant did her soul become.

Now she had two immediate objectives in view. The first was to convert Makhin, or rather, as she expressed it to herself, to return him to his true self, to his own good and beautiful nature. She loved him, and by the light of her love she was able to perceive the divine element in his soul, common to all human beings, yet she saw in this fundamental element of life shared by all men and women a goodness, a tenderness and a distinction which were his alone. Her other objective was to cease to be rich. She had wanted to get free of her property in order to put Makhin to the test, but beyond that she desired to do this for her own sake, for the sake of her soul – and she wanted to do it according to the principles of the Gospel. She started the process by planning to give away her land, but she was thwarted in putting this idea into practice first by her father, and then even more so by the flood of suppliants who applied to her in person or in writing. Then she decided to turn to an Elder, a man well known for the holiness of his life, and to ask him to take her money and to use it in whatever way he thought fitting. On hearing of this her father was very angry, and in a furious exchange he called her a madwoman and a psychopath, and announced his intention of taking steps to protect her from herself, as a person of unsound mind.

Her father's irritable, exasperated tone of voice affected her powerfully and she lost control of herself, bursting into angry tears and calling him a despot, and even a monster of selfishness.

She asked her father's forgiveness and he said that he was not angry with her, but she could see that he was hurt and that inwardly he had not really forgiven her. She was unwilling to talk to Makhin about any of this. Her sister was jealous of her attachment to Makhin and had become quite estranged from her. Thus Liza had no one to share her feelings with, no one she could confide in.

'God is the one I should be confiding in,' she told herself, and as it was now Lent she decided that she would observe the Lenten fast and make her confession, telling her confessor everything and asking his advice about what she should do next.

Not far from the city there was a monastery where the Elder lived who had become famous for his way of life, his teaching, his prophecies, and the healings which were attributed to him.

The Elder had received a letter from Yeropkin senior, warning him of his daughter's visit and of her abnormal, hysterical state and expressing his confidence that the Elder would put her back on the right path – the path of the golden mean and the good Christian life lived in harmony with the existing order of things.

Tired out from his regular session of receiving visitors, the Elder nonetheless agreed to see Liza and gently counselled her to behave with moderation and to submit to the existing circumstances of her life, and to her parents. Liza said nothing, merely blushed and perspired, but when he had finished she began to speak meekly, with tears in her eyes, about the words of Christ who had said, 'Leave thy father and thy mother, and follow me'; then, becoming more and more animated, she began to explain to him her whole conception of what Christianity really meant. At first the Elder smiled slightly and brought out some conventional points of teaching, but then he fell silent and began to sigh, repeating to himself, 'O Lord, O Lord.'

'Very well then, come to me tomorrow and make your confession,' he said, blessing her with his wrinkled hand.

The next day he heard her confession, and without continuing their conversation of the previous day, sent her away, having briefly refused to take upon himself the disposal of her property.

This young woman's purity, her utter devotion to the will of God, her fervour, impressed the Elder deeply. He had long wanted to renounce the world, but the monastery needed his activities, which were a source of income for the community. And he had accepted this, although he was vaguely aware of the falsity of his position. People were turning him into a saint, a miracle-worker, but in reality he was a weak man carried along by the current of his own success. And the soul of this young woman which had just been opened to him had revealed to him the truth about his own soul. And he had seen just how far he was from what he wanted to be and from the goal towards which his heart was drawing him.

Soon after Liza's visit he withdrew to his cell, and it was only after three weeks had gone by that he emerged again into the church to conduct a service; and after the service he preached a sermon in which he reproached himself and denounced the wickedness of the world and called it to repentance.

He took to delivering a sermon every two weeks. And more and more people came to hear these sermons. And his fame as a preacher spread further and further. There was something special, bold and sincere in his sermons. And this was why he had such a powerful effect upon other people.

XIII

MEANWHILE Vasily had been carrying out his plans as he had intended. One night he and some companions got into the house of a rich man named Krasnopuzov. He knew that Krasnopuzov was a miser and a man of depraved character, and he broke into his writing-desk and stole thirty thousand rubles in cash. And Vasily did with it as he pleased. He actually stopped drinking, and gave money to poor girls so that they could get married. He financed weddings, paid off people's debts, and lay low himself. His only concern was how best to distribute the money. He even gave some to the police. And they stopped looking for him.

His heart rejoiced. And when eventually despite everything he was arrested, he laughed and boasted at his trial, saying that when it was in paunchy old Krasnopuzov's possession the money had never done any good, in fact the owner didn't know how much he'd got, 'Whereas I put the stuff into circulation and helped good folk with it.'

And his defence was so cheerful and good-hearted that the jury almost acquitted him. He was sentenced to be exiled.

He thanked the court and gave advance warning that he intended to escape.

XIV

THE TELEGRAM which Sventitsky's widow sent to the Tsar produced no effect whatever. The committee which dealt with petitions decided initially that they would not even report it to the Tsar, but then one day when the Tsar was at luncheon and the conversation turned to the Sventitsky case, the chairman of the petitions committee who was at table with the Sovereign informed him about the telegram they had received from the wife of the murdered man.

'*C'est très gentil de sa part,*'* remarked one of the ladies of the Imperial family.

---

* 'It is extremely nice of her.'

The Tsar merely sighed, shrugged his shoulders beneath their epaulettes and said, 'The law is the law.' And he held up his glass, into which a chamber-footman poured some sparkling Moselle. Everyone tried to look as though they were impressed by the wisdom of the Sovereign's remark. And nothing further was said about the telegram. And the two peasants – the old man and the young man – were hanged with the assistance of a Tatar executioner, a cruel and bestial murderer who had been summoned from Kazan especially for the purpose.

The old man's wife wanted to dress her husband's body in a white shirt, white foot-cloths and new shoes, but she was not allowed to do so and both men were buried in a single grave outside the fence of the cemetery.

'Princess Sofya Vladimirovna was telling me that he is a most wonderful preacher,' said the Tsar's mother, the Dowager Empress one day to her son. *'Faites-le venir. Il peut prêcher à la cathédrale.'**

'No, it would be better to have him preach to us here,' said the Tsar, and he gave orders that the Elder Isidor should be invited to come to the court.

All the generals and highest officials were assembled in the court chapel. A new and unusual preacher was something of an event.

---

* 'Have him sent for. He can preach at the cathedral.'

A small grey-haired, thin old man came out and cast his eye over them all. 'In the name of the Father, and of the Son, and of the Holy Ghost,' he said, and began his sermon.

To begin with all was well, but the further it went, the worse it became. '*Il devenait de plus en plus aggressif*,'* as the Empress put it immediately afterwards. He fulminated against everyone and everything. He referred to the death penalty. He said that the need for the death penalty was a symptom of bad government. Could it really be permissible, in a Christian country, to kill people?

They all looked at one another, all of them concerned exclusively about the impropriety of the sermon and about how disagreeable it was for the Sovereign, but no one said anything out loud. When Isidor had said 'Amen' the Metropolitan went up to him and asked him to come and have a word with him in private.

After his talk with the Metropolitan and the Chief Procurator of the Synod the old man was sent straight back to a monastery – not to his own monastery, but to the one at Suzdal, where the Father Superior and commandant of the prison was Father Misail.

---

* 'He grew more and more aggressive.'

XV

THEY ALL pretended that there had been nothing disagreeable about Father Isidor's sermon, and no one made any mention of it. Even the Tsar felt that the Elder's words had left no impression in his mind, nevertheless on two occasions later that day his thoughts turned to the execution of the two peasants and to the telegram sent by Sventitsky's widow appealing for their pardon. That afternoon there was a parade, followed by a drive to an outdoor fête, then a reception for ministers, then dinner, and in the evening the theatre. As usual the Tsar fell asleep the moment his head touched the pillow. That night he was wakened by a terrible dream: in a field stood a gallows with corpses dangling from it, and the corpses were sticking out their tongues, and the tongues protruded further and further. And someone was shouting, 'This is your doing, this is your doing.' The Tsar woke up sweating and started to think. For the first time ever he started to think about the responsibility which lay upon him, and all the things the little old man had said came back to him . . .

But he could see the human being within himself only as if from a great distance, and he was unable to yield to the simple demands of the human being within him because of all the other demands coming at him from all sides as Tsar; and to acknowledge the demands of the human being within as taking precedence over those of the Tsar – that was beyond his strength.

XVI

AFTER SERVING his second term in prison Prokofy (Proshka), that lively, proud, dandified young fellow, had come out an utterly broken man. When he was sober he simply sat about doing nothing, and however much his father shouted and swore at him, he went on living an idle life consuming the family's bread, and furthermore whenever he got the chance he would steal things and take them off to the tavern to get drunk on the proceeds. He lounged about, coughing, hawking and spitting. The doctor whom he went to consult listened to Prokofy's chest and shook his head.

'What you need, my lad, is what you haven't got.'

'I know that, it's what I've always needed.'

'You need to drink plenty of milk, and you mustn't smoke.'

'But it's Lent now, and anyway we don't have a cow.'

One night that spring he could not get to sleep the whole night, he felt rotten and he was longing for a drink. There was nothing in the house for him to get his hands on and sell. He put on his fur hat and went out. He walked down the street until he came to where the clergy lived. Outside the deacon's house there was a harrow standing propped up against the wattle fence. Prokofy went over, slung the harrow up onto his back and walked off with it to Petrovna at the inn. 'Maybe she'll give me just a little bottle of vodka for it.' He had not gone far before the deacon came out onto the porch of his house. It was now fully light, and he could see Prokofy making off with his harrow.

'Hey, what are you up to?'

The deacon's servants came out, seized Prokofy and threw him in the lock-up. The Justice of the Peace sentenced him to eleven months in prison.

Autumn came round. Prokofy was now transferred to the prison hospital. He was coughing all the time, fit to tear his lungs out. And he could not get warm. Those other patients must have been in better shape than he was, because they were not shivering. Prokofy, though, kept on shivering day and night. The warden was trying to economize on firewood and did not heat the prison hospital until November each year. Prokofy suffered physical agonies, but what he suffered spiritually was worse than anything. Everything seemed to him disgusting and he hated everybody: the deacon, the warden who refused to heat the hospital, the orderly, and the patient next to him who had a red, swollen lip. He also conceived a deep hatred for the new convict who was brought in to join them. This convict was Stepan. He had developed a severe inflammation of the head and had been transferred to the hospital and placed in a bed alongside Prokofy. To begin with Prokofy detested him, but later he became so fond of Stepan that his main aim in life was to have a chance of talking to him. It was only after talking to him that the pain in Prokofy's heart was ever eased.

Stepan was constantly telling the other patients about the

most recent murder he had committed and about the effect it had had on him.

'She didn't scream or anything like that,' he would tell them, 'she just said, "Here you are, cut my throat. It's not me you should feel sorry for, it's yourself."'

'Yes, I know that well enough, it's a terrible thing to do a person in. I once cut a sheep's throat, and I didn't feel too good about it myself. And here am I that's never killed anybody, but they've gone and done for me, the swine. I've never killed anybody . . .'

'Well and good, that'll be counted in your favour.'

'And where will that be then?'

'What do you mean, where? What about God then?'

'God? You don't see much of him about, do you? I don't believe all that stuff, friend. The way I see it is, you just die and the grass grows over you. And that's all about it.'

'How can you think that? I've done in that many, but she, she was kind-hearted, never did anything but help people. All right then, do you think it will be the same for me as it'll be for her? No, just you wait and see . . .'

'So you think that when you die, your soul goes on?'

'That's it. I reckon that's the truth.'

Dying was a hard process for Prokofy as he lay there gasping for breath. But when his last hour came he suddenly felt easier. He called Stepan over to him.

'Well, brother, goodbye. I can see it's time for me to die

now. I was really scared, but it's all right now. I'd just like it
to be quick.'

And Prokofy died in the prison hospital.

XVII

MEANWHILE Yevgeny Mikhailovich's business affairs were
going from bad to worse. His shop was mortgaged. Trade
refused to pick up. Another shop had opened in the town and
the interest on his mortgage was due. He had to take out another
loan to pay the interest. And in the end he was obliged to put
up the shop and all the contents for sale. Yevgeny Mikhailovich
and his wife rushed hither and thither but nowhere could they
find the four hundred rubles they needed in order to save their
business.

They had faint hopes of the merchant Krasnopuzov, whose
mistress was friendly with Yevgeny Mikhailovich's wife. But
now it was all over town that an enormous sum of money had
been stolen from Krasnopuzov. People said that it amounted to
half a million.

'And who do you think stole it?' Yevgeny Mikhailovich's
wife was saying. 'Vasily, the one who used to be our yardman.
They say he's throwing the money about all over the place, and
the police have been bribed to take no notice.'

'He never was any good,' said Yevgeny Mikhailovich. 'Look

how ready he was to perjure himself that time. I'd never have thought it of him.'

'They say he actually came round to our place one day. The cook said it was him. She says he paid the dowries for fourteen poor girls to get married.'

'Well, no doubt they're making it up.'

Just at that moment a strange-looking elderly man in a woollen jacket came into the shop.

'What do you want?'

'I've got a letter for you.'

'Who is it from?'

'It says on it.'

'I presume they will want a reply. Just wait a moment, please.'

'I can't.'

And the strange-looking man handed over the envelope and hurriedly departed.

'Extraordinary!'

Yevgeny Mikhailovich tore open the bulging envelope and could hardly believe his eyes: inside there were hundred-ruble notes. Four of them. What on earth was this? And there was a semi-literate letter addressed to Yevgeny Mikhailovich. It read:

'In the Gospel it says to retern good for evil. You did me a lot of evil with that cupon and I offended that peasant to but now I am sorry for you. So take these 4 Cathrines and remember your yardman Vasily.'

'This is absolutely amazing,' said Yevgeny Mikhailovich, to his wife and to himself. And whenever he subsequently remembered it or spoke of it to his wife, the tears would come into his eyes and her heart would be filled with joy.

XVIII

IN THE PRISON at Suzdal there were fourteen clergymen who were there primarily for having deviated from Orthodox teaching; and this was where Isidor too had been sent. Father Misail admitted Isidor in accordance with the written instructions he had received and, without interviewing him, gave the order that he should be placed in a solitary cell, as befitted a serious offender. In the third week of Isidor's stay in the prison Father Misail was making the rounds of the inmates. Going into Isidor's cell, he asked whether there was anything he needed.

'There is a great deal that I need, but I cannot talk about it in the presence of other people. Please allow me the opportunity to speak to you on your own.'

They looked at one another, and Father Misail realized that he had nothing to fear from this man. He ordered that Isidor should be brought to his cell in the monastery, and as soon as they were left alone he said:

'Well, tell me what you have to say.'

Isidor fell to his knees.

'Brother!' said Isidor, 'what are you doing? Have mercy on yourself. There cannot be a villain alive worse than you, you have profaned everything that is holy . . .'

A month later Father Misail sent in applications for the release, on the grounds of repentance, not only of Isidor, but of seven of the other prisoners, together with a request that he himself should be allowed to withdraw from the world in another monastery.

XIX

TEN YEARS went by.

Mitya Smokovnikov had long since graduated from the technical institute and was now working as an engineer on a large salary in the Siberian gold-mines. He was due to go on a prospecting trip in a certain area. The mine director recommended that he should take with him the convict Stepan Pelageyushkin.

'But why should I take a convict with me? Won't that be dangerous?'

'There's nothing dangerous about him. He's a holy man. Ask anyone you like.'

'So why is he here?'

The director smiled.

'He murdered six people, but he's a holy man. I'll vouch for him absolutely.'

And so Mitya agreed to take Stepan, now bald, thin and weather-beaten, and they set off together.

On the journey Stepan looked after everybody's needs as far as he could, and he looked after Mitya Smokovnikov as if Mitya had been his own offspring; and as they travelled on he told Smokovnikov his whole story. And he told him how, and why, and on what lines he was living now.

And it was a very strange thing. Mitya Smokovnikov, who until that time had lived only to eat and drink, to play cards, and to enjoy wine and women, fell to thinking for the first time about his own life. And these thoughts of his would not leave him, in fact they started an upheaval in his soul which spread out wider and wider. He was offered a job which would have brought him great benefits. He turned it down and decided to settle for what he had, to buy an estate, to get married, and to serve the common people as best he could.

XX

AND SO he did. But first he went to see his father, with whom his relations were strained on account of his father's new wife and family. Now, however, he had decided to make things up with his father. And so he did. And his father was quite astonished, and ridiculed him at first, but then he stopped criticizing his son and recalled the many, many occasions when he had been at fault with regard to him.

Esarhaddon, King of Assyria*

THE ASSYRIAN KING, Esarhaddon, had conquered the kingdom of King Lailie, had destroyed and burnt the towns, taken all the inhabitants captive to his own country, slaughtered the warriors, beheaded some chieftains and impaled or flayed others, and had confined King Lailie himself in a cage.

As he lay on his bed one night, King Esarhaddon was thinking how he should execute Lailie, when suddenly he heard a rustling

---

* In this story Tolstoy has used the names of real people. Esarhaddon (or Assur-akhi-iddina) is mentioned three times in the Bible (2 Kings xix, 37; Isaiah xxxvii, 38, and Ezra iv, 2), and is also alluded to. in 2 Chronicles xxxiii, 11, as, 'the King of Assyria, which took Manasseh in chains, and bound him with fetters, and carried him to Babylon'. His son, Assur-bani-pal, whom he promoted to power before his own death, is once mentioned in the Bible, under the name of Asnappar (Ezra iv, 10). Of Lailie history does not tell us much; but in Ernest A. Budge's *History of Esarhaddon* we read: 'A King, called Lailie, asked that the gods which Esarhaddon had captured from him might be restored. His request was granted, and Esarhaddon said, "I spoke to him of brotherhood, and entrusted to him the sovereignty of the districts of Bazu."'

near his bed, and opening his eyes saw an old man with a long grey beard and mild eyes.

'You wish to execute Lailie?' asked the old man.

'Yes,' answered the King. 'But I cannot make up my mind how to do it.'

'But you are Lailie,' said the old man.

'That's not true,' replied the King. 'Lailie is Lailie, and I am I.'

'You and Lailie are one,' said the old man. 'You only imagine you are not Lailie, and that Lailie is not you.'

'What do you mean by that?' said the King. 'Here am I, lying on a soft bed; around me are obedient men-slaves and women-slaves, and tomorrow I shall feast with my friends as I did today; whereas Lailie is sitting like a bird in a cage, and tomorrow he will be impaled, and with his tongue hanging out will struggle till he dies, and his body will be torn in pieces by dogs.'

'You cannot destroy his life,' said the old man.

'And how about the fourteen thousand warriors I killed, with whose bodies I built a mound?' said the King. 'I am alive, but they no longer exist. Does not that prove that I can destroy life?'

'How do you know they no longer exist?'

'Because I no longer see them. And, above all, they were tormented, but I was not. It was ill for them, but well for me.'

'That, also, only seems so to you. You tortured yourself, but not them.'

'I do not understand,' said the King.

'Do you wish to understand?'

'Yes, I do.'

'Then come here,' said the old man, pointing to a large font full of water.

The King rose and approached the font.

'Strip, and enter the font.'

Esarhaddon did as the old man bade him.

'As soon as I begin to pour this water over you,' said the old man, filling a pitcher with the water, 'dip down your head.'

The old man tilted the pitcher over the King's head, and the King bent his head till it was under water.

And as soon as King Esarhaddon was under the water, he felt that he was no longer Esarhaddon, but someone else. And, feeling himself to be that other man, he saw himself lying on a rich bed, beside a beautiful woman. He had never seen her before, but he knew she was his wife. The woman raised herself and said to him:

'Dear husband, Lailie! You were wearied by yesterday's work and have slept longer than usual, and I have guarded your rest, and have not roused you. But now the Princes await you in the Great Hall. Dress and go out to them.'

And Esarhaddon – understanding from these words that he was Lailie, and not feeling at all surprised at this, but only wondering that he did not know it before – rose, dressed, and went into the Great Hall where the Princes awaited him.

The Princes greeted Lailie, their King, bowing to the ground, and then they rose, and at his word sat down before him; and the eldest of the Princes began to speak, saying that it was impossible longer to endure the insults of the wicked King Esarhaddon, and that they must make war on him. But Lailie disagreed, and gave orders that envoys should be sent to remonstrate with King Esarhaddon; and he dismissed the Princes from the audience. Afterwards he appointed men of note to act as ambassadors, and impressed on them what they were to say to King Esarhaddon. Having finished this business, Esarhaddon – feeling himself to be Lailie – rode out to hunt wild asses. The hunt was successful. He killed two wild asses himself, and, having returned home, feasted with his friends, and witnessed a dance of slave-girls. The next day he went to the Court, where he was awaited by petitioners, suitors, and prisoners brought for trial; and there as usual he decided the cases submitted to him. Having finished this business, he again rode out to his favourite amusement: the hunt. And again he was successful: this time killing with his own hand an old lioness, and capturing her two cubs. After the hunt he again feasted with his friends, and was entertained with music and dances, and the night he spent with the wife whom he loved.

So, dividing his time between kingly duties and pleasures, he lived for days and weeks, awaiting the return of the ambassadors he had sent to that King Esarhaddon who used to be himself. Not till a month had passed did the ambassadors return, and they returned with their noses and ears cut off.

King Esarhaddon had ordered them to tell Lailie that what had been done to them — the ambassadors — would be done to King Lailie himself also, unless he sent immediately a tribute of silver, gold, and cypress-wood, and came himself to pay homage to King Esarhaddon.

Lailie, formerly Esarhaddon, again assembled the Princes, and took counsel with them as to what he should do. They all with one accord said that war must be made against Esarhaddon, without waiting for him to attack them. The King agreed; and taking his place at the head of the army, started on the campaign. The campaign lasts seven days. Each day the King rode round the army to rouse the courage of his warriors. On the eighth day his army met that of Esarhaddon in a broad valley through which a river flowed. Lailie's army fought bravely, but Lailie, formerly Esarhaddon, saw the enemy swarming down from the mountains like ants, over-running the valley and overwhelming his army; and, in his chariot, he flung himself into the midst of the battle, hewing and felling the enemy. But the warriors of Lailie were but as hundreds, while those of Esarhaddon were as thousands; and Lailie felt himself wounded and taken prisoner. Nine days he journeyed with other captives, bound, and guarded by the warriors of Esarhaddon. On the tenth day he reached Nineveh, and was placed in a cage. Lailie suffered not so much from hunger and from his wound as from shame and impotent rage. He felt how powerless he was to avenge himself on his enemy for all he was suffering. All he could do was to deprive his enemies of the pleasure of seeing his sufferings; and he firmly resolved to endure courageously, without a murmur, all they could do to him. For twenty days he sat in his cage, awaiting execution. He saw his relatives and friends led out to death; he heard the groans of those who were executed: some had their hands and feet cut off, others were flayed alive, but he showed neither disquietude, nor pity, nor fear. He saw the wife he loved, bound, and led by two black eunuchs. He knew she was being taken as a slave to Esarhaddon. That, too, he bore without a murmur. But one of the guards placed to watch him said, 'I pity you, Lailie; you were a king, but what are you now?' And hearing these words, Lailie remembered all he had lost. He clutched the bars of his cage, and, wishing to kill himself, beat his head against them. But he had not the strength to do so; and, groaning in despair, he fell upon the floor of his cage.

At last two executioners opened his cage door, and having strapped his arms tight behind him, led him to the place of execution, which was soaked with blood. Lailie saw a sharp stake dripping with blood, from which the corpse of one of his friends had just been torn, and he understood that this had been done that the stake might serve for his own execution. They stripped Lailie of his clothes. He was startled at the leanness of his once strong, handsome body. The two executioners seized that body by its lean thighs; they lifted him up and were about to let him fall upon the stake.

'This is death, destruction!' thought Lailie, and, forgetful of his resolve to remain bravely calm to the end, he sobbed and prayed for mercy. But no one listened to him.

'But this cannot be,' thought he. 'Surely I am asleep. It is a dream.' And he made an effort to rouse himself, and did indeed awake, to find himself neither Esarhaddon nor Lailie – but some kind of an animal. He was astonished that he was an animal, and astonished, also, at not having known this before.

He was grazing in a valley, tearing the tender grass with his teeth, and brushing away flies with his long tail. Around him was frolicking a long-legged, dark-grey ass-colt, striped down its back. Kicking up its hind legs, the colt galloped full speed to Esarhaddon, and poking him under the stomach with its smooth little muzzle, searched for the teat, and, finding it, quieted down, swallowing regularly. Esarhaddon understood that he was a she-ass, the colt's mother, and this neither surprised nor grieved him, but rather gave him pleasure. He experienced a glad feeling of simultaneous life in himself and in his offspring.

But suddenly something flew near with a whistling sound and hit him in the side, and with its sharp point entered his skin and flesh. Feeling a burning pain, Esarhaddon – who was at the same time the ass – tore the udder from the colt's teeth, and laying back his ears galloped to the herd from which he had strayed. The colt kept up with him, galloping by his side. They had already nearly reached the herd, which had started off, when another arrow in full flight struck the colt's neck. It pierced the skin and quivered in its flesh. The colt sobbed piteously and fell upon its knees. Esarhaddon could not abandon it, and remained standing over it. The colt rose, tottered on its long, thin legs, and again fell. A fearful two-legged being – a man – ran up and cut its throat.

'This cannot be; it is still a dream!' thought Esarhaddon, and made a last effort to awake. 'Surely I am not Lailie, nor the ass, but Esarhaddon!'

He cried out, and at the same instant lifted his head out of the font . . . The old man was standing by him, pouring over his head the last drops from the pitcher.

'Oh, how terribly I have suffered! And for how long!' said Esarhaddon.

'Long?' replied the old man. 'You have only dipped your head under water and lifted it again; see, the water is not yet all out of the pitcher. Do you now understand?'

Esarhaddon did not reply, but only looked at the old man with terror.

'Do you now understand,' continued the old man, 'that Lailie is you, and the warriors you put to death were you also? And not the warriors only, but the animals which you slew when hunting and ate at your feasts, were also you. You thought life dwelt in you alone, but I have drawn aside the veil of delusion, and have let you see that by doing evil to others you have done it to yourself also. Life is one in them all, and yours is but a portion of this same common life. And only in that one part of life that is yours, can you make life better or worse – increasing or decreasing it. You can only improve life in yourself by destroying the barriers that divide your life from that of others, and by considering others as yourself, and loving them. By so doing you increase your share of life. You injure your life when you think of it as the only life, and try to add to its welfare at the expense of other lives. By so doing you only lessen it. To destroy the life that dwells in others is beyond your power. The life of those you have slain has vanished from your eyes, but is not destroyed. You thought to lengthen your own life and to shorten theirs, but you cannot do this. Life knows neither time nor space. The life of a moment, and the life of a thousand years: your life, and the life of all the visible and invisible beings in the world, are equal. To destroy life, or to alter it, is impossible; for life is the one thing that exists. All else, but seems to us to be.'

Having said this the old man vanished.

Next morning King Esarhaddon gave orders that Lailie and all the prisoners should be set at liberty, and that the executions should cease.

On the third day he called his son Assur-bani-pal, and gave the kingdom over into his hands; and he himself went into the desert to think over all he had learnt. Afterwards he went about as a wanderer through the towns and villages, preaching to the people that all life is one, and that when men wish to harm others, they really do evil to themselves.

Three Questions

I T ONCE OCCURRED to a certain king, that if he always knew the right time to begin everything; if he knew who were the right people to listen to, and whom to avoid; and, above all, if he always knew what was the most important thing to do, he would never fail in anything he might undertake.

And this thought having occurred to him, he had it proclaimed throughout his kingdom that he would give a great reward to anyone who would teach him what was the right time for every action, and who were the most necessary people, and how he might know what was the most important thing to do.

And learned men came to the King, but they all answered his questions differently.

In reply to the first question, some said that to know the right time for every action, one must draw up in advance, a table of days, months and years, and must live strictly according to it. Only thus, said they, could everything be done at its proper time. Others declared that it was impossible to decide beforehand the right time for every action; but that, not letting oneself be absorbed in idle pastimes, one should always attend to all that was going on, and then do what was most needful. Others, again, said that however attentive the King might be to what was going on, it was impossible for one man to decide correctly the right time for every action, but that he should have a Council of wise men, who would help him to fix the proper time for everything.

But then again others said there were some things which could not wait to be laid before a Council, but about which one had at once to decide whether to undertake them or not. But in order to decide that, one must know beforehand what was going to happen. It is only magicians who know that; and, therefore, in order to know the right time for every action, one must consult magicians.

Equally various were the answers to the second question. Some said, the people the King most needed were his councillors; others, the priests; others, the doctors; while some said the warriors were the most necessary.

To the third question, as to what was the most important occupation: some replied that the most important thing in the world was science. Others said it was skill in warfare; and others, again, that it was religious worship.

All the answers being different, the King agreed with none of them, and gave the reward to none. But still wishing to find the right answers to his questions, he decided to consult a hermit, widely renowned for his wisdom.

The hermit lived in a wood which he never quitted, and he received none but common folk. So the King put on simple clothes, and before reaching the hermit's cell dismounted from his horse, and, leaving his bodyguard behind, went on alone.

When the King approached, the hermit was digging the ground in front of his hut. Seeing the King, he greeted him and went on digging. The hermit was frail and weak, and each time he stuck his spade into the ground and turned a little earth, he breathed heavily.

The King went up to him and said: 'I have come to you, wise hermit, to ask you to answer three questions: How can I learn to do the right thing at the right time? Who are the people I most need, and to whom should I, therefore, pay more attention than to the rest? And, what affairs are the most important, and need my first attention?'

The hermit listened to the King, but answered nothing. He just spat on his hand and recommenced digging.

'You are tired,' said the King, 'let me take the spade and work awhile for you.'

'Thanks!' said the hermit, and, giving the spade to the King, he sat down on the ground.

When he had dug two beds, the King stopped and repeated his questions. The hermit again gave no answer, but rose, stretched out his hand for the spade, and said:

'Now rest awhile – and let me work a bit.'

But the King did not give him the spade, and continued to dig. One hour passed, and another. The sun began to sink behind the trees, and the King at last stuck the spade into the ground, and said:

'I came to you, wise man, for an answer to my questions. If you can give me none, tell me so, and I will return home.'

'Here comes someone running,' said the hermit, 'let us see who it is.'

The King turned round, and saw a bearded man come running out of the wood. The man held his hands pressed against his stomach, and blood was flowing from under them. When he reached the King, he fell fainting on the ground moaning feebly. The King and the hermit unfastened the man's clothing. There was a large wound in his stomach. The King washed it as best he could, and bandaged it with his handkerchief and with a towel the hermit had. But the blood would not stop flowing, and the King again and again removed the bandage soaked with warm blood, and washed and rebandaged the wound. When at last the blood ceased flowing, the man revived and asked for something to drink. The King brought fresh water and gave it to him. Meanwhile the sun had set, and it had become cool. So the King, with the hermit's help, carried the wounded man into the hut and laid him on the bed. Lying on the bed the man closed his eyes and was quiet; but the King was so tired with his walk and with the work he had done, that he crouched down on the threshold, and also fell asleep – so soundly that he slept all through the short summer night. When he awoke in the morning, it was long before he could remember where he was, or who was the strange bearded man lying on the bed and gazing intently at him with shining eyes.

'Forgive me!' said the bearded man in a weak voice, when he saw that the King was awake and was looking at him.

'I do not know you, and have nothing to forgive you for,' said the King.

'You do not know me, but I know you. I am that enemy of yours who swore to revenge himself on you, because you executed his brother and seized his property. I knew you had gone alone to see the hermit, and I resolved to kill you on your way back. But the day passed and you did not return. So I came out from my ambush to find you, and I came upon your bodyguard, and they recognized me, and wounded me. I escaped from them, but should have bled to death had you not dressed my wound. I wished to kill you, and you have saved my life. Now, if I live, and if you wish it, I will serve you as your most faithful slave, and will bid my sons do the same. Forgive me!'

The King was very glad to have made peace with his enemy so easily, and to have gained him for a friend, and he not only forgave him, but said he would send his servants and his own physician to attend him, and promised to restore his property.

Having taken leave of the wounded man, the King went out into the porch and looked around for the hermit. Before going away he wished once more to beg an answer to the questions he had put. The hermit was outside, on his knees, sowing seeds in the beds that had been dug the day before.

The King approached him, and said:

'For the last time, I pray you to answer my questions, wise man.'

'You have already been answered!' said the hermit still crouching on his thin legs, and looking up at the King, who stood before him.

'How answered? What do you mean?' asked the King.

'Do you not see?' replied the hermit. 'If you had not pitied my weakness yesterday, and had not dug these beds for me, but had gone your way, that man would have attacked you, and you would have repented of not having stayed with me. So the most important time was when you were digging the beds; and I was the most important man; and to do me good was your most important business. Afterwards, when that man ran to us, the most important time was when you were attending to him, for if you had not bound up his wounds he would have died without having made peace with you. So he was the most important man, and what you did for him was your most important business. Remember then: there is only one time that is important – Now! It is the most important time because it is the only time when we have any power.

The most necessary man is he with whom you are, for no man knows whether he will ever have dealings with anyone else: and the most important affair is, to do him good, because for that purpose alone was man sent into this life!'

Work, Death and Sickness

A Legend

THIS IS A LEGEND current among the South American
Indians.

God, say they, at first made men so that they had no need
to work: they needed neither houses, nor clothes, nor food, and
they all lived till they were a hundred, and did not know what
illness was.

When, after some time, God looked to see how people were
living, he saw that instead of being happy in their life, they had
quarrelled with one another, and, each caring for himself, had
brought matters to such a pass that far from enjoying life, they
cursed it.

Then God said to himself: 'This comes of their living separ-
ately, each for himself.' And to change this state of things, God
so arranged matters that it became impossible for people to live

without working. To avoid suffering from cold and hunger, they were now obliged to build dwellings, and to dig the ground, and to grow and gather fruits and grain.

'Work will bring them together,' thought God. 'They cannot make their tools, prepare and transport their timber, build their houses, sow and gather their harvests, spin and weave, and make their clothes, each one alone by himself.

'It will make them understand that the more heartily they work together, the more they will have and the better they will live; and this will unite them.'

Time passed on, and again God came to see how men were living, and whether they were now happy.

But he found them living worse than before. They worked together (that they could not help doing), but not all together, being broken up into little groups. And each group tried to snatch work from other groups, and they hindered one another, wasting time and strength in their struggles, so that things went ill with them all.

Having seen that this, too, was not well, God decided so to arrange things that man should not know the time of his death, but might die at any moment; and he announced this to them.

'Knowing that each of them may die at any moment,' thought God, 'they will not, by grasping at gains that may last so short a time, spoil the hours of life allotted to them.'

But it turned out otherwise. When God returned to see how people were living, he saw that their life was as bad as ever.

Those who were strongest, availing themselves of the fact that men might die at any time, subdued those who were weaker, killing some and threatening others with death. And it came about that the strongest and their descendants did no work, and suffered from the weariness of idleness, while those who were weaker had to work beyond their strength, and suffered from lack of rest. Each set of men feared and hated the other. And the life of man became yet more unhappy.

Having seen all this, God, to mend matters, decided to make use of one last means; he sent all kinds of sickness among men. God thought that when all men were exposed to sickness they would understand that those who are well should have pity on those who are sick, and should help them, that when they themselves fall ill, those who are well might in turn help them.

And again God went away; but when He came back to see how men lived now that they were subject to sicknesses, he saw that their life was worse even than before. The very sickness that in God's purpose should have united men, had divided them more than ever. Those men who were strong enough to make others work, forced them also to wait on them in times of sickness; but they did not, in their turn, look after others who were ill. And those who were forced to work for others and to look after them when sick, were so worn with work that they had no time to look after their own sick, but left them without attendance. That the sight of sick folk might not disturb the pleasures of the wealthy, houses were arranged in which these poor people suffered and died, far from those whose sympathy might have cheered them, and in the arms of hired people who nursed them without compassion, or even with disgust. Moreover, people considered many of the illnesses infectious, and, fearing to catch them, not only avoided the sick, but even separated themselves from those who attended the sick.

Then God said to Himself: 'If even this means will not bring men to understand wherein their happiness lies, let them be taught by suffering.' And God left men to themselves.

And, left to themselves, men lived long before they understood that they all ought to, and might be, happy. Only in the very latest times have a few of them begun to understand that work ought not to be a bugbear to some and like galley-slavery for others, but should be a common and happy occupation, uniting all men. They have begun to understand that with death constantly threatening each of us, the only reasonable business of every man is to spend the years, months, hours, and minutes, allotted him – in unity and love. They have begun to understand that sickness, far from dividing men, should, on the contrary, give opportunity for loving union with one another.

After the Ball

'WHAT YOU ARE saying is, that a man is incapable of deciding for himself what is good and what is bad, that everything depends on the environment, that man is the victim of his environment. But as I see it, everything really depends on chance. Listen, I will tell you about something that happened to me personally . . .'

These words were spoken by our universally respected Ivan Vasilyevich at the end of a discussion we had been having about whether, in order to achieve individual perfection in life, it was first necessary to alter the conditions in which people live. In fact no one had actually argued that it is impossible to decide for oneself what is good and what is bad, but Ivan Vasilyevich had a curious way of answering questions of his own which had arisen in the course of discussion, and using these thoughts of his as a pretext for telling us about episodes which had occurred in his own life. He would frequently lose sight of the reason which had originally set off his narrative, and get carried away by the story, all the more so since he was an exceptionally sincere and truthful story-teller.

And so it was on this particular occasion.

'I will tell you about something that happened to me personally. My whole life has been like this – not influenced at all by environment, but by something else altogether.'

'By what, then?' we asked him.

'Well, it's a long story. It will take some telling if you are really going to understand.'

'Then please go on, and tell us.'

Ivan Vasilyevich reflected for a moment, then nodded his head.

'Yes,' he said, 'my whole life was changed by what happened one night, or rather one morning.'

'So what was it?'

'The thing was, I had fallen deeply in love. I had been in love many times before, but this time my feelings were something far stronger. It's a long time ago now; she even has married daughters of her own. Her family name was B———, yes, Varenka B———' (here Ivan Vasilyevich mentioned the family name). 'Even at fifty she was still an outstanding beauty. But when she was young, at eighteen, she was absolutely enchanting: tall, shapely, graceful, and imposing – yes, really imposing. She always held herself very erect, as though it was not in her nature to do otherwise, with her head thrown slightly back, and this, together with her beauty and her tall stature, and despite her thinness, boniness even, gave her a sort of regal air which might have been intimidating, had it not been for the charming, always joyful smile of her mouth and her wonderful shining eyes, and the general effect of her lovely, youthful being.'

'What a picture Ivan Vasilyevich is painting for us!'

'Well, describe her as I may, it is impossible by describing her to make you see her as she really was. But that is not the point. The events I want to tell you about took place in the 1840s. At that time I was a student at a provincial university. Whether it was a good thing or a bad thing I have no idea, but in those days our university contained no intellectual groups, no theories whatever; we were simply young men and we lived as young men typically do – studying, and enjoying ourselves too. I was a very jolly, lively young fellow, and well off into the bargain. I was the owner of a really spirited horse, an ambler; I used to go tobogganing with the young ladies (skating having not yet come into fashion); and I was much given to celebrating with my companions (in those days we never drank anything but champagne; and if there was no money we didn't drink at all – we never drank vodka instead, as they do nowadays). And my chief delight was going to evening parties and balls. I was a good dancer, and not at all bad-looking.'

'Come now, there's no need to be quite so modest,' put in one of the ladies in our company. 'We are quite familiar with your daguerreotype portrait. It isn't true to say that you were not bad-looking – you were handsome.'

'That is as may be, but that is not the point either. What matters is that just as my love for her was reaching its peak, on the last day of Shrovetide, I attended a ball at the house of the district marshal of the nobility, a genial old man who was wealthy, well known for his hospitality, and a chamberlain at court. His wife, as good-natured as he was, received the guests wearing a puce-coloured velvet gown, a diamond ferronnière on her forehead, and with her ageing, puffy shoulders and bosom on display, as in those portraits of the Empress Elizaveta Petrovna. It was a splendid ball: a beautiful ball-room with galleries for the musicians, and an orchestra, well known at that time, which was made up of serfs belonging to a landowner who was an amateur musician, and a veritable ocean of champagne. Although I was fond of champagne I didn't drink any, for I was already drunk without wine, drunk with love; but I still danced to the point of exhaustion – quadrilles, waltzes, polkas; and as far as possible of course, I danced them with Varenka. She was wearing a white dress with a pink sash, white kid gloves reaching almost to her slender, pointed elbows, and white satin shoes. The mazurka was filched from me by a most unpleasant engineer by the name of Anisimov – even today I cannot forgive him – who had asked her for this dance almost the moment she arrived, whereas I came in late, having called at the hairdresser's to collect my gloves. So I did not dance the mazurka with her, but with a German girl whom I had been pursuing some time before. But I'm afraid I treated her quite rudely that evening – not talking to her, not looking at her: I had eyes only for that tall, shapely figure in the white dress with the pink sash, her flushed, radiant face with its dimples, and her gentle, affectionate eyes. I wasn't the only one either: everybody looked at her and admired her, men and women alike, though she eclipsed them all. It was impossible not to admire her.

'By decree, so to speak, I danced the mazurka with someone else, but in fact I danced practically all the rest of the time with her. Without the least sign of embarrassment she would walk the whole length of the ball-room and come up to me, and I would jump up from my seat without waiting to be asked, and she would thank me with a smile for my quick-wittedness. When we were led before her so that she could choose a partner, and she was unable to guess the particular "quality" I was supposed to be representing, she was obliged to give her hand to some other young man, but she shrugged her slender shoulders and smiled at me as a sign of her regret and as a consolation.

'When the figures of the mazurka were being danced to a waltz I danced with her for quite a long time and she, breathless and smiling, said to me "encore". And I waltzed on and on with her until I was hardly aware of my body at all . . .'

'What do you mean, you were hardly aware of your body? I should think you were well aware of it when you had your arm round her waist; and not just your body, but hers as well,' said one of the guests.

Ivan Vasilyevich suddenly blushed, and replied with annoyance, almost shouting: 'Yes, that's modern young people for you. You don't see anything except the body. In our day it was not like that. The more deeply I was in love, the more disembodied she became for me. Nowadays you look at women's feet, their ankles, and more besides: you mentally undress the women you are in love with; but for me, as Alphonse Karr would say – he was a good writer, too – the object of my love was always clad in robes of bronze. Not only did we not undress them in our minds, we did our best to cover their nakedness, like the virtuous son of Noah in the Bible. But of course you wouldn't understand that . . .'

'Don't bother with him. What happened next?' said one of us.

'Yes. So there I was dancing with her, and losing all sense of time. The musicians were by now pretty desperately tired, you know how it is towards the end of a ball, and they kept on repeating the same section of a mazurka, and the mothers and fathers had already got up from the card-tables and were waiting for supper to be served, and the man-servants were running about faster than ever, carrying things. It was gone two o'clock. I had to make the most of those last minutes. Yet again I asked her to dance, and for the hundredth time we floated down the ball-room.

'"So may I have the quadrille after supper?" I asked as I led her back to her seat.

'"Of course, if they don't take me home before then," she said, smiling.

'"I won't allow it," I said.

'"Hand me my fan," she said.

'"It makes me sad even to do that," I said as I returned her simple white fan to her.

'"Well, here you are, just so that you won't grieve," she said, plucking a feather from the fan and giving it to me.

'I took the feather, and could only by a look express my delight and gratitude. I was not only happy and content, I was in a state of bliss, full of goodwill to all; I was no longer myself, but some unearthly being who had no knowledge of evil and was capable only of doing good. I hid away the feather in my glove and stood there, without the strength to walk away from her.

'"Look, they are trying to get papa to dance," she said to me, pointing to the tall, stately figure of her father, a colonel in silver epaulettes, standing in the doorway with the hostess and some other ladies.

'"Varenka, come over here," we heard the hostess, with her diamond ferronnière and Empress Elizaveta shoulders, calling in a loud voice.

'Varenka went across to the doorway, and I followed.

'"Do persuade your father to take a turn with you, *ma chère*. Come, Pyotr Vladislavich, do please dance with her," said the hostess to the Colonel.

'Varenka's father was a very handsome, stately, tall and

youthful-looking elderly man. His face had a high colour, he had white, curled moustaches *à la* Nicholas I, with white side-whiskers curving down to meet them, and his hair was combed forward over his temples; and the same joyful smile as his daughter's played in his brilliant eyes and around his lips. He was splendidly built, his broad chest thrust out in the military manner and adorned with just the right quantity of medals, his shoulders powerful, his legs long and well-shaped. He was a military commander with all the bearing of a veteran of the time of Nicholas I.

'As we approached the doorway the Colonel was making excuses, saying that he had quite forgotten the art of dancing; nevertheless he smiled, reached across with his right hand to draw his sword from its scabbard and handed it to an obliging young man; and putting a suede glove on his right hand – "all according to regulations" as he said with a smile – he took his daughter's hand and made a quarter turn, waiting for the music to strike up.

'As soon as the music of the mazurka began, he stamped one foot smartly on the floor and advanced the other, and his tall, bulky figure began, now gently and smoothly, now noisily and energetically with a clicking of soles and of one boot against the other, to move around the ball-room. The graceful figure of Varenka sailed along beside him, imperceptibly shortening or lengthening the steps of her little feet in their white satin shoes. The whole room followed the couple's every movement.

I gazed at them not just with admiration, but with a feeling of rapturous tenderness. I was particularly moved by the sight of his boots, fastened with little straps – good calf-skin boots, not the fashionable pointed sort but old-fashioned boots with square toes and without built-up heels. They were clearly the work of some battalion cobbler. "To bring out his beloved daughter and show her off he doesn't buy fashionable boots, he puts on his everyday home-made ones," I thought, and those foursquare toecaps continued to move me. It was obvious that he had once been an excellent dancer, but now he was stout and his legs were not supple enough for all the quick and elegant dance steps he was attempting to execute. All the same, he completed two accomplished circuits of the floor.

'And when he swiftly parted his feet and brought them together again and, although somewhat heavily, dropped on one knee, and she, smiling as she smoothed down her skirt where he had caught it, described a smooth circle round him, everyone burst into loud applause. Rising again with some effort to his feet, he tenderly and affectionately clasped his daughter's head between his hands and, kissing her on the forehead, led her across to me, assuming that I was dancing with her. I told him that I was not her escort.

' "Well, never mind, you dance this one with her," he said with a kindly smile as he put his sword back into its scabbard.

'Just as a single drop poured from a bottle is followed by all the liquid contained inside gushing out in great streams, so my love for Varenka released the entire capacity for love which I had in my soul. At that moment I embraced the whole world in my love. I loved the hostess with her ferronnière and her Imperial bosom, I loved her husband, her guests, her footmen, even Anisimov the engineer who was regarding me with dislike. And for her father with his home-cobbled boots and the same tender smile as his daughter's, for him I felt at that moment a sort of rapturous affection.

'The mazurka came to an end and the host and hostess invited their guests to sit down to supper, but Colonel B—— declined, saying that he had to be up early in the morning, and took his leave of them. I was terrified that Varenka too would be taken away, but she and her mother stayed on.

'When supper was over I danced the promised quadrille with her. And although it seemed to me that I was already infinitely happy, my happiness kept on growing and growing. We neither of us mentioned love; I did not ask her, or indeed ask myself, whether she loved me. It was sufficient for me that I loved her. My only fear was that something might come and spoil my happiness.

'When I had got home, undressed, and thought about going to sleep, I realized that sleep was quite out of the question. In my hand was the feather from her fan and one of her gloves, which she had given me on leaving just as I was helping first her mother and then her into their carriage. I gazed at these objects, and without closing my eyes saw her standing there before me just as she had looked at the moment when, faced with a choice between two partners, she had been trying to guess the quality I represented, and I had heard her lovely voice say "*Pride?* Yes?" – and she had joyfully given me her hand; or when at supper she was sipping from her goblet of champagne and had given me a sideways look with her caressing eyes. But most of all I saw her with her father, smoothly circling round him, then surveying the admiring spectators proudly and joyfully, both on her own account and on his. And I could not help including them both in a single feeling of tender affection.

'At that time I was living with my brother, who has since died. My brother in general had no time for society life and did not go to balls, and now he was preparing for his final examinations and leading a very regular life. He was asleep. I looked at his head buried in the pillow, half-hidden beneath the flannel blanket, and felt affectionately sorry for him – sorry that he neither knew nor shared the happiness I was experiencing. Our household serf Petrusha came in with a candle to help me undress, but I sent him away. The sight of my brother's sleepy face and tousled hair seemed to me deeply touching. Trying not to make a noise, I tiptoed to my room and sat down on the bed. No, I was too happy, I could not possibly sleep. What was more I felt too warm in the heated rooms, and without taking off my uniform I went quietly into the hallway, put on my overcoat, opened the front door and went out into the street.

'It was after four a.m. when I had left the ball, and what with the journey home and the time spent in the house, two hours had gone by, so that now, when I went out, it was already light. It was regular Shrovetide weather: it was foggy, the snow, saturated with water, was thawing on the roads, and water dripped from every roof. At that time the B——s lived at the far end of the town next to a large meadow, one end of which was used as a public pleasure-ground and the other was the site of an institute for young ladies. I walked along the deserted lane where our house stood and emerged into the main street, where I began to meet people on foot and draymen with loads of firewood on their sledges, which grazed the underlying surface of the roadway with their runners. And the horses rhythmically swaying their sopping wet heads under the glistening shaft-bows, and the cab-drivers with bast matting on their backs trudging along in enormous boots beside their vehicles, and the houses on each side of the street looming tall in the fog – all this seemed to me extraordinarily precious and filled with meaning.

'When I came out on to the field where their house was situated I saw at the far end, towards the pleasure-ground, something large and black, and I heard the sounds of fife and drum coming to me from that direction. All this time my mind was still full of music, and now and again I could still hear the melody of the mazurka. But this music was of quite a different kind – harsh and unpleasant.

'"Whatever is it?" I wondered as I made my way along the slippery path which had been beaten across the middle of the field, towards the place the sounds were coming from. When I had gone some hundred yards I managed to make out through the fog a crowd of dark figures. They were obviously soldiers. "Most likely a training exercise," I thought, and I went closer, walking just behind a blacksmith in a greasy sheepskin jacket and an apron, who was carrying something. Some soldiers in black uniforms were standing quite still in two rows facing one another, their rifles at the rest position. Behind them were some drummers, and a fife-player who kept on playing the same shrill and unpleasant tune over and over without a break.

'"What are they up to?" I asked the blacksmith, who had stopped beside me.

'"They're thrashing a Tatar for trying to desert," said the blacksmith angrily, his eyes fixed on a point at the far end of the ranks of men. I too looked in that direction and saw between the rows a fearful sight coming towards me. What was approaching was a man stripped to the waist and lashed to the rifles of two soldiers, who were leading him along. Alongside them walked a tall officer in a greatcoat and peaked cap, whose figure looked to me familiar. His whole body twitching, his feet slapping on the thawing snow, the man who was being punished moved towards me under a hail of blows which poured down on him from both sides, now throwing himself backwards – whereupon the NCOs leading him along on their rifles would thrust him forward, now plunging forward – whereupon the NCOs pulled him back, preventing him from falling. And keeping pace with them, walking with a firm, slightly quivering step, came the tall officer. It was her father, with his rubicund face and his white moustaches and side-whiskers.

'At each stroke the man being punished, as if in astonishment, turned his face contorted with suffering to the side from which the blow came, and baring his white teeth, kept repeating the same few words. Only when he had got quite close to me could I make out what these words were. He was repeating, in more of a sob than a voice: "Have mercy on me, lads. Have mercy, lads." But the lads did not have mercy on him, and as the procession drew level with me I saw the soldier standing opposite me step decisively forward, brandish his stick vigorously in the air and bring it whistling down on to the Tatar's back. The Tatar jerked forward but the NCOs restrained him, and another similar blow fell on him from the other side, followed by another from this side, another from that . . . The tall Colonel kept alongside: looking now down at his feet, now at the man being punished, he was drawing the air deeply into his lungs, blowing out his cheeks, then slowly letting it out through his protruding lips. When the procession had passed the place where I was standing, I caught between the ranks of soldiers a glimpse of the man's back. It was such a lurid, wet, red and unnatural-looking sight that I could not believe I was looking at a human body.

'"Jesus Christ" – said the blacksmith standing beside me.

'The procession was now moving away from us. The blows kept on falling from both sides on the stumbling, contorted

371

man, the drums kept on beating and the fife shrilling, and the tall, stately figure of the Colonel kept on walking with the same firm step beside the man who was being punished. All at once the Colonel stopped and quickly approached one of the soldiers.

'"I'll teach you to miss the mark," I heard his wrathful voice saying. "Going to miss it, are you? Are you?"

'And I saw his powerful suede-gloved hand strike a puny, terrified soldier full in the face for having failed to bring down his stick hard enough on the Tatar's bleeding back.

'"Give them some fresh sticks!" he shouted, looking round, and as he did so catching sight of me. He pretended not to recognize me, and frowning angrily and menacingly he turned hastily away.

'I was filled with such a pitch of shame that not knowing where to look, as though I had been apprehended in some shameful act, I lowered my eyes and hurried off home as fast as I could. All the way I had in my ears the beating of the drums and the shrilling of the fife, and I could still hear the words "Have mercy on me, lads", followed by the self-confident, angry voice of the Colonel shouting "Going to miss it, are you? Are you?" And meanwhile I felt in my heart an almost physical anguish, rising to the point of nausea, so that several times I had to stop and I thought I was going to vomit up all the horror with which this spectacle had filled me. I do not remember how I reached home and got into bed. But as soon as I began to fall asleep I heard and saw it all again, and I leapt out of bed.

'"It's obvious that he knows something which I don't," I thought with reference to the Colonel. "If only I knew what he knows, then I should understand what I have just seen, and it would not upset me like this." But however much I thought, I could not imagine what it was the Colonel knew, and it was not until that evening that I managed to fall asleep, and then only after I had been to visit a friend of mine and we had got completely drunk.

'Well then, do you suppose I decided there and then that what I had seen was something evil? Not at all. "If it was carried out with such conviction and everyone involved recognized that it was necessary, then they must certainly have known something I did not know," I thought to myself, and I tried to discover what it was. But however much I tried, discover it I could not. And since I was unable to discover it, I was unable to go into the army as I had earlier intended, and not only did I not serve in the army, but I did not enter government service of any kind, and as you see, I ended up not doing anything very much.'

'Well, we know about that, how you ended up not doing anything much,' said one of us. 'But just tell us this: how many men would end up the same way if there were not men like you to give them the example?'

'Now that is plain nonsense,' said Ivan Vasilyevich with genuine irritation.

'Well, and what happened about that love of yours?' we all wanted to know.

'My love? From that day on my love went into a decline. Whenever she fell into a pensive mood, as she frequently did, with that smile on her face, I would immediately remember the Colonel on the square, and I would feel somehow awkward and sickened, so I began to see her less often. And so my love for her gradually dwindled away to nothing. That is how it just is with some affairs, and it is things like that which can alter the whole direction of a man's life. But you say . . .' he concluded.

Alyosha Gorshok

ALYOSHKA WAS THE youngest boy in his family. People started calling him 'Gorshok' because his mother once sent him to fetch some water for the deacon's wife, and he tripped up and smashed the pot [*gorshok*] he was carrying it in. His mother beat him, and the children took to mocking him by calling him 'Pot'. So 'Alyoshka Gorshok' – Alyoshka the Pot – became his nickname.

Alyoshka was a thin boy with lop-ears (his ears stuck out just like wings) and he had a big nose. The other children would taunt him by saying, 'Alyoshka's got a nose like a dog on a hillock.' There was a school in the village, but Alyoshka never managed to learn reading and writing, in fact he had no time to study. His elder brother was living in a merchant's household in the town, and from his earliest childhood Alyoshka began helping his father. At the age of six he was already minding the sheep and cows on the common pasture with his sister who was not much older, and when he had got a little bigger he started minding the horses, by day and by night. From his twelfth year he was ploughing, and driving the cart. He was not particularly strong, but he had the knack of doing things. And he was always cheerful. The other children made fun of him, but he would just keep quiet, or laugh. If his father cursed at him, he kept quiet and listened. And when the cursing was over he would smile, and get on with the job in hand.

Alyosha was nineteen years old when his brother was taken away to be a soldier. And his father sent Alyosha to take his brother's place as a yardman at the merchant's house. Alyosha was given his brother's old boots, his father's cap and a coat, and went off on a cart to the town. Alyosha himself was not too delighted with his outfit, but the merchant was quite displeased at the look of him.

'I reckoned I was going to get something like a man in place of Semyon,' said the merchant, giving Alyosha the once-over, 'but this is a proper little milksop you've brought me. Whatever use is he going to be?'

'He can do anything you want – he can harness up, and fetch and carry anywhere, and he's a glutton for work. He may look like a yard of wattle fencing, but in fact he's a wiry young chap.'

'Well, I can see what he looks like, but I'll give him a try.'

'And the best thing about him is, he doesn't answer back. He's really keen to work.'

'There's no getting round you. All right, you can leave him with me.'

So Alyosha came to live at the merchant's house.

The merchant's family was a small one: the master's wife, his old mother, an elder son with only a basic education, married, who helped his father in the business, and another son who was a scholar – after leaving the grammar school he had gone to the university, but he had been expelled from there and was now living at home; and there was a daughter, a young schoolgirl.

To begin with Alyosha was not happy there – for he was a real country bumpkin, poorly dressed and without manners, and he called everyone 'thou'; but they soon got used to him. He worked even harder than his brother had done. He really was meek and didn't answer back: they sent him on all kinds of errands and he did everything willingly and quickly, and switched over from one task to the next with no break whatever. And as it had been at home, so too in the merchant's house, all manner of work fell on Alyosha's shoulders. The master's wife, the master's mother, the master's daughter and the master's son, the steward, the cook, they all sent him running hither and thither and told him to do this, that and the other. You would never hear anything but 'Run and fetch this, lad', or 'Alyosha, you sort it out', or 'You did remember to do that, didn't you, Alyosha?' or 'Look here, Alyosha, don't forget this'. And Alyosha ran, and sorted out, and looked, and didn't forget, and managed to do it all, and all the time he never stopped smiling.

He soon wore his brother's boots to pieces and the master told him off for going about with his boots full of holes and his bare toes sticking out, and gave orders for some new boots to be bought for him at the bazaar. The boots were brand new and Alyosha was delighted with them, but his legs were still the same old pair, and towards evening they ached from all this running about, and he would get cross with them. Alyosha was afraid that his father, when he came to get his money, might take offence if the merchant was to deduct part of his wages in payment for the boots.

In winter Alyosha would get up before it was light, chop the firewood, sweep the yard, give the horse and the cow their fodder and water them. Then he would heat up the stoves, clean the master's boots and brush his clothes, and take out the samovars and clean them; then either the steward would call him to help get out the wares, or the cook would order him to knead the dough and scour the saucepans. Then he would be sent into town, sometimes with a note for somebody, sometimes to take something to the master's daughter at the grammar school, sometimes to fetch lamp-oil for the old lady.

'Wherever did you get to, you wretch?' now one of them, now another would say to him. 'Why go yourself? Alyosha will run and get it. Alyoshka! Here, Alyoshka!' And Alyosha would come running.

He ate his breakfast as he went along, and rarely managed to have his dinner with the others. The cook swore at him for not bringing everything that was needed, but then felt sorry for him all the same and left him something hot for his dinner or his supper. There was a particularly large amount of work for him on high days and holidays and on the days leading up to them. And Alyosha took special pleasure in the feast days, because on feast days they would give him tips, not much, of course – not above sixty kopeks all told – but still, it was his own money. He was able to spend it as he wished. His actual wages he never set eyes on. His father would arrive and receive the money from the merchant, merely reprimanding Alyoshka for getting his boots looking worn so quickly.

When he had collected two rubles' worth of this 'tea-money', he bought, on the cook's advice, a fine knitted jacket, and when he put it on he was unable to stop grinning from sheer pleasure.

Alyosha spoke little, and when he did speak it was always short and fragmentary. And when he was ordered to do something, or asked whether he could do such and such a thing, he always replied without the slightest hesitation 'I can do that', and at once threw himself into the task, and did it.

Of prayers, he knew none at all. Whatever his mother had taught him he had forgotten, but he still prayed morning and evening – he prayed with his hands, by crossing himself.

Alyosha's life went on in this way for a year and a half, and then in the second half of the second year, something happened to him which was the most remarkable event in his life. This event had to do with his astonishing discovery that apart from the relationships between human beings which arise from their mutual needs, there are other, quite special relationships: not the ones which cause a person to brush the boots, to bring home some shopping, or to harness the horse, but the sort of relationship in which a man, although he is not needed at all by the other person, feels the need to devote himself to that other person, to be nice to them; and he discovered that he, Alyosha, was just such a man. He got to know about all this through the cook, Ustinya. Little Ustinya had been an orphan, and a hardworking child just like Alyosha. She began to feel sorry for Alyosha and Alyosha felt for the first time that he, he himself and not his services, was actually needed by another human being. When his mother had shown him that she was sorry for him, he had not really noticed it; it seemed to him that this was how things must be, that it was all one and the same, just as if he had been feeling sorry for himself. But now all of a sudden he realized that Ustinya was quite separate from him, but she did feel sorry for him and would leave him some buttery porridge at the bottom of the pot, and while he ate it she would rest her chin on her arm, the sleeve rolled up to her elbow, and watch him. And he would glance at her, and she would laugh, and then he would laugh too.

All this was so new and strange to him that at first it quite frightened Alyosha. He felt it was preventing him from carrying out his duties as he used to do. But all the same he felt glad, and when he looked at his trousers which Ustinya had darned, he shook his head and smiled. Often when he was working or as he walked along, he would think of Ustinya and say, 'Oh yes, Ustinya!' Ustinya helped him where she could, and he helped her. She told him all about her past life, how she had lost her parents, how her aunt took her in, then sent her to the town, how the merchant's son had tried to talk her into doing something stupid, and how she had put him in his place. She loved talking, and he loved listening to her. He had heard that in towns it often happened that peasant workmen ended up marrying cooks. And on one occasion she asked him whether his family would soon be marrying him off. He said he didn't know, and that he wasn't keen to take a country girl for a wife.

'Well then, who have you got your eye set on?' she said.

'Ah, I'd like to marry you, of course. Would you be willing to marry me?'

'Just look at him, he may be only Alyosha the Pot, just a pot, but see how he's contrived to speak out and say what he wanted,' she said, giving him a whack on the back with the towel she was holding. 'And why shouldn't I marry you indeed?'

At Shrovetide the old man came to town to collect his money. The merchant's wife had heard how Alexei had hit on the idea that he was going to marry Ustinya, and she did not like it. 'She'll go and get pregnant, and what use will she be with a child?' she said to her husband.

The master paid over the money to Alexei's father.

'Well then, and how is the boy behaving himself?' asked the peasant. 'I told you he was a meek one.'

'Meek or not meek, he's thought up a thoroughly stupid scheme. He's got it into his head that he's going to marry the cook. But I'm not going to start employing married people. That sort of thing doesn't suit us.'

'He's a fool, nothing but a fool. Look what he's thought up here,' said the father. 'You wouldn't credit it. I'll tell him straight out he's got to give up this notion.'

Going into the kitchen, the father sat down at the table to wait for his son. Alyosha was out running errands, and he was panting when he came in.

'I thought you were a sensible lad. But now what's this you've gone and thought up?' said the father.

'I haven't thought up anything.'

'What do you mean, you haven't thought up anything? You've decided you want to get married. I'll marry you off when the time's right, and I'll marry you off to the right person, and not to some town slut.'

The father went on talking for some time. Alyosha stood there and sighed. When his father had finished talking, Alyosha smiled.

'So I'm to give the whole thing up.'

'That's right.'

When his father had gone and he was left alone with Ustinya, he said to her (she had been listening behind the door while the father was talking to his son):

'Our plan wasn't right, it didn't work out. Did you hear him? He got real angry; he won't allow it.'

She said nothing, but burst into tears and buried her face in her apron.

Alyosha made a clicking noise with his tongue.

'It's no use going against it. It's clear we must just give the whole thing up.'

That evening, when the merchant's wife ordered him to close the shutters, she said to him:

'Well then, did you listen to your father, and have you given up your silly notions?'

'Stands to reason I've given them up,' replied Alyosha; and he laughed, then immediately burst into tears.

From that time on Alyosha said nothing more to Ustinya about marriage, and he went on living as he had before.

One day in Lent the steward sent him to clear the snow off the roof. He had climbed up on to the roof, and had got it clear and was just starting to pull away the frozen snow from the gutters, when his feet slipped, and he fell off the roof, holding the shovel. Unfortunately he landed not on the snow, but on the iron-covered entrance gate of the yard. Ustinya came running up, as did the master's daughter.

'Are you hurt, Alyosha?'

'I reckon you could say that again. But not to worry.'

He tried to stand up, but could not, and he began to smile. They carried him into the yardman's lodge. The doctor's assistant arrived. He examined Alyosha and asked him where it hurt.

'It hurts all over, but it's not too bad. But the master's going to be upset. And they ought to send word to my old man.'

Alyosha lay in bed for two days and nights, and on the third day they sent for the priest.

'And what if you should be going to die?' asked Ustinya.

'What if I am? We don't go on living for ever, do we? You've got to go sometime,' said Alyosha quickly, in his usual tone of voice. 'Thank you, Ustinya, for having pity on me. But it was really better that they didn't let me get married, it wouldn't have been any good. And now we're on friendly terms, you and me.'

He accompanied the priest's prayers only with his hands and in his heart. But in his heart was the knowledge that life here on earth is good if you do what you are told and don't offend people, and there too it will be good.

He did not say very much. He just asked for something to drink, and as he drank it he looked as if he was surprised at something.

He looked surprised, stretched himself out, and died.

What For?

A Story from the Time of
the Polish Insurrections

I

IN THE SPRING of 1830 Pan Jaczewski, who was living on his ancestral estate of Rozanka, received a visit from his late friend's only son, the young Josif Migurski. Jaczewski was an old man of sixty-five with a wide forehead, broad shoulders and a broad chest and long white whiskers on his brick-red face, and he was a patriot from the time of the Second Partition of Poland. As a young man he had served alongside Migurski the elder under the banner of Kosciuszko and he detested with all the strength of his patriotic soul the 'whore of the Apocalypse', as he called her, the Empress Catherine II, and her loathsome, traitorous lover Poniatowski, and he likewise believed in the restoration of the Commonwealth of Poland and Lithuania,* just as he believed at night that the sun would rise again by the next morning. In 1812 he had commanded a regiment in the army of Napoleon, whom he worshipped. Napoleon's downfall grieved him but he did not abandon the hope of a restoration of the Polish kingdom, were it only a mutilated one. The opening of the Sejm† in Warsaw by Alexander I revived his hopes, but the Holy Alliance and the triumph of the general reaction across the whole of Europe, and the petty tyranny of the Grand Duke Constantine, put off indefinitely any realization of his cherished longings ... After 1825 Jaczewski made his home in the country, spending his time without interruption at Rozanka and occupying himself with farming, hunting, and the reading of newspapers and letters, by which means he continued ardently to follow political events in his homeland. He had taken as his second wife a beautiful but impoverished woman from the *szlachta*,‡ and the marriage was not a happy one. He neither loved nor respected this second wife of his: he felt her to be an encumbrance and treated her harshly and rudely, as if her were punishing her for his own mistake in remarrying. He had no children by his second wife. From the first marriage there were two daughters: the elder, Wanda, a stately beauty

---

* The Rzecz Pospolita, instituted in 1569 by King Sigismund II Augustus, last of the Jagellon dynasty.

† Representative assembly, Diet.

‡ Polish aristocracy.

who was aware of the value of her attractions and was bored by country life; and the younger, Albina, her father's darling, a lively, bony little girl with curly blonde hair and, like her father, large widely spaced sparkling blue eyes.

Albina was fifteen years old at the time of Josif Migurski's visit. Migurski had in fact stayed with the Jaczewskis before as a student, in Wilno where they spent the winters, and had paid court to Wanda, but now he was coming to visit them in the country for the first time as a grown-up and independent young man. The arrival of young Migurski was agreeable to all the inhabitants of Rozanka. The old man liked Josif Migurski because he reminded him of his friend, Josif's father, of the time when they were both young, and of how they had talked together with great passion and the rosiest hopes about the current revolutionary ferment – and not only in Poland but also abroad, whence he had just returned. Pani Jaczewska liked him because when there were guests present old Jaczewski restrained himself and did not scold her for everything in his usual manner. Wanda liked him because she was sure that Migurski had come for her sake and that he intended to propose to her: she was preparing to accept, but she intended, as she expressed it to herself, to '*lui tenir la dragée haute*'.* Albina was glad because everyone else was glad. Wanda was not the only one convinced that Migurski had come with the intention of asking for her hand. The entire

---

* Literally: 'to hold the sweetmeat high' – i.e. to put him through his paces first.

household, from old Jaczewski down to nanny Ludwika, thought so, although nobody said anything.

And they were correct. Migurski had arrived with that intention, but at the end of a week he left again, somehow confused and downcast, without having made any proposal. They were all surprised by this unexpected departure and no one, with the exception of Albina, understood the reason for it. Albina knew that the cause of his strange departure was she herself.

The whole time he had been at Rozanka she had noticed that Migurski seemed particularly animated and cheerful only when he was with her. He treated her like a child, joking with her and teasing her, but with her feminine intuition she sensed that underneath this treatment of her there lay not the attitude of an adult towards a child, but that of a man towards a woman. She could see this in the admiring expression and affectionate smile with which he greeted her whenever she came into the room and took his leave of her when she left. She had no clear awareness of what was happening, but his attitude towards her made her feel happy, and she unconsciously did her best to please him. In fact anything she could possibly have done would have pleased him. And so when he was present she did everything with a special kind of excitement. He was pleased when she ran races with her beautiful greyhound and it jumped up and licked her flushed, radiant face; he was pleased when at the slightest pretext she broke into loud and infectious laughter; he was pleased when, continuing her merry laughter in the expression of her eyes, she put on a serious face to listen to the Catholic priest's boring homily; he was pleased when, with exceptional accuracy and humour, she mimicked first her old nanny, then a drunken neighbour, and then Migurski himself, switching in an instant from the depiction of one to the depiction of the next. Most of all he was pleased by her enthusiastic *joie de vivre*. It was just as though she had only just realized the full charm of life and was hastening to enjoy it to the utmost. He liked this special *joie de vivre* of hers, and this *joie de vivre* was aroused and heightened especially when she was aware that it was delightful to him. And so it was that Albina alone was aware why Migurski, who had come to propose to Wanda, had gone away without doing so. Although she could not have brought herself to tell anybody and did not confess it directly even to herself, in the depths of her soul she knew that he had wanted to fall in love with her sister, but had actually fallen in love with her, Albina. Albina was greatly astonished at this, counting herself totally insignificant in comparison with the clever, well-educated and beautiful Wanda, but she could not help knowing that it was so and she could not help rejoicing in the fact, because she herself had come to love Migurski with all the strength of her soul, to love him as people only love for the first, the only time in their lives.

II

AT THE END of the summer the newspapers brought the news of the July Revolution in Paris. After that news began to arrive of impending disorders in Warsaw. With a mixture of fear and hope Jaczewski awaited with every post news of the assassination of Constantine and the beginning of a revolution. At last in November the news arrived at Rozanka — first of the attack on the Belvedere Palace and the flight of the Grand Duke Constantine Pavlovich; then that the Sejm had pronounced that the Romanov dynasty had been deprived of the Polish throne and that Chlopicki had been proclaimed dictator and the Polish people were once more free.

The insurrection had not yet reached Rozanka, but all the inhabitants followed its progress, awaiting its arrival in their home region and making ready for it. Old Jaczewski corresponded with an acquaintance of long ago who was one of the leaders of the insurrection, received a number of secretive Jewish commercial agents not on economic but on revolutionary business, and prepared to join the insurrection when the time should be right. Pani Jaczewska concerned herself as always, but now more than ever, with her husband's material comforts, and by that very fact managed to irritate him more and more. Wanda sent off her diamonds to a girlfriend in Warsaw so that the money obtained for them could be given to the revolutionary committee. Albina was interested only in what Migurski was doing. She learnt via her father that he had enlisted in Dwernicki's detachment and she tried to find out all she could about that particular detachment. Migurski wrote twice: the first time to inform them that he had joined the army; and the second time, in mid-February, an enthusiastic letter about the Polish victory at the battle of Stoczek, where they had captured six Russian guns and some prisoners.

'*Zwyciestwo polakòw i kleska moskali! Wiwat!*'* – he wrote at the conclusion of his letter. Albina was in raptures. She scrutinized the map, trying to work out when and where the decisively defeated Muscovites must be, and she went pale and trembled as her father slowly unsealed the packets brought from the post-office. On one occasion her stepmother chanced to go into Albina's room and came upon her standing before the mirror wearing trousers and a *konfederatka*.† Albina was getting ready to run away from home in male attire to join the Polish army. Her stepmother went and told her father. Her father summoned Albina to him, and concealing the sympathy, even admiration, he felt for her, delivered a stern rebuke, demanding that she should banish from her head any stupid ideas about taking part in the war. 'A woman has a different duty to fulfil: to love and comfort those who are sacrificing themselves for the motherland' – he

---

* 'Victory to the Poles, destruction to the Muscovites! Hurrah!'
† A Polish man's hat, with a square base and a tassel on top.

told her. Now he needed her, she was a joy and a comfort to him; but the time would come when she would be needed in the same way by her husband. He knew how to persuade her. He reminded her that he was lonely and unhappy, and kissed her. She pressed her face against him, hiding the tears, which nevertheless moistened the sleeve of his dressing-gown, and promised him not to undertake anything without his agreement.

III

ONLY THOSE who have experienced what the Poles experienced after the Partition of Poland and the subjection of one part of the country to the power of the hated Germans and another part to the power of the still more hated Muscovites, can understand the rapture which the Poles felt in the years 1830 and 1831 when, after their earlier unsuccessful attempts to liberate themselves, their new hope of liberation seemed about to be fulfilled. But this hope did not last long. The forces involved were too disproportionate and the attempted revolution was once again crushed. Once again tens of thousands of dumbly obedient Russians were herded into Poland, and at the command first of Diebitsch, then of Paskevich, quite without knowing why they were doing it, proceeded to soak the earth with their own blood and that of their Polish brothers, to crush them, and once more to set in power weak and worthless men who desired neither the freedom of the Poles nor their suppression, but simply and solely the satisfaction of their own greed and their childish vanity.

Warsaw was taken and the independent Polish detachments utterly defeated. Hundreds, thousands of people were shot, beaten with rods, or sent into exile. Among those exiled was young Migurski. His estate was confiscated, and he himself assigned as a common soldier to a line battalion at Uralsk.

The Jaczewskis spent the winter of 1832 at Wilno for the sake of the old man's health: since 1831 he had been suffering from a heart ailment. Here a letter reached him from Migurski, written in the fortress where he was serving. He wrote that however hard were the experiences he had already gone through and which still awaited him, he rejoiced that it had been his destiny to suffer for his native land, that he did not despair of the sacred cause to which he had devoted part of his life and was ready to devote that which remained, and that if a new opportunity were to present itself tomorrow, then he would act again in precisely the same way. Reading the letter aloud, the old man burst into sobs when he reached this passage and for some time could not go on. In the final section of the letter, which Wanda read out, Migurski wrote that *whatever his hopes and longings might have been* at the time of his last visit to them, which would ever remain the brightest point of his whole life, now he could not and would not speak further about them.

Wanda and Albina each understood these words in her own way, but neither confided to anyone else exactly how she understood them. Migurski concluded his letter with greetings to all of them: among these he addressed Albina in the same playful tone he had adopted with her at the time of his visit, asking her whether she was still rushing about as she used to, running races with the greyhounds, and mimicking everyone so beautifully. To old Jaczewski he wished good health, to the mother success in household affairs, to Wanda that she should find a husband worthy of her, and to Albina that she should keep her *joie de vivre*.

IV

OLD JACZEWSKI'S health grew ever worse and in 1833 the whole family went abroad. In Baden Wanda met a wealthy Polish emigré and married him. The old man's condition rapidly declined, and at the beginning of 1833, while they were still abroad, he died. His wife he had not permitted to follow him, and to the very last he was unable to forgive her for the mistake he had made in marrying her. Pani Jaczewska returned to the country with Albina. The chief interest in Albina's life was Migurski. In her eyes he was the greatest of heroes and a martyr, to whose service she had resolved to dedicate her own life. Before going abroad she had already struck up a correspondence with him, at first on her father's behalf, then on her own. After her father's death she returned to Russia and went on writing to him; and once her eighteenth birthday was past she declared to her stepmother that she had decided to travel to Uralsk to join Migurski and there become his wife. Her stepmother at once began accusing Migurski of selfishly wanting to relieve his own difficult situation by captivating a rich young woman and compelling her to share his misfortune. Albina grew angry and informed her stepmother that no one but she could think of imputing such base thoughts to a man who had sacrificed everything for his own nation, that Migurski had on the contrary refused the help she had offered him, and that she had decided irrevocably to join him and become his wife, if only he was prepared to grant her that happiness. Albina was now of age and had some money – the thirty thousand *zlotys* which her late uncle had left to each of his two nieces. So that there was nothing to hold her back.

In November 1833 Albina, as if for the last time, said farewell to the family who were tearfully seeing her off on her journey to this distant, unknown realm of barbarous Muscovy, took her seat alongside her devoted old nurse Ludwika whom she was taking with her, in her father's old covered sleigh, newly repaired for this long journey, and set off on the highroad.

V

MIGURSKI WAS living not in the barracks, but in separate quarters of his own. Tsar Nicholas I required that Polish officers who had been reduced to the ranks should not only have to put up with the hardships of an austere military life, but also suffer all the humiliations to which private soldiers were subjected at that time. But the majority of the ordinary men whose duty it was to carry out his orders were fully aware of the harshness of treatment meted out to these demoted officers, and without regard to the danger involved in any failure to carry out the Tsar's will, deliberately failed to carry it out whenever they could. The semi-literate commander of the battalion to which Migurski had been assigned, a man who had been promoted from the ranks, understood the situation of this once wealthy, well-educated young man who had now lost everything: he felt sorry for him, respected him, and made all kinds of concessions in his favour. And Migurski could not help appreciating the generous spirit of the Lieutenant-Colonel with the white side-whiskers on his puffy military face, and to recompense him Migurski agreed to give lessons in mathematics and French to his sons, who were preparing for entry to the military academy.

Migurski's life at Uralsk, which had now been dragging on for some six months, was not only monotonous, dreary and dull, but very hard into the bargain. Apart from the battalion commander, from whom he attempted as far as possible to distance himself, his sole acquaintance was an exiled Pole, an uneducated and disagreeable man of a thrusting disposition who worked in the fishing trade. The principal hardship for Migurski lay in the difficulty he experienced in getting used to a life of poverty. Following the confiscation of his estate he had been left quite without financial means, and he was making ends meet by selling off whatever gold objects still remained to him.

The single great joy of his life in exile was his correspondence with Albina, and the charming, poetic image he had formed of her during his visit to Rozanka remained in his soul and now in his banishment grew ever more beautiful to him. In one of her first letters to him she asked him, among other things, about the meaning of his words in the earlier letter: 'whatever my dreams and longings might have been'. He replied that now he was able to confess to her that his dreams were connected with his desire to call her his wife. She wrote back that she loved him too. He responded that it would have been better if she had not written that, for it was dreadful for him to think about something which was now most likely an impossibility. She said in her reply that it was not only possible, but would most certainly come about. He wrote back that he could not accept her sacrifice, and that in his present circumstances it simply could not be. Shortly after writing this letter he received a package of money to the value of two thousand *zlotys*. By the postmark on the envelope and the handwriting he could see that it had been sent by Albina, and recalled having jokingly described in one of his earliest letters the satisfaction he felt now at being able by the lessons he gave to earn enough to pay for all the things he needed – tea, tobacco, even books. He transferred the money to another envelope and returned it to her with a letter begging her not to destroy the sacred nature of their relationship by bringing money into it. He had enough of everything he needed, he wrote, and he was completely happy in the knowledge that he possessed such a friend as she was. With that their correspondence came to a stop.

One day in November Migurski was at the Lieutenant-Colonel's house giving his sons their lesson, when the approaching sound of the post-sleigh bell was heard, and the runners of a sledge came crunching over the frozen snow and stopped in front of the house entrance. The boys jumped up from their seats to find out who had arrived. Migurski stayed behind in the room, looking at the door and waiting for the boys to return, but through the doorway came the Lieutenant-Colonel's wife in person. 'Some ladies have come asking for you, Pan,' she said. 'They must be from your country – they look like Polish ladies.'

If anyone had asked Migurski whether he thought it possible that Albina might come to see him, he would have said that it was unthinkable; yet in the depths of his soul he was expecting her. The blood rushed to his heart and he ran out gasping for breath, into the hall. In the hall a stout woman with a pock-marked face was untying the shawl which covered her head. A second woman was just going through the doorway which led to the Lieutenant-Colonel's quarters. Hearing steps behind her she looked round. From beneath her bonnet shone the joyful, widely spaced radiant blue eyes of Albina, their lashes covered with hoarfrost. Migurski stood rooted to the spot, not knowing how he should greet her or what to say. 'Juzio,' she cried, calling him by the name his father had used, and she herself had used in the old days, and she flung her arms round his neck, pressing her face, rosy with cold, against his, bursting into laughter and tears at one and the same time.

When she had found out who Albina was and why she had come, the Lieutenant-Colonel's kind-hearted wife took her in and gave her lodging in her own house until it should be time for the wedding.

VI

THE GOOD-NATURED Lieutenant-Colonel managed after considerable trouble to obtain an authorization from the high command. A Catholic priest was dispatched from Orenburg to marry the Migurskis. The battalion commander's wife acted as proxy for the bride's mother, one of Migurski's pupils carried the icon, and Brzozowksi, the Polish exile, was best man.

Albina, however strange it may appear, loved her husband passionately but did not know him at all. Only now was she really getting acquainted with him. It stands to reason that she discovered in this living man of flesh and blood a great many commonplace and unpoetic things which had not been part of the image of him which she had nurtured and carried in her imagination; yet on the other hand, precisely because he was a man of flesh and blood, she discovered in him much that was simple and good, which had also not been part of her abstract image of him.

She had heard from friends and acquaintances about his bravery in war and she knew for herself how courageously he had faced the loss of his status and his liberty, so that she imagined him in her own mind as a hero, invariably living a life of exalted heroism; whereas in reality, for all his exceptional physical strength and bravery, he turned out to be as gentle and mild as a lamb, the simplest of men, with his talent for genial jokes and the same childlike smile on his sensitive mouth with its small blond beard and moustache, the smile which had attracted her long ago at Rozanka – but also in his mouth the never-extinguished tobacco pipe which proved particularly trying for her during her pregnancy.

Migurski too was only now getting to know Albina, and getting to know the woman within her. From the women he had known in the period before his marriage he had never gained any understanding of woman herself. And what he discovered in Albina, as in woman in general, surprised him and might well have made him disillusioned with woman in general, had he not felt for Albina a special and grateful tenderness. For Albina and for woman in general he felt a tender, slightly ironic indulgence, but for Albina herself and for her alone he felt not only loving affection, but also an awareness of and an admiration for the unrepayable debt created by her sacrifice, which had given him such totally undeserved happiness.

The Migurskis were blessed in that, directing all the power of their love on one another, they felt amid so many alien people like two half-frozen wanderers who had lost the winter road, yet managed by their mutual contact to keep each other warm. The joyful life the Migurskis spent together was enhanced by the contribution of Albina's nurse Ludwika, who was utterly self-sacrificing, devoted as a slave to her mistress, full of good-natured grumbles, amusing, and ready to fall in love with any man whatever. The Migurskis were blessed too with the gift of children. At the end of a year a little boy was born; a year and a half later, a girl. The boy was the image of his mother: the same eyes, the same playfulness and grace. The little girl was a fine, healthy child, like a little wild thing.

Yet the Migurskis were still far from blessed by their separation from their homeland, and most of all by the harshness of their unaccustomed humble situation. Albina in particular suffered from this humiliation. He, her own Juzio, a hero and a model of humanity, was obliged to stand to attention before any and every officer, to carry out rifle maintenance, to do guard duty and to obey every order without complaint.

On top of all that, the news they received from Poland

continued to be extremely miserable. Virtually all their close relatives and friends had either been exiled or, having lost everything, had taken refuge abroad. For the Migurskis themselves there was no prospect of any end to this situation. All attempts to petition for a pardon or at least some improvement in their conditions, or for promotion to officer rank, failed to reach their destination. Tsar Nicholas conducted inspections, parades and exercises, attended masquerades and flirted under the cover of his masks, and galloped unnecessarily through Russia from Chuguyev to Novorossiisk, St Petersburg and Moscow, frightening ordinary people and riding his horses to exhaustion; and when a bold spirit plucked up the courage to ask for some alleviation of the lot of the exiled Decembrists or of the Poles who were now suffering precisely because of that patriotism which he himself extolled, he would stick out his chest, fix his pewter-coloured eyes on whatever happened to be in front of him, and say: 'Let them go on serving. It is too soon.' As if he knew when it would no longer be too soon, when it would be time to do something. And all the members of his entourage – the generals, the chamberlains and their wives, who were busy around him looking after their own interests, would feel moved at the extraordinary perspicacity and the wisdom of this great man.

All the same, there was on the whole more of happiness than of unhappiness in the lives of the Migurskis.

So they lived for a period of five years. But suddenly there came upon them an unexpected and terrible sorrow. First the little girl fell ill, then two days later the little boy: he had a high fever for three days, and in the absence of medical help (there was no doctor to be found) on the fourth day he died. Two days after him the little girl also died.

The only thing which stopped Albina from drowning herself in the river Ural was that she could not imagine without horror the state her husband would be in on receiving the news of her suicide. But it was hard for her to go on living. Hitherto always active and solicitous, she now handed over all her concerns to Ludwika and would sit for hours doing nothing, gazing mutely at whatever met her eyes, then suddenly jump up and run off to her tiny room and there, ignoring the consolations offered by her husband and Ludwika, she would weep silently, merely shaking her head and begging them to go away and leave her alone.

In the summer she would go to her children's grave and sit there, lacerating her heart with memories of what had been and of what might have been. She was particularly tormented by the thought that her children would still have been alive, had they all been living in a town where medical aid was to be had. 'Why? What for?' she thought. 'And Juzio and I, we want nothing from anybody, except for him to be able to live in the way he was born to live, as his grandparents and his forefathers lived, and all I want is to live with him and to love him, and to love my little ones and to bring them up.

'Yet suddenly they start tormenting him, and send him into exile, and they take away from me what is dearer to me than

403

the whole world. Why? What for?' – she hurled this question at men and at God. And she could not conceive of the possibility of any kind of answer. Yet without an answer there was no life for her. And so her life came to a standstill. This wretched life of banishment, which she had previously managed to beautify by her feminine good taste and elegance, now became intolerable not only to her, but to Migurski, who suffered both on her account and because he did not know how to help her.

VII

AT THIS MOST terrible time for the Migurskis there appeared in Uralsk a Pole by the name of Rosolowski who had been involved in a grandiose plan for a rebellion and escape, drawn up at that time in Siberia by the exiled Catholic priest Sirocynsky.

Rosolowksi, like Migurski and thousands of others condemned to Siberian exile for having desired to live in the manner to which they were born, that is as Poles, had got involved in this cause and had been flogged with birch rods and assigned to serve as a soldier in the same battalion as Migurski. Rosolowksi, a former mathematics teacher, was a long, thin stooping man with sunken cheeks and a furrowed brow.

So it was that on the very first evening of his time in Uralsk, Rosolowski, as he sat drinking tea in the Migurskis' quarters, inevitably began in his slow, calm bass voice to recount the circumstances which had led to his suffering so cruelly. It appeared that Sirocynsky had been organizing a secret society with members all over Siberia whose aim was to incite a mutiny among the soldiers and convicts with the help of the Poles enlisted in the Cossack and line regiments, to rouse the deported settlers to revolt, seize the artillery at Omsk and set everyone free.

'But would that really have been possible?' inquired Migurski.

'Quite possible, everything had been prepared,' said Rosolowski frowning gloomily, and slowly and calmly he proceeded to tell them all about the plan of liberation and the measures which had been taken to assure the success of the enterprise and, in case it should fail, to ensure the safety of the conspirators. Their success would have been certain, but for the treachery of two villains. According to Rosolowski, Sirocynsky had been a man of genius and of great spiritual power, and his death too had been that of a hero and a martyr. And Rosolowski began in his calm, deep, measured voice to recount the details of the execution at which, by the order of the authorities, he and all the others found guilty in the case were compelled to be present.

'Two battalions of soldiers stood in two ranks forming a long corridor, each man holding a pliant rod of such a thickness, defined by the Emperor himself, that no more than three of them could be inserted into a rifle muzzle. The first man to be brought out was Dr Szakalski. Two soldiers led him along and the men with the rods lashed him on his exposed back as he came level with them. I was only able to see what was happening when he came near to the spot where I was standing. At first I could hear only the beating of the drum, but then, when the swish of the rods and sound of the blows falling on his body began to be audible, I knew he was approaching. And I could see that the soldiers were pulling him along on their rifles, and so he came, shuddering and turning his head first to one side, then to the other. And once, as he was being led past us, I heard the Russian doctor telling the soldiers, "Don't hit him too hard, have pity on him." But they went on beating him just the same: when they led him past us for the second time he was no longer able to walk unaided, they had to drag him. His back was dreadful to behold. I screwed up my eyes. He collapsed, and they carried him away. Then a second man was brought out. Then a third, and a fourth. All of them eventually fell down and were carried away – some looked as if they were dead, others just about alive, and we all had to stand there and watch. It went on for six hours – from morning until two in the afternoon. Last of all they brought out Sirocynsky himself. It was a long time since I had seen him and I would not have recognized him, so much older did he look. His clean-shaven face was full of wrinkles, and a pale greenish colour. His body where it was uncovered was thin and yellow and his ribs stuck out above his contracted stomach. He moved along as all the others had done, shuddering at each stroke and jerking his head, but he did not groan and kept repeating a prayer in a loud voice: *'Miserere mei Deus secundum magnam misericordiam tuam.'**

'I myself could hear it,' said Rosolowski rapidly in a strangled voice, and he shut his mouth and breathed heavily through his nose.

Ludwika, sitting by the window, was sobbing and had covered her face with her shawl.

'And you had to describe it to us! They are beasts, nothing but savage beasts!' cried Migurski, and throwing down his pipe he jumped up from his chair and hurried out into the unlit bedroom. Albina sat there as if turned to stone, gazing into the dark corner of the room.

VIII

THE FOLLOWING day Migurski, on his way home from a lesson, was surprised to see his wife hurrying to meet him with light steps and a radiant face. When they got home she took him into their bedroom.

'Juzio, listen to me.'

'Listen? What do you mean?'

'I have been thinking all night about what Rosolowksi was

---

* 'Have mercy upon me, O God, according to Thy great mercy.'

telling us. And I have decided: I cannot go on living like this, in this place. I cannot. I may die, but I am not going to stay here.'

'But what can we possibly do?'

'Escape.'

'Escape? How?'

'I've thought it all through. Listen,' – and she told him the plan she had worked out during the night. Her plan was this: he, Migurski, would leave the house in the evening and leave his greatcoat on the bank of the Ural, and beside it a letter saying that he was going to take his own life. They would think he had drowned. They would hunt for his body and send in a report of what had occurred. Meanwhile he would be hiding – she would hide him so that he could not be found. They could go on like that for a month at least. And when all the fuss had died down, they would run away.

Migurski's first reaction was that her scheme was impracticable, but by the end of the day her passionate confidence in it had convinced him, and he began to be of the same mind. Apart from that, he was inclined to agree with her, for the very reason that the punishment for an attempted escape, the same punishment Rosolowski had described to them, would fall on him, Migurski, but if they succeeded she would be set free, and he saw that since the death of the two children life here had been bitterly hard for her.

Rosolowski and Ludwika were let into the scheme, and after lengthy discussions, modifications and adjustments the plan was complete. To begin with they arranged that Migurski, once he had been presumed drowned, should run away alone on foot. Albina would then take the carriage and meet him at a pre-arranged place. This was the first plan. But later, when Rosolowski had told them of all the unsuccessful escape attempts which had been made in Siberia over the past five years (during which only one fortunate man had escaped to safety), Albina put forward a different plan – namely, that Juzio should be hidden in the carriage and travel with her and Ludwika to Saratov. At Saratov he would change his clothes and walk downstream along the bank of the Volga to an agreed spot where he would board a boat which she would have hired in Saratov and which would take the three of them down the Volga as far as Astrakhan and then across the Caspian Sea to Persia. This plan was approved by them all, as well as by its principal architect Rosolowski, but they were faced with the difficulty of fitting the carriage with a hiding-place big enough to take a man without attracting the attention of the authorities. And when Albina, having paid a visit to the children's grave, told Rosolowski that she felt bad about leaving her children's remains in an alien land, he thought for a moment, then said:

'Ask the authorities for permission to take the children's coffins away with you – they will grant it.'

'No, I can't do that, I don't want to!' said Albina.

'You must ask them. Everything depends on it. We shall not take the coffins, but we shall make a large box for them and into that box we shall put Josif.'

For a moment Albina wanted to reject this suggestion, so painful was it for her to associate any such deception with the memory of her children, but when Migurski cheerfully approved the project, she agreed.

The final version of the plan was thus as follows: Migurski would do everything to convince the authorities that he had been drowned. As soon as his death had been officially recognized she would apply for permission, following the death of her husband, to return to her native land, taking with her the mortal remains of her children. Once the permission had been granted, everything would be done to give the impression that the graves had been opened and the coffins taken out, but the coffins would remain where they were and instead of the coffins it would be Migurski who would take their place in the specially constructed box. The box would be loaded on to the tarantass and so they would reach Saratov. At Saratov they would transfer to the boat. In the boat Juzio would emerge and they would sail down to the Caspian Sea. And there Persia or Turkey awaited them – and freedom.

IX

FIRST OF ALL the Migurskis purchased a tarantass on the pretext that Ludwika would soon be leaving to return to her homeland. Then began the construction of the box to allow Migurski to lie in it, if only in a contorted position, without suffocating, to emerge quickly and unobtrusively, and to crawl back into it when necessary. The designing and fitting out of the box was the work of all three of them together – Albina, Rosolowski, and Migurski himself. Rosolowski's help was particularly vital, since he was an accomplished carpenter. They made the box to be fixed against the front-to-back struts at the rear of the coach body and flush with it, and the wall of the box which lay against the bodywork could be slid out, allowing a person to lie partly in the box and partly in the bottom of the tarantass. In addition airholes were bored in the box, and the top and sides were to be covered with bast matting and tied up with cords. It was possible to get in and out of the box by way of the tarantass, which was fitted with a seat.

When tarantass and box were ready, and when her husband had yet to make his disappearance, Albina began to prepare the authorities by going to the Colonel and telling him that her husband had fallen into a state of melancholia and was threatening to kill himself, and that she feared for his life and begged that he might be released before it was too late. Her acting ability stood her in good stead. The fear and anxiety she expressed for her husband appeared so natural that the Colonel was touched and promised to do all he could. After that Migurski composed the letter which was to be discovered in the cuff of his over-coat left lying on the river-bank, and on the evening they had chosen he went down to the Ural, waited until it was dark, laid the clothes and the coat containing the letter on the bank, and returned home. They had prepared him a hiding-place in the loft, secured by a padlock. That night Albina sent word to the Colonel by Ludwika to say that her husband had left the house some twenty hours earlier and had not returned. Next morning her husband's letter was brought to her, and she, with every appearance of deep despair, went off weeping to show it to the Colonel.

A week later Albina submitted her request to be allowed to leave for her own land. The grief displayed by Madame Migurski affected everyone who saw her: all were filled with pity for this unfortunate wife and mother. When permission had been granted for her departure, she made a second request – that she might be allowed to exhume the bodies of her children and take them with her.

The military authorities were astonished at such a display of sentimentality, but agreed to this as well.

On the evening of the day after this permission had been given, Rosolowski, Albina and Ludwika drove in a hired cart, containing the box, to the cemetery where the children were buried. Albina fell to her knees before the grave, said a prayer, then quickly got up, and turning to Rosolowski said:

'Do what must be done, but I cannot have any part in it,' and went off by herself.

Rosolowski and Ludwika moved the gravestone aside and turned over the whole of the top surface of the plot with a shovel so that the grave looked as though it had been opened. When all this was done they called to Albina and returned home taking the box, filled with earth.

The day fixed for their departure came at last. Rosolowski was rejoicing at the success of the enterprise which seemed almost complete, Ludwika had baked biscuits and pies for the journey, and repeating her favourite turn of phrase, '*jak mame kocham*',* said that her heart was bursting with fear and joy at the same time. Migurski was filled with joy, both by his release from the loft where he had spent more than a month, and still more by the renewed vitality and *joie de vivre* of Albina. She seemed to have forgotten all her former grief and the dangers, and as she might have done in her girlhood, ran to see him in the loft, radiating rapture and delight.

At three in the morning their Cossack escort arrived, bringing with him the coachman and a team of three horses. Albina, Ludwika and the little dog took their seats on the cushions of the tarantass which were covered with matting. The Cossack and the driver got up on the box, and Migurski, wearing peasant clothes, was lying in the body of the tarantass.

They were soon out of the town, and the team of good horses pulled the tarantass along the beaten roadway, smooth as stone, through the endless unploughed steppe overgrown with the last season's silvery feather-grass.

---

* 'As I love my mother.'

X

ALBINA'S HEART had almost stopped beating from hope and delight. Wishing to share her feelings with someone else, she now and then, almost smiling, made a sign with her head to Ludwika, indicating now the broad back of the Cossack seated on the box, now the bottom of the tarantass. Ludwika stared motionlessly ahead with a meaningful expression, only slightly pursing her lips. The day was bright. On all sides stretched the limitless deserted steppe and the silvery feather-grass shining in the slanting rays of the morning sun. Occasionally, first on one side, then on the other side of the hard road on which the rapid, unshod hooves of the Bashkir horses rang out as if on asphalt, the little earth-covered mounds made by gophers came into view; one of the little creatures would be sitting up on sentry duty, and anticipating danger would give a piercing whistle and disappear into the burrow beneath. On rare occasions they met with passers-by: a string of Cossack carts full of wheat, or some Bashkirs on horseback with whom their Cossack exchanged animated remarks in the Tatar tongue. At all the posting-stations the horses were fresh and well-fed, and the half-rubles provided by Albina for vodka ensured that the drivers drove the horses, as they put it, like *Feldjägers*,* galloping all the way.

---

* Couriers or special messengers.

At the first posting-station when the first driver had led away the horses and the new driver had not yet brought out the new ones and the Cossack had gone into the yard, Albina bent down and asked her husband how he was feeling and whether he needed anything.

'Excellent, don't worry. I don't need anything. I wouldn't mind lying here for two whole days.'

Towards evening they drew into a large village called Dergachi. To give her husband the chance to stretch his limbs and refresh himself Albina told the driver to stop not at the posting-station but at a coaching-inn, then immediately gave the Cossack some money and sent him off to buy milk and eggs. The tarantass was standing beneath a projecting roof. It was dark in the courtyard, and having stationed Ludwika to watch out for the Cossack, Albina released her husband and gave him food and drink, after which he crawled back into his hiding-place before the Cossack returned. They had a new team of horses brought round and continued on their way. Albina felt her spirits rising more and more and was unable to contain her cheerfulness and general delight. There was no one to talk to other than Ludwika, the Cossack and her little dog Trezorka, so she amused herself with them. Despite her plainness, at every contact with a man Ludwika would immediately detect him sending amorous glances in her direction, and she now suspected something of the sort in her relations with the burly and genial Ural Cossack with unusually bright and kind blue eyes who was escorting them and behaving most agreeably towards the two women, treating them with gentle and good-humoured kindness. Apart from Trezorka, whom Albina had to threaten to prevent him from sniffing about under the seat, she now found amusement in watching Ludwika's coquettish advances to the Cossack, who was quite unaware of the intentions being ascribed to him, and smiled agreeably at her every remark. Albina, stimulated by her sense of danger, by her growing conviction that their plan was succeeding, and by the splendid weather and the fresh air of the steppe, was enjoying the return of those youthful high spirits and merriment which she had not felt for such a long time. Migurski could hear her cheerful chatter and he too, despite the physical discomfort which he concealed from them (for he was extremely hot and tormented by thirst), forgot about himself and rejoiced in Albina's joy.

Towards evening on the second day something came into sight in distance through the mist. It was the town of Saratov and the Volga. The Cossack with his far-sighted steppe-dweller's eyes could distinguish the Volga and the masts of the ships, and he pointed them out to Ludwika. Ludwika said that she could see them too. But Albina could make out nothing, and remarked loudly, for her husband to hear:

'Saratov, the Volga' – and as though she was talking to Trezorka, Albina described to her husband everything as it came into view.

XI

ALBINA DID NOT let the carriage drive into Saratov but made the driver stop on the left bank of the river at the settlement of Pokrovskaya directly opposite the town itself. Here she hoped that in the course of the night she would be able to talk to her husband and even get him out of the box. But throughout the short spring night the Cossack did not go away from the tarantass but sat next to it in an empty cart which was standing beneath a projecting roof. Ludwika, on Albina's instructions, stayed in the tarantass and, convinced that it was on her account that the Cossack would not leave the tarantass, laughed and winked and hid her face in her shawl. But Albina could see nothing amusing in this and grew more and more worried, unable to understand why the Cossack was so doggedly attached to the vicinity of the tarantass.

Several times that short night in which dusk almost merged into morning twilight, Albina left her room in the coaching-inn and walked along the stuffy verandah to the porch at the back of the building. The Cossack was still not asleep but was sitting on the empty cart, his legs dangling. Only just before dawn when the cocks were already awaking and calling from one farmyard to the next did Albina, going down to the yard, find an opportunity to exchange a few words with her husband. The Cossack was now snoring, sprawled in the cart. She cautiously approached the tarantass and knocked on the box.

'Juzio!' – No answer. 'Juzio, Juzio,' she repeated more loudly, now becoming alarmed.

'What is it my dear, what is the matter?' came Migurski's sleepy voice from inside the box.

'Why didn't you answer me?'

'I was asleep,' he replied, and from the sound of his voice she knew that he was smiling. 'Well, and can I come out?' he asked.

'No, you can't, the Cossack is here.' And as she spoke she glanced at the Cossack asleep in the cart.

And strange to say, although the Cossack was snoring, his eyes, his kindly blue eyes, were open. He looked at her, and only when his glance had lighted on her, closed his eyes.

'Did I just imagine it, or was he really not asleep?' Albina wondered. 'I expect I imagined it,' she thought, and turned back to her husband.

'Try to put up with it a little longer,' she said. 'Do you want anything to eat?'

'No. But I should like to smoke.'

Albina again turned to look at the Cossack. He was sleeping.

'Yes, I imagined it,' she thought.

'I am going to see the Governor now.'

'Well, it is as good a time as any . . .'

And Albina took a dress out of her trunk and went back to her room to change.

When she had changed into her best widow's dress Albina took a boat across the Volga. On the embankment she hired a

418

cab-driver and drove to the Governor's residence. The Governor agreed to see her. This pretty little Polish widow with her sweet smile, speaking beautiful French, made a tremendous impression on the Governor, an elderly man who liked to appear younger than his age. He granted all her requests and asked her to come to see him again the next day to receive a written order to the Town Governor of Tsaritsyn. Rejoicing in the success of her petition and the effect of her own attractiveness which she could see from the Governor's manner, Albina, happy and full of hope, drove back in a carriage down the unmetalled street towards the jetty. The sun had already risen above the woods and its slanting beams were already playing on the rippling water of the mighty river. To right and left on the hillside she could see apple-trees like white clouds, covered in fragrant blossom. A forest of masts came into view by the river-bank and the sails of the boats showed white on the water lit up by the sun and rippling in a light breeze. At the landing-stage, having consulted the driver, Albina asked whether it was possible to engage a boat to take her to Astrakhan, and at once dozens of noisy, cheerful boatmen offered her their boats and their services. She came to an arrangement with one of the boatmen she particularly liked the look of and went to inspect his open-hulled barge which was lying amid a crowd of others at the wharf. The boat had a mast which could be stepped at will and a sail to allow it to use the power of the wind. In case there should be no wind there were oars provided, and two healthy, cheerful-looking barge-haulers-cum-oarsmen, who were sitting on the boat enjoying the sun. The jovial pilot advised her not to leave the tarantass behind but to remove the wheels and install it in the boat. 'It'll go in just right, and you'll be more comfortable sitting in there. If God grants us a bit of good weather we shall make the run down to Astrakhan in five days clear.'

Albina bargained with the boatman and instructed him to come to the Logins' inn at the Pokrovskaya settlement so that he could have a look at the tarantass and collect a deposit. The whole thing worked out more easily than she had expected. In a state of rapturous happiness Albina crossed the Volga once more, and bidding farewell to the driver, made for the coaching-inn.

XII

THE COSSACK Danilo Lifanov came from Strelyetski Outpost* in the highlands between the Volga and Ural rivers. He was thirty-four years old and he was just completing the final month of his term of Cossack service. His family consisted of an old grandfather of ninety who still remembered the time of Pugachov, two brothers, the daughter-in-law of the elder brother (sentenced to exile with hard labour in Siberia for

---

* A settlement inhabited by descendants of the Streltsy (archers), a state security force established by Ivan the Terrible and disbanded by Peter the Great (1708).

being an Old Believer), Danilo's wife, and his two daughters. His father had been killed in the war against the French. Danilo was the head of the household. On the farm they had sixteen horses, two ploughing teams of oxen, and fifteen hundred *sazhens* of private land, all ploughed and sown with their own wheat. He, Danilo, had done his military service in Orenburg and Kazan, and was now getting to the end of his period of duty. He kept firmly to the Old Faith: he did not smoke or drink, did not use dishes in common with worldly people, and also kept strictly to his word. In all his undertakings he was slow, steady and reliable, and he carried out everything his commander instructed him to do with his complete attention, not forgetting his purpose for a single moment until the job was properly finished. Now he was under orders to escort these two Polish women with the coffins to Saratov, to see that nothing bad befell them on the journey, to ensure that they travelled quietly and did not get up to any mischief, and on reaching Saratov to hand them over decently and in order to the authorities. So he had delivered them to Saratov with their little dog and their coffins and all. These women were charming and well-behaved despite being Polish and they had done nothing bad. But here at the Pokrovskaya settlement last evening he had seen how the little dog had jumped up into the tarantass and begun yelping and wagging his tail, and from under the seat in the tarantass he had heard somebody's voice. One of the Polish women – the older one – seeing the little dog in the tarantass had looked very scared for some reason, and grabbed hold of the dog and carried it away.

'There's something in there,' thought the Cossack, and he started to keep his eyes open. When the younger Polish woman had come out to the tarantass in the night he had pretended to be asleep, and he had distinctly heard a man's voice coming from the box. Early in the morning he had gone to the police-station and reported that the Polish women such as were entrusted to him and not travelling of their own free will, instead of dead bodies were carrying some live man or other in their box.

When Albina, in her mood of jubilant happiness, convinced that now it was all over and that in a few days they would be free, approached the coaching-inn she was surprised to see in the gateway a fashionable-looking carriage and pair with a third trace horse and two Cossacks. A crowd of people thronged round the gateway, staring into the yard.

She was so full of hope and vitality that it never entered her head that this carriage and pair and the people clustering round might have anything to do with her. She walked into the inn-yard and at once, looking under the canopy where the tarantass was standing, saw that a crowd of people were gathered round it, and at the same moment heard the anguished barking of Trezorka. The most dreadful thing that could have happened had happened. In front of the tarantass, his spotless uniform with its bright buttons, shoulder-straps and lacquered boots shining in the sun, stood a portly man with black side-whiskers, saying something in a loud imperious voice. Before him, between two soldiers, in peasant clothes and with wisps of hay in his tousled hair, stood her Juzio, raising and lowering his powerful shoulders, as if perplexed by what was going on around him. Trezorka, unaware that he was the cause of the whole disaster, stood with bristling coat, barking with carefree dislike at the chief of police. On seeing Albina, Migurski winced and made to go towards her, but the soldiers held him back.

'Never mind, Albina, never mind,' said Migurski, smiling at her with his gentle smile.

'And here is the little lady in person!' said the chief of police. 'Welcome to you, madam. And are these the coffins of your babies? Eh?' he said, pointing to Migurski.

Albina made no reply, but simply crossed her arms on her breast and gazed in open-mouthed horror at her husband.

As often happens in the very last moments of life and at other crucial points in human experience, she felt and foresaw in an instant a multitude of thoughts and feelings, while not yet grasping her misfortune or believing in it. Her first feeling was one long familiar to her – the feeling of wounded pride at the sight of her hero-husband, humiliated before these coarse, bestial men who now had him in their power. 'How dare they hold *him*, the very best of men, in their power!' Her second feeling, which swept over her almost at the same time as the first, was an awareness of the disaster which was now complete. And this consciousness of disaster revived in her the memory of the chief disaster of her life, the death of her children. And now once again the question came to her: what for? why had her children been taken away? The question 'Why have my children been taken away?' called forth a further question: Why was her beloved, the best of men, her husband, now in torment, now being destroyed? What for? And then she remembered that a shameful punishment awaited him, and that she, she alone, was to blame.

'What is your relation to this man? Is this man your husband?' repeated the chief of police.

'What for, what for?!' she screamed out, and bursting into hysterical laughter she collapsed on to the box, which had been removed from the tarantass and was standing on the ground nearby. Her whole body shaking with sobs and with tears streaming down her face, Ludwika went up to her.

'Panienka,* my dearest Panienka! *Jak Boga kokham,*† nothing will happen to you, nothing will happen!' she said, distractedly running her hands over her mistress.

Migurski was handcuffed and led out of the inn-yard. Seeing what was happening, Albina ran after him.

'Forgive me, forgive me!' she cried. 'It is all my fault, I alone am to blame!'

'They'll sort out who is to blame in court. And I've no doubt

---

* Diminutive of 'pani' (mistress).

† 'As I love God.'

the case will involve you,' said the chief of police, pushing her out of the way.

They led Migurski down to the river-crossing and Albina, not knowing herself why she was doing so, followed him and refused to listen to Ludwika's advice.

All this time the Cossack Danilo Lifanov was standing leaning against a wheel of the tarantass and glaring angrily now at the chief of police, now at Albina, and now at his own feet.

When Migurski had been led away Trezorka, now left alone, wagged his tail and began to fawn on him. The Cossack had grown used to the dog during the journey. Suddenly he pulled himself upright, tore his cap from his head and hurled it with all his strength onto the ground, pushed Trezorka away from him with his foot, and went into the eating-house. Once inside he ordered vodka and drank solidly for a day and a night, drinking away all the money he had on him and everything he had with him, and only on the next night, when he woke up in a ditch, was he able to stop thinking about the question which had been tormenting him: why had he done it, informing the authorities about the little Polish woman's husband in the box?

Migurski was tried and sentenced to run the gauntlet of a thousand rods. His relatives and Wanda, who had connections in St Petersburg, managed after much trouble to obtain a mitigation of the punishment, and instead he was sent into permanent exile in Siberia. Albina travelled after him.

And Tsar Nicholas Pavlovich rejoiced that he had crushed

the hydra of revolution not only in Poland, but throughout Europe, and took pride in the fact that he had not betrayed the ordinances of the Russian autocracy, but for the good of the Russian people had kept Poland in Russia's power. And men wearing decorations and gilt uniforms lauded him for this to such an extent, that when he came to die he sincerely believed that he was a great man and that his life had been a great blessing for humanity in general and for Russians in particular, those Russians to whose corruption and stupefaction he had unwittingly directed all his powers.